LEGEND OF ELBERKHAN

LEGEND OF ELBERKHAN

YUXIAO CHEN

Yuxiao Chen

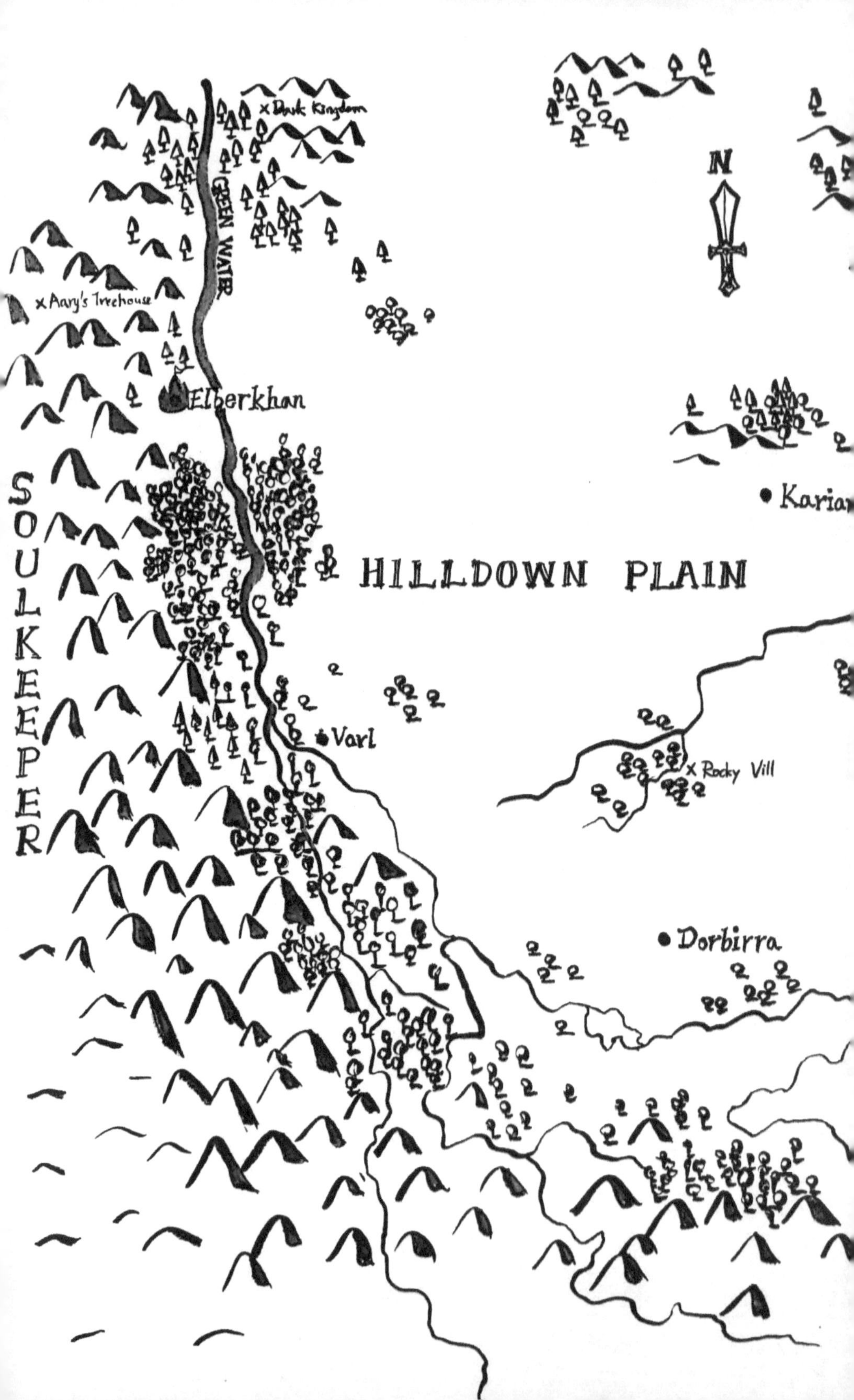

x Dark Kingdom
GREEN WATER
x Aary's Treehouse
Elberkhan
SOULKEEPER
HILLDOWN PLAIN
N
Karian
Varl
x Rocky Vill
Dorbirra

Prologue

The sky was getting dimmer outside the window. At the horizon, the color turned from blue to gray, and then gradually developed into a kind of elegant magenta, like paint extracted from the petals of a delicate flower, but scrubbed onto a dimmed blue-gray canvas. I looked out of the window, through the thick and heavy shades of dusk, and scoured the mountains aimlessly, while my mind drifted through a faded old memory, to a similar dusk many, many years ago, until my eyes fell on the distant castle. The mountains were covered with a blanket of thick forest, which looked almost completely black at this hour. Standing out among the sea of black woods was the pale figure of the ancient castle, firmly established at the foot of the mountains. Being unceasingly washed and brushed by the river of time, the castle always remained, and forever would be, the same.

All living things will fade and die in the rush of time, being replaced or regenerated by vibrant new lives. Even the most dazzling and vigorous fire of life will burn out eventually, gradually dimming with the light in the eyes of its body, until the last spark turns into a wisp of smoke, then nothing at all. No matter how long and lasting a life is, it cannot stand the trial of time. In the course of history, it is more fleeting than the blink of an eye.

However, some things bear witness to eternity. Mountains, rivers, castles... and words. I closed the wooden paneled window, picked up the half-burnt candle and with it, lit the oil lamp on the desk. I took out the quill pen dipped in the ink, and left a long dark-colored mark on the yellowed parchment.

Prologue

Chen Yuxiao

PART ONE

I

Twilight

The Soulkeeper Mountain stood with its back against the setting sun, casting a clear and beautiful silhouette. A warm red halo was gently caressing the wavy border outlined by the mountains, shrouding the mountain range and the plain below in a dreamy orange light.

It was a quiet and sleepy dusk. Even the birds had stopped chattering and hurried back to their nests to unite with their nestlings, share the fruits of their day's work, and watch the nestlings eat the supper they brought back in sheer happiness. Only a few giant eagles were still hovering high above in the sky, patronizingly looking down onto the mountains that were gilded by the sunset.

At the foot of the mountains, a very old, but strong castle was crouching in the shadow, snuggling up to a corner of the magnificent mountain range. The castle was built out of numerous giant stone ashlars. Having endured years of erosion, the once light gray ashlars had turned slightly yellowish, showing a kind of bleak color resembling the yellow dirt of the ground. Green mosses squeezed out from the gaps between the stones, adding a bit of energy to this heavy city of rocks.

In front of the castle, a river steadily flowed by, occasionally reflecting a bit of light in the dark. "Green Water" was the name people called it, not that the water was really green, but because of the reflection of the green woods on the mountains dancing in the river when people looked at it from the side of the plain. That was in the day, of course. Now the river was as black as all of the mountain woods. The river ran around the castle in half a circle, forming a natural moat for the rock city, and then continued to run, along the foot of the hills, winding and meandering, until the end of the earth. If it hadn't been for a sharp horizon intercepting the river, no doubt it would keep on flowing into the sky, and turn into the stars that should appear any time soon. Probably the Milky Way was just a mischievous river, released by a horizon somewhere that hadn't stuck to its duty.

As the sky became darker and darker, the shadow of the mountains grew longer, swiftly crossing the Hilldown Plain beneath, and covering more villages in the shadow. The people that had gone out hunting or farming were rushing towards their homes, hoping to set foot into their sweet homes before sundown, to hold their children into their arms and kiss their wives who had been waiting for them. Lighting up oil lamps, families gathered around the warmth of light. People gently held the hands of their beloved ones, and softly told each other about their day. It was not completely dark yet. The stars were just showing their faces, and there were already drops of starlight lighting up beneath the sky across the whole plain. For every light of oil lamp glittering in the dark, there was a loving and happy family. Before the darkness falls, there's still time for everything.

All was so calm and peaceful, on this evening at the end of summer and the start of fall.

But the tranquility was only superficial. On one side of the mountain, about half way up, hustling in the shades of the lush green woods, there was a small dark figure, furtively sneaking around.

The woods were the most terrifying at dusk. The remaining light of the sun could no longer illuminate the gloom in the murky forest, but the protection of the night had not yet come. There was no boundless darkness thick as ink, to act as camouflage and hide everything inside.

It was a tiny little thing, less than four feet tall, covered in a huge olive-colored robe of rough fabric with worn edges on the cuffs and hemline. He looked like an underfed human child from behind, if it was not for his dark gray wrinkled skin wrapped around his stick-like arms and legs. His head was way too large for his body, and neck way too thin for his head. Two huge ears were mostly cloaked by the big hood, only leaving two pointy ends at the rim, and his face was hidden in the dark shade of the hood, showing only a pair of alert and suspicious big eyes. The little black eyeballs were spinning suspiciously in the overly large sockets, occasionally flickering with some greedy and vicious light.

A skinny, but strong, hand reached out from under the robe. Oh no, it might be better to be called a claw. Not the kind of fluffy paw-claws that belonged to felines, but the kind of skin-tight claws that could be found more often in predatory birds like hawks or falcons. Each of the talons was extended by a deadly sharp nail, with some residue of a kind of small animal's blood. This hand was tensely half open, constantly bending and stretching in an extremely unfriendly manner. Two bare claw feet under the robe had the same kind of hook-like nails, making every step he took look very steady. But one of the little toes on one foot was pricked by a thorn when passing through a bush of thistles not long ago, and was bleeding a wisp of dark red blood. He tried to lift that toe while walking, but it would still wince in pain whenever it accidentally ran into some leaves or sticks.

He murmured quietly as he walked, endlessly cursing the thorn, and every little pebble, every small branch he had met along the way. He slowly walked through the woods, carefully, his long and skinny toes leaving a long trail of uneven footprints on the moist earth. Judging from his look and behavior, he would be a tree elf, and was about a hundred years old. But for elves that are famous for their super long lifespans, about seven hundred years in average, he's indeed just a child.

Suddenly, a tiny bit of movement in the bushes in front of him made the little elf shut up and stop. He held his breath and stared attentively at the bushes. Time slipped away one second after another. He just froze there and didn't move at all, not even the slightest. But that movement did not appear again.

Just when the little elf started to doubt if it was just a trick of his eyes, finally, the bushes were slightly disturbed again. In a trice, a big fat rabbit hopped out!

The little elf's eyes shined bright, and he shot straight out like an arrow from a bow. He pounced on the rabbit in no time, catching the rabbit in the air as it tried to leap off and pressing his own weight upon it. His sharp claws hooked onto the rabbit's brown fur, and gripped it tightly in his arms.

The rabbit shivered violently in fear. The claws didn't pierce through its skin to make it bleed, but it wouldn't dare to struggle. The little elf was lost in ecstasy. This plump rabbit could keep him fed for days! No more rat meat, no more choking on grass roots! He could almost smell the greasy, burnt smell of cooked meat...

He was too excited drooling over this wonderful vision, and feeling too good about himself, to notice the slight sound of twig breaking behind him.

Snap.

* * *

She was born and raised in a small distant village deep in the mountains, and had never set foot out of the village since her birth. She had never met with anyone apart from the villagers, never seen the colorful world outside. She didn't even know that there was a Hilldown Plain. She only lived in a small world in the mountains, and was happy with it. Why wouldn't she be? It was quiet and peaceful. It was her whole world. Of course, the outside world was rich and exciting, but what did it have to do with her? She had always led a tranquil life, like all the people that had been living in this small village, generation after generation. Until one day, her world was turned upside down, by his intrusion.

2

A Hidden Crisis

The sun had almost sunk behind the back of the mountains. A few rays of red light shot out from the edge, shining the final golden glory upon the clouds at the edge of the sky. The sky faded from red at the edge of the mountains, to violet in the middle, and when it came to the opposite side across to the mountain range, there was only an endless deep blue. Rippled by a few strands of horizontally spread light clouds, it looked almost like it was under the ocean.

The excited mutter of the little elf after catching the rabbit and the ensuing commotion in the woods caused by his hunt masked the tiny sound behind him.

Just as the elf was considering how many meals he could split this rabbit into, and how he would cook it, suddenly, a deathly cold hand clasped his long ears and yanked him backwards, almost pulling his ears off, a second before saliva came pouring out of his mouth. His hood must have fallen off his head when he jumped for the rabbit, leaving his pair of huge pointy ears unprotected. He gave out a desperate and tragic sounding howl and shut his eyes. At the sound of his cry, a group of crows lifted into the air somewhere in the woods, cawing and flapping into the dark of night. For a moment, terrorized, his breath escaped his skinny chest, and his whole body turned numb in great fear. Yet, he was still holding tightly onto his beloved rabbit, as if his life hung on it.

A few seconds later, when he could breathe again, he realized that he had been lifted off the ground and turned around, his ears aching fiercely because of the weight of his body, his legs dangling in the air like a pair of crooked sticks. But he dared not open his eyes. His tongue moved silently in his mouth, busy praying that his predator could be quick about killing him thus causing him less pain. With nothing else in his mind, he waited for the judgment of fate...

Another half minute had passed, and the prayers said had already been repeated several times, but the little elf found himself still alive. Surprised and confused, but mostly terrified, he gingerly opened a slight crack in one eye. Appearing into his sight was a pair of eyes green like emeralds, almost shinning in the dimmed light of the forest, cunning and cold like a black cat observing its prey, staring at him with attentive interest and a bit of ridicule.

Frightened, the little elf closed that eye and fell back into darkness. When still nothing happened, finally, he couldn't help but open his eyes. This time, he had both of his large eyes wide open, and clearly saw the whole picture of his captor.

It's a human, no doubt, he thought, with his absurdly long limbs and wide shoulders. The little elf had not lived long among many of his own kind, so he was more used to the look of humans than other elves, and would definitely know one when he saw one. The eyes he saw were very beautiful even to him, but filled with unconcealable cruelty. The lowered eyelids covered half of the eyes, concentrating a vicious and sly gaze at him. The elf believed that this was a pair of eyes that only belonged to the devil, with the contempt of a spoiled teen examining his supper, and the mockery of a big cat playing with its prey before the kill, embedded on a pale, delicate visage.

He seemed to be just a boy not much older than fifteen, with a clean chin that no hair had grown on whatsoever, but his body build showed no hint of juvenility, firm yet smooth muscles shown from his shoulders and the upper arm with which he was holding the elf, whereas his face looked much younger. His straightly shaped nose and pale skin was as exquisite as silver which gave him a kind of chilling nobility. A strand of raven black hair hanging in front of his forehead formed a great contrast to his pale face. His angular cheeks drew a contour with two perfect arcs. The sinews of his neck seemed to be neither coarse nor awkward, nor lacking hardness, connecting to two collarbones with beautiful curves, casually half hidden by the open collar of his shirt, which was of a pale color, white or light green or light blue, it was hard to tell in the dim light of the woods at dusk. No details of his shirt could be clearly seen, except that there was a dark colored button around his neck below the collar.

He was leaning against a big rock and sitting on his feet, his right hand supporting his head with his elbow on the rock, the left hand extended out grabbing the elf by the ears. The youth's arm looked slimmer than most male humans his age, but it was obviously very strong, as it was carrying the whole weight of the elf like he was holding an apple by the stalk. The little elf looked up into his face after a quick scan over the hunter's full appearance, and came across that pair of eyes that were still staring at him.

The elf hesitated for a moment, then tentatively mumbled a few words in the human language.

"It is a lovely evening, isn't it?"

When he saw an interested and amazed look emerging on his enemy's face, showing that he understood, he saw a light of hope. A captor that would listen to his talk was far better than a roaring bear or a howling wolf. If he had to be captured by something, a human might be the best he could hope for. They could understand the value of a bargain. Hoping for the best, he began to use his innate elf talent, and burst out in a lengthy speech like a flood.

"Oh my most valiant and handsome captor, please, please don't eat me. I can see it is a noble lord you are, aren't you? My lord can surely see that I'm not tasty at all, not at all. Elves are never tasty. I won't taste better than a piece of wood. Look at these fleshless dry sticks of arms and legs, my lord. I don't have much meat, do I? My lord won't be satisfied even after eating the whole of me. You might as well just set me free. You won't regret it, I promise you. I'll catch animals for you every day, every month, and every year. And each one of them will be tastier and fatter than me, I promise! You won't even have the slightest need of hunting on your own anymore. And there's no need for you to worry that I will escape. Even if I do, you can catch me again easily, no? Or you can put a chain on my feet to keep me. Anyway please just don't eat me. I'm of more value to you alive than dead don't you see? Anything, anything I'll do for you if you would just spare my life... Oh and this big fat rabbit I caught..." he looked down in frustration at the rabbit in his arms, "It's yours now. If it's not enough, I'll catch you plenty more. You won't have that if you kill me."

The boy didn't move or make a sound, but was still looking at him with an "amused" look. The little elf didn't know if his pleadings were working or not. Perhaps not. But he might have already been eaten by now if he hadn't kept on talking and talking. So he'd better keep going. If his captor didn't do as much to release him, at least he could buy himself some time to find a way to escape. His eyes quickly and clandestinely spotted a small sharp stone not very far away from his right foot. Not daring to look down, his toes started reaching out blindly towards the stone on the ground as he continued to talk.

"We tree elves are blessed with the talents of controlling the growth of trees and doing woodwork. Do you need anything to be made out of wood? A slingshot maybe? I can make colorful clothes too like the other elves. How about if I'll make you a very, very beautiful hat, how about that? I promise it will satisfy you. I'm a really good hat maker. Or if you don't like it, a pair of boots will definitely satisfy you. If you let me go, I'll make you anything, anything you name."

When the little elf saw that the youth had still not reacted, he was a bit frustrated, even beginning to doubt if the lad could understand what he was saying. But the pair of green eyes looked down at the elf's bare feet with a bit of a smile. Maybe he did understand, but just cared not to answer. The little elf continued anyway, with all his hopes clinging to those toes of his. He still dared not look that way in case the predator noticed his plan, but he could feel that his toes were getting ever closer to that stone.

"If you like, I'll even build a house for you. I can also find a wife for you, a very, very beautiful girl. Isn't that a desirable thing? I'll be your loyal servant and friend forever, to help you with all your difficulties and..."

The elf felt a slight shake from the hand holding him, giving him the chance to finally reach that stone. In the meantime, the green eyes froze. For the first time, cruelty seemed to leave those eyes, and the thin lips beneath were also opening for the first time. They moved silently as if he was saying something, but no voice came out.

Just when his enemy was staring blank for a moment, and his lips moving repeatedly like saying a spell, the elf nimbly grabbed the sharp stone with the claws of his foot using his fastest speed, and fiercely threw it aiming at one of the emerald green eyes.

* * *

He, was a wanderer forever, going from this mountain to that peak, from this river to that creek. He walked through the wild and savage territories, far beyond the reach of the fire of civilization; he walked past ancient cities and castles, drenched in long eventful histories and rich magnificent cultures. No one knew where he came from, nor the place he was going. He didn't even have a destination himself. He just kept on going forward. When he was hungry, he picked some berries to eat alongside the road or shot a little animal or two with a simple self-made bow he carried around. When he was thirsty, he sipped the dew in the mountain woods or paid visits to some nearby mountain springs, streams, or tarns. He might be walking on and on like this forever. Until one day, his life became totally different than before, when she appeared.

3

A Failed Escape

"Ah!"

With a slight cry, the hand that was grasping the ears of the little elf let them loose. As soon as his feet touched the solid ground, the elf quickly turned around and ran for his life as fast as he could, still with the rabbit in his arms.

The elf heard an angry snarl came from behind him, and only two seconds later, that hand once again clutched him, this time by the neck, like a pair of pincer jaws, and pushed him against a nearby tree trunk.

In a great panic, the elf lost his grip on the rabbit in an effort to raise his claws to the hand that held him. The struggling rabbit escaped the moment his claws left its fur, when it landed on its feet. The rabbit realized that it had just escaped from hell and regained its life. It stomped its feet several times in gratitude and disbelief, and ran its heart out into the bushes, away from this damned place that had almost become its grave, never looking back. This time at last, the little elf couldn't care about his rabbit any more. Actually, that was the last thing he needed to worry about at the moment. Even if there was any bit of a chance that his captor intended to set him free, he lost it when he tossed that stone at him. Now there could be nothing waiting for him but death. Cold, cold death. He wouldn't even have a grave, he thought mournfully. Who cared if he could have that rabbit for dinner, in no time, he would become someone else's dinner. If the human didn't care to eat him, he could still kill him and leave him for the crows. Left as a pile of sticky bones, that was his future, if anything at all.

He tried his best to rip away the hand around his neck with his claws, but that only made the youth's hold tighter. With his back against the trunk, he heard the lad's fingernails digging into the bark behind his neck while his own nails were digging into the flesh of this hand. His thin neck was stuck in the arc between the fingers. He could still move a bit, but there was no way that he could get his big head out of the youth's grip, and it was ever closing in around his neck. He felt the hand becoming tighter and tighter, making his breath more and more difficult. The little elf knew that he was certainly doomed this time. The failed attempt had crushed all his hopes. There was nothing he could do than to face whatever was coming for him.

He opened his eyes with a stronger fear than before. The angry eyes he met made him shudder. He couldn't look into them, so he had to look away. But with that quick glance, he could still see that the stone hadn't hit the boy's eye. Instead, it had struck a little above his brow ridge. Fresh red blood bled from the wound on his forehead making his face look even paler. His hand was bleeding too, a river of wet blood running down along the little elf's sharp claws. He was glaring at the elf with extreme anger, his rapid breath pushing through his clenched teeth.

But once more, nothing happened. The little elf plucked up his courage and looked up again. This time, the green eyes weren't staring at him, but were painfully shut. His captor seemed to be in great agony. A lot of strength and will seemed to be needed to keep the pain inside, instead of showing it on his face. Although he had already closed his eyes, those eyes still gave away the agony he was suffering from behind those thin layers of eyelids. His breath became shaky and unstable, like he was choking on something. His face turned as pallid as a piece of paper, and he lowered his head. It seemed to the little elf that the lad was swallowing some large and rough object, so that his

Adam's apple was moving up and down with great difficulty. The little elf was worried that his enemy would begin to cry. He was confused, even developing a little sympathy for his captor. With a sudden absurd feeling of guilt, he released the grip of his claws on the hand, which in turn caused the grip around his neck to loosen up a little. He hoped the agony was not caused by his attack or his claws, or he would really die a horrible death.

Several minutes passed until the boy finally overcame the pain in his heart and slowly opened his eyes. This time, there was no cruelty, no anger, only tenderness. The elf doubted if his eyes tricked him, but he thought he saw also a tiny bit of helplessness and begging. Blood was running down the boy's face, diverted by his eyebrow around his eye, and dripping from his chin onto the grass one drop after another. What once had been a strange and ruthless predator now seemed more like a sad little boy.

The lad closed his eyes again, took a deep breath, swallowed hard, and finally weakly began to talk for the first time since the elf had encountered him:

"If... if I let you go, will you really... are you really willing to... become my friend?"

This time it was the elf's turn to be frozen. He would never would have thought that the youth would ask this specific question. He sounded innocent and pitiful, without the slightest shadow of the frightening hunter the elf had seen. The little elf was still frightened for a moment, judging the boy suspiciously, worrying if it was some kind of a cruel trick. But when he saw the boy's eyes, he understood. He had seen more than one kid like this one in his one hundred years of life. They appeared to be hard and cruel in the face of strangers, but were actually so lonely inside and all they ever needed was a friend. The youth didn't catch him for food in the first place. He just did it to dissipate the loneliness in his heart. Thinking of this, he finally knew why his captor never hurt him, not a tiny bit, even though he had all the capabilities for it. And in return, he threw a stone at him and dug his claws in his hand. He was overcome by strong guilt and would have flushed if his skin hadn't been so dark and wrinkled. He already knew the answer and hoped that his sincerity could comfort the boy and make up for his reckless actions. For a talkative little elf that loved to bring people happiness, there was nothing in the world that he should be better at. He forced himself to come to his senses, and answered with great pleasure:

"Absolutely!"

* * *

No one had ever thought that his life and hers would intersect. He belonged to the whole world. No single place, absolutely not one tiny village, could ever trap him inside. And she belonged to her little village. No place outside the village, not even the whole world, would have anything to do with her. However, people say that for two beautiful souls, even if they were just passing by the other in a trice, they would be able to find each other. On a day that couldn't be more ordinary, at a moment that couldn't be more accidental, a tiny ripple was created and spread out, like the shining water of a lake swept by a sweet summer breeze.

4

A Strange Company

The youth stared at the little elf, his pair of green eyes wide open with misbelief. He was not moving at all. Time seemed to become still, and the silence in the air seemed to have frozen their breath. To appease this awkward situation, the elf continued: "Of course I would love to be your friend! I'm sorry for the misunderstanding before and terribly sorry for hurting you." When the lad made sure it was not a lie or a trick, he released a breath of air that had been stuck in his chest. His body was also loosening a little, though his look was still a little uncertain and he was still quite guarded. He asked doubtfully:

"You promise that you won't run away again the moment I let you go?"

The little elf patted his chest hard and said: "I promise! Anyway, why would I run away again? I thought you were going to eat me! Now, I'm not only not going to be eaten, but also have a new friend! This is the best day of my life!"

The teenager was amused by the elf's funny actions, smiled and shyly lowered his head.

It was the first time the little elf saw his smile.

The youth finally rested his body and pulled his fingernails out from the bark behind the elf's neck, his hand still bleeding but he didn't seem to care. The little elf was just about half his height, so the lad had been kneeling and leaning forward to trap him, pressing his weight onto the tree. But since he no longer needed to hold the elf captive, he shifted his weight backwards and altered his position to sit on the ground. The little elf moved his head with gratitude. It was good to regain freedom. Even this movement made the lad became a little alert again. But the elf pretended that he hadn't seen it. The elf sat down against the tree with a look of total relaxation and even enjoyment. That made the youth fully let his guard down at last. This pair of new friends still needed time to get to know each other.

The lad didn't seem to know how to start a conversation because he was quietly waiting for the elf to speak. He was looking at the little elf without blinking, but his expression had totally changed from the precaution and doubt he had previously shown to expectation and interest now. Only the bleeding wound on his forehead was still a reminder of the unpleasant incident a while ago. The little elf guiltily looked at the wound, apologized to him and stood up to wipe the blood away using his dirty robe. The boy still looked a bit uneasy, but he smiled gratefully.

When the elf realized that his new friend was actually pretty friendly, he forgot all about the frightening experience right away and began to introduce himself.

"My name is Rudi. I'm a tree elf and I'm 112 years old now. We don't grow so fast like you humans do, in case you're wondering. Although I'm 112 years old, I'm not even fully grown yet. I live on my own by catching small animals like rabbits and pheasant in these woods."

He stopped when he finished and waited for the teenager to speak. But the lad was still looking at him delightedly. Left with no choice, Rudi asked some questions to break the awkward silence.

"Would you like to tell me your name?"

"I'm Aary."

"Oh, Aary, good name! Nice to meet you! And... where do you come from?"

"The Kingdom of Elberkhan" Aary said, as one of his fingers pointed towards the ancient castle lying in the shadows down the hills. Regardless of the thick layers of trees, shining lights of torches could still be seen on the castle walls, flickering in the dark.

"Wow! Really?" Rudi cried with excitement. It had always been his dream place to go, "Can you take me there?"

Aary's smile grew dimmer and a kind of sadness appeared on his face. He lowered his eyelids and murmured something Rudi didn't catch. Rudi was really bewildered. He didn't think he said anything inappropriate. But considering this was a very new friend, he dared not to push, in case it might fracture their newly built friendship. But before he could come up with another, easier subject, Aary suddenly thought of something and became jolly again. He asked Rudi as he stood up and brushed the grass debris off his pants: "Would you like to see my treehouse?" "Um... sure!" Before the little elf could finish his answer, Aary excitedly dragged him on the way like a little child. Rudi followed him, his little legs quickly moving to try to keep up with Aary's fast pace, and in the meantime, he tried not to trip over Aary's long legs.

The sky had turned completely dark. The moon hadn't come out yet, only the shimmers of bugs and fairies had appeared, and the glimmers of light reflected by the leaves lit up the whole forest. Nocturnal creatures were ready to begin their activities, and the woods became more and more gruesome in the dark.

Rudi watched warily for any movements in the forest around them. His eyes seemed to have better sight at night. He could feel many eyes staring at them from the bushes beside them as they hurried along the trail, while they were making huge noises around them. This made Rudi follow closer to Aary and hold his hand tighter. The howling of a beast came from a distance in the mountains sounding shrillingly and chillingly. Rudi shuddered unconsciously. But when he felt a firmer grip on his hand from Aary, he regained a bit of courage.

After walking a while, Aary brought the elf to a very old and magnificent redwood tree. The tree was located at a peak of the mountain. It was so thick that even if 10 elves were hiding behind it, Rudi wouldn't be able to tell.

"We're here." Aary said in a cheerful voice. "Right on the top."

At the same moment, a beam of bright moonlight shone through the treetops. Rudi looked up along the tree trunk. When his sight was almost vertical to the skyline, he finally spotted a wooden little cabin sitting on the tree's crown halfway into the dark sky. He probably wouldn't even notice it if Aary hadn't pointed it out for him. It wasn't big, and even though lit by the moonlight, its wooden color was nicely hidden among the branches and leaves. From the ground, they couldn't see much apart from the wooden platform it was sitting on, and a ladder leading to the platform from a nearby branch.

Rudi looked at it until his neck was stiff and sore and his head a bit dizzy, then he turned to Aary. Aary had also just looked back at Rudi after appreciating his own cabin in the heights. He asked Rudi with a proud smile:

"So? Not bad?"

* * *

It was a warm and gentle afternoon. She was rinsing clothes by the creek beside her village. As he passed by that village and casually lifted his head, he saw her beautiful silhouette in the setting sun. Her dark hair was gilded with golden sunlight beside her face, and he was completely fascinated. After years of drifting and wandering, his heart had become dried by darkness and weariness. But now, it was nourished by something, and he felt an unprecedented feeling of sustenance that he never had before. Like withered lips meeting a gush of fresh water or cracked soil welcoming a heavy rain, his hardened heart suddenly became soft as silk. It was as if the sunlight had leaked through the leaves and lit up all the dark dusty corners in his heart, reviving them to life. That feeling, peculiar and beautiful, captivating and intoxicating, gave him a sudden urge to settle down.

5

The Boy's Treehouse

Aary blinked at the elf, waiting for his comments, not even trying to conceal the pride on his face.

Naturally, the little elf was really generous complimenting Aary, even though he couldn't really see much of it. The height of the treehouse itself was impressive enough, and he couldn't wait to go up and take a closer look. That was when he realized, that the ladder didn't extend all the way down to where they were. In fact, apart from the very short section of ladder that he just saw, he couldn't spot anything at all: no ladders, no stairs, not even branches on the three trunk that anyone could hold onto for the most height of the tree. They were still a long distance away from where the bottom of the ladder disappeared into the air, and that's not just from a short little elf's point of view. Rudi estimated, that even for Aary, the height of the treehouse from the ground was more than five times his own height, and there was nothing on this tall, thick tree trunk that could lead them up there.

He asked confusedly: "But how do we go up there? Is there a hidden ladder somewhere?"

Aary grinned: "No need for ladders." He reached out a hand to Rudi: "Come on, I'll take you up there."

Aary threw him over his shoulder the moment Rudi took his hand. "Hold tight!" He shouted.

Rudi did not need Aary to tell him that. He clutched his hands tightly over Aary's chest, one arm over his shoulder and the other under his arm, as if his life depended on it, which was sort of true. As Aary started climbing, Rudi felt like he was starting to fly.

The tree on which the house stood had a thick trunk that was hard to grasp, without any branches close to the ground. So Aary used the branches of nearby trees for help, swinging and jumping from one branch to another. He raced up the trees like a skillful monkey, grabbing onto thick branches, or vines twining around the trunks when there were no branches, or nodes on the bark of the trees when there were no vines. Most of the time, Aary was hanging with the weight of them both entirely in his hands as he pulled them both up and up. Leaves brushed their cheeks and fell to the ground as they went by. The elf looked down and saw the ground rushing away from them swiftly, and closed his eyes in fear.

Only after a few seconds, Rudi found himself on solid footing again. He opened his eyes and saw a really beautiful wooden door. It was made from a whole thick piece of wood. The material's texture was a little coarse, but it was carved with delicate patterns. He truly loved this extraordinary piece of work in front of him, and his eyes were filled with admiration and expectation.

As they were almost at the top of the trees, the moonlight shone brightly on the carved wood without obstruction of the leaves. Compared to the gloomy darkness under the trees, the night up here was peaceful and beautiful. Afraid, but curious, he timidly turned around. When he saw the ground beneath him, he felt a wave of dizziness. If Aary hadn't given him a pull, he might have fallen down. He quickly turned back around and tried to calm his heart before it popped out. *Don't ever do that again*, he warned himself, and walked in through the wooden door that Aary had held open for him.

It was pitch dark inside. With the sound of a flick in the dark, a candle lit up. When Rudi's eyes adjusted to the candlelight, he opened them wide to see the furnishings in this room. To his surprise, there wasn't even a bed in the room, only a couple of wooden chairs around a square wooden table, and a wooden bookshelf holding some books and bottles and other peculiar objects against a wall. At the bottom of the bookshelf was a big wooden box that was too big to fit completely in, a wooden bucket next to the box, and some folded and piled up clothes. There was also a round stone bucket-like container sitting on the floor at a corner of the room, with some black charcoaled leaves and sticks inside. Rudi guessed that it was some type of a stove. Apart from the door that they just came in, there was only one closed wooden window on the wall of the opposite side.

Aary carefully put the candle down on the table. The wooden walls and furniture glowed yellowish in the warm orange light, and the shadows in the room danced as the flame flickered.

"Come sit." Aary dragged over a chair for Rudi and sat on the one next to it. Rudi climbed onto the wooden chair that was a little too tall for him, and sat facing Aary.

"Would you like some water? Or anything else to drink?" Aary asked.

"Really? You have something else?"

"Hmm... no, not really. Sorry."

A little disappointed, Rudi agreed to water and thanked Aary. He knew that humans also drank some other liquids, like milk from other animals' breasts or different kinds of colorful water with the same spicy taste that could make one's head dizzy or even crazy. He had some many, many years ago and had almost forgotten the taste.

But a life in the forest meant that even sufficient clean water was a luxury, so he wouldn't complain about that. The river currents on the plain were often busy places and therefore dangerous, even the one at the foot of the mountains. Humans, horses, dogs, and forest beasts all came down to the river for water, and Rudi wouldn't dare to go there unless he really needed to.

Small mountain creeks ran down from the top of the mountains. The water was really nice and fresh there, but it was too far and too long a climb. The mountain tops were stonier and more barren, which could keep the water running above the surface, while at the bottom, thick layers of earth covered the surface, and rich plantations grew. Before the creeks ran down the side of the mountains, they often went underground into the spongy soil to moisturize the roots of the plants. Even these creeks were often dried up after weeks without rain or snow during the autumn and winter seasons. Surely, there would be water enough for everyone when it rained, but raining meant also wet and cold, and it was not a very good thing to wish for. Most of the time, he needed to chew on grassroots to keep himself from dehydrating to death.

Aary took a large bronze jug and two stone cups from the book-shelf. He removed the heavy lid from the jug, and poured water into the cups, filling them to two thirds of the height. He handed one to Rudi. Rudi thanked him, tasted the water from the rim of his cup and began to wonder how Aary managed to get all these jars and bottles, and the water, up the tree. The water tasted a little sweet, probably taken from one of the mountain creeks.

"So...uh..." Aary began, a little nervously, "I'm sorry for scaring you... and for your rabbit. I could catch you another if you want."

"No, no, don't be." Rudi felt himself unnaturally polite, "I should be the one to feel sorry for hurting you, your head and your hand. How are your wounds by the way?" Only then did Rudi realize that Aary's left hand, the one which he had clawed, was still bleeding. Deep claw marks spread through the back, to the fingers and the wrist. Rudi felt guilty all over. He didn't even notice that Aary had climbed this tall tree with a bleeding hand carrying Rudi on his back. "Please let me help you with the wound."

"It's nothing. Don't worry about it." Aary hid his left hand behind his back and didn't even look at it, as if it was someone else's, as if he was ashamed of it.

Rudi wanted to insist, but Aary didn't give him the chance.

"I want to know about you. You must have had a lot of stories in all the 112 years of your life so far."

By then, Rudi was already filled up with questions. But he did love to tell people stories about himself, and decided that maybe it would be better if he started his own story before asking all the questions he had about Aary. So he agreed as soon as he heard this proposal, and began his lengthy narrative.

"Alright then. I do have an interesting story, now you've asked. But where should I start...?" and when he saw Aary's expectant look, "Ok, I'll tell the longer version. Let's start from before I was born..."

* * *

He came to this village, put his bags down for the first time in his long and endless journey, and found an empty house to stay in. He even found a decent job. He bought some necessities, got some furniture, and put everything properly in place inside his little cabin. He had not yet gotten the chance to meet the girl formally, but he wasn't anxious or worried. He was still young, only 16. No need to rush. He told people his name was Jerre, and that he came from a place very far away, but he loved this village, so he wanted to settle here.

6

The Little Elf's Tale

Hundreds of years ago, in the woods on the side of the Soulkeeper Mountain, there was a huge tree with a hole. Inside the tree hole was a spacious and comfortable room. My mother, who was a very young elf at the time, lived in that room.

She used to live with her grandfather. Sadly, before she came of age, her grandfather was taken from her by a serious disease. You should know that it's really dangerous for a young elf girl to live alone in the ancient and treacherous woods. But she was never afraid, because she had a red cloak that could keep her away from all harm and danger. It was protected by an ancient spell, and no foul or evil things could ever get near it. That spell was one of the strongest in the magic of the elves, one that could date back tens of thousands of years, when the elves were still one of the most powerful species in the world. I know that magic is considered evil and unnatural now, and anyone who practices it is seen as wicked, but that's only after the humans became the dominant species of the world. I don't know if you are familiar with the history, but thousands of years ago, there was a time when all magic prevailed, and the world was dominated by elves and other magical species. Humans also existed back then, but only had a relatively small population, and didn't play a very important role in the course of history.

But of all the magical species, there were always a small number of individuals that preferred to use their great power to feed their own selfish desires instead of for good purposes. They were the practitioners of dark magic. They used spells that were forbidden by the magic law to get eternal lives and extra powers for themselves at the expense of others. They had always existed, yes, but secretly, and posed no real threat to the main world, until seven thousand years ago, the dark power grew so strong that they didn't need to hide themselves anymore. It was referred to in history as the Dark Era, and the whole world, magical or non-magical, was a miserable place.

That was when the remaining kind and selfless individuals of all the magical species decided to unite their strengths and fight back against the dark powers. The Great Magic War lasted for hundreds of years, millions of magical creatures died on either side, until the dark side was finally subdued and went back into hiding. But the sacrifice was also severe for the winning side. The remaining magical species had trouble recovering from the cost of that war for a very long time.

In the meantime, the human species, who did not suffer much from the war, grew larger and more powerful at great speed, until about three thousand years ago, when all the magical species were forced to bend their knees to the ancient human kings and give up all magic practices, or endure the fate of being hunted down to the last one. Looking back to the Dark Era and the Great Magic War, humans, who had no inborn magic power, came to the conclusion that all magic is bad. So they banned all magic, good and evil, and forbade magic to be used for any purpose, regardless of the fact that it was also magic that had conquered the dark magic in the first place.

The magical species tried to defy at first, but even with magic, they were no match against the humans that outnumbered them a hundred to one. So in the end, all the remaining magical species obeyed, in order not to cost their species even more. But without magic, they found it hard to even survive in the perilous world full of humans and wild beasts. By now, many species have completely disappeared, and there are no more than a thousand elves left in the whole world. Sorry Aary, I mean no offense, but your ancestors did subjugate my ancestors among the others, and drove magic out from the world, not that it has anything to do with you and me, of course. Don't worry, I don't hate you humans. Oh, I've digressed, haven't I? Sorry, back to my mother.

So the words of the spell were lost with the decay of our species and the loss of our power. Only the cloak remained to protect the elves of my family, including my mother. It belonged to her grandmother, and her grandmother before that. It was given to her by her grandfather before he passed away. As his last breath faded away, he became part of the tree, as all the tree elves do when our lives come to an end.

In her red cloak, she walked around in the woods, looked for food in the woods, and played in the woods. She especially loved to sing. Nearby residents and the animals in the woods called her the Red Elf. Day by day she matured, and day by day, she became more beautiful than ever before, and her singing voice mellower and sweeter. In the woods, the flowers that had seen her face, only for her would they blossom, the birds that had heard her songs, only for her would they sing.

One morning, a travelling human hunter rode to the foot of the Soulkeeper Mountain, and heard a maiden's singing coming from above, in the woods on the side of the mountain. He pulled the reins and halted the horse. He stopped in his journey, which he hadn't done for a very long time, to listen. It was a song he had never heard in all the places he'd been to, in a language he didn't understand. But he was totally lost in the beautiful voice. The song ended and he came back to reality, but the next one began right away. He turned his horse towards the sound. Following the singing, he rode slowly up the hill and into the woods. Even his horse was enchanted by the songs and ambled towards the fountainhead of the voice by itself. Strands of morning mist tangled around the trees, leading the man and the horse deep into the gloomy forest.

Eventually, he saw a red figure dancing around in the woods. He could vaguely see her behind all those trees. The huntsman urged his horse to keep moving, until there was just one row of trees between him and the red figure. He stopped for a moment, and hopped off his horse.

The girl was only half the size of a human and had long ears sticking out between her beautiful red hair. But she had a face that would make any human girl jealous, and her voice was making the bottom of the hunter's heart tremble and tickle. And the next thing, like in the fairy-tales, the huntsman couldn't help but join in at a break of the song, in human language. The Red Elf was startled by his abrupt entry and halted her singing. But the magnetic, passionate singing of the hunter didn't stop. It became more sonorous.

The Red Elf calmed down and carefully inspected this intruder. He was very tall. His lean cheeks were covered in an unruly black beard, and his skin showed a gloss like bronze under the light of the morning sun bursting through the leaves. He was carrying a strong but rough looking wooden bow, and a long spear was strapped to his back. The weapons looked scary to the Red Elf, but also fascinating. The black stallion he held was as sturdy as its owner, its mane moving in the light breeze. A worn leather quiver was hanging over the saddle, with a dozen well-used arrows inside. The horse was listening quietly with its head down. The hunter was not looking at her, but looking into the sky. His soulful eyes captivated the beautiful elf. She felt herself melting into the hunter's songs. Soon, she began singing again, responding to the hunter's song with her own language. The hunter lowered his head and looked into the elf's beautiful eyes. Two mellifluous voices entangled together. All the animals in the woods fell silent and held their breaths. Even the plants were softly swinging with the rhythm. The two singers looked each other in the eyes and ambled closer and closer in their dancing steps. At last, at the end of the song, they turned the last note into an affectionate kiss.

A wonderful and happy life began in this song. The hunter ended his years of life on the road and settled in these woods. He couldn't live in the tree hole the elf had once lived in, because only tree elves were able to fit in. So, he built a wooden cabin and she moved inside with him. After they met, she completely threw away her old life of a tree elf and lived with him like a human girl, living in a human house and eating human food. He hunted and brought home food for her, and she also played her part as a responsible wife by taking good care of the housework and preparing dinners. They had to learn each other's language, but the power of love made learning an enjoyable and easy thing. Their cabin was forever filled with singing and laughter. They became the spring of joy in the woods and made the whole forest more alive.

A year later, they gave birth to a child. Of course, that child was me. They were like all the other parents, caring for and protecting their baby with all their hearts. I looked more like my mother than my father, with my long ears and short size, but my lifestyle was totally human. I learned both the language of elves and of humans. Actually, the only thing that I ever learned from my mother is the elfish language, which is already quite rusty now.

I was never afraid in the woods, with my mother's cloak and my father's bow. I couldn't sing beautifully like them, as much as I wished I could, but they were always patient in teaching me, and encouraged me a lot, so even I could sing with them in a chorus of three. The perfect life went on, until I was 28. As you know, for us, 28 could still be considered as an infant. In my mother you couldn't see even the slightest change from the day my parents met. But for my father, it was different. Actually, the problem became obvious only a few years after they met: my father was aging day by day: his raven black hair grew greyer and greyer, and finally white, his hands became weaker and trembled more; wrinkles crawled on his once radiant face; his eyes could no longer see things clearly, and he began to miss shots during his hunt, which had never happened before. My mother retained the look of a young girl, beautiful and vibrant. Time slid away from her without leaving any trace, while it peeled away my father's youth and life piece by piece. Only neither of them would mention it, neither wanted to admit the truth. Mother loved father as always, and father tried to show his strong and healthy state like the first day they met. But he was indeed getting old.

In the end, tragedy happened. Inevitably. One day in the year I turned 28, he went out hunting as usual. He struggled to climb onto his old steed and left for the forest, but he never came back. We went looking for him, and found him on the ground, face down, His steed stood by his side, gently sniffing him with its nose and making a mourning sound, its hoofs stomping the ground beside him. He had no serious wounds, so it couldn't be a bear or a boar, nor any other wild beasts. My guess is that he tried to chase some game, but the horse was too old to run steady, and he lost his balance. His feeble hands couldn't hold tight enough onto the reins anymore, so his whole body probably tipped over. At last, he fell onto the ground, and never got up again.

* * *

Only weeks after his arrival, he had helped the villagers solve several difficult, long unsolved problems with his intelligence. Everyone knew there was a new teenage boy in the village. He was kind and friendly, warmhearted and helpful. Everybody loved him, and he fitted into this little village right away. But before long, his distinguished noble bearing gradually emerged, making him stand out from the others in this remote little mountain village. Another thing was, unlike those people who spent their whole lives living and dying in this small village, he had seen the world.

Rudi's Theme

Chen Yuxiao

7

A Sad Memory

With my father gone, my mother became a totally different person. I noticed a few days after my father passed, when she told me to call my father home for dinner. We had just buried his bones together, under the tree in front of our house. I looked at her confusedly and told her he was gone. She seemed like she suddenly remembered this and started to cry. I didn't know what to do but pat her on the shoulder. I knew I must stop acting like a baby and grow up, for her.

I started making meals for us, since she could no longer do anything but sit still, staring blankly and crying. I didn't know how to hunt, but we did have some food in stock that would be enough for the both of us for weeks. I hoped that after some time she would get better and come back to me, then we could figure out how to pull through this together.

But days passed, and she didn't get any better. I'd say she turned even worse. She had almost become completely mad, often crying and laughing at the same time. Although she remained very beautiful, she never sang again. When the birds in the woods came to visit her, she just shut them all out. She also completely forgot about my existence. I was like the air to her eyes. When I spoke it was nothing more than a blow of wind. She would walk straight past me, not pausing for one second or even glancing in my direction. She always locked herself in the room and cried. Even when I checked on her there, she would be completely indifferent to me. She just lay in bed with my father's old clothes clutched tightly between her fingers. Gradually, I learned to not care anymore. For me, I didn't just lose my father, my mother died on that very same day.

Weeks passed like this. One day, she finally came to me. On that day, she seemed particularly clear-minded. She came to my room early in the morning, wearing her red cloak. I was both surprised and happy about her behavior. I thought my mother had finally come back to me. But before I could speak, she gently pressed her finger to my lips and stopped me. She closed her eyes and kissed me on my forehead. Then she walked out of the house in silence and closed the door behind.

Later, I realized that she was gone. She quietly left the wooden cabin in the woods, riding father's old horse that was almost unable to walk, and wearing her red cloak. She didn't take anything else with her. I looked for her around the cabin without any actual hope, and when I couldn't find her, I never looked for her again. Since then, I have never seen her. But even if I found her, what difference would it make? ...

Rudi said these words without any emotions. He didn't even try to hide his disappointment and frustration. His gloomy big eyes were half covered by the lids as he sat there in a trance.

Aary interrupted his thoughts and urged him on: "I'm sorry to hear that Rudi. But what happened next? How did you grow up on your own?"

"Ok, ok." Rudi placated his emotions and continued, "my parents were gone, but for me, life had to go on..."

After that, I lived in the wooden cabin by myself. My habits were all human so I couldn't live with the other elves or live in a tree. But I was too queer-looking to join the humans either. The only thing I knew well, and felt comfortable with, were these woods and my parents' cabin. So that was where I stayed, even if it meant living alone.

It was not so bad at first, living alone. Although I didn't have the red cloak to protect me, I managed to keep myself safe by staying in the cabin and eating the food in stock. But the stock was getting emptier every day. Finally, when I ate up the last pieces of hard cookie and dried meat, I knew that I must find food for myself. I had the bow my father left, grasped in his hand the day he passed, but I didn't know how to use it. He never taught me. He always went hunting alone. When I asked him to take me with him, he always smiled kindly and told me that it was dangerous for children, and that he would teach me later, when I was older. In the end, he never got the chance to. I tried to pull the string once but nearly knocked my own arm off, and I have never dared to touch it again.

So, I had to return to my wild nature and hunt for prey with my sharp claws. Actually, elves don't eat meat. My fellow brothers and sisters eat only pies and cakes specially made from the leaves of trees, and their claws are only used for delicate woodworking. But I had lived my life as a human child and didn't know anything about the recipes of the elves, so I had to hunt.

Before I hunted for the first time, I was really afraid, and would have rather chewed mud than dare to kill an animal. But I was so hungry that I finally made up my mind to catch a raccoon. When I noticed it, it was moving slowly on the ground through the trees. It was a lot slower than normal raccoons, perhaps too old or had had too much food. Anyway, it made a perfect target for me. I kept really still and watched it closely from behind a tree, and when it got near me, I sprang off and pounced on it. It struggled in my hands as I strangled it as hard as I could. At last it finally stopped moving. When I looked down, its bloody mutilated look made me nauseous. My hands were all bloody, with hairs stuck in the nails. I didn't even want to eat it anymore. Luckily, I know how to build a fire. So, I cooked it over the fireplace in my house. That kept me fed for a week, but my hand stunk of blood for even longer. The contact with blood hardened my claws, and hardened my heart. That day I began my life as a hunter with claws.

I always thought that, even if I lost everything, I would still have my father's little cabin. It could keep me away from the attacks of beasts. Little would I have expected, that one time when I was out hunting, I forgot to put out the fire from the last time I cooked, and it set the wooden house on fire. I was still out hunting when a little bird came to me in a hurry and told me to go back home. When I saw her terrified look, I knew something was wrong. I raced home with her, but by the time I got back, the fire was already burning to the sky. Thick black smoke was rolling up to break through the crowns of the trees and rushed straight into the sky. The pungent burning smell and gusts of heat came at me so that I couldn't open my eyes. The crackling sound of the burning wood and booming sound of structure falling down came from inside the house. I was petrified. The terror and desperation of losing everything I had made me unable to move. My head was a total blank, and the crushing noise sounded like the sky tumbling down. I even felt like I was in that house myself, and my life was fading away with its destruction, perishing together with it. The picture in front of me blackened out as I lost my balance and passed out on the ground.

When I opened my eyes again, I found myself surrounded by a flock of concerned little birds. From them, I came to know that after I fainted the day before, a human troop that was passing by the woods on the way to Elberkhan put out the fire. They found me unconscious on the ground and wanted to bring me with them. But their leader said it was not allowed. At last they decided to put me in a more comfortable position and left some clothes on me to prevent me from being frozen to death at night before they resumed their journey. I have been filled with gratitude for the Kingdom of Elberkhan and the people living there ever since, though I have never dared to go there, considering my look. That, as you can imagine, was the reason why I was so excited when you mentioned Elberkhan.

But anyway, the house was totally ruined. Only piles of blackened wood and a piece of scorched land covered with ashes were all that's left behind, like the remaining firewood on a hearth. All I had left were those clothes the men left for me, and my sharp claws.

Aary listened to the little elf's experience with sympathy and felt the deepest condolence for his misfortune. He never thought that this inattentive looking little elf had been through such miserable things.

Rudi looked at him with an expression longing for consolation. Aary thought he should say something to comfort him, but he didn't know what to say. He felt a bit embarrassed, needing to think for a long time before he could organize the words. He finally took a deep breath and said carefully: "Good thing that you weren't home and saved yourself. Everything could start again as long as you're alive, right?"

When he said this Aary felt those words weren't enough to comfort Rudi, and felt a little ashamed. But Rudi cooperatively appeared to be greatly encouraged, and nodded hard with gratitude and inspiration in his eyes, and continued his tale. Aary realized that Rudi didn't really need the comfort, the response from the audience was only part of his storytelling.

"You are right. I didn't stay homeless for too long. With the blood of tree elves running through my veins, though I hadn't spent a day in a tree, I found a wonderful tree hole using my natural instincts, and made it my home. Living like a normal tree elf isn't so bad after all. The tree closes its hole and protects me from the beasts when I'm inside, and all I need to do is to keep it company, and make sure that it has enough water. I still keep myself alive by hunting small animals though. I can't eat raw leaves, they are impossible to swallow. I don't know how the other elves manage with them, but I'm sure they aren't eating them directly from the trees. I can't survive only on berries either. There are too few in the woods, and none in the winter, not to mention some are poisoned. I still cooked meat on open fires, but I was more careful with the fire... well, at least I thought I was, until I burnt down the tree again."

"What?? Seriously?" Aary asked in disbelief, his eyes wide open.

"Ha ha, of course not. That one was a joke. How stupid do you think I am?"

Aary smiled. Although it was not a very good joke, he felt a kind of gratitude for how Rudi ended his story in a humorous and easy way, and was moved by how cheerful and positive he remained after all that he had been through. He knew he would feel sad for days if the story ended when the fire burned down everything.

"Do you... still feel sad when remembering it?" He asked tentatively.

"Nah, it all happened many, many years ago, and I am long past weeping for it. Remember one thing Aary, time is always the best antidote for sorrow and the best healer for wounds. And a hundred years is a really long time."

The little elf who had looked like an innocent and heartless little child previously, now seemed for the first time to Aary, a wise and profound elder of 112 years old. Aary gave a heartfelt smile to the little elf which he very much deserved.

* * *

Because of his outstanding wit, bright humor and extraordinary makings, he gradually became a star among the girls in the mountains. The girls surrounded him every day, sang for him, danced for him, and he repaid them with a graceful manner, remaining charming and debonair with the girls. However, none of them knew, that he was only attracted to one of them. Little by little, he found out that the girl's name was Maire. She was the village elder's youngest child and only daughter. She was 23 years old, 7 years older than him. But what did it matter?

8

The Cookie Jar

A golden sun rose up from behind the peaks. Sunlight gradually crept towards the shade under the mountains, slowly crawling over the villages on Hilldown Plain and bringing vitality to the earth. The morning air smelt so fresh that you could almost squeeze juice out of it. People and animals all began to stretch themselves and move their bodies which had been motionless for the whole night. Eyes were opened lazily in the morning sun, but returned to squinted lines the moment they met the dazzling light. The rivers on the plain gleamed again with shimmering gloss, and spread across the plain like veins of light. In the shallow spots, pebbles that had been smoothed and bleached by the flow of water appeared from the water's surface, and were as exquisite and glistening as eggs freshly boiled and peeled under the sunlight. Giant eagles emerged from their stony caves on the cliffs, and were standing at the top of the peaks, shaking their wide black wings in the warmth of the rays carried by the sunlight. Suddenly, they rose up into the sky, circling around and around, casting giant shadows on the earth, like a piece of dark cloud on the light blue sky.

Sunlight slowly shone through the opened wooden window of the treehouse in the woods, and enveloped every dusty corner with light. It crawled onto Rudi's face and woke up the little elf from his deep slumber. He struggled to open his eyes in the sun and was surprised to see the room he was in. The wooden furniture and floor seemed to be glowing in the warmth of the morning light, and his back ached a little from the hardness of the floor he had been lying on. Only then did he recall what happened the evening before and the friend he just met. He also remembered that he entered and stayed at Aary's place only moments after they met, not to mention that this friend almost killed him in the beginning. He had never been so careless. It was lucky that he was still alive and he felt a bit scared even thinking of it. But it was fun, and worth it. If he hadn't woken up to find himself in Aary's treehouse, he would have thought that everything that happened the day before was all a dream.

When Rudi scanned the room for Aary, he realized Aary was already up. He was standing by the window, looking outside with his back to Rudi, putting on a black hooded cape over his shoulders. The morning air breezed in, bringing a mixed scent of autumn leaves, pine needles, and wet dirt into the room, and stirring the fringe of Aary's black cape, as well as his black hair. Birds were chirping loudly outside, bringing the whole forest alive with tuneless songs.

Rudi yawned aloud to let Aary know that he was awake. When he heard Rudi, he had just finished his last movement of pinning the cape onto his shirt, and turned around. He seemed to be in high spirits. He smiled to Rudi, the kind of innocent, hearty smile that lit up his face with the sunlight that shone from behind him, and asked: "Did you sleep well?"

"Yes! Very well. Thanks for asking. I haven't slept in a human house for ages." Rudi said cheerfully, "It totally agrees with me."

Another big yawn came to Rudi. He rubbed his eyes and said: "You're up early."

"I've been awake for a while. I hope you didn't find the floor too hard. It was not made for sleeping, I'm afraid."

"It's fine enough for me." Speaking of this, Rudi was suddenly curious, "You don't usually stay here?"

"No."

The conversation ended abruptly. Rudi felt like there was more to the story. He wanted to ask where he usually stayed, but Aary didn't give him the chance to.

"I'm going out for some time," said Aary, with the slightest bit of anxiety hidden in his voice, "Do you need my help getting down? Or if you want, you could stay here until I return. I will be back before sundown."

Rudi had been waiting for the chance to explore the house, so he answered right away: "If it's alright for you, can I stay here?"

"Sure, great. Make yourself at home. You can use anything, the chairs, the books, anything. Oh, only, try to keep away from the medicine bottles, some of them might be a bit dangerous if you don't know how to handle them. I wouldn't want you to burn down my house too." Aary stuck out his tongue and made a face to Rudi.

"Ha ha, don't worry, I won't. Just do your thing. I'm a big boy now. I can take care of myself."

Aary laughed and headed to the door. Before Aary could reach the door, a sudden rumbling noise sounded from Rudi's stomach. That's when he realized how hungry he was. He hadn't eaten for a while, even before the rabbit ran away.

"Oh, wait! Do you have anything to eat?"

"Of course! Where are my manners! Here!" Aary reached for a pottery jar from the bookshelf and took it down. Compared to some other delicate wares on the bookshelf, this jar looked pretty plain and simple. The base of the jar was made with coarse yellow clay. The uneven shape made it look handmade. The brown colored enamel dripped down from the opening like melted caramel, forming an upside down crown shape. Aary popped open the cork lid of the opening and shoved the jar into Rudi's arms: "Eat as much as you want. I'll see you later."

Rudi looked down and, *wow*, it was a whole jar of sweet cookies! Not the kind of hard cookies for storage, but freshly baked soft cookies that smelled like childhood. He joyfully reached his hand inside and grabbed out a handful of cookies and stuffed them into his mouth. That instant, he felt like he was in love, and the rest of the world disappeared. The rich taste of the cookies filled his head from his mouth. He had never had anything so good, so delicious. The cookies tasted like honey and butter, and something else, something he couldn't name, something like... a dream? They were so richly-flavored and crunchy, he could almost die at that instant so that his always-hungry life would end with these lovely things in mouth and belly. Before he even had the chance to chew, the second handful was already on its way. His hands seemed to be out of control, just continually delivering cookies to his mouth.

When he was ready to grab for the fifth time, he looked down at the jar, worrying that he was already finishing the cookies. Surprising, he found that the jar still seemed full, without any trace of his past plunders. He stared confusedly at the cookies and shook the jar a little. Nothing seemed amiss, just a *whole jar* of ordinary cookies. Suspiciously, he grabbed the next handful and watched closely without distraction. Then he saw. Magically, the cavity made from the missing cookies rose up from below and was restored almost immediately. More cookies seemed to be "growing" from the bottom and refilled the hole! His eyes opened wide in shock, like two boiled eggs. He lifted his head: "Hey Aary, what's with this..."

Before he could finish his question, he realized that Aary had already left. The door was still slightly swinging behind him, the hinge making a squeaking sound.

* * *

In his eyes, she had a unique kind of tranquil beauty that was different from all the others. She never flattered him or disgraced herself by being ridiculously pretentious in front of him like the other girls. Her hair and eyes were as black as the deepest night. They trapped him inside and he could not escape. As for Jerre, he was casual, even a bit raffish with the other girls, but he never allowed himself to overly flirt with Maire. She had something in her that fascinated him, bewitched him, something that both attracted him and intimidated him. She had the sharpness and wisdom of a woman. She had a unique temperament that no one else had. And she had an unreleased passion like fire deep inside her heart, he could tell.

9

The Mysterious Assortment

The sky turned bluer as the sun climbed higher. Fat white clouds began to gather in the sky, so pure and fluffy, like cotton, or a herd of sheep scattered on a vast blue grassland. A flock of black birds flew up from the forest, chattering as they pushed past each other into the sky.

After filling his belly with loads of cookies, Rudi finally felt that he could eat no more. With the jar continually filling up, he lost count of how many cookies he had eaten, but could guess that he finished at least 10 entire jars. After swallowing the last piece of cookie that he could manage, he stuffed the cork lid back into the jar in his arms, which still seemed as full as if he had done nothing with it. When he stood up, his tummy felt it was about to explode. The great pain caused by an overly stretched stomach forced him to sit back down and relax for almost an hour rubbing his belly, before he could stand steadily. He tried to put it back to its original place on the bookshelf with his little short arms but failed, so he put it on the table for now. He picked up some of the cookie crumbs he found on himself and put them into his mouth. Then he finally lifted his head, ready to take a formal look at this house.

As noon drew near, the magical golden light that shrouded the room in the morning was gone. The area lit up by the sunlight grew smaller but brighter, until it turned into a dazzling bright line of light on the floor under the window frame right before it disappeared. When it was almost the middle of the day, most parts of the room seemed dimmer than in the morning, even as the sun burned as bright as ten thousand candles above the roof. Although it was turning chilly at nights as the autumn drew near, at noon it still felt like summer, and the sun was still bright and hot. A light wooden scent filled the room as the cabin basked in the midday sun. The smell made Rudi feel safe and relaxed. Outside the opened wooden window, layers of tree leaves shivered lightly in the wind. A few of the leaves were beginning to turn slightly yellow, but the forest still seemed thick and green.

Rudi stretched himself and felt that the cookies in his stomach went down a little, so he could move again. He leaped down from the chair to take a walk around the room. As if he had just arrived, he looked at the room curiously. Everything in the cabin was made of wood. The walls, the floor, the celling, and all the furniture were made in the same fashion. Judging from the color, Rudi thought it looked like the pinewood from this forest. No nails were used as far as Rudi could see, and all the wood was joined together with mortises and tenons. It was nicely made, Rudi thought. He wondered if Aary did it all by himself, and if so, how long it took him. He knew that as a tree elf, he was supposed to be good at woodwork, but he was not, and he lied about it when he was trying to get Aary to free him. Had he known how good Aary was, he'd never have said that. But that didn't matter anymore.

His legs stopped in front of the bookshelf. The first thing that caught his attention was the box next to his feet. Rudi bent down to pull out the big wooden box and opened the lid, and was surprised to see that inside the box were all kinds of simple handmade musical instruments. It looked like they were all made from materials gathered in this forest. They weren't painted, but were all very elegantly made and carved with delicate patterns. Rudi was totally amazed by the maker's techniques. If the house was made by a skilled builder, these were definitely made by a great master. There were all kinds of wooden instruments that he did and didn't recognize. Holes were cut out from some, others were attached with strings. Every edge and every hole, smooth or sharp, was crafted almost perfectly, without any bit of carelessness. Rudi gingerly took out a few to take a closer look at. There were patterns and words carved on the exteriors, all very delicate as well. He could recognize some of the words written in the curlicue letters of human language, even a few in his own language – Elvish. But there were also words in peculiar languages that he had not seen before. From the sentences he understood, he could see that they were mostly beautiful poems and verses, and each one of the instruments was signed with Aary's name.

Rudi took out a little wooden box with the shape of a tear drop cut in half. One side of the box was flat, while the other was round. A spiral shaped hole was cut out on the flat surface, and a few strings were attached across the hole. On the right side of the box, there was a line carved in human letters: *A tear of the autumn falls from the sky, before the sunset and the evening tide.* Rudi read the words out loud, and read them again. It was beautiful, he thought, and fitted the time of autumn. But he hadn't read many poems in his 112 years, and he could not tell if it was a famous line or written by Aary himself. The left side had only Aary's name, carved in cursive letters. He held the box in one hand, and gently stroked one string with another. As the string vibrated, the wooden board around the spiral hole trembled with the vibration, and a very sweet sound came out from the little box. He was fascinated by that sound, and couldn't help sticking all his fingers out to play it. But he didn't know how to play and just managed to make a few awkward notes in the end. The notes bounced floppily in the air and quickly vanished. Rudi reached out a hand, trying to grab them in the air, but couldn't catch a tail. That made him quite frustrated.

After he put the instrument back into the box and closed the lid, he turned to examine the wooden bucket beside it. Inside the bucket were some white cloths with chocolate-colored stains. It looked like a waste bucket, so Rudi lost interest and stood up to look at the bottles and jars on the higher tiers of the bookshelf. He took a long time to carefully inspect everything within his reach. There were some other big clay jars like the one he ate the cookies from, but they were on the top layers of the bookshelf and he could not reach it, being only half the height of Aary. Of those he could reach, most were bottles made of colored crystal, and he could see the substances inside. The bottles were of different shapes, tall and short, fat and thin, big and small. He was certain that these were not made by Aary himself, because there was no way to find the materials in the forest. Some bottles contained things he was familiar with, like herbs and leaves, nuts and berries. Others with stuff that looked like some kinds of mysterious and dangerous remedies as if they came from black sorcerers' drawers, like thick black syrup, clear blue liquid with bubbles, yellow pearly liquid, small green crystals... He tried to open a bottle with some sort of clear colorless liquid inside that looked absolutely harmless, and instantly a purple tongue of flame burst out, together with a pungent heat wave. He was completely terrified and almost threw the bottle away. But somehow, he managed to keep it in his hand. Not feeling like touching it for even one more second, he hastily closed the lid and put it back in place with shaking hands. Then he remembered Aary's words before he left. How could he have forgotten! The one thing that Aary had asked of him! It must have been the cookies. He had so many cookies that all his wits were pushed out by them. It must have been. He felt so lucky that he decided to hold onto the bottle instead of throwing it on the floor, or else, he might really have burnt down Aary's wooden house, and himself with it. He never dared to open anything again. He didn't even dare to look anymore, as if the act of looking itself could be dangerous and cause trouble.

Then he took a look at the books. There were more than 20 of them. The covers all looked very old and worn-out, but quite clean. He thought carefully and was certain that Aary didn't warn him about the books. So, he took one with a red-brown leather cover off the bookshelf. *The Art and History of Alchemy in Healing*, Rudi read the title silently. Well, that somewhat explained the peculiar bottles on the bookshelf and the dangerous contents. Driven by curiosity, he looked at other books one by one. He hadn't done much reading in the human language, but his mother had a lot of books in Elvish passed on to her by her grandfather, and Rudi read most of them before they were burnt down with the house. He hadn't seen any books since. Therefore, even though reading human language was more difficult for him, Rudi couldn't help himself going through every one of the books. Even just flipping those pages, feeling the weight of it in his hands, made him feel somewhat nostalgic.

On Aary's bookshelf, there were fictional novels and ancient legends, such as *The Dawn of the Silent Kingdom*, whose Elvish version was one of Rudi's favorite books when he was younger, telling a fascinating story about an ancient legendary kingdom controlling the world with a new religion. There were some practical books, like *A Carpenter's Cabinet*, or the one about alchemy that he saw earlier. There was even a book about elves, *The Hidden Masters of Nature*, Rudi was quite interested in this book about his own species, but after reading a few pages and finding that it was mainly telling the history of elves, which was in fact quite boring, he closed it and put it back on the bookshelf along with the others.

Rudi went on like this, looking and touching things in the cabin, and before he realized it, half the day had already passed. The sun was not as dazzling now and the sky became gentle and mild. Birds in the forest fell silent, and bugs buzzed lazily in the leaves of the trees. He wondered where Aary had gone and when he would come back. He walked to the window and stood in front of the opening, where Aary stood in the morning. The windowsill was about the height of Aary's waist, but Rudi could barely stick his head above it and look outside. The forest looked peaceful and undisturbed in the lazy afternoon warmth. Rudi felt a gush of sleepiness and yawned aloud. If Aary wasn't coming back, he would have to eat a second meal of cookies... A cool, refreshing breeze broke the peace and blew onto his face, bringing in the scents of autumn, of fallen leaves and ripe fruit. He closed his eyes, feeling the soft wind touching his face evenly. Nothing could be more blissful.

BANG!!

Suddenly, the door behind him popped open with a loud sound. Rudi almost had a heart attack. He turned around frightened and startled, and saw Aary. The black-haired boy tumbled in through the door, and crashed onto the floor.

* * *

He was thinking of her day and night. Maire, this name echoed in his ears all the time. He carefully approached her, with patience and discretion, lest any step he took be too hasty and cause him to lose his chance. He began to invite her for walks from time to time. The topics of their conversations gradually evolved from the affairs in the village to the whole world. He told her about many of the interesting things he came across in his journey and many peculiar stories he had seen or heard of. His narration of the beautiful world outside was vivid and fun, and he always added some humorous comments of his own. When talking with her, his eyes were full of radiant sparks and endless tenderness at the same time, and she listened, with her shiny eyes.

10

The Healing

Rudi was totally terrified. He stood there for several seconds before he realized that he should hurry forward to check on Aary and see what was going on. Aary was lying weakly on the floor, pressing his chest against the cold hardwood floor. Rudi watched his shoulders move up and down with each difficult breath he took. His breath was feeble and rapid, very unsteady and shaky. Blood soaked through his light blue shirt, fresh blood, newly stained.

Rudi was anxious but didn't know what to do. He reached out a hand, but froze in the air before it touched Aary when he saw the blood, and drew it back. He felt useless. He wanted to help Aary up but was worried that he would hurt him. He didn't even know if Aary could stand at all. Seconds felt like hours, and Rudi's head was a chaotic mess, but a total blank in terms of ideas.

Finally, he asked, attentively: "Are... are you alright... Aary? What happened?"

Aary just seemed to have realized Rudi's existence, and noticed his embarrassment. He struggled to support his upper body with his arms, lifted his head and forced a pale smile:

"Sorry... Rudi... I... I just need a moment... please. Don't worry."

His voice was trembling, and Rudi could hear pain in the pauses between the words. He also saw a bloody gash on Aary's left cheek, all the way from his chin to the corner of the eye. But instead of scolding Rudi for his uselessness, Aary almost sounded like he was feeling bad for not being able to attend to Rudi. Now Rudi felt even worse. He was not only doing no good, but also making Aary spend extra energy on comforting him!

He dared not speak again, but watched worriedly as Aary's breath gradually steadied.

Aary rested for a few more minutes before he finally gathered enough strength and propped himself up painfully with his arms. Little by little, he dragged himself to the bookshelf, with apparent difficulty. Then he realized that Rudi was still staring at him in horror. He smiled again, and said to Rudi with feigned easiness:

"It's nothing. Could you... close the window for me, please, and would you excuse me...? I mean... just look away?"

Rudi could see pinpricks of sweat on Aary's forehead. He felt the great effort Aary was making in concealing the pain, and knew that he was asking him to look away. He was completely puzzled, but seeing how weak Aary was, he couldn't allow himself to ask any more questions. So, he turned around and shut the wooden windows obediently, leaving the room in almost total darkness, and sat on a chair facing away from Aary.

After Rudi sat down, he heard some soft noises coming from behind, clothes rustling, wooden floor squeaking, and Aary's trembling breath. Then he heard a light noise that sounded like Aary had taken a bottle from the bookshelf and opened it. Then, there was a sound of tearing clothes, which startled Rudi a little bit, and, after a moment of silence, another tearing sound, and another, and another. Between the tearing sounds, he could hear Aary's staggered breath, and from time to time, a slight muffled moan of pain.

Rudi wiggled uncomfortably in his seat and struggled in his mind. He forced himself to focus on something, staring at a corner of the room in the darkness, or nibbling at his fingernails. He tried to get his mind off of what was happening behind him and stop picturing the sounds he heard, but he couldn't. At last, he couldn't contain his curiosity anymore and looked around.

At a sudden glance, Rudi was completely terrified of the sight he was seeing and almost called out. The room was very dark, but there was still enough light coming from the crack of the window for Rudi to see what Aary was doing.

Aary sat on the floor with his legs crossed, facing away from Rudi. His bloodstained shirt was already taken off, crumbled in a pile on the floor beside him, so now Rudi could see his skin covered with wounds and blood. Several long, deep gashes spread across Aary's pale skin, from the bottom of his waist to his neck and shoulders. Fresh blood oozed from the open wounds and the skin around the torn flesh was red and swollen. Numerous small cuts spread between the gashes, all swollen and bleeding. Aary's back looked like a twisted web of blood.

What in the name of hell happened to Aary? He left this morning looking perfect and pleased, and within half a day... Did he get into a fight? Who in world would do such a monstrous deed? Although he had only known Aary for a day, he could already tell that he was as gentle and kind as a deer. And who would hurt him like this?

Rudi wanted to shout, to help Aary, to get revenge for him. But he knew, he could do nothing. Whoever did this to this sweet boy was a monster no doubt, yet he was only a useless little elf. Rudi suddenly felt dizzy so he turned his head back around. Tears of fear and worry gathered in Rudi's eyes. He rubbed them with his dirty sleeves before the tears began to flow, and sat in silence.

After a while, curiosity got the better of him again and he couldn't help but turn around once more. This time, he did not turn back. He watched Aary take off a reel of gauze from the bookshelf and rip a piece off with his teeth. Under the chink of light that leaked from the gap in the wooden window, he carefully used the cloth to wipe up the blood on his skin around every wound.

After cleaning each wound, he threw the bloodstained cloth into the wooden bucket under the bookshelf. Now Rudi knew what the chocolate-colored stains on them were.

Aary moved really gently and slowly, but he still accidentally hurt himself when he touched the wounds, making him wince and gasp. Rudi could hear the hissing sound of cold air passing through Aary's teeth. Rudi couldn't see the wounds on Aary's chest and stomach, but he spent quite a long time dealing with them too. There were also some on his arms. His eyes looked calm and tired, without any anger or hatred.

Rudi watched in the darkness as Aary cleaned all the wounds on his body. He seemed to have recovered some energy after that. He got up on his knees to reach for a bottle on the bookshelf with some thick white liquid in it. He poured the liquid onto a piece of gauze and applied the medicine to each wound.

Although he looked pretty calm, Rudi could see that he was in pain from the slight trembling every time the cloth touched his skin. When treating the wounds on his back, Aary saw that Rudi was watching. Rudi hurriedly turned his head the other way. But Aary was too weak to say anything, so he just pretended he didn't know and continued with his own business.

When Rudi turned around for the third time, Aary had just finished the treatment, and he looked much better than before. He moved his head around to ease his rigid neck, put the white bottle back on the bookshelf and took another one. This bottle was very large and contained a colorless liquid like water. But Rudi didn't think it was water. Aary poured the liquid on his bloodstained shirt. Rudi was surprised to see that the blood vanished as the liquid spread. A few seconds later the shirt looked clean as new. Aary put it over an empty tier on the bookshelf for it to dry and pulled out a new shirt from the pile of folded clothes.

Finally, he stood up, put the new shirt on with difficultly, and fastened the buttons at the collar. Then he looked up at Rudi. By that time, Rudi had already turned around and was staring at the dark ceiling as if nothing had happened. Aary smiled, he walked up to Rudi and patted him on his shoulder, and said to him in a very lighthearted tone:

"Sorry about that. You can open the window now."

* * *

However, he seldom spoke about his childhood. The only time Maire ever heard about it was when she asked him about a queer-looking bracelet, probably made from wood, that he always wore around his ankle. He answered, slightly sentimentally, that it was a memory from his past, his childhood. There was something in his eyes when he said it, a bit of sadness, a bit of softness, and it captivated her. Yes, she had fallen deeply in love with this young man, even though he was 7 years younger than her. His heart, whether in terms of depth or maturity, was far beyond his actual age. She loved his stories, his maturity, his smile, and the subtle hint of sadness and mysteriousness he carried. Finally, little by little, they became more and more intimate.

11

A Friend's Concern

Rudi opened the window and was unable to keep his eyes open due to the sunlight pouring in. The warm afternoon light reflected on the leaves in the forest and brought liveliness back into Aary's treehouse. Aary didn't look much different than before he left. If not for the wound on his face and the few pieces of cloth added on the top of the bucket with fresh colored blood, Rudi couldn't even believe that what he had just seen with his own eyes was real. He smiled at Rudi apologetically, and poured two cups of water.

Rudi stared at Aary with his puzzled eyes wide open, waiting for his explanation. But Aary didn't seem to be going to explain anything.

"How was your day?" asked Aary, as he handed Rudi a cup, "Do you like it here?"

"Wh... what?" Rudi couldn't believe what he had heard.

"How was your day in my treehouse? What did you do today?"

"Seriously? Are we not talking about what happened to YOU? You walked in, all wounded and bloody, and looked like you were dying. You spent at least one hour treating your wounds. Even now I can see blood on your face, and now you're asking about MY day??"

Aary was a bit startled by Rudi's reaction. He pulled his head back and lifted a hand, palm to Rudi, as if protecting himself from his attack:

"Hey, okay, okay. I'm sorry. I'm sorry you had to wait an hour, okay? I won't die, if that's what you're worrying about. It's nothing, really."

"Nothing?" Rudi was getting more and more confused, but his voice was softer, "Just tell me, Aary, what happened to you? What on earth did you do after you left the treehouse today?"

Aary scratched at his ear with a nervous look on his face: "It's... it's nothing you should worry about."

"Tell me." Rudi's voice was firm, but soon enough he added, "Please." When he saw Aary's troubled face, he put a clawed hand on Aary's knee, looked into his eyes and said: "Aary, I'm your friend now, remember? You can tell me anything. Don't worry. I won't tell anyone."

Aary sighed. "Well... if you have to know... it was just my master. I made some mistakes. But it's nothing. I'm long used to it."

"Master?" Rudi asked, "Who is your master? And what do you do for him? Why don't you find another master?"

"Well, just the normal stuff... tending to his needs, fetching food and water, some paperwork, horses... nothing peculiar."

Rudi realized that Aary was answering only one of his questions. But he wouldn't let that pass. He was determined to dig to the bottom of this. So he needed to ask the questions one by one.

"Who is that?"

"Just some man... high lord..."

"What lord?"

"Well... emm... actually... he's the King of Elberkhan."

"What??" Rudi gaped at Aary, "You're the king's servant?"

"Yeah, kind of."

"But why did he hit you?"

"Told you, I made some mistakes. It's not important."

"He does that a lot?"

"Yeah, so I'm already used to that. Don't make it a big deal. Let's find some fun things to do. You want to read a book?"

"Like once a week?" Rudi knew that Aary was trying desperately to change to another topic, but he didn't give him the chance to. Instead, he ignored Aary's random suggestion and followed up tightly to his previous question.

"Yeah... or a little bit more." Aary answered reluctantly, frustrated that his attempt had failed.

"Then why don't you leave him? You can surely live well on your own. You can build houses and instruments. Those are really amazing skills. You must be a good hunter too considering how you caught me. You don't need to suffer this!"

"Yeah, well, the thing is, I can't. But it's a long story... quite difficult to explain. I'd have to tell you my whole life story before you could really understand."

"How long? Longer than mine? My story started from hundreds of years ago!"

Aary smiled: "Not so long in time. But it might take longer to tell."

"Then tell me. I don't care how long. I've already told you my story, now it's time you tell yours, in return. You know, friends have to give and get equally. It's not fair if you know mine and hold yours secret."

Aary realized that there was no escape from this today. He gave a resigned shrug, and asked once more: "You sure you want to hear it? It might not be as good as yours."

"Yep, I'm sure. Don't worry, I won't judge. I just want to know the reason for this all."

Aary signed: "Alright. Here's the thing..."

* * *

Every spring, when the river broke the ice, the people in the village held a dance party to celebrate the time of revival. It was 7 months after the arrival of this new youth, and the whole mountain village was alive. They lit a bonfire and sang and danced around it. The little village band came into the square in the center of the village with instruments in their arms. Huge wooden barrels were carried out from the cellars and wine was poured into small bottles and goblets. People cheered and drank, celebrating the birth of a new year. The whole village was immersed in the festive joy and happiness of celebration.

12

Rocky Vill's Tale

When I was young, when there was still more than one kingdom on Hilldown Plain, and the villages in the southmost area still belonged to the old king of the kingdom of Dorbirra, everything was peaceful and happy, and the hardworking people there were living lives of prosperity and tranquility.

I lived in a little village on the northern border of Dorbirra called Rocky Vill, by the side of Maiden River. Across the river was another kingdom's territory. The villages there belonged to the kingdom of Varl. But even so, the people on the two sides of the river got along very well. There hadn't been a war between the kingdoms on Hilldown Plain for decades, and the occasional trades of land between the kings didn't bother us small folks at all.

Like all the other villages around us, Rocky Vill was a lovely and friendly place. You can tell by the name of the village that there were a lot of rocks. All the houses there were made of rocks, all the roads and streets were paved with gravel, and there was a stone pillar on either side of the road that marked the entrance to the village.

My parents had untimely deaths. I never met my father, and my mother passed away when I was very young. I don't even remember her face. So, I've been an orphan for as long as I can remember. But

I never felt self-pity or suffered from loneliness, because I was never really alone. It was the kind and good villagers that brought me up. They took turns keeping me in their homes, letting me eat and play and sleep with their own children, and taught me to read before I was old enough to go to school with the others. Not a single family had any reluctance taking me in, and every single person treated me as if I were his or her own son.

I was a very weak child when I was young, always ill and smaller than other kids my age. But the villagers didn't forsake me. They fed me well and took care of me. I got even more milk and meat than their own children. So under their care and protection, I grew healthier and stronger. By the time I went to school, I was even taller than some older kids.

Children's lives in small villages are really joyous and carefree. We had plenty of free time to play and fool around, even after we were in school, as the school was easy and fun too. At the time, there were several kids in the village, and I was the youngest, but not a single kid bullied me or made me feel abandoned. I grew up happily just like the others. I even became a little leader among them, leading all the kids older than me everywhere I went: saving the boy that was captured by the nearby villagers as a chicken thief because he accidentally ran into the henhouse, or catching big fish in the river to bring to the grown-ups for dinner. When any kid caused trouble, I would take the blame for them, but the grown-ups wouldn't punish me too hard, because I always did more chores than they asked me to do. So the kids all liked me very much. When anyone had something nice they would think of me first, and I would share it with everyone. I spent a childhood filled with happiness and laughter in Rocky Vill, and never thought that my lack of mother and father was a sorrowful thing.

There was an old man in the village that could make all kinds of musical instruments and play wonderful music with all of them. In the year that I first started school, one morning on the way there, I wandered by his door and my soul was captivated by the enchanting sound of the music, and I just stood there like that for a whole day.

When the old man found me, he took me in as his apprentice at once. I was punished for missing school, but it was totally worth it.

He was alone too. His wife died and his sons and daughters had all moved out of the village. So I was like a grandson to him. To many of the villagers, he was a little bit eccentric and hard to get along with. He was always invited to village activities for music performances, which he always attended. But after the performances, he seldom talked to other people, and was really quiet in the crowd. To me, however, he was really nice and kind, always smiling, willing to teach me anything, and was always very patient.

He lived in a stone house behind his workshop. There were several empty rooms, where his children had lived when they were young. So he invited me to move in. From then on, I stopped moving from one family to another and stayed with him. I learned how to make and play musical instruments from him and learned many songs. Some songs were so old that no one even sings them anymore. He told me that we were the only ones that kept those songs from dying. Later, when I learned enough, I started performing in the village activities with him. I could also help him with some small things, do all the things that he was too old to do, like climbing trees to saw off branches, or threading strings into small holes. His eyes weren't as good as in his younger days, his hands weren't as steady, and his legs were slow and limping, so I could be his eyes, his hands, and his legs.

Sometimes when the work was done, I could read books. The old man had a room full of books in his house and he allowed me to take any of them. Now to think of it, there weren't a lot of books there. Compared with the libraries in the cities, it was like a drop of water in the ocean. But at that time, it seemed like all the books in the world. I thought I could never finish reading them even if I kept reading my whole life. So I was never bored, and spent countless wonderful afternoons there.

As I got older, I spent less time playing with other kids and more time in the workshop. Apart from making musical instruments, playing music, and reading, there were also times when I would go to farms and houses to help with some jobs. As my carpentry skills improved, and I grew taller and stronger, I was no longer a weak kid that needed care and help. Instead, I could help with almost anything any villager needed. Whenever anyone asked for help, whether it was a broken cabinet waiting for repair or a field being harvested that needed extra hands, I would stop what I was doing and help. My life was provided by the villagers of Rocky Vill, so I never asked for anything in return for my work and would do anything needed with all my effort. If I could be of even the tiniest bit of help to these selfless villagers that brought me up, I was very happy.

I thought I'd continue to grow up like this, to become a music master myself, then marry a girl and have some lovely children of my own. I thought I would live in Rocky Vill forever, along with my children and grandchildren, and all the generations after, just like my father and mother and their parents before that. I thought I'd never have to leave Rocky Vill and the kind villagers. Life would have been happy and peaceful like this forever, if it wasn't for that war...

* * *

She was sitting beside the dancing crowd with her female companions, happily watching this joyful celebration. She heard the jolly sound of the accordion, her favorite sound of all, and was enchanted by it as always. She couldn't help but swinging her head lightly to the music. Her eyes were searching in the crowd for his figure. She didn't know if he would come or not. He didn't grow up in this village, didn't know the dance they grew up dancing, and didn't know how much this village loved singing, dancing, and festival celebrations.

Rocky Vill

Chen Yuxiao

13

The War

You must have known, seven years ago, there was a great war on Hilldown Plain. It started in the north and spread really fast. In no time, the whole plain was burning with the fire of battles and blood, and the peaceful kingdom of Dorbirra wasn't spared.

Too many years of peace and quiet left this southern kingdom with no decent armed forces, like most of the kingdoms on the plain. All that was left of the army were a number of untrained people, mostly old and poor, who joined it only for a bowl of soup to last the day. Their duties were no more than patrolling around the cities, or strolling, to be more accurate, and settling minor disputes among people. They knew nothing of fighting a war, or even any fighting at all.

The poor old king of Dorbirra loved his people, but his strength was fading day by day, and he spent more and more of his time inside his bed chamber. He had no interests in training an army and preparing for wars. It's not that he wasn't a good king. Actually, he was a really considerate king and did many good things for the people, especially in his younger days. He cared for his people. He cared about whether they were well fed, about whether they could keep warm in the winter, and about their happiness. He was the one who opened the royal granary for the starving people in times of famine, and the one who went around the country on foot for a whole year dressed as a poor peasant to see what the people's lives were really like. He was a king that was loved by all.

But that didn't save his kingdom, nor his life. By the time the catastrophe came, he wasn't able to defend and protect his people from the foreign invasion. In fact, he couldn't even protect himself. The city army collapsed before the enemies even reached their border. No one wanted to die for a battle they had no chance of winning. Thousands of village people rushed into the capital city for protection. Desperately, the old king did one last thing for the people he loved: he closed the city gate, hid as many people as possible behind the castle walls, and awaited their fate.

The invader, even if you didn't know you would have guessed by now, was Elberkhan. Their young king, Elior, was filled with will, energy, ambition, and determination. He is a cold-blooded killer himself, and a marksman of archery, with preeminent skills with the sword. He is very good at tactics and strategies too. People say he is a born fighter and military commander.

At that time, he hadn't been the king for long. He was the son of the old king of Elberkhan, or so as they say, but before the old king died and he came out of nowhere to claim the throne, the people of Elberkhan had never seen him. At first, no one trusted this young king that looked so frivolous and unconcerned. But before long, people realized his abilities.

Soon after his succession in Elberkhan, he sent out words to all the other kingdoms on the plain, that their kings needed to come and bend their knees to him, submitting their kingdoms under the rule of Elberkhan, acknowledging that Elior, the king of Elberkhan, was the only king that ruled the entire Hilldown Plain, or else he was going to take them by force. Of course, none of the other kings obeyed. Elberkhan wasn't even a big and powerful kingdom among all the kingdoms on the plain. The other kings laughed at this young pup who didn't know his place, and offered nothing but insulting words.

Elior did not reply to their insults, but started putting all the kingdom's efforts into training the army. And before anyone realized, an invincible army was born. His troops had the finest equipment and the most advanced weapons, and the whole army was made up of strong, tough, cold-hearted grown-up men who were absolutely allegiant and loyal to their king, willing to die for him if they must. Every single man in the army was picked and trained by the king himself. It wasn't a very large army, but it was all that he needed: a troop of killing machines that obeyed him under all circumstances.

No sooner had the army been formed than he led them into the war. This army of invaders started out from the castle of Elberkhan in the north, easily fought their way across the plain and went all the way south, conquering all before them. All the regions on the way became new territories of this little kingdom that wasn't taken seriously before.

Only after several weeks of battles, the army of Elberkhan arrived at Dorbirra. By that time, it was the only kingdom left on the whole plain that hadn't been conquered by them, and the biggest one. One morning, they broke into Rocky Vill.

They must have thought that it was just an ordinary village like the other thousands of villages on Hilldown Plain, and not even a big one. But they were wrong. The people in Rocky Vill were like the rocks we used to build the houses: hard, strong, unbreakable. Unlike other villages, which were mostly deserted and vacant by then, the little village of Rocky Vill did not move. While the other villagers fled from their homes to seek refuge in the castle or ran into the mountains and wilderness to hide away from the war, the people in Rocky Vill were prepared to stand our ground and fight to the end.

Actually, right after the invaders left the castle, word spread across the whole plain following deserters and refugees, and we started preparing. Every person in the village between the age of 12 and 70 got a weapon: hoes, shovels, axes or hammers. Younger children, the elderly, including the old instrument master and me, were arranged to stay in the town hall, the strongest stone house in the village.

I was nine years old at that time, but I wanted to fight with the grown-ups. I told them I was taller and stronger than other kids of my age, and I was a good fighter. But they told me that they needed me to stay with the women and children to protect them. Thinking that I could indeed help defend them if it ever came to that, I agreed. Little did I know they just said that to keep me safe away from the fight. I took my task seriously and found a small blunt knife that was used to cut cheeses from the old instrument master's kitchen. I sharpened the edge of its blade so that it would be able to slit a man's throat, and I practiced with a stick and a tree day and night. My arms were already quite strong from the daily wood carving works in making instruments but the practice made them stronger.

Before the enemy came, the fighting people hid in the stone houses to surprise them, while the rest of us stayed in the stone town hall. I volunteered to be on the lookout, so I climbed up the clock tower of the town hall and watched from behind the clock face. When the invaders broke into the village with the arrogance of winning so many battles, they thought it was just another empty village that was abandoned in fear of war.

They must have spread their men out to raid many villages at the same time, so it was just a very small troop with only dozens of men that came to Rocky Vill. I saw that they were starting to search the houses for any valuables left around, when our good men and women emerged from their hideouts and hit them in the faces. I was watching all this from the tower and was so excited by the progress.

Our folks gave them such a hard blow. Only after a few minutes, several of their men were lost to our blades, fully armed and well-trained men, to the blades of our working tools! And the ones that were left saw what was happening, and fled from the village on their horses. It was no doubt a great victory. I ran down the tower to report the inspiring progress to update the anxious people waiting in the hall.

But that wasn't the end. Before we could even start celebrating, the few soldiers that ran away came back, and this time with more people, and this time, they were prepared for a battle. We had to bar the doors of the town hall again, and I had to climb back up to the clock tower to watch.

The fighting villagers met with the invaders once more. But this time, it wasn't as easy. We had some success hitting them unexpectedly last time, but after all, knifes and daggers couldn't defeat a well-trained army. Chaotic fighting soon began. The streets were filled with the sound of people shouting and metal crushing, and blood, the blood of their men and ours. It's sad to admit, but they had much better blades and skills. Even though they were still smaller in number, when they took it seriously, our people were no match for them.

I saw the villagers die one by one by the swords of the soldiers. I watched a soldier pressing his sword into the chest of Tommy's dad, who spent many weekends teaching me and his son Tommy to read before we went to school. I watched another one catching Mrs. Gita, the gentle woman who made so many clothes for me stitch by stitch. He caught her by the wrist, like seizing a little lamb, and slit the poor woman's throat with an easy cut.

Even the younger ones, the older kids whom I grew up with, played with, and studied with, who were like big brothers and sisters to me, were not spared. I watched them, the people closer to me than my own kin, successively fell into pools of blood, and my heart ached more than a cut from a knife. I just couldn't stay there and watch anymore as these men died for me. What if they killed everyone out there, and came to our town hall to slaughter all the unarmed children and old people too?

I held the cheese knife tightly in my hand and ran down the tower steps. I didn't enter the main hall, because I didn't want the others to know, fearing that they would stop me. I peered through the gap in the back door of the main hall to look at the people in it for the last time, feeling guilty for abandoning them. The old instrument master was sitting in a corner alone, drilling holes in a wooden pipe to make a flute.

He didn't want to come to the Town Hall at first. He said he wouldn't hide away from enemies. Even if his legs couldn't walk properly, he would prefer to just sit in his own house when they came and let them kill him. But I begged him to come, and he agreed at last. I knew he would come out after me if he knew I was leaving the hall to join the fight, and I could never let it happen. That was the last time I saw him.

I found a narrow window in the back corridor outside the main hall. The window was high above the floor, so I found a chair to step on and climbed through it with the knife between my teeth. Luckily, I was small and could just manage to crawl through the window. I jumped down to the ground, knowing that I could never come back. But I was ready to risk it all. Everything I loved in the world was being destroyed. If they had all died, what would be the meaning of me being alive all alone?

I ran towards the streets where the most intense fighting was happening. When I turned around the last corner, I saw a soldier fighting against the village baker Phil. Phil was using a long, sharpened bread knife. He was on the downside and kept on stepping back towards the wall of the house. And at the same time, another soldier was running towards them to finish off the poor baker. I ran after him, and before he could reach Phil, I shoved my knife into his neck. Blood poured from the wound onto my hand. He tried to shout but choked on his own blood, and then tumbled down like a falling leaf. That was the first person I ever killed. I was so shocked by how easy it was for a man to die. A life ended, just like that, without even a struggle. My hand lost grip of the knife as the man fell to the ground with it, and tears filled my eyes. I didn't like the feeling of killing him at all, but I told myself that if I didn't do it, he would kill Phil.

The other soldier turned his head on hearing the sound behind, and Phil grabbed this chance to stab him in the belly with his bread knife. He pulled my knife out of the dead man's neck and handed it to me, saying in a very anxious tone: "What are you doing out here? You shouldn't be here! It's dangerous! You'll get yourself killed! Go back to the Town Hall and bar the door..." Before he could finish his words, an arrow came out of nowhere and pierced through his chest. Blood came out of his mouth as he fell against the wall. "Run...." He managed to mumble out the word in a fountain of blood before he was completely gone. I turned around and jumped at the archer that was nocking his next arrow, and pushed my knife into his chest with all my strength.

Then I found myself running blindly in the streets hacking and stabbing at every soldier I came across. Their swords were much longer than my little knife, and that made me suffer quite a lot. But I was much quicker and more flexible than them because I was small and wasn't wearing heavy armor. I could always hit their fatal spots when they were off guard, so I wasn't always the underdog, and I didn't care about what could happen to me since I was ready to die at any moment. Strangely enough, I didn't even feel any pain even though I was bleeding all over.

But after all I was only nine. I was so tired at the end and suffered from so many injuries. My blood was pouring, my legs were limping, and my hands were shaking. I knew I had little time left. The last thing I remembered was using up my remaining strength to throw my knife towards an attacking soldier's eyes, before the world blackened in front of my own eyes.

I had a long, dreamless sleep. I thought I was going to be together with the dead villagers, I never thought I'd wake up in a little cell in the dungeon of Elberkhan with my wounds already wrapped up. Beside me were other prisoners of war. From them I learned the inevitable result of the war: most of the villages and small cities in Dorbirra were taken easily. The few large cities that were not yet abandoned had surrendered. No one fought back, like the people in Rocky Vill did. They were not to be blamed though. Facing such powerful enemies, no one worried about anything else but his own life. Maybe that was the right thing to do.

The invaders marched across the kingdom and struck the old king's fortress. When they crushed the outer gate and started ramming the inner gate, with the Dorbirran army nowhere to be found, all the people and the old king knew that they stood no chance. In order to save the people, the king made the hard choice of surrendering the kingdom, and ordered the city gate opened to their enemies. It was the only reasonable choice at that moment. Even if he didn't open the gate, the people might have. Anyone might want to trade a city they did not own, for the lives of themselves and their families.

However, when the Elberkhan army entered the king's palace, they found that the old king had already hung himself in his bedchamber. He just could not accept the fact that the kingdom he had loved so much and built so well, and that was run by his family for hundreds of years, had fallen to a foreign kingdom within a week, and the people that he cared so much for, would even willingly die for, wouldn't even fight for him in the face of the enemy. Well, sadly he didn't know about Rocky Vill, and would never have the chance to.

After that, I started a period of prison life. Actually, they treated their prisoners pretty well. There were four other people in my cell, who were all captured during the war, though not all from Dorbirra. But other nearby cells also held robbers, thieves, and people that committed other crimes. They gave us food, not very much or very tasty, but true, edible food, not pig feed or something like that. There were prison medics that came to treat our wounds once every few days, and I felt my strength was coming back to me. I tried to ask around if anyone knew what happened to Rocky Vill in the end, if they had found the people in the Town Hall and killed them, or imprisoned them. How I wished they hadn't found them at all! But no one knew, and I hadn't seen anyone from Rocky Vill. Days passed, and my hope gradually faded.

Then one day, totally unexpectedly, the king himself came to the prison for inspection. He wore a long, snow white gown, which was more than conspicuous in this dark and dingy prison, and he was accompanied by a group of soldiers and high lords. He said he was looking for a person to be his attendant, who would be pardoned for all former crimes, and even be rewarded if served him well.

Many were rushing to offer themselves to him, but I would have rather rotted in the dungeon than serve the tyrant who killed everyone I knew. Then the king announced his conditions. He was looking for a boy under ten, who had to be an orphan with no other relatives. I knew I fit these requirements, but I lowered my head and kept quiet, hoping that there were other orphan boys who would like to do it.

But sadly, I was the only one in the whole prison that fit these terms. When the prison fell silent, the other prisoners in my cell called me out. They were actually happy for me, not knowing that I didn't want to be his attendant at all. The jailers dragged me out, and the king had two guards escort me from the dungeon to his castle.

The king Elior was very young, not even thirty at that time, and the cruelest man I have ever known. He always looked indifferent and cold, full of contempt, as if no one in the rest of the world could be half as good as him. You could seldom read any emotion from his expressionless face, nor guess what was on his callous and fickle mind. He always has a bit of a sneer on his face, and never fully opens his eyes. Also, his face is as clean and exquisite as a woman's. He doesn't look at all like the ambitious king that conquered the whole plain within a fortnight, but rather a dandy who spent all his father's money and brought down his family. His eyes are of a very light color, something between yellow and green. They are like the eyes of a snake, full of guile and cruelty. These extraordinarily colored eyes are like some kind of amber, impossible to see through, cold like they open into another world. His hair is also very light. It is supposed to be faint golden, but is so pale that it looks like it's silvery. His silver string-like hair makes him look special, and evil.

I've never seen him lose his temper, or be excited with any kind of emotion. His voice is always calm and quiet. But something in his voice and his look gives me goosebumps. As far as I can tell, the whole kingdom is afraid of him, especially when he wears that sinister smile. No one knows anything about him, but he seems to know everything about everyone.

When he gave me orders for the first time and told me to fetch his cloak, of course I didn't obey. I did nothing and said nothing. I hoped that he would just kill me or send me back to prison and find another attendant for himself, or better, maybe I could find a chance to kill him. I was determined that I would never serve him, even if disobeying him would cost me my own life. My life wasn't worth anything to me anymore, not after everyone I cared about was gone. But seeing my reaction, he wasn't surprised or angry at all. He just said calmly, his words even sounded gentle if you didn't know what was happening:

"Your Rocky Vill villagers haven't all died out, including your instrument master. If you care for them, you'd better do what I tell you. You be a good boy, and I'll let them live. They can even live a well-fed, worriless life like before. But if you don't obey, or escape, or even try to kill yourself, none of them will remain in this world."

His words flowed out like a gentle stream, but it seized my heart tightly at once. So, some people from my village were still alive! My instrument master, the kind old man that taught me everything, was still alive! I would do anything to keep them safe. But how could Elior know that they were so important to me? What would he do to them? For a moment I couldn't breathe, overwhelmed by both hope and dread at the same time. He knew that my only concern was them, and he ruthlessly used my weakness against me.

"Why are you still standing there?" He asked, "Do you really want them to die because of you?"

I bit my lips and did as he bid, as well as every time after that, and I still haven't been able to escape from the palm of his hands up to now.

He asked me to follow him all the time, serving drinks, holding horses, and sometimes doing paperwork. This kind of work should have been pretty easy, but often enough, he would also send me to perform hard labor like carrying rocks for the extension of the castle. But those were totally okay for me, it was what came next that made my life a living hell.

Not long after I started working for him, once I accidentally broke a plate, and he had me flogged with a whip, so hard that it made me fall onto the ground and I wasn't able to get up for a long time. After that, his punishments grew more and more frequent, and more and more unreasonable. And then, he began to use me as his venting object. Even if I didn't make mistakes, he would still pick on me, like saying that the water's too cold or too hot, and find any excuse to beat me almost to death. I don't think he even needed a servant, only someone to torture without any consequences. That was why he asked for a young boy under ten, so that I wouldn't be able to fight back, and an orphan so that there wouldn't be any family to protect me. I was more and more sure that he was just a madman that simply enjoyed torturing people.

Sometimes, he asks me to fight against him. But I can only use a lame weapon, like a wooden stick or a shovel, like the ones we used in the war, while he uses a sword, mace, or spear. To be honest, we aren't really fighting at all. It's just another way for him to beat me and humiliate me. I can't defeat him even if we exchange weapons. He is really strong, skillful in fighting. Even in speed I can't beat him. The best I can do is to keep myself away from the sharp edge as much as possible. He doesn't stop until I lose all ability to fight back and curl up on the ground in a pool of blood. Every time, I hope that he will just kill me, but he always leaves me just enough strength to crawl away. Of course, I have gotten better through the years, but he degrades my weapons, and the results have all been the same. Sometimes when he breaks some of my bones, or if my wounds are too severe and bleeding too much, he asks the royal physicians to treat me to keep me alive. But more often he just leaves me there. For countless nights, I couldn't even lie on my back because of the pain, let alone sleep. But later, I grew used to these punishments and grew used to the pain. Now, I don't care a pin anymore.

* * *

Suddenly, behind the dancing crowd of people, she saw him. He was dressed in a brand new white suit, which looked really dashing and neat, catching every eye in the crowd. He moved elegantly through the noisy, revelrous crowd, passed countless girls captivated by him and screaming for him, and arrived in front of her. He wore a smile as warm as the sunlight in winter, and a little shyly, he reached out his hand and invited her to dance.

14

A Question without Answers

Rudi listened attentively to Aary's story. At this point, disgust and anger was showing on his face. He looked at the wound on Aary's face. The place where the skin opened was wet with blood, but it was nothing compared with the big ones on his back.

"How can there be such a vicious man in the world! How can he do that to you!" He exclaimed with indignation.

Aary shrugged: "I told you it's not so fun to listen to. Don't let it bother you, though. It doesn't bother me anymore. See, I'm almost as good as new now." He lifted his arms up and down, rotated his upper body to the left and right, to show Rudi that he was ok, and smiled.

Rudi smiled back, uncertainly, and asked: "Was that some kind of medicine you just used?"

"Yes!" Aary answered proudly, "I made it myself, and all the other medicines on the shelf. There's this book I found."

He took down the thick book covered in brown leather from the wooden shelf and placed it on Rudi's lap. *The Art and History of Alchemy in Healing.* Rudi had noticed this book before, when he was fumbling around the room during Aary's absence. He turned the pages and saw drawings of all kinds of herbs and plants.

Aary continued: "It included the recipes of many kinds of medicines for different purposes. I collected herbs and leaves from the forest and cooked them on my stove according to the instructions in the book. After I was familiar with the functions of each kind of herb, I experimented to create a special medicine to cure exterior wounds, especially whip wounds. When I put it on, the wounds that normally wouldn't heal for months will be cured in a couple of days. See, this one was from 2 days ago, and it's already healing."

He rolled up the sleeves of his right arm to show Rudi a gash on his forearm. It was a cut, probably from some kind of a sword or knife, from the middle of his forearm all the way to the elbow. Rudi could see scabs growing where the skin had opened. It looked like a 2 week-old wound.

Rudi asked concernedly: "Did he do that too?"

"Well, yes. How else would I get this?"

"Damn him." Rudi cursed. He thought for a moment and asked: "But how could Elior let you come here and build your own house in the forest? Don't you need to be with him all the time?"

"No, actually, I'm allowed to leave him for some time on my own when I don't have work to do, as long as I come back when he wants. But it is not some kind of reward, though. He told me on the first day that he wouldn't waste any food on me, so I would have to find food for myself, whether I begged, robbed, or ate rats in the gutter he didn't care. Then he threw a dagger on the ground in front of my feet, like he was throwing away a piece of junk, and said calmly: 'If I were you, I'd pick it up and keep it safe. It will be the only weapon you'll ever have.' He smiled at me, the kind of mocking smile he always wears, 'Try to rob some old woman or pick some bugs with it if you can. Just remember one thing, don't you ever try to use it on me, or it will easily become the thing you'll regret the most in your life. Now, get out of my sight, please.' He was still smiling.

"I have never tried to use it on him, though I think about it all the time. How I wish to stab this dagger right through his heart and end it all, to get revenge for my friends and myself. But I have never been able to. He is always surrounded by fully armed guards and soldiers. I know that I could never even reach his side. Even if I am alone with him, it will be hard for me to beat him. He always carries his sword and bow with him, no matter where he goes. Plus, they always take my dagger away when I'm near him.

"But I am quite grateful for this, I can tell you that."

Aary unfixed his dagger from his belt and handed it to Rudi. Marveling, Rudi pulled it out of the sheath and looked at the shining blade. There wasn't any decoration on the hilt, or on the sheath, but the steel blade itself looked fine enough.

Aary continued: "It's probably just the least fancy weapon he had and didn't want any more. But I like it very much. It was forged in one piece of metal, very simple but very handy. I might be imagining it, but it even seems to have a special connection with me. Although I'm sure he didn't know that it would be so handy to me. As far as I know, if he knew I liked it so much, he would take it away from me. That's just how he is.

"Anyway, so I needed to find my own food. Of course, I wouldn't rob some poor old woman. It wouldn't be fair. Nor would I beg on the street. Having been educated at Rocky Vill, I would rather die of hunger than rob someone else or put a bowl out to beg.

"Then I remembered that I once buried a magical cookie jar somewhere in the mountains before the war. I pledged the dagger to borrow a horse from a city inn and rode to where I remembered the jar was. It took me three days to get there and find the jar buried under a tree I marked. By then I was almost fainting with starvation. I was glad to find the jar intact and the magic still working. I ate quite a lot of cookies and so was able to get my energy back. I knew that when I returned to the castle there would be a terrible beating waiting for me, and I had to hide the jar again in the woods beside the castle, or Elior would surely take it or smash it. But I have it now to keep me from starving to death.

"But with all the labor he has me do, cookies aren't really enough, and I got tired of them after some time. So, I started to try hunting. At first, I wasn't very good at it. This dagger was no bow and arrow, thus it was difficult to catch something from a distance. And I was often too tired after the work he had me do. So, I spent most of my free time trying to catch animals but ended up with nothing. But after some time, I got the hang of it. Now I can throw my dagger to catch a flying pheasant from hundreds of feet away."

"That's amazing!" Rudi said in wonderment. He handed the book and the dagger back to Aary. As Aary stood up to put the book back on the shelf where it was, Rudi asked: "Where did you get all these books?"

"Oh, yes, here comes the best thing about being in Elberkhan. The library in the castle was really an eye-opener for me. It's the grandest, most significant architecture in the Kingdom of Elberkhan, and one of the oldest. It's like a maze of rooms that grows towards the sky, with numerous hallways and staircases. And there are books in every dusty corner. You can see a rare and precious book lying beneath a bench, or a book that is thousands of years old between the arm rails of the stairs. There's even a secret vault underground that stores more books than all of the people in the world. There are countless words and endless knowledge in its collection, some lost to the rest of the world. Any book you can or cannot imagine, you can find it there. Before that, I thought the books in the old music master's book room were all that there were.

"Common people can access most areas of the library during opening hours and borrow books as long as there are still copies left. But there are some restricted parts of the building, forbidden to the public. There the most precious books of all are stored, many the only copies in the world. Only Elior himself and his most trusted scholars can enter. Being his attendant, I sometimes got the chance to enter with him. After a while, he started sending me to get books on his behalf. Gradually, I got familiar with the librarians and book keepers. And now, I don't even need a royal parchment to enter the restricted areas or go to the library during closed hours. Now I can surf this sea of knowledge any time without restrictions, like the king himself. That's a special privilege few people have.

"At first, I spent many hours in the library, like I did before the war in the old master's book room. Then later, after I built this treehouse, I could borrow the books and bring them up here to my own little space to read. Up to now, I've been reading for seven years and haven't even finished a hundredth of the library's collection of books. And whenever I found a book that I really love and want to keep, I take it out in the king's name, so that I won't have to return it in a limited period of time. Of course, I would never let him know this or it will certainly be painful for me." Aary made a face to Rudi.

"Ow that sounds dangerous!"

"Don't worry. He doesn't notice such small things. He only hits me when he likes, not really when I deserve it."

"That's not fair. I'm so sorry for you Aary." Rudi sighed, "What about ruling? Is he a good king?"

"Hmm, it's a hard thing to say. Some people think he is, but others... well, though I have to admit that he's a good military commander - he seems to have the gift for that – I'm not sure if he's a good monarch. When I served him in the court, I sometimes overheard some of his discussions with the ministers. After he won the battle and united the plain with a single army he trained and led himself, he maintained the country as if it was still at war. He continued spending much money in the training of his army and the manufacture of arms, when all his advisors were trying to persuade him to put more efforts into maintaining the country he had won, in the development of an economy, and winning people's hearts. But he was really arrogant and never listened to anyone. He had no intention of making his people love him, like the old king of Dorbirra did. He had a different strategy, aiming to control the kingdom through fear. Do you think he's a good king?"

Rudi shook his head firmly.

"So that's all. That was my story, nothing particularly interesting. Just a story of my life destroyed by a man named Elior. You can see why I'm not particularly fond of remembering it."

Rudi patted on Aary's hands and said: "I'm sorry Aary. But I'm glad that you told me."

He lingered in Aary's story for a few more minutes, before he finally made up his mind and carefully let out the concern in his mind: "Have you seen the villagers of Rocky Vill since the war?"

"No." Aary frowned.

"Do you really believe that they are still alive?"

Aary felt like someone had clutched his throat, making him unable to breath. He knew this was the question he always worried about but didn't want and didn't dare to think about. Rudi once again struck Aary's nerves, pushing him to think of this question. Aary felt a thunderstorm going on in himself.

Yes, on countless sleepless nights, the same questions circled in his head.

What if everyone from Rocky Vill had died?

What if all of this was just a lie Elior made up to make me obey and endure everything?

What if I spent my whole life under oppression and humiliation, just to find out in return that it was all a suffocating lie?

Even if they are still alive, what then? I may never see them, not now, not in the future.

A beautiful illusion, that's all it was. He'd never know if it was real or not. Elior would never let him see them. This was a riddle without solutions, a maze without exits.

Actually, he did try to get back to Rocky Vill once, not long after he was captured and made attendant of the king, to see if the villagers were still there like Elior said. Like the time when he went to get his cookie jar, he borrowed a horse, left a note to Elior that he would be away for a few days but would come back, and rode off towards the south. He was really excited in the beginning, thinking that he would see everyone once again. But as he got further into his journey, the excitement faded and fear came instead.

He dreaded the possibility that Elior was telling a lie and everyone was dead. He dreaded that he would see an empty ghost town in the place of the lovely little village in his memory. Even if some of the villagers were alive as Elior said, he still dreaded that he would bring disaster to them by seeing them. And what if most people were dead but a few? If the old instrument master was dead, would he still have the strength to carry on enduring all the pain for the lives of the rest of them? As he got nearer and nearer, the fear grew stronger and stronger, until it finally took over him, when he was only one day's ride from Rocky Vill. That was when he stopped.

The devastation and disappointment was overwhelming. He just sat there on the back of the horse, and cried like a baby. He cried until he was exhausted, and turned his horse around.

When he got back, Elior broke several of his ribs, but he didn't mind at all. The pain in his heart made the pain in his body seem so frivolous. He spent a whole month in the sickbed, blaming himself for cowardice, for not even being brave enough to face the truth. He told himself that if he didn't see the village, there was always a chance that they were indeed still living there happily. Apart from the people that he saw dead with his own eyes, all the others could still have remained, alive and healthy. This desperate hope was the only string that he was clinging onto, that his life was based upon. He never tried to go back again.

He remained silent for a few seconds with his eyes shut, then bit his lips and took a deep breath. When he reopened his eyes, he saw Rudi with guilt and worry on his face. He gave a bitter smile and said in a firm tone: "Whether they are alive or not, as long as there's hope, I will carry on to the end. If I escaped and they suffered because of me, their deaths would be on me, and I could never forgive myself. I would rather be fooled and bear pain for the rest of my life, than hurt the ones I love because of some doubts. Even if it is a lie, I hope my persistence can bring solace to their souls in heaven. Actually, to be honest, it's more about me than it is about them. Call me selfish if you want, but I want to live with peace in my heart, not guilt."

* * *

He held her hand gently and led her into the dancing crowd. She was surprised to see that his dancing moves were elegant and light. There were steps that she was familiar with, but also moves that she had never seen. Even the best dancing experts in the village couldn't help stopping for a moment to enjoy his dance. Accompanied by the joyful music played by the band, the two of them danced happily to the drum beats, light and graceful like a pair of white doves. They circled one round after another. With the music becoming more and more enthusiastic, the atmosphere of the party grew more exciting still. A passionate dance tune pushed the celebration to the climax.

15

A Weird Pause

"This treehouse," Aary stood up and looked around his house, "I built it behind Elior's back in my free time. This is my own space of freedom, my oasis amid the cruelty of the world. It's far enough from the castle and deep in the woods. He can never find me here. When I am here, I don't have to worry about anything, and can forget about all my troubles.

"But I can't stay here during the night, which is why you don't see any beds. I have to go back to the dungeon and stay in a small cell every night, in order to 'remind me of my prisoner's identity' as Elior declared. If I don't go back for a whole night, he'll beat me hard when I return. I think you've already had some clue of that."

Now Rudi understood why Aary was beaten this time. It was actually because of him. He felt a rush of guilt and unease, and blamed Aary for not telling him before. Of course, he wouldn't mind him leaving in the evenings, so that he wouldn't have to be punished for that.

"You should have told me that and avoided this beating! You fool!"

But Aary just smiled lightheartedly, like it was not a big deal. He shrugged.

"I always get more free time after the beatings. Now I won't need to go back until evenfall. It's just a fair price to pay."

He sat back in his chair and tilted his head like a little boy: "One story for another. Now you know everything about me as well. If you have no more questions, we should probably get down and find us some food."

Rudi felt the hunger indeed. The cookies that once stuffed his stomach so densely had totally vanished, and it was rumbling again at that moment. Now he understood why Aary thought the cookies were not as filling as meat. That was when he remembered to ask:

"Where did the magical cookie jar come from? You said you buried it before the war, but how did you get it in the first place."

"Oh, it was given to me by..."

Aary hesitated, his eyes froze and his mind seemed to have drifted away. A complicated, uneasy expression crawled onto Aary's face and wrinkled his brows. He quickly lowered his eyes and looked to the ground, but Rudi caught a glimpse of it anyway.

Rudi watched Aary confusedly as he sat there in silence staring at the ground.

A moment later, Aary let go of a breath of air and swallowed hard. When he finally looked back at Rudi, he could see that something was shining in Aary's eyes.

"...by someone I knew."

His voice was so soft that Rudi almost didn't catch him. He was totally puzzled about Aary's strange behavior and perfunctory reply. But he didn't have the chance to ask any more questions before Aary nervously shifted to the other topic:

"We should really get some food now. The sky is getting dark. I need to get back to the castle after dinner. Even I find it difficult to take another beating before the wounds from the last one heal. Let's go. What do you fancy for dinner?"

Rudi still felt really confused about the short pause just a moment ago. He believed that Aary was trying to hide something. *Who was that "someone"? Was it a girl? Someone from Aary's past? What happened to this person? Something must have happened or why would he try to hide it and not be willing to speak about it? Not his instrument master, that's for sure, or he would just say it. Or maybe there was something more to the story of his late parents? Aary buried this jar before the war, why? Who would ever want to bury a magical cookie jar that creates infinite cookies?*

He wanted to ask these questions so badly, but instead, he swallowed them down and simply followed Aary's lead: "Yeah, sure. I'm quite hungry actually. I would kill for a roast chicken right now!"

Rudi decided not to push Aary again into telling him something that he didn't want to, at least not now. Apparently, this youth had many secrets hidden away from the rest of the world. Young as he was and cheerful as he might seem, he had some terrible memories from the past, memories that could still bite and hurt him even now if they were recalled. As a way of protecting himself, he locked all the bad memories away in a box and buried them deep in his mind to keep himself away from the harm in his past. If it's too hard to face and fight the monster, avoiding it might be a good option as well.

Rudi respected his choice, and he didn't want to make him suffer any more than he already had. So he pretended that he didn't notice the peculiar pause, and followed Aary towards the door. To break the slightly awkward atmosphere and ease Aary's nerve, he asked something that he was certain Aary *would* like to talk about.

"Oh, and, I saw that box of musical instruments. They look wonderful! I'm sure you made them yourself as well?"

Aary showed relief and gratitude. Then Rudi saw a look emerge on his face that was full of pride and joy:

"Of course! I'm an excellent musician too! I'll play a piece for you if you like. When we get back from our hunt and are waiting for whatever we caught to cook on the fire, I'll play a tune to accompany our dinner. What kinds of music do you like? Brisk or melodious? Any song you particularly like? Not to brag but I know all the songs, just name it..."

* * *

During the break between the music, he led her by the hand to the side of the crowd. Emboldened by the sip of wine he had just now, he asked the question he had wanted to ask since the first day he saw her: "Maire, will you marry me?" Time seemed to have frozen and was hanging between the two of them. She was stunned and dizzied by this sudden surprise, and couldn't believe that it was all real. It took her a few seconds to make sure that she wasn't dreaming. But to him, these few seconds seemed like ages.

16

An Unexpected Letter

The sunshine was always warm in the afternoon. Some heat from the summer that just ended still remained in the sunlight, but it was not as disturbingly hot anymore. Trees are the messengers that filed the first reports on autumn. Of the leaves that were slightly turning yellow, the laziest few had already left the branch, searching for their destinations, following the lead of the cool autumn breeze.

A chink of light leaked through the skylight in the roof of the Elberkhan palace, running side by side with the sunlight that shone through the window and poured onto the king's marble throne. The throne reflected the highest power and grace a king could have. The dark velvet cushion on the seat was even softer than a kitten's paws. The stone was sculpted with complicated and exquisite carved out patterns and engraved with the purest gold. But actually, the mere existence of such a whole and massive piece of invaluable marble would be enough to make people believe that this was the throne of the king that rules over the whole plain.

Two guards were always standing by the side of the throne, even when the king was absent. Both of them were dressed in the armor of knights. Their shining silvery armor reflected blinding lights as bright as the sun. One of them held a halberd, and the other a spear. The steel edges of their weapons also glimmered with chilling rays, as both men stood resting the ends of the shafts of their weapons on the ground. A sword with a decorated sheath hung from the belt of both men. Neither of them was wearing a helmet, but they looked even more imposing with their thick, dark hair and substantial beards.

The throne room was overflowing with magnificent decorations which seemed to be showing off power in every corner and every detail. Several weapons were hanging on the walls, all shiny and spotless, reflecting the fire in the hearth. Around one corner of the half built-in fireplace crawled a lizard-like creature made from bronze, snarling at the fire while the flickering flames shone in its emerald eyes. All the scales on the creature were made with extreme delicacy, reflecting out a hundred little flames. The bronze gloss made it look antique and mysterious, calling to the ancient fire god to bring out its vicious, but extremely powerful forces.

The frame of the fireplace was stacked with thick ashlar, already blackened after years of close contact with the fire. Above the mantelpiece hung a stag's head sculpture made of black iron heated up by the fire. Behind the head were two crossed long knives as old as the castle itself. Although they were used merely for decoration purposes, the edges had been honed properly and were extremely sharp. Several torches fixed on the wall were blazing pointlessly in the intense sunlight and gave out a slight scent of burning wood together with the fire on the hearth. It was actually not that cold yet to be needing a fire, but the fireplace did make the glossy stone floor look less chilly.

With a deep rumbling noise, the heavy marble doors of the throne room opened, and in came two lines of armed soldiers. They split as soon as they entered and arrayed themselves evenly on both sides of the throne room. When all of them found their spots and stood still, all the soldiers struck their spears on the ground making one unified sound. Following the soldiers, two men came in. One of them was tall and heavily built, dignified looking, with a grey beard and wearing heavy dark-grey armor.

"Your Grace, recently there's been a widespread rumor in the army that the crops will fail this year. I don't think that augurs well." The man said in a serious tone as he reached out his hands to take the white cloak the king had just taken off.

The young king ignored him and lightly walked up the steps in front of the throne. He was an inch shorter than the other man and much slenderer. But no one would mistake one for the other. He was wearing a snow-white shirt, made of the finest silk and embroidered with silver threads on the sleeves and collar. The white laces in the front were slightly loosened around the collar, baring his sharp collarbones. His shirt was tucked into the black leathered sword belt fastened around his waist. A sword and a dagger hung from the belt, both with delicate carved sheaths and handgrips. A beautiful long bow and a leather quiver hung over his shoulder.

He always carried his bow with him whenever and wherever he went, like it was part of his own body. This bow was really lightweight and exquisitely made. But it was said that he was the only one in the world that could draw it to the full. No one knew if it was true or only a myth though, since he never let anyone touch it. No one knew where this bow came from, too, for it was as if it came to this world with Elior. Since he showed up at Elberkhan to claim the throne, till he conquered the whole plain and ruled for more than seven years up to now, no one has ever seen him without his bow.

After climbing to the top of the dais, he took his bow and quiver off his shoulder, and hung them casually over the beautifully sculptured beast heads on the back of the throne chair. Then he turned around to sit on the soft cushion of his throne.

When the king seated himself, a line of serving girls emerged from a little door behind the throne to bring in drinks and food for the two of them. The king took a tall goblet of white wine and sipped, while the tall man waved them away. His eyes were on the king, waiting for his response. His upper body was bent towards the king to show respect, even though he was twice as old. His once thick black beard was spotted with white, but his eyes were as bright and fierce as any young valiant knight. His skin was dark colored and coarse from years of exposure to the sun and rain in the field trainings. Compared to him, the young king looked like a fair little boy.

Elior leaned casually on the seat, with his left leg bent so that his boot rested directly on the delicate cushion. The long black leathered boots enveloped his shins all the way up to the knees and were covered with intricate patterns of silver threads embroidered onto it by hand. He hung his left arm over his knee, fingers knocking randomly at his kneecap, with an emerald set in a silver ring on the index finger. His right arm propped up his chin while the elbow balanced on the low armrest on the right side of the chair. His silver hair was tied casually and loosely behind his head, but there was still some unfastened hair hanging by his ears, even a wisp over his eyes. Even his eyelashes were light silver. His half-closed eyelids could not conceal the crafty glow in his unnaturally light-colored eyes, which showed as much indifference as the glimmer of the scornful sneer that appeared at the corner of his lips.

"Oh, my dear Bobor," the king said lazily, "when did you become such an alarmist and start to believe in rumors? Don't be a little girl. You are a commander. Mind your troops. What do the crops have to do with you?"

"But, Your Grace, I don't think that it's just rumor, people are saying that..."

"Was the training schedule for this month finished?"

"No... not yet, Your Grace."

"Then what are you still doing here?"

"Forgive me, sire..." Commander Bobor lowered his head and knelt down on one knee, still holding the king's white cloak in hand, "the morale of the troops and common people is not very high these days. It's been seven years since your grace conquered the plain, and the whole kingdom has been living in peace and harmony. Hilldown Plain is naturally protected by the surrounding mountains, with only some small villages and cities nearby that would pose no threat at all... What I'm trying to say, Your Grace, is that the kingdom is safe. But... there are increasing problems in our own cities. The frequencies of robbery and rape are increasing, and the gap between the rich and poor is also broadening. If Your Grace doesn't mind me saying, many people, including myself, believe that maybe... maybe it would be better if Your Grace withdrew some of the investment in military and put more effort in ruling the kingdom..."

"I do mind you saying, Bobor. What are you telling me? Are you questioning my ability to rule?" Elior interrupted him abruptly, and bent forward a little in his throne.

"Please forgive me, Your Grace. No, I would never dare..."

"You don't dare? So you think so, but don't dare to say?"

"No, of course not." Commander Bobor panicked. He pressed both of his knees on the floor and held his hands together in a fist in front of his face, "Your Grace misunderstood me...please forgive me, I'm just..."

"Just what?" Elior's tone became impatient, "Raise your head and look at me. Look me in the eye."

Unsure of what the king was meaning to do, Commander Bobor lifted his head, and saw the king's pair of yellow-green eyes as cold as a snake.

"My dear Bobor," his tone grew softer, "look at me, and tell me. Who is the king of Elberkhan?"

"Your Grace is, of course."

"I am. And do you think that I care, even for a tiny bit, what the others say, about how I should rule MY kingdom?"

"Your Grace... I..."

"Stop hemming and hawing. You know the answer."

"Yes, Your Grace... I mean, no, you don't, Your Grace."

"No. I don't, care, at all. And I'm never having this conversation again. How I want to rule my kingdom is my business, and your business is to follow my orders, nothing else. Is it really that hard? Remember your place, Bobor. You are a military commander, and if you intend to keep being one, do what you are supposed to do as a military commander. In case you forgot, I gave you a training schedule to follow. I will have an inspection of the army next week, and if you're behind schedule... you know the consequences." The king showed a contemptuous smile at the corner of his lips and lifted his left hand to wave him off without even looking at him, "Now leave me."

"But... Your Grace..."

"Why are you still here? That was an order!"

Commander Bobor was still hoping to give it another try. But when he heard the king's tone was getting firm, he dared to say no more.

"Yes...Your Grace."

Sighing in chagrin, he handed the white cloak in his hands to one of the serving girls, and walked out shaking his head in small movements so that the king wouldn't notice. While walking through the door with his head down, he almost ran into a white bearded old man in a linen robe, and emitted an unhappy grumble. But when he looked up and saw the old man's face, he apologized respectfully at once and hurried away.

When the king saw the visitor, the subtle smile at the corner of his lips faded. But when he spoke, his tone was still very calm. He said to the guards: "Go on. Leave us." Then he turned around to talk to the two by his throne: "You too. Take a break. Be back before dinner time."

The old man nodded lightly at the king. Any expression on his face was concealed by his heavy wrinkles and white beard. He was holding a letter in his hand. On the envelop a few words were crookedly written in fresh red ink. The uneven edges of the letters caused by running ink made it look ominously like blood. Among them only two words were recognizable: Dark Kingdom.

* * *

When the delightful music started to play again, the bustling crowd went back to dancing in circles. Her eyes were filled with tears of joy and excitement, and solemnly she nodded her head. He almost cried out with happiness. He closed his eyes and leaned his head towards hers. She didn't dodge but touched his cold lips with her own. He put his arms around her neck and all the hectic surroundings disappeared. Even the whole world had nothing to do with them anymore. Now, it was just the two of them. He loved her. She loved him.

17

Big Straw Hat

The chilly autumn wind led the red and yellow leaves into elegant dances in the sky, before leaving them to fall onto the ground. The fallen leaves on the ground were swept up by the wind again, and fell onto the ground once more... It had been over a month since the two friends met each other. Rudi wasn't staying at Aary's treehouse all the time, but since his own tree hole wasn't very far away, he could often hang out with Aary there. After all, Aary couldn't possibly fit in the little elf's tiny tree hole. Aary needed to stay in the castle at nights and his work there was mostly in the mornings. So, during many afternoons, when the sun started going down and the shadows of the woods were getting longer and longer, there would be music coming out from a little wooden house at the top of a tree's crown. The beautiful melody filled the forest, and even the trees seemed to be swinging with the rhythms.

When Rudi wasn't around, Aary spent most of his time on the trees just outside his treehouse enjoying the autumn view. It was his favorite season of all. He loved the yellow, orange, and red colors of the world and the sound of the wind sweeping through the drying leaves. Somehow it reminded him of his childhood in Rocky Vill, where in autumn times people celebrated the harvest by baking all kinds of bread with the freshly grown wheat.

He remembered how he used to knead the dough with the other children, making it into little pigs, cows, ducks, and dogs, and how they used to throw flour at each other so that at the end of the day, everyone would look as white from head to heel as the floury dough they made. The grown-ups would hold them by the ears as if they were angry, and they would howl and wail as if they were hurt, but no one was really upset and everyone was smiling and laughing. Those were such happy times. Even now, when Aary thought of how naughty they were and what a mess they made, it would make him smile. And yet everyone in his memory was gone now or somewhere far away from him. It was a sweet memory from a long time ago, and now he was all alone. The happy memories always made him sad in the end. There was no dough now, no bread, no villagers or other children, but the autumn leaves were the same year after year.

He tried not to think too much and forced himself to focus on the beautiful leaves. After all, these thoughts would not change anything that had already happened. It would be a crime to dwell on useless thoughts that would only cause him frustration, and leave the beautiful scene before him unnoticed. He found himself a nice thick branch on a tree and then settled into a comfortable position. His branch wasn't high, so he could lie down and watch the leaves falling from above. The leaves on this tree were the reddest, and that was exactly why he picked this branch. It even made him feel absurdly a little proud.

The lazy sunshine of the afternoon shone through the treetops onto Aary's face. It soon made him sleepy. Yawning, he watched the sunlight, and the falling leaves swirling in the cool air were dappled by the rays of sunlight shining through. Feeling the autumn breeze lifting up his hair and tickling his face, Aary listened to the soft crunchy sound of dry leaves crackling. The big yawn left tears in his eyes, and blurred his sight, making the sun look like a giant bright halo floating atop the tree crowns. At this moment, there was nothing in the world that could worry him, nothing.

Except that, in the woods, not far from where he was, a small, energetic figure wearing a large linen overcoat was capering through the leaves, picking out the most beautiful red leaves to hold in his hands. A huge straw hat covered his face and shoulders, and he was not much taller than Rudi the little tree elf, but the small white hands holding the leaves suggested that it was a human child instead of an elf, strange as it was to see a child alone in the treacherous woods. That being said, the woods didn't seem so treacherous at the moment. The afternoon sun shone down through the flying shower of red and yellow and green leaves, decorating the world in red and yellow and green lights, making the woods look beautiful and peaceful, even magical.

The kid had collected a handful of pretty leaves in his left hand now, but he was still looking for more, going for each pile he saw, running here and there and squatting down to pick up the ones he wanted. The overcoat seemed ill-fitting on the child's small stature, really big and loose especially around the child's narrow shoulders. Being almost longer than its owner's height, the hem of the coat constantly brushed the ground, tripping him from time to time. When he squatted or kneeled down to pick up leaves, he always stepped on the coat. And when he tried to stand up again, he always found himself pinned to the ground by the coat under his feet. But he didn't seem to mind, and kept wearing it all the time. The hat was obviously too big for him as well, dangling and wobbling from side to side as he jumped and ran around. The coat and the hat looked pretty old from the worn-out edges and faded color, but rather clean and in good condition.

Random was his path, he was moving slowly towards Aary's tree. But neither did the child see someone on the tree above him, nor did Aary notice someone on the ground. Aary was lying on the branch facing the sky, sleepy and daydreaming, and the child's whole attention was focused on the leaves on the ground, with the big hat blocking his view to the sky. The sound of wind and crackling leaves dangling on the tree and sweeping on the ground also covered the child's footsteps, and Aary noticed nothing unusual.

While walking past the tree Aary was laying on, and suddenly intrigued by the particularly red fallen leaves under that very tree, the child let go of all the leaves in his hand, and ran excitedly towards the tree. He knelt down on the thick pile and started picking up leaves greedily. He seemed pretty fastidious, always throwing away the one in his hand when he saw a redder leaf. After a while, he was so convinced that the reddest leaves in the whole forest lay under this tree, he decided that he wouldn't have to go anywhere else. He finally took off his large overcoat that consistently got in his way, folded it neatly and laid it on the ground beside him. In order not to dirty the shirt, the child rolled up his sleeves to the elbows and stretched out two thin arms to dig into the pile for the reddest leaves.

Baked by the sunshine, Aary felt totally drowsy. He stretched himself, reaching out his arms, and caught a beautiful dancing red leaf in his right hand. He put it in front of his squinting eyes and examined it carefully under the sun. The sunlight shone through the thin leaf into Aary's green eyes. The main veins on the leaf were red like blood vessels, but as they grew thinner and more delicate towards the edge, they became almost transparent, letting the sunlight through and making them shine like glowing golden threads. The thickest parts of the leaves between the veins seemed the darkest as less sunlight could shine through, with a smudge of dark green mingled in the dark red. And at the edge of the leaf were tiny zig-zags with a golden fringe painted by the sun.

Aary was blown away by the magnificence of life in this little leaf. He never realized how many different colors could be seen in a single leaf. He thought about how in one autumn, millions of leaves like this would fall from the trees to the earth, and become soil to fertilize the trees, so that they could grow new leaves again in the coming year. The cycle of trees went on and on, year after year, like everything on earth: the death of the old and the birth of the new, on and on, forever. Aary knew perfectly well that he himself would die someday, and the world would continue to exist, on and on. He couldn't tell how he felt about this, maybe a little sad? Or maybe more peaceful than sad. He turned the leaf in his hand by rubbing the stalk between two fingers, then loosened his grip. The leaf was immediately taken away by a gust of passing wind. Aary's eyes followed the leaf into the air, dancing and circling, swirling and twirling, until it fell all the way down, onto a huge straw hat.

People!!!

Aary panicked. Someone else was here, in this depth of woods! His private space was no longer private! Had Elior's scouts already found him? What would they do to him, and his treehouse?

He jerked himself up suddenly, trying to sit up on the branch, but the sudden movement made his head feel dizzy, and the branch under him wasn't so thick after all. His body slipped on the branch. He tried to grip the tree branch with his legs, but it was too smooth. Losing his balance, he fell from the tree into the air. He tried to grab onto other branches as he fell, but there weren't any beneath him. After a short period of "gliding", he fell heavily on his back onto a pile of leaves. The small wind created by his fall made all the fallen leaves swirl up around him. Some of these leaves met the wind near the ground and followed it somewhere else, some circled around and then fell back onto Aary. The last thing he saw before he blacked out, was a wisp of long golden hair falling from beneath a huge straw hat.

* * *

Suddenly, he withdrew his lips from hers. The next thing she knew, he held her around the waist, lifted her up in the air, and began spinning her around in the crowd. Her light dress was raised up by the wind, like an early blossoming lily. She was the most beautiful woman that night, and the happiest. The joy and excitement of this pair of love birds overflowed from the two of them, and affected everyone around them. They became the brightest stars at that party.

18

The Coat Awaits

Aary didn't know how long he was unconscious for, but when his eyes slowly opened, the sun was gone and the world was dark. Oh, wait, it wasn't dark. As he struggled to open his eyes, and more light came into them, he realized that the sun was still there, only something had blocked it out. A large cloud of a shadow hovered over his head. He couldn't make out what the shadow was, as the shape was too dark and the rest of the world too bright. The sun was shining behind it and framing a particularly bright halo around the fringe, making it harder to see. And his eyes weren't helping either. Everything looked a bit fuzzy... Before he could adjust his eyes and see things clearly, the shadow suddenly tore away, and his whole world turned completely white as the bright light of the sun shone straight into his eyes, painful like a stab of a sword, making him almost blind.

Then he knew it must be someone, a person. He didn't catch the appearance. He opened a tiny crack in his eyes that he had shut against the sun. There was no one there anymore. He wanted to turn his head to look, but it just wouldn't move. It seemed that his head had nothing to do with him. In fact, as he tried, he realized that he couldn't move any part of his body. His limbs felt unattached, only his eyelids were able to move up and down, but even that was difficult, and it felt too painful to open his eyes to the sun.

That was when he realized the pain. It was no less blinding than the sun itself. He didn't know if the pain had just come now or if he had just been too numb to feel it. But now it felt real as hell. Everywhere in his body hurt. It seemed like a mountain had fallen on top of him, pressing his body into the ground, making him unable to move, and pushing all the air out of his chest. He struggled to breathe, to shout, to move, to raise himself up, but he failed to do any of that. As if that was not enough, the only little strength he had was fading away. His eyelids felt heavier and heavier, and he found it harder and harder to keep them open. Desperately, he gave up the fight. *So, this is the end of me,* he thought bitterly, *I'm not dying for killing Elior as I had wished, or even fighting with him, but falling off a damn tree limb. How funny is that?*

Yet, only a short moment later, the pain was gone. In fact, he could no longer feel anything at all. His sight came back to him too. Aary felt time had become still, or just extremely slow. The flying leaves seemed to be hanging in the windless air, and the sunlight was frozen on the surreally blue sky. He lay on the leaves, like he was floating in the water, without any sensation in his body. He couldn't say that his mind had any feeling either. If that was death, maybe it wasn't so bad after all. He was just lying there, not tired but wanting to sleep. No, maybe, he was already asleep. How big was the difference between dreams and reality? And what's the boundary?

What came into his mind was a face, the face he saw in the last second before he passed out.

Someone was here, deep in the forest. But it wasn't Elior, or any of his soldiers. It wasn't Rudi, his little elf friend. It was someone else, an unfamiliar face, someone Aary had never seen before.

As he lay there unmoving, more detail started coming back to him.

The face looked startled. Aary remembered the pair of big frightened eyes staring at him before they vanished. *The owner of the face looked as scared as myself, so it couldn't be one of Elior's men. No, wait... the big eyes, the frightened face... it wasn't a man at all, it was a child. A child that was terrified when I fell, but leaned over me curiously a moment later, and ran away when I opened my eyes. That's it. That was the only person that I saw, a child, and no one else.* Then it all made sense to him, except... how was it possible? A child alone in the forest?

Then he remembered something else.

The hair. That wisp of long, golden, curly hair.

Was it a girl?

No, what are you thinking! Listen to yourself, it's getting more and more ridiculous. How could there be a girl alone in a dangerous forest like this, or any kid at all? Maybe it was all just a dream. Did I really see someone? Or was it just my imagination? A shadow of a tree or even a pile of leaves. That must be it.

Yet, it seemed so real. The face, the big straw hat. It had to be a real person. But who?

Why was the person here? Was it an embassy of death sent from above to take me away?

It must have been. I am dying now. That person was my guide.

Aary seemed to have fallen asleep again. He dreamed of heaven, of people in Rocky Vill, and even imaginary figures of his own mother and father. Their faces resembled everyone that he knew, and yet they were not anyone that he knew. But somehow, in his dream, he knew perfectly well that they were his parents, and he felt an unprecedented sense of security and happiness when he was with them. In his dream, they were like the other kids' parents in his village, but even more loving and caring. Not only them, everyone he knew before the war was there, alive. Old instrument master, Tommy's dad, Phil the baker, everyone was around him, happy and laughing... at least until he was woken up by Rudi when the little elf passed by.

Rudi was patting him violently on the shoulders. That woke him from the deep slumber. As he was yawning sleepily, the little elf stared at him like he was seeing a man talking without a head: "Why in the name of trees are you lying here in this cold weather? How tired were you that you must sleep HERE, on the ground in the middle of the forest? I thought you were dead!!!"

Aary lifted his fingers and realized that his body was his again, and the pain was gone. It all felt just like a dream. Only his back still ached a little from the fall he took. He blinked at Rudi blankly. Aary didn't know what to say or even what to think. *I'm not dead. So, it was all just a dream. How could it be?*

Rudi waved a hand in front of Aary's eyes: "Have you lost your wits? What happened?" Aary turned his eyes from Rudi to the tree branch he had fallen from. It looked so high from here. How could he not have died? Dubiously, Rudi looked towards the direction where Aary was looking at, and found the tree branch above. After staring and thinking for a while, he suddenly turned his head back and cried out: "Oh no, did you fall from the tree?? But wait... but why are you covered in that coat? It looked like you were taking a nap here. How can you be so prepared for a fall?"

That was when Aary saw the coat. He lifted his head and stared incomprehensibly at the brown linen overcoat on himself. *Where did that come from? I've never seen it. And it's definitely not Rudi's, from his reaction. So, there was a person here. At least that part was not completely a dream or I wouldn't have this.*

Rudi saw Aary's confused look and shook his head, deciding that he wouldn't get any answers from his buddy today. He looked up to the sky. "It's almost dark. Don't you need to get back to Elberkhan?" "Oh damn!" Aary suddenly came back to reality. He jumped up from the ground and as soon as his feet landed on the ground, he bolted away like a bird in flight, holding the coat in his hand, kicking up leaves and dirt behind him. As he ran, he called back to Rudi: "Thank you! I'll see you soon!"

For the next couple of days, Aary had been waiting for the owner of the coat to show up, but he hadn't seen him again. He started to doubt his memory of the event. Was it a fictional character in his own mind that he created when he was in a trance that came out of his imagination when he was knocked unconscious? But then how could he explain the coat hanging in his treehouse that still smelled nice? *Or maybe, was it just a ghost hunting the forest looking for someone to keep its coat? And now that it found me, it could finally rest?* He was amused by his stupid thoughts. *Don't think about it anymore. What will be will be. If it was not meant to come, it wouldn't show up, even if I wait until the end of time.*

Autumn silently slipped away and winter was about to come. The forest was not green and luxuriant anymore like it used to be. The dreary yellow leaves were like fallen souls as they withered and fell off the branches one by one. The animals started storing food for the winter, stuffing more leaves and feathers in their nests to help keep them warm. Little by little, the autumn wind grew cooler, grew colder, and grew chillier... He almost forgot about the peculiar experience and stopped noticing the coat hanging in his home.

Until one day, just before winter came, on the way from Elberkhan back to his house in the forest, he saw that straw hat again.

* * *

Looking into her beautiful and blissful eyes, he felt that his whole world had lit up. At that moment, he didn't have anything else on his mind. He would give her happiness. He would be with her his whole life. He would never ever let her feel sad or let her down. He would live with her, grow up with her, grow old with her, and die with her. He already seemed to be able to see the picture after many decades, when the two of them were already old and grey, but would still hold their hands together happily, and he would still have the strength to hold her and raise her up high in the air.

19

A Hungry Bear

"Wait!"

Aary shouted. But it was no use. There was no way that his voice could reach whoever it was. It was a really windy day, and the sound of his voice was torn to pieces right after it left his mouth. Not to mention that the whole forest was shaking, leaves flying violently in the air, making thunderous noises.

He could only run towards the hat, hoping to catch it before it disappeared. He ran through the trees, while pushing aside the leaves blowing into his face, which scratched his arms and made him really itchy.

"Please wait!"

He could see the hat vaguely through the leaves hanging on the trees and those flying in the air. It was moving swiftly, jumping left and right and left again. It seemed like it was running away from something. But Aary didn't feel like it was running away from him, because it was actually moving towards his direction.

However, when he was only a few meters away from the other person, the hat disappeared from his sight suddenly. Aary was surprised. He stopped moving to see the area more clearly. But that huge straw hat was just nowhere to be seen.

Aary was confused. As he was pondering the situation, he heard a horrified scream behind him. He turned around at once, and the scene in front of his eyes made the hair on his neck stand up.

A small, lean human kid was standing against a tree, with a giant bear in front of him. The bear had already stood up on its back paws, ready to attack. It was more than twice the boy's height. The kid backed up a final step and almost tripped over a root under his feet. The tree blocked his way of escape. He had a huge straw hat on his head, hiding his face in the shadows. But it was still clear enough to see his terrified face.

The child looked not much older than ten. His panicking eyes were staring straight at the bear in front of him. He was only wearing a thin cotton shirt. Although he tried hard to straighten up his thin body to appear to be brave and fearless, he couldn't stop from shaking in the chilly wind and in front of the sharp teeth of the bear. Neither the bear nor the child noticed Aary.

Suddenly, the bear roared and pounced forward.

At that very moment, Aary also jumped forward. He grabbed the kid in his arms, pushed him away from the paws of the bear, and rolled over to stand up. He shouted to the frightened kid: "Run!" as he pulled out his dagger and crouched down fully prepared, ready to deal with the bear with full strength.

The bear was furious that someone had messed up its dinner. It roared angrily and turned to pounce on Aary. Aary dodged its attack. Taking advantage of the bear's own thrust forward, he turned to give a hard knock on the bear's ribs with his elbow. The bear howled in pain, and struck towards Aary in return.

His face managed to avoid the bear's paw by an inch, but the huge clawed paw hit his right hand that was on its way to stab the bear's stomach. Aary withdrew the hand quickly in order not to lose it to the paw, but the strong paw still knocked the dagger out of it and left some bloody claw marks on the back.

With no time to pick up the dagger, Aary seized the short interval when the bear hadn't yet found its balance and kicked its knee with all his strength. The bear fell on the ground like a fallen tower, but as it was waving the paws desperately on the way down one of them hit Aary's back. He went down together with the bear.

He felt his lungs and heart were almost cracking, and could hardly breathe after the smack. It felt as if he had fallen from the tree again. He tried but just couldn't get up. And yet, the bear was crawling up. Aary could already feel the hot, stinky breath from the bear's mouth through its frightful teeth blowing on the back of his neck.

He took a deep breath with difficulty, bit his lips and clenched his fists, ready to roll over and fight. But then, the bear suddenly collapsed onto the ground beside him, face down, with a loud crash.

Confused, Aary struggled to turn around, and saw the kid with the huge straw hat opening his eyes wide with terror, trembling like the tree leaves in the wind. His arms were stretched forward and shaking in the air, and about an arm's length down from his frozen hands, the bear had a big rock on its head.

The kid was still not fully recovered from the shock of just a moment ago. He cautiously helped Aary get back on his feet, hands still shaking violently, and said in a soft, trembling voice: "Thank you for saving my life... are you alright?" Aary smiled tenderly and said: "I'm alright. You?" The child nodded. Aary swept away some dirt and broken leaves off his elbows and continued: "I wasn't of much help actually. You were the one that defeated the beast..."

"Is it dead?" The child asked.

Aary put a hand in front of the bear's mouth with its scary teeth sticking out. He felt that there was still some weak hot air pushing out from its nose and mouth, but he estimated the weight of the rock, and thought that it would probably keep the bear unconscious for a while, enough for them to get away. Plus, he doubted that the bear would dare to go near them ever again, or any human. So he decided to just let it be. *It's not evil, it's just hungry. Poor old thing.*

"Don't worry, it won't bother you again." Aary answered.

"Did I kill it?" The kid seemed tense.

"It's still alive, but..."

The child let out a breath of relief. Aary just realized then that he was worried about killing it, instead of the bear coming at him again.

"I should go." The boy said, "thank you again for saving my life."

"Oh wait! I believe I have something that belongs to you. It's getting cold, I want to return your coat as soon as possible. Would you mind coming with me to pick it up?"

To Aary's surprise, the child looked a bit startled instead of happy, and took a step back: "That's ok. I really should go now." Before finishing his sentence, he turned around to leave.

Seeing that the person he had long been waiting for was about to go away, when he was still full of doubts and questions, Aary hastened to call out: "Wait! Please..." He reached out a hand wanting to stop him, but only caught his huge straw hat.

A head of long, beautiful golden hair tumbled down with springy curves and smelt like the fragrance of petals and barley. It hung down to the child's waist like silk, reflecting the golden sunlight. Aary was stunned.

So, it was a girl.

Aary stood there, feeling crude and silly. The girl looked quite skinny, probably a little underfed; her hair strewed with some dirt and leaves; her lips a little chapped and blue in the cold wind; and her face had some tiny bruises and cuts. But when a spot of sunlight shone through the leaves of the trees and onto the girl's face, lighting up a few strands of golden hair hanging in front of her forehead, Aary just felt his mind going completely blank. The feeling he just had of not being able to breathe came back to him again.

But the girl seemed to be totally startled by this abrupt action. She opened her big eyes wide, with a mixed expression of shock, fear, confusion, and helplessness. Aary had never been so close to a girl before, let alone such a beautiful girl. He stared at her for a long time, not willing to spare a second to blink. But he soon realized how rude it was of him and hurriedly looked away. Then he realized that she was shivering in the cold wind, her bluish frozen lips constantly trembling.

He lowered his eyes in shame and guilt, and blamed himself in his mind. He had her coat, so she had only a thin shirt left to defend her from this cold weather, and all he did was stare at her so rudely. How could he not notice this earlier?! He hastened to hand back the hat, clumsily took off his own cloak, and awkwardly wrapped it around the girl's shoulders.

The girl gave out a startled tremble when his hands touched her as he put the coat on her, and took another small step back. Aary quickly drew back his hands, and smiled apologetically at her. The girl looked like a frightened little deer, eyes warily fixed on Aary, but her hands caught the corner of the cloak before it fell off.

Aary thought carefully about how he could stop frightening the little girl, and began: "I... I'm so...I'm really sorry about that. I shouldn't have..." he felt that his tongue was not really his, "please... don't be afraid. I won't hurt you..." He thought about Rudi's conversational skills, and wished so much that he was here. But Rudi wasn't here, and Aary was never good at this.

"Mmm.. my name is Aary. I'm 16 and work and live at the castle of Elberkhan. Oh, but that's not where I kept your coat. I have a treehouse not far away from here in the woods. I built it myself to keep away from all dangers. You must be cold. Would you like to come and have a hot drink at my place? I can fetch you the coat. Please trust me, I would never hurt you. Here," he bent over to pick up the fallen dagger and sheathed it before untying it from his sword belt and handed forward to the girl, hilt first, "you hold the dagger. If you think that I'm going to hurt you, you can stab me with it. No, I mean, you can stab me, but please don't do that, I would never hurt you. Oh, and..." he pulled out the belt and handed it to the girl too, "you can tie my hands up behind my back. Here, so I can't do anything."

Aary said as he turned around and put his hands together behind his back for the girl to tie up. But his pants were starting to fall off now that his belt was gone. Embarrassed, he awkwardly hurried to pull them back up. Amused by Aary's clumsy words and actions, the girl finally let her guard down a little bit and giggled.

On seeing her smile, Aary felt something melting in his heart. It was a timid smile, but very lovely and pure. She was not the prettiest girl Aary had seen, but when he saw her smile, he just knew that he was willing to do anything to keep her smiling. She had a pair of sapphire blue eyes, as pure and clean as lakes reflecting the sky, with lights of intelligence and spirit shining from within. She had a pair of cute little canine teeth that showed up when she smiled, and a pointy little nose that curved slight up, just like a little cat. Her hands were grabbing onto Aary's cloak and wrapping it around herself. Her trembling became less noticeable, and her lips got back some redness. Aary thought she looked even prettier as the color of blood returned to her face. Still smiling, she handed back his belt, and softly nodded.

"Ok. I believe you. But I'll keep the dagger, just in case."

On the way neither of them spoke. They just walked quietly, one after the other. Only the fallen sticks and leaves made rustling sounds under their feet as they stepped on them. It seemed as if a beautiful and colorful soap bubble was floating between the two, and the slightest disturbance of the air by anyone opening their mouths would make it burst in the blink of an eye. The girl was wrapped up in Aary's cloak, and sniffed her nose from time to time.

Without the cloak, Aary had only a thin layer of shirt left on him, but he didn't feel the slightest bit of cold. Instead, he felt that his face was burning as if he had a fever. Even some beads of sweat came out on his forehead. He almost wanted to take off the shirt and walk in the freezing wind barebacked – this seemed like the only way that he could cool down the fiery heat inside of him. His hands were dangling rigidly and unnaturally by his sides as he if didn't know where to put them. Strangely enough, he never noticed where he normally put his hands when he walked, but now they felt like two awkward animal hoofs, not even from the same pair, and seemed so superfluous no matter how he moved them. So, he put them in the pockets of his trousers.

The girl followed behind. She sneaked a peek at this strange boy with gentle green eyes, who fell from the sky last time, and had just risked his life to save her from the paws of the bear. She secretly decided that he was not a bad guy, because a bad guy would never give away his own belt allowing his pants to fall down just to comfort someone. She noticed that the collar of his shirt was a little soaked with sweat, and his hands were in his pockets unnaturally. She bit her lips and quietly giggled.

Later, the girl climbed up to the treehouse by herself under Aary's protection. Aary was quite worried about that beforehand. He wanted to invite her up for a drink, but thought that she might not want to enter the house of a stranger she had just met, and even if she wanted, how could she get up there? He didn't even dare to suggest that he carry her up. But his worry soon proved to be frivolous. Apparently, the little girl was super excited on seeing his treehouse and couldn't wait to climb.

When climbing the tree, the girl finally seemed more like the child she was, laughing and calling out to Aary when she was ahead or left behind. The fun of the climb seemed to have made her forget about the frightening experience she had just had, and the worry and fear on her face were finally replaced by happiness and freedom from care. By the time they got up to the treehouse, the barrier between them seemed to have dissolved, and they were both laughing and breathing heavily.

Aary carefully boiled a kettle of water on the little stone stove in his house, and poured a cup for the girl with a few calming herbal leaves in it. The girl held the hot stone cup with both of her hands to warm them up, slowly delivering it to her lips and took a sip. She felt the warmth flowing in her body as the delicate, calming fragrance of the leaves surrounded her.

"So," Aary considerately raised his eyes to look at the girl, his hands locked nervously and thumbs rubbing against each other, "Can you tell me about yourself? How old are you? What's your name? Where did you come from? And what are you doing here alone in the winter forest? It's really dangerous for a little girl like you. I mean... you don't have to tell me if you don't want to. But if you're here for a reason, maybe I can help..."

The girl raised her head and looked at him, the worried look came back to her again. She took a deep breath and began in a soft voice: "My name is Lyna. I just turned 13 last month. And I live on the other side of the Soulkeeper Mountain."

* * *

He asked the musicians for an accordion, and played a soulful song for her. He hadn't known how to play the accordion, but he knew that she always liked the sound of it very much. So, he had been secretly taking lessons from the accordionist for the past few weeks, only to see her surprised and touched smile, right here, right now. As she watched the man she loved performing on the stage only for her, tears of happiness filled her eyes.

20

Lyna's Tale

My mom and I live on the other side the Soulkeeper Mountain, in a place called the Garden Valley, which must be unfamiliar to you. Although it's not a very tall mountain, the climate over there is nothing like it is here. As the name suggests, the place is like a beautiful garden, forever green and feels like spring all year round, with flowers and butterflies everywhere. The weather is always very placid and comfortable, and the people friendly and peaceful.

My dad passed away when I was seven years old. We miss him dearly. But even if it's just me and my mom, we have always lived a happy life. My mom works as a seamstress. She made beautiful clothes for everyone in the village and that supports us so that we are able to live a mostly worriless life. I help her with her designing and tailoring work sometimes when I finish my schoolwork, make all the material purchases needed for the clothes, and deliver the finished clothes to the families. Because of this I have been able to build close friendships with the villagers.

Our village is a small one, there aren't many people in it, so everyone knows each other, and everyone is kind and helpful. Although my mother and I tend to do everything on our own, there are times when we meet with something that is out of our capabilities, and so our neighbors would come and help without hesitation. Although I lost my father, I have a mother that loves me very much, and we live in a little village full of harmony. I am more than grateful for the life I had.

However, it all changed last month, when my mom got a strange disease – she lost the ability to sleep. She couldn't sleep, not even for a little bit, for days and nights. No one knew what it was or what caused it, not even the doctor in our village or any of the doctors in nearby villages. In order to figure out how to help my mom, I started skimming through all the medicine related books in our village library, and soon everyone in the village joined to help me.

Finally, someone found the answer in a dusty old book. The disease is called the Watchman's Curse. It is a very old and rare kind. The cause of the disease is unknown, but the book says that it might be related indirectly to dark magic, because it was more commonly seen thousands of years ago when dark magic prevailed, and it's very seldomly heard of since magic has been gone from the world. But the infection of the disease seemed very random, and the people infected are usually not related to magic themselves. It's not contagious, but nevertheless deadly. Without proper treatment, it will gradually and painfully eat the person away, and judging from the description, my mom might not make it through the winter.

The only cure, the book says, is a remedy made from three of the reddest leaves, three flowers that blossom in the ice and snow, and the blood from the three fiercest beasts in the world. Where I live, there are no red leaves, no ice and snow, and absolutely no beasts. Her condition was getting worse day by day, I could see her getting weaker and thinner, and I just couldn't watch it anymore. I can't let my mom die. So, I put on the big straw hat and the overcoat my dad used to wear when he was alive, dressed up as a boy and hid my hair in the hat for a bit more safety, and secretly left. I am determined to find the cure for mom's disease.

When I climbed over the hill, I was happy to find that there are red leaves all over these mountains. I easily found the three reddest leaves that were so red they didn't even have any spots or specks. And on that day, when I finished picking out the leaves, suddenly a person fell from the sky, it was you. You really startled me. I scampered away at once. But I left the leaves and the coat there in a hurry. After a while, when I made sure that you hadn't followed me, I went back to look for them, and saw you lying there...

Lyna raised her eyes from the hot steaming water in her cup to look at Aary, and Aary blushed. Lyna smiled in return, and looked back to her cup. What she decided to keep to herself was that when she saw him, she felt a strange feeling inside her. She didn't know this boy, and had never seen him in her life before. But she didn't know why at that very moment, when she saw him lying there on a pile of leaves, eyes closed, she was so afraid that he was going die.

For all she knew, he could be some bad guy in the storybooks that would kidnap her or do something worse. But he looked so innocent and harmless at that moment. She ran to him and kneeled by his shoulder. The boy didn't move an inch. He was as still as a piece of wood. Worried, she put her hand gently on his chest, and when she felt his heartbeat, she felt a sudden relief. His heart had the same beat as her own.

Assured that the boy was still alive, she picked up her leaves and coat, and was ready to go. But she didn't have the heart to leave him alone lying on the freezing ground. She didn't dare stay either. A tall, strange, almost-grown man was no danger when he lay there unconscious, but who knew what he would do when he woke up. So, she took off her coat again, and covered him gently up to the neck. Maybe it was her movement or the weight of the coat, but at that moment, suddenly, his eyes moved and started to open. Startled, she quickly hopped away before he could fully open his eyes, and ran away from that place.

After that, she tried to forget this peculiar incident, but could not get this strange boy out of her head, the boy that came from the sky.

As the weather grew colder, she felt a little challenged without the coat. She was also running out of the food she brought from home, thus, she was afraid that she couldn't make it through the winter. But the flowers that blossom in the ice and snow could only be found in the winter. Just when she decided to go home first to collect more clothes and food, a bear broke up all her dreams.

The hungry bear, which was probably grabbing its last meal to make sure that it stored enough fat for its imminent hibernation, chased her till there was nowhere to escape. She thought heartbreakingly that her poor mother was going to lose her one and only daughter... She never dreamt that the boy who fell from the sky would show up again right at that moment.

Lyna smoothed a strand of golden hair in front of her forehead to the back of her ear, and raised her head to say to Aary: "Thank you for saving my life and inviting me here. But I think I should go. I just want to find the cure for my mom as soon as possible."

"Actually," Aary said sincerely and anxiously as he saw Lyna standing up, "you can stay for longer." Lyna turned around and saw Aary's concerned look. "You can stay here until you've collected everything. This is my house, but I don't live here, so you don't need to worry about inconvenience. You can lock the door from the inside when you're alone. It will keep you safe. Although it's quite simple and unrefined, even without a proper bed, it can keep you from the cold and danger. I can share with you the food that I hunt and gather, as I usually found more than I would need anyway. And I can get other stuff too, from Elberkhan, where I work. Blankets, medicine, books, anything that you would need. It should be enough for you to wait until the snow comes. And the blood from the three beasts you talked about, I'll help you get it. It's too dangerous for a little girl like you to be around those beasts, but I'm tough, I can beat them for sure."

"What?" Lyna was so shocked that she didn't know what to say.

"I mean it. I can help you with this. You will have much better chances of collecting the things you want than if you look on your own. I assure you I'm not a bad guy."

"But... why?"

Aary blushed: "Well, I just thought that it would be easier for you, that's all."

Lyna already felt tears welling up in her eyes, so she dropped her eyelids and hid her eyes behind her long, beautiful eyelashes. Her mother had taught her to be independent and strong since she was young, to finish things by herself and not bother anyone else, which she had tried to do very hard in the past few weeks. But she also knew the difficulty of achieving this on her own, and knew that this boy might be her only hope to save her mom, or the closest she'd ever get. She was confident about the red leaves and the flowers, but today a single bear in the forest almost took her life, how could she ever possibly be able to defeat those three fierce beasts and get their blood?

This strange boy, who fell from the sky and saved her from a bear, offered to help her do something so dangerous shortly after they met each other. Is he human, or an angel sent from heaven? She knew she shouldn't accept his offer of help. You don't ask someone to risk his life for you when you barely know him. But when her mother's face appeared in her head, she also couldn't bring herself to refuse his help. She didn't know how to respond to an offer like this. How she wished that her mom was here to tell her the right things to do. The anxiety and pressure she had felt since her mother got ill, the fear she bore from being alone in a strange and dangerous place, and all the challenges and difficulties she suffered those past days and weeks, all at once rushed towards her like the evening tide. The hard shell she built to protect herself and keep her strong crumbled down in front of this gentle boy, and tears poured out like a flood that broke the dam.

She buried her head into the sleeves of her shirt, and sobbed like a little kid. Not knowing what to do, Aary awkwardly leaned forward and put a hand on her shoulder, feeling her twitching and trembling, his own heart trembling with it. He wanted to put his arms around her and hold her tight, telling her it's alright, telling her that he'll protect her and help her no matter what, but he just didn't have the courage to do that. Instead, he simply said: "You won't lose your mom. I promise."

After Lyna cried for a while, she rubbed her eyes with the back of her hand, then she blinked her eyes still shining with tears and looked at Aary: "Thank you, my angel."

* * *

After the party was over, people scattered home with joyful moods and tired bodies, and fell into deep slumbers. But the two of them didn't want to part. They wanted to be together forever, or at least for the night. They went back to his home together. The messy environment and the subtle fragrance of pine wood made her feel safe and comfortable. As light from the candles outdoors shone in, the dim room looked sweet and cozy. Their happiness and sweetness filled the whole cabin. The door softly closed behind them.

Lyna's Theme

Chen Yuxiao

21

Three Animals

Lyna started living in Aary's little cabin. Aary tied up some bundles of dried hay into a block, and covered it with some clothes and blankets on top, making a crude bed for Lyna. It was not the most comfortable bed Lyna had slept on, but it was the first bed she'd had in a while.

She didn't expect that when she finally relaxed her strung-out nerves after a long time, her body also let its guard down, and as a result, a fever started as soon as she settled down. Because Aary seldom got ill, he had absolutely no idea of how to take care of a sick person. Lyna begged him again and again not to bother doing things for her anymore, saying that she'd get better after some rest. She struggled and pretended to look like she was in good spirits every time he came back, but each time Aary touched her forehead he felt it burning hotter, as he himself burned with anxiety.

Aary dug out all his clothes and wrapped them around Lyna. He also looked up fever medicine recipes in his book *The Art and History of Alchemy in Healing*, and collected the ingredients to cook for her on his stove in the cabin. He had much experience in making medicines, but mainly for external use, and the ingredients for this were totally new to him. He burnt the medicine several times, and almost set fire to the house. Lyna sat against the wall by the stove wearing her own coat and thick layers of Aary's clothes, watching him flurry about, and smiled weakly with gratitude.

When Aary was not around, Lyna just sat by the stove and read his books to distract herself from the awful feeling of sickness. Aary came to see her every afternoon, bringing her new books. He also tried to get some fresh fruits to Lyna every day. Since it was almost impossible to find any fruits in the forest at that time of the year, he had to buy some in the market of Elberkhan. Fortunately, he had saved some coins from selling hunts that were excessive to his needs. Apart from that, their diet was not much different from his old one, mainly consisting of cookies and meat.

When they were together, they often read together or talked freely. Both of them enjoyed each other's company very much. Lyna was also getting well because of Aary's medicine, and always felt content and grateful.

From their talks, Aary learned that Lyna liked animals very much, although she mostly meant the kinds of animals from her hometown, little puppies, kittens, mild cows, horses, chickens, and beautiful little birds. She wouldn't dare to declare the same love for the dangerous beasts over his side of the mountain.

He also knew that she went to formal schools in her village. Because crops can grow very easily in the mild climate of Garden Valley, and there were seldom wars as well because of its remote location, the people there put much of their time and energy into knowledge and culture. Although Lyna's village was only a very small one, the people were all well-educated. Every child needed to go to school for many years until they were full-grown, and learn not only reading, but all sorts of knowledge, from how to make crops grow stronger, to the history of magic and wars.

It was totally different from Aary's Rocky Vill where people were busier doing hard labor without the leisure time to read. In fact, most people couldn't read at all. The school he went to was really more for fun than learning, and there wasn't even a library in the whole village. The old instrument master had the most books in Rocky Vill, but even those weren't many. Aary was so amazed by how much knowledge Lyna knew at such a young age. She had read almost all the books he had ever known, especially the fantasy novels because they were her favorite type of books. And she read so much faster than him too. She would finish the books he brought back in no time, so he was driven to get more books for her every day.

Lyna also met Rudi when he came by to visit Aary. She was quite shocked to see him because she thought that elves only existed in history books and novels. But she had seen a lot of unbelievable things since she left home and came here, so this short, friendly, and talkative little creature was not very hard to accept. Rudi was really happy to see Lyna and liked her very much, even though Lyna couldn't help stroking his 112-year-old ears again and again. When he heard that Lyna was staying in Aary's treehouse, he gave Aary a wink with a funny look on his face. However, judging from Aary's totally confused look, Rudi guessed that Aary probably didn't understand what he meant.

Aary tried to hide his beatings from Lyna because he didn't want to scare the little girl. He would ask Rudi to get his medicine from the treehouse every time so he could take care of the wounds before he went back. But Lyna still noticed that there was something wrong. She noticed that on some days his movements would be unusually rigid, and he would be slightly frowning and panting even while doing some easy tasks. She asked several times if he was alright, but he always just smiled nervously and acted as if nothing was wrong.

One day, when Aary came home, he found that Lyna was crying. Rudi was standing beside her comforting her. Aary anxiously ran towards them:

"What happened? Did someone hurt you?"

Lyna looked up at him, tears shining in her big watery eyes: "No. Someone hurt YOU." She stood up and hugged him, gently but tightly.

Aary was really confused for a moment, then he understood. Rudi was looking at him apologetically. Aary wanted to blame Rudi, but just couldn't do it. The only things he felt right now were the girl's arms wrapping around his waist, her head and cheek leaning on his chest, and the delicate fragrance of petals and barley on her golden curly hair. At that moment, all the hardness suppressed in himself over the years dissolved at once, and any resentment or anger he had for this world suddenly disappeared too. He had never felt such a sense of security, such a feeling of being loved, like in that moment.

"Why didn't you tell me?" Lyna asked, sobbing, with her face still buried in Aary's chest. "Why would they hurt you? I won't let anyone hurt you. I will fight them. I will protect you. I will kill the king if he hurts you again. Why didn't you tell me? Why?"

"I..." Aary didn't know how to answer. He put his own arms around the girl's lean shoulders, "I... I'm sorry..." *From now on, I will tell you everything I know. There will be no more secrets. I won't be afraid to reveal my deepest wounds to you, because I know you will always protect me.* He made a silent promise in his heart.

Later that afternoon, after Rudi left, Aary and Lyna sat shoulder to shoulder in a corner of the house, each with a book in hand, until the sky was dark. Neither of them spoke, and neither needed to. They merely enjoyed each other's company. Two lonely wandering souls in a perilous and cruel world found each other. They both felt a little bit of warmth, a little bit of comfort, just like two little kittens cuddling together to pass through a severe cold winter, seeking warmth in each other's fur. At that time, they both felt the exact same feeling in their hearts, and any word lost its meaning.

Lyna had been staying in Aary's place for two weeks now. The weather was getting colder day by day as winter drew near. Aary was determined to help Lyna get the blood of the beasts she needed. But he had no idea what they were or where to find them. He borrowed a high pile of books on animals from the castle library, and the two of them spent days reading through everything, but there was still not a single clue.

After finishing the last book, Aary sat against the wall in frustration. "All these books are about how people can make use of the animals, if we can eat them or make them do labor for us, or keep them as pets. I don't know so much about animals, but I'm guessing that the fiercest animals shouldn't become common dishes on humans' dining tables. Humans seem to be scarcely afraid of any animals. The scariest animals I know are batwing dragons and even they have been killed by humans for their skin."

"Wait! Batwing dragons exist?" Lyna's eyes widened.

"Yes of course." Aary answered, "You don't have them where you live? Oh, you're so lucky. They are a nightmare. They are the number one cause of death for hunters here. That's why their skin is so valuable. More than half the people trying to hunt them down were killed by them first."

"Maybe this is silly. But I once read a fantasy book when I was young." Lyna told Aary, "It's called *The Evil Spirits*. In that book, the author told stories about three kinds of the most dangerous animals. They are the Batwing Dragon, the Sea Monster and the Lava Demon. I didn't mention it because I thought it was completely fictional. But if batwing dragons are real, the other two may be real as well!"

"I think that's our answer! Would you also happen to know where to find them?"

"Yes! That was one of my favorite books. I have read it many times and remember every detail." Lyna called out in joy, "In the book, it's said that they were the nightmares of the sky, the ocean, and the underground world. So, you already know where batwing dragons are. Sea monsters only roam where the saltwater flows, and they can't breathe in the air. They mostly wander in the deep ocean, but they do get close to the shore sometimes and kill sailors. Fishermen should know where to find them. And lava demons live in mountain caves. When you go deep into the caves, the air should become colder. But where lava demons are, it gets extremely hot and that turns stone into liquid..." a sudden look of worry appeared on her face, "If what the author said in the book is true, they are extremely dangerous animals. Any of them could kill us without any effort. How will we ever be able to get their blood?"

"We won't." Aary answered firmly, "But I will. You don't need to worry about that. Just stay here and rest well until you're fully recovered from your fever, while I get the blood for you. Remember? I promised you before."

"No." Lyna's response was firmer, "I won't let you risk your life for me. This is my task. You can help me, but that's it. Promise me that you won't try to do this by yourself."

Aary looked at the determined expression on the girl's face that was so haggard and weary from the sickness, and lied:

"Ok, I promise."

* * *

He and she had a wedding in the little main hall of the village. Her father, the village elder, personally held the ceremony. Everyone in the village was present to witness the important moment of this enviable little couple. The hall was decorated with fresh flowers that were pure white, and the people were also holding bundles of beautiful flowers in their hands. The bright sunlight cast a dreamy luster inside the hall though the colorful stained-glass windows high in the walls, and the fragrance of flowers gently suffused the hall till every corner was immersed in the mood of joy.

2 2

A Wounded Beast

Aary decided that he will get the blood by himself without letting Lyna know. Because if she knew, she would insist on going with him, and that may put her in danger. In preparation, he took a tiny metal flask with a cork lid from his bookshelf to collect and store the blood. He had used it for medicine before, but it was empty now. Aary tied it on his belt next to the scabbard of his dagger. He planned to go for the batwing dragon first, since he thought that would be the easiest of the three and the only kind that he had seen before. But even that was more difficult than anything he had done, and he had no idea how to go about it.

They are extremely large, about five times the size of the giant eagles, which already seemed like a nightmarish size for humans. And even though they are gigantic, they move incredibly fast and swiftly, just like the bats that they were named after. Also like the bats, they like to hunt at night, when the darkness gives their black skin the perfect cover. That's why, even though they are enormous, they are seldom seen, and even less known about.

But the fear of them couldn't be more widespread or real. If anything, their mysteriousness only adds to their dreadfulness. It's no exaggeration to say that they are like the death gods of night, because when night comes and everything slumbers, they emerge as huge black shadows soaring across the sky and every place their huge black wings covered, death followed.

Every batwing dragon would start its massacre after dusk, with its transcendent night vision and deadly claws, and nowhere under the night sky would be safe until the first light of dawn breaks through the darkness. Animals are murdered in their sleep and devoured whole, with nothing left but a pile of bones they spat out. Entire herds of livestock would disappear from pens or sheds over a single night. Even human casualties could be heard of from time to time. Not a single life would be spared if it had been chosen by one of these almighty monsters for its prey. Batwing dragons are what made it so dangerous to be outdoors during the night, especially in open fields.

Aary had heard that hunters usually used huge mechanical crossbows to shoot them, with iron arrows as thick as a man's wrist. But because they fly so fast and unpredictably, the chances of shooting one from the sky is one in a thousand. During the other nine hundred and ninety-nine times, the arrows would miss and worse, provoke them. And no one had ever made a batwing dragon angry and lived to brag about it. But why was Aary even worried about that? The only weapon he had was the dagger. That was like a toy in the face of batwing dragons.

He was secretly thinking about ways to find a batwing dragon, but never had he thought that one would find its way to him. One evening, he was on his way back to the castle after saying goodbye to Lyna, and considering whether he could find the habitat of batwing dragons on land, or plot a trap high in the air. He estimated that going to their nests would be suicide. Even when they slept, they were dangerous, being able to kill a man in less than a second. Setting a sky trap might be a better option. But how could one of these smart, agile creatures fall into his trap...?

BANG!

A tremendous crash in the forest behind him abruptly stopped his thoughts and steps, and almost stopped his breath too. He turned around and held still for a moment waiting for any more movement.

But nothing happened. Scared, but curious, he gathered up his courage and walked cautiously towards the source of the sound to see what had happened. He quietly approached the spot and poked his head from behind the tree trunk where he was hiding, and saw a behemoth lying in a pool of blood. He couldn't believe his eyes. Although the sun was already gone and the day pretty dark, there was no mistaking what he was looking at. The monstrous size, the scary look, the pitch-black color, this could be no other but the batwing dragon he was looking for! He hadn't even started actually looking, and yet there it was. Aary was overthrown by excitement and surprise.

That creature was about ten times a man's height from head to tail and completely covered in dark, smooth skin like black satin. One of the bat-like thin wings was folded at the side of its body, the other feebly spread on the ground. The membrane of the wings was so thin that it seemed almost transparent at the edges. The wings were supported by very strong but lightweight bones, and Aary could see every one of them on the spread-out wing.

The main bones were like those of a human arm, connecting to its shoulder on one end, and had a joint that could bend like an elbow, enabling the wing to spread and fold. Those main bones supported the upper edge of the wing, and connected to all the other bones at the end. Four thinner bones spread out in different directions like four fingers of a hand, supporting the main area of the wing, each with a sharp, spike-like end sticking out the edge. There was also a fifth bone, the thumb, short and sturdy, that stuck out from the wing like a strong hook. The dragon only had two legs, and they were quite short for its body size. So Aary imagined that if they ever needed to walk on the land, they would probably need to use the hooks on the wing as front legs to support the weight of their bodies. But who would walk if they could fly?

Its head was long and huge. The shape was somewhere between a dog's head and a horse's head, perfectly smooth and optimized for flying at very high speed. But what made it different from a dog or a horse was the long, pointy, bony crest extending backwards from the skull. That, and of course, the giant size, the sharp fangs visible even when its mouth is closed, and the eyes. The dragon's eyes were half-closed, but Aary could still see the light shining out from those red eyes. The eyes glimmered in the dark, like rubies, or sparks of fire in the amber. The color of red made it look scary and evil. It gave Aary a chill down his spine.

Speaking of spines, Aary could see hard ridges down the dragon's spine all the way from the back of the long neck to the tip of the long tail, becoming sharper and longer towards the end of the tail. At the tip of the tail, the last four ridges were so sharp and long that they looked like swords sticking out towards both sides. It looked ferocious and majestic, just as he had been told.

But now, this one was seriously injured. Aary saw a very thick iron arrow sticking out from its chest, around where the spread wing joined the body, and fresh red blood was pouring out from the wound like a gushing fountain. The dragon looked like it was already at its last gasp, with its head weakly lying on the ground, not even moving a little. Aary observed long enough to make sure that there was absolutely no need to worry that it would hurt him, and approached the dragon carefully.

The dragon saw him, and tried to prop its body up with the folded wing. But the struggle just made it bleed faster, so it gave up the fight soon enough and collapsed again to the ground. Aary walked slowly and carefully, until he reached the wound. He opened the lid of the little flask and held it near its wound. The wound was bleeding violently, and the dragon was not moving, so it wasn't hard at all to catch enough blood in the flask. He couldn't believe that he got the first animal's blood so easily.

Certain that he acquired more than enough blood from the dragon, Aary closed the lid and stood up to leave. But then, he saw the dragon's eyes again, when he was taking one last look at the magnificent beast, and strangely, he could not take another step. The dragon opened its eyes up all the way, and looked at Aary. And now he could see, those eyes weren't evil. Instead, they were pleading, begging, filled with desperation and agony, glittering in the wetness of tears. They firmly seized Aary's heart with sympathy.

Unable to just walk away from those eyes, Aary took another look at the dragon's wound. The arrow was buried at least an arm's length deep in the flesh, and Aary could almost feel the pain himself. Pain had been a daily routine for him since he came to Elberkhan, but now, he believed, that the dragon was suffering more deeply than all his pain combined. Although it might be a cruel beast, and it may have done quite a lot of terrible things, it was still a living soul. Even devils were not completely unforgivable, right?

He couldn't bear the inner torment anymore, so he kneeled back down near the dragon's wound and inspected it carefully and thoroughly. The wound was deep, but Aary judged from the size of the dragon that the arrow didn't pierce through its heart, so there was still a chance to save it. Aary was certain that this arrow must have been shot by an incredible hunter, and he was probably on his way here to claim his prize. Time was short.

Aary searched anxiously in his head for possible solutions to help this poor creature, and then, the medicine in his treehouse came to his mind. He patted the huge wing of the dragon and gently comforted it: "I'm getting medicine for you, and will be back in a minute. Don't be afraid."

The beast seemed to have understood his words and made a docile moaning sound. Aary stood up and ran back to his treehouse at his fastest speed. As soon as he broke through the door, he rushed to the cabinet to get the medicine. Lyna was shocked by his sudden intrusion, and knew something serious had happened from his anxious look. But he had just left minutes ago, and he didn't seem to be wounded.

"What happened Aary? Are you alright? Are you hurt?" She asked concernedly.

"No. This is not for me." Aary tried to explain in the briefest words possible, "Someone else needs help. Got to hurry. Sorry, I'll explain later."

Lyna called out worriedly as Aary rushed out the door: "Please be careful!"

He went back to the batwing dragon. Fortunately, the hunter still hadn't arrived yet and the beast was still breathing. He checked the wound again, and warned the dragon: "Sorry. This is going to hurt."

He held two hands around the thick shaft of the iron arrow, and pulled it out with all his strength. The dragon howled and shivered in pain, knocking Aary to the ground. He curled into a ball and covered his head with his arms, thinking that the dragon was going to kill him for causing the pain. But it didn't. The howl was long and echoed in the mountains. It sounded heartbreaking and penetrating. When Aary looked back up, the dragon was looking at him piteously with its watery red eyes. "Sh..." Aary calmed the dragon down with his patting hand, "it will be alright." He poured the whole bottle of medicine on the dragon's wound. It took him a very long time to concoct and could heal his whip wounds for a year. But now, this poor creature needed it more than him.

Then, a miracle happened. The recovery speed of the dragon was beyond anything he'd imagined. The skin where the medicine had touched reacted like it was enchanted by spells. New black skin grew at a speed visible to human eyes. In a few seconds, the wound closed, just like that in front of Aary's eyes. He knew that his medicine was specially made and healed his wounds three times faster than usual, but it still amazed him to see how well his medicine worked on the dragon. When the wound recovered, the dragon regained its spirit right away, and all its strength also came back to it. It arose slowly with the support of the wings, and when it stood up, its head stuck out over the top of the trees. It spread out its wings and raised its neck, giving out a bright and sharp cry to the sky that was even louder than the last one. This tremendous cry almost broke Aary's eardrum. He happily looked up at the huge dragon.

Suddenly, Aary heard the sound of galloping hoofs from a distance coming towards them.

"Go on! The hunter is coming to get you." He gave the dragon's wing a push, "if he could shoot you once, he could do it twice. You're still very weak. Don't let him get you again."

But the batwing dragon didn't leave. Instead, it lowered its head and bent over its neck beside Aary, and gave a low cry. Aary understood when he saw its meek and gentle eyes: "You want me to climb on?" The dragon answered by giving Aary a gentle shove with its head. Nervous and excited, Aary mounted the dragon's shoulder and wrapped his arms around the dragon's neck, even though his arms couldn't close around the thick dragon neck.

The dragon stood up at once, thrust hard against the ground with its strong feet and spread its wings, lifting straight up into the air. The sudden and powerful impulse almost made Aary fall from its shoulder. He closed his eyes and griped firmly onto the dragon's neck. When he finally had the courage to reopen his eyes, he carefully stuck out his head and looked down over the dragon's wide shoulder. The ground was moving away from them at a great speed. A man appeared on a horse in the opening of the forest where the dragon had just lay, but it was already too far and too dark to see him clearly. Aary could just vaguely see that the man stopped there and lifted his head to watch them fly off into the sky.

* * *

The village elder liked this friendly, polite, erudite, and cheerful young man very much, although he was a little worried that he might be a bit too young to take good care of his precious, only daughter. But when he saw the infinite affection in the young man's eyes when he gazed at her, the delicate care and attention he had for her, and the unconceivable happiness on her face when he was near, he passed his daughter's hand into the young man's with trust, and offered them his most sincere wishes.

23

Lyna's Magical Power

Aary had plenty of experience riding a horse when he was young, but this was his first time riding a dragon, and the first time flying too. In the beginning he was really nervous. Bumping up and down with the movements of those huge wings so high up in the air, he was afraid that if he didn't hold on tight, he'd fall and end up with nothing but being smashed to a thousand pieces.

However, soon enough, he discovered that riding the dragon was such a wonderful feeling. He loved riding horses, that's for sure, but this was a thousand times better. The magnificent mountains covered in the twilight looked like black waves from this height, and the fastest birds couldn't keep up with them, but all receded with the wind, chattering past his ears. He was riding the fastest animal in the world, and completely enjoyed it as they circled above the plain.

What's more amazing was that he didn't even need to learn how to ride the dragon or use a reign, this dragon seemed to have an amazing connection with him. Anywhere he wanted to go, without him saying anything, the dragon would go, as if it could read his mind. They even tried some special moves like rolling, diving, and sudden rising, and all finished perfectly together. Aary felt that he and the dragon had become one soul, and he was flying in the air himself. The dragon didn't speak, but he could feel that it was equally delighted as him. After a while, Aary thought the dragon might need a rest and that he should probably go and explain this to Lyna. Before he said anything, the dragon landed right beside his little treehouse, stirring up a cloud of dust and shaking off a rain of leaves. The shoulder of the dragon when it was standing straight was so high that Aary could just hop off onto the platform in front of his treehouse.

Aary hugged the dragon on its neck and asked: "Do you have a name? How should I call you? I'm Aary, by the way."

The dragon gently gave Aary a nudge with his huge black head. But even that gentle nudge almost knocked Aary to the ground.

Aary laughed and patted on its hard skull: "How about if I call you Blackwind? Do you like it?"

The dragon squeaked happily.

Startled by the dramatic sound of the dragon landing, Lyna, who was alone in Aary's treehouse, nudged the door open a little and gingerly poked out her head. At first glance, she was totally freaked out by the black giant in front of her that seemed even higher than the trees. She darted back inside at once with her heart thumping. But for a moment she thought she saw Aary in that short glance, so she ventured to peek back out again. This time she realized that Aary was hugging a gigantic, imposing dragon. Her eyes, which were already round and big, opened up like they were going to pop out.

Blackwind turned his head towards the crack of the door to see Lyna, and made a long rumbling noise. Aary turned around as well. Seeing Lyna, Aary couldn't wait to start telling her about everything, about how he ran into the injured dragon on his way, how fast the dragon healed with his medicine, how they just managed to avoid the hunter, and how cool it was to fly in the sky. But just when he opened his mouth, Lyna laughed and stopped him: "I already knew."

"What? I just wanted to tell you what happened."

"Yes, I already knew what happened."

"But... how? Did you watch us from here?"

"No, he told me." Lyna nodded towards the dragon.

"Wh... what??"

"I'll explain later. He said he owes you his life, so your two souls will be connected from now on. You need to set a signal, so that whenever you need him, he can be there in no time, something that he can hear from far away."

"Wait, but..."

"I told you, later. Do this first. You must have something among all your musical instruments that could work?"

Still totally confused, Aary went back to his treehouse and took a little wooden whistle with a string attached from his box of instruments. He put the string around his neck, pressed his lips against it and gently blew out some air. The whistle made a melodious and beautiful sound that echoed around the mountains.

"Will this work?"

Blackwind hummed in satisfaction and give him another nudge. Then suddenly, he spread his long wings that almost broke the trees around them, gave the ground a big push, and vanished into the night sky.

"Now are you going to explain?" Aary turned to Lyna, with the most curious and unbelieving expression on his face.

Lyna made a naughty face, and asked: "Don't you need to go back to Elberkhan? It's almost dark."

"No please, I can't wait until tomorrow. Just tell me in the briefest words, please! How could you understand him?!"

Lyna laughed, "Ok. I'll keep it short. You remember I told you I love animals? So, I grew up amongst many animals, and just like a child learning to speak, I gradually picked up their way of expression, like their body language or the sound they make. I could understand what the animals say and feel. Dogs, cats, pigs, sheep, cows, they would all come talk to me. The more intelligent the animal is, the easier I can understand. Like I can understand a lot from cats and dogs, but not so much from chickens. It was only until I was about 7 or 8 that I realized this was a special skill that not everyone has, because it came so natural to me, and my mother can also do this, so I thought everyone in the world had this capability. I also realized that even for animals that I was not very familiar with, I could still understand them. Maybe it's like a family gift? I don't know."

"But, what about that bear that almost killed you...?"

Lyna sighed: "I couldn't stop him. He was too hungry and needed to store fat for the winter sleep. It's an animal. They have their feelings and emotions, but they are not always as reasonable as humans. And also bears are not very clever so it's harder to communicate for me. However, as *The Evil Spirits* said, batwing dragons are one of the most intelligent animals on earth. So, with Blackwind it was so much easier. By the way, he loves this name."

"Wow that's amazing. I was just wondering if he could understand when I said that."

"To be more precise, he didn't understand your speech, but he understood your thoughts. Batwing dragons are one of the oldest species in the world, just like elves, and they still have ancient mind-reading abilities. So, when you touch him, he understands completely what you have in mind."

So, he DID read my mind when we were in the sky. Aary thought.

"They are also very faithful and have long-lasting memories. They always pay back what is owed, no matter if it's revenge or favor. They can spend their whole lives avenging a wrong that was done to them, or spend their whole lives repaying a kindness that they received. So, since you saved his life, he will try to repay you with his life."

"Wow! Did he tell you all of this just now?"

"No, this part I learned from the book. Although it mainly focused on the revenge part, like how they would sense people's fear or hunt down and tear hunters into pieces if they tried to hurt them. It made them sound so scary. I never thought they were such lovely creatures. Blackwind was so joyful."

"Wait! Does that mean that Blackwind will kill the hunter that shot him?"

"Oh no! You're right! He probably will try."

"No!! I'll have to stop him then! He'll listen to me." Aary blew the whistle they just agreed on, and looked into the sky for Blackwind's huge black wings. The stars were filling up the darkness. Then he remembered the dragon blood he got for nothing. He patted the little flask on his belt proudly and said: "By the way, I got the first blood too. That was a really good and safe start."

Lyna hugged him and stood on her toes to kiss him on the lower cheek. Aary blushed. Luckily it was dark enough, and the dragon arrived just in time. Aary climbed on Blackwind's shoulder, and waved to Lyna: "I'll use a ride to get back to Elberkhan. I'll see you tomorrow."

What he didn't see was that Lyna stayed standing there, in front of the treehouse, for a long time, even after they were gone. Tears of gratitude and bliss ran down her face as she watched the two of them disappear in the night sky.

* * *

He couldn't afford the most expensive and lavish ring, but he still wanted to give her the best. So, he bought a small piece of gold, and went to the goldsmith's shop in his leisure time to learn and work. In this way, he crafted a ring for her with his own two hands. The ring wasn't even a perfect circle, but he engraved delicate patterns on it, and her name. On their wedding day, he put the ring he made himself gently on her fingers. She touched the beautiful carvings on the ring, and was lost in fascination.

24

The Sea Monster

At the foot of the Soulkeeper Mountain, there was a place where the sun never shone. There, the hideous darkness bred evilness.

It was a land without sunlight, with a name that made the whole plain shiver with dread. The citizens there were called the Shadow Knights, because they never came out of the shadows into the sunlight, and they moved quietly and swiftly like shadows too. Black hooded cloaks that hid them from the light were their symbol, and they rode black horses wearing horned helmets made from giant buffalo skulls. They were the nocturnal devils, invincible and cruel, but they never fought anyone face to face. They mainly lived on carrion and sucked the rotted sticky blood, but badly injured animals or humans often became their prey too, as they could smell blood and death from miles away. They always came and went without a trace, leaving nothing behind.

However, it's their control of individuals' minds that put true fear into people. Whenever they were near, dark thoughts and emotions would silently creep into people's bodies and tamper with people's minds. Distrust, hatred, jealousy, violence... Their victims would be affected without even noticing. They made brothers fight brothers, friends kill friends, and all they needed to do was to come and collect their prizes after the damage was done. But no one, nor even any kingdom, dared to challenge them, as it meant nothing more than suicide. Their lack of enemies made them grow ever stronger, and meant their evil deeds went unpunished. Their prince was the cruelest of all. No one had ever seen him, or more accurately, no one that was still alive. Because he never let a single soul live. No one knew how big this place really was, or what it was like. The Dark Kingdom was what people called it.

Ever since Aary got the blood of a batwing dragon, he had been looking for a chance to go in search of the other two beasts. He saw the perfect opportunity when Elior needed to visit a few other cities on the plain to get new recruitments for his army. He knew Elior would want to bring him along, as he never left any chance for Aary to rest or be away from his punishments. But Aary came up with a clever trick. There was a bottle of medicine he made that was used to treat food poisoning. It would make people vomit anything they had in their stomach, so that the bad food could be flushed out. He pretended that he was getting ready to go with Elior, but secretly drank the whole bottle the night before the royal journey, and ended up throwing up crazily for the whole night. It was a really terrible feeling, but it served its purpose. When Elior saw him in the morning, kneeling beside the loo looking like he was dying, with vomit all over the floor, Elior gave him a really disgusted look and let him be.

Right after Elior left the castle with his royal escort, Aary started his journey to look for a sea monster. He packed some food, a water skin, and borrowed a copy of the book Lyna mentioned about the three beasts from the library, hoping that he might have some time to read. But he didn't tell Lyna that he was going after the beasts. He told her all about Elior's journey and said he had to go with Elior for a couple of days, and there was nothing he could do about it. He knew he promised Lyna that he wouldn't do this. But even if the quest was not that dangerous and Lyna not that young, the girl was still not fully recovered from her sickness and really weak. How could he take her on a journey that could kill someone when she was not even able to say a full sentence without being interrupted by coughs? Instead, he would give her a nice surprise when he came back, with the little flask full of all three kinds of beast's blood. He couldn't wait to see the surprised and happy look on her face.

He asked Blackwind to take him to the seaside and then sent him away, despite the loyal beast pleading with his eyes to stay with him and protect him. He needed to talk to the local people to learn more about the sea monster, and the presence of a monstrous dragon could hardly have encouraged conversation. So, he walked the last mile on foot, until he saw the infinite blue horizon appearing in front of his eyes.

The castle of Elberkhan was not too far away from the sea. He felt like he could almost see it from the window of the highest tower in the city. And he could definitely see the large surface of water that only ended at the edge of the world when he was flying on Blackwind's back. But this was his first time to actually go near the ocean. As the ground below him turned into soft white sand, the magnificence of the vast deep blue unveiling before him truly captured his breath. The water was deep and calm where it met the sky, with clouds rolling above the air. But where the water hit the rocks by the seaside, huge angry waves higher than man a reached up to the sky, breaking into ten thousand white pearls that fell back and disappeared into the sea again. The waves on the beach were less violent and more soothing. Layers of white and clear water rushed onto the shore one after another, carrying back some sand when they returned to the ocean. There were some simple shacks on the beach that belonged to the fishing village, and a shabby wooden deck that reached out into the sea with some boats tied along its side. He took off his shoes that were already full of sand, rolled his pants up to his knees, and felt the cool soft sand with his bare feet.

But while enjoying the beautiful view of the seaside, he was also starting to worry about his task. The ocean was so vast and infinite, how could he possibly find something in there, and even harder, to battle it? For all he knew, sea monsters could be even larger than the batwing dragons, and the sea is their home field.

A little boat with a ragged old sail appeared from far away and slowly came towards the shore. Aary watched as an old fisherman with a grey beard and bald head stowed the sail and started rowing the boat to the wooden pier. The old man looked skinny, but quite healthy. Years of exposure to the sun and rain left his face dark and coarse like a piece of crumpled parchment.

Aary walked slowly towards the old man as he pulled in next to the pier, and tried to tie the rope cable of the boat onto a wooden pillar. *An old fisherman like him must know something about sea monsters.* Aary thought confidently. Then he realized that the old man was having a bit of trouble. Part of the cable was stuck in a gap between the wood of the deck and the old man was trying his best to pull it out. Aary quickly ran across the sand and helped the fisherman get the cable out.

"Thank you, son." The fisherman smiled to Aary as he skillfully tied a knot after coiling several rounds around the pillar. Aary could see a net full of fish in the small boat. "You're not from around here, eh? High-born boy coming to the beach for fun?"

"Hmm not really. I'm not high-born, and I came here to look for a sea monster. Do you happen to know where I could find one?"

On hearing the words "sea monster", the old man's face turned immediately. The smile disappeared without a trace and fear crawled onto his brown wrinkled face.

"Why... why on earth are you looking for that, boy? That's no joking stuff aye! If you want to listen to me, be a good lad and go back home to your dad. He wouldn't like you to be eaten, eh?"

"I have no dad, mister, and I have not come here to be eaten. However, maybe I'll kill it instead."

After hearing him, the fisherman was suddenly full of reverence, like seeing a god. He held his palms together in front of his chest and said:

"So, you've come to deal with **it**, eh? Oh, thank heavens, our miserable days are finally coming to an end! The Fisher God didn't forget about us! He's finally sent us our savior! Thank you! Thank you!" He knelt down in front of Aary and was planning to bow down to him, but Aary stopped him in time and reached out his arms to help him back onto his feet.

"Sorry, uncle, you've mistaken. I'm not sent by anyone, and I can't promise you that I will kill it. I'm just a boy, but I will try my best. Could you please tell me everything you know about this sea monster?"

"Aye, boy. That's what I thought." The old man looked a little disappointed, but his voice was gentle, "You're good lad. But you won't kill it. Good men have tried and failed. Good men have died for it."

The old man sat on the flat surface of a wooden column of the pier, and began: "Our little village has been here by the sea for thousands of years, eh. And for thousands of years, men have lived by catching fish from the sea. We're not especially wealthy, but no one ever needed to worry about starving or freezing. Until 'bout a hundred years ago, **it** came from the bottomless trench under the ocean to the sea just outside our village. That's when our nightmare started, aye. Whole boats disappeared. Only small broken boards would be washed up to shore. Every week someone'd go out to the sea and never return. Every day when men set sail, they'd say goodbye to their families because they didn't know if they would come back.

"Every fisherman knows the ancient legends of sea monsters dragging boats and ships into the deepest sea, devouring everyone and everything on them, but no one imagines that this nightmare will actually come true for their own village. 'Tis a small village, and if it went on like this, not long and everyone would be dead, aye. No one knew what it was. Until some really lucky fellas caught sight of the hideous monster when they were out there, and somehow managed to stay alive. They said it was a giant fish the size of five fishing boats with teeth as long as a man's arm. But if 'twas a fish, it's possible to be killed by men, eh? To end this, all the strongest men in the village formed a team, every one of them muscular and experienced at sea. They took all kinds of weapons, set sail on the biggest and strongest sailboat in the village, and went off to kill the monster. But no one thought that the whole boat and everyone on the boat... alas... would be left with only a few shattered planks of wood." he sighed in sadness.

"Then what happened?" Aary asked anxiously.

"After that, all that was left in the village were old men with one leg in their graves, children that couldn't even hold an oar, and wenches that still had babes suckling at their breasts. My old man, I tell you, he was a baby at that time. Those that were left still needed to survive, aye? To beg for peace, they did what they thought was the only thing they could do. They took out all the fish they had left and put them in a little boat. With a long rope they tied the boat to the pier and pushed the boat into the sea. The most prestigious old man of the village stood by the pier and called out to the ocean: 'Dear Sea God, please come and eat the fish as our sincere offerings. We will serve you with all the fish we can spare, but please spare the fishing boats and people on the sea.' Guess what? The monster really came. It devoured the whole boat and all the fish in it.

"No one knew if it understood what the old man said, but after it finished the fish and went back to the ocean, there was truly a time when no more accidents happened. But not long after, the monster came again, so they had to give it more. That really gave the villagers a hard time, aye. Since then a hundred years has passed, and every month for these hundred years we need to feed it a large amount of fish, and barely have enough left for ourselves. But life still went on and we survived, until just recently. We don't know if it got bored with what we provided, or gained a bigger appetite, but a few months ago, it started causing troubles again. There hadn't been an accident in all these years since we started the sacrifices, but there have already been several just since the beginning of this year. We attended the funerals of those poor lads. All good, honest, lads. But we didn't even have their bodies to bury, how funny is that? We don't know what to do apart from increasing the amount of fish. But if it goes on like this, everyone in this village will soon starve to death, eh?" The fisherman gave out a bitter laugh.

"Then there's even more reason to something about it, and fast. Do you think the villagers would help me?" Aary asked.

The fisherman seemed shocked: "You still want to try and kill it, child?"

"Of course." Aary answered, "I actually wasn't planning on killing it before. I just need a little bit of its blood, that's all. But after hearing what you told me, I just made up my mind now. I promise you. I won't give up until I kill it and return the villagers to the life you had before it came."

"So, you are sent by God? Or are you God Himself? 'Cause if not, why else would you risk your own life for ours?"

"I told you uncle, I need its blood. It's a win-win situation. Could you tell me how I can find it?" Aary urged.

"The day after tomorrow is our next date of offering. At sunrise, we will provide it with fish, and it will come to the shore. If you need us, I will gather everyone in the village to help you. We will do whatever you ask if you can help us kill this beast."

"That would be great!" Aary said, "Thank you uncle."

"What? Thank me? If you kill it, you're the savior of this whole village. We'll do whatever you need. Do you have a place to stay? We have a spare room in our house if you don't mind. Now come home with me for dinner. My wife makes the best clam soup ever. And our son is about your age, you two will get along."

Aary squinted to look at the last smear of red at the end of the sky before darkness arrived, and realized how hungry he was. He only had some bread on the way, and it was after throwing up everything in his stomach. He smiled and gratefully accepted the offer. He was worrying that he wouldn't be able to deal with the sea monster alone, and didn't expect that the sea monster would be so vicious and have made so many enemies. Now he had hopefully gotten the help of a whole village. Even better, instead of harming an innocent creature, he was actually doing something good for all the people in the village. It made him feel more certain about what he was going to do.

He went home with the warmhearted fisherman and met his wife and children. The old fisherman told him that they had one son and four daughters, but the three older daughters were all married and had moved out. Only their son and the youngest daughter were at home. The daughter was about the same age as Aary, and the son was two years older.

The fisherman's wife was very friendly and nice, like the fisherman himself. Every time Aary finished his bowl of soup, the fisherman's wife would insist on giving him another bowl with extra clams and shrimp, even though he was constantly telling her that he was too full.

The girl was also very good to Aary. And when she heard that he was going after the sea monster, she went back to her room and took out a colorful rope with a wooden pendant. She asked for permission to tie it around Aary's wrist, telling him that it was a lucky charm she made herself, to keep him safe in this dangerous mission. She was really beautiful too, with chestnut hair and brown colored eyes, like her brother, but with much more delicate features.

Her brother, on the other hand, didn't seem to like Aary very much. He appeared to be a little arrogant and was looking down on Aary. Indeed, although he was not much older than Aary, he was a lot bigger in stature. He was at least a foot taller, and his muscles looked much thicker and stronger. The hard, chestnut stubble on his chin also made him look more mature and dignified. Compared with him, Aary looked just like an undergrown little boy. It was understandable that he didn't believe this skinny boy would kill the sea monster. But Aary didn't care too much. He was long used to all the disdain Elior directed at him all the time. When this big guy looked at him sideways and confronted him with a bunch of contemptuous doubt, Aary didn't take offence at all. Instead, he just smiled politely and answered all the questions calmly. He tried to keep it modest and prudent, so many of the answers were "perhaps", "I'll try", "I can't promise", which made the fisherman's son more arrogant and filled with scorn and disbelief for him.

Not long after dinner, the old fisherman started knocking on every door in the village, asking people to gather together in the open space of the village. Everyone came, including the fisherman's son. Under the dim light of an oil lamp hanging on a long fishing pole, Aary stood on a big rock and said: "If you are willing to help me with it, I believe we will be able to kill the beast. But we can't go into the sea, it's the monster's territory. We have to trick it to come to the land. Now I will tell you about my plan..."

* * *

Finally, under the attention and witness of everyone, they recited their vows and became husband and wife. He felt that he had spent his whole life preparing for this moment, to embrace his beloved into his arms and give her a kiss with the deepest affection, with people's applause and the beautiful sunshine in their hair. From this moment until forever on, he would not be who he had been anymore. His world would revolve around the axis of her, his life would blossom for the beauty of her.

25

⟨∾⟩

A Deliberate Plan

Every morning, people in this little village would get out of bed very early to start the day's work. Today, they were up as early as usual, but no one would go out fishing this day. The night before, Aary explained his plan to the villagers and they broke into heated discussions. Some people understood what he was trying to do, but many didn't. Of those who didn't understand his plan, some said that since Aary was so sure about this, they might as well give it a try. If it succeeded of course that's the best they could hope for, but even if it failed, their situation couldn't get any worse. Some, like the old fisherman when he first met Aary, thought that Aary was help sent to them from above, and were willing to obey him no matter what. However, there were also some villagers that thought Aary was a fraud, who was trying to use them for his own purposes, which was what the fisherman's son had been telling everyone. Luckily, in the end, many villagers chose to believe in Aary. And on the morning of Aary's second day in the village, almost half of the villagers started to prepare according to his plan.

All the men gathered by the seaside, including the old fisherman and Aary himself. But his son did not come, as Aary expected. It didn't really matter to him, though. They started digging a giant pit at the location Aary pointed out. Aary borrowed a shovel from the fisherman and was digging the hardest of all. The tide had just receded, so the sand was wet and solid, very easy to dig. That morning by the seaside it was quite chilly, but everyone warmed up when they began to dig. However, as noon drew near, it became much more difficult. The sand was drying up and getting hard to control. The sand on the surface would be dried by the sun and slip to the bottom of the pit. As if that was not hard enough, the sun was getting hotter and fiercer, baking everyone into a sweat. Since there were only men, many of them took their tops off, but sweat would still pour down their backs like rivers. Luckily, when it was getting almost too hot to bear, they could just jump into the waves and cool themselves down with the chilling sea water. They dug the pit deeper and larger, and used some rocks to fortify its sides and bottom, so that sand wouldn't fall back in and refill the hole.

Meanwhile, all the women were sitting together in a big circle in the open space of the village where they had gathered the night before, trying to weave a giant web. It was not like their normal fishing nets. The web was extraordinarily strong, and they used the thickest ropes for the threads. After they were finished with the web, they brought it to the seaside, where the men collected some big rocks around the stony shore, and tied them to the edges of the web. The people in the fishing village had never seen this. Many were questioning how they would even be able to use it with all the heavy rocks tied to it, saying that it would just sink into the ocean. Aary explained to them that the purpose of it was to keep the beast trapped on the ground instead of getting out of the water. When they continued to doubt the plan, Aary decided to just let them be. *They will understand when it happens.* He thought.

Aary was still staying with the fisherman's family. The fisherman's son grew more and more hostile and rude to Aary, even though his father and mother told him again and again to be good to their guest. He kept complaining to other people that Aary was just a fraud and was wasting their time and labor, and succeeded in persuading many of his friends not to help him. Fortunately, his little sister was as nice to Aary as she could be, bringing him water and food when he was digging sand with others, and calling all her girlfriends to join the web weaving.

On the third day, the whole village was excited and anxious. When the sky was still at its darkest without even the slightest hint of dawn, no one could sleep anymore. Some were excited to fight and kill the beast, others were excited to see how these people would fail so that they could laugh at them with an "I told you so". As the first glimmer of light appeared from the night sky, everyone went towards the seaside, some with weapons in their hands, to the huge pit they dug the day before. Some kids ran in the front, laughing, chasing, and fighting with each other.

"It's GONE!!!" The first kid screamed.

Tumult flooded through the crowd as they started running towards it. And it was true, the huge pit had completely disappeared, and all that was there was water, endless water. Then someone recalled, the tide was still high at that hour. The whole pit was under the seawater by several meters. Aary's followers were stunned, someone started scolding him loudly:

"You stupid inlander! You didn't even consider the tide! Now what? The pit's gone. All our hard labor yesterday was for nothing! We should have never believed you!"

The fisherman's son sneered at him contemptuously and said to the others: "I always knew that he was a bluffer, from the very beginning. What do you say, guys? Feed him to the monster instead?"

"Yeah! Feed him to the beast!" Several voices echoed.

Aary sighed and shook his head, feeling a strong bitterness in his heart. He looked at them sadly. Those people, that he was trying so hard to help, were talking about killing him. He felt so heartbroken that he didn't even want to kill the monster anymore, not for these foolish ungrateful people. But he forced himself out of that thought. *It was not for them*, he reminded himself, *it was for Lyna, to get the blood. I was the one that needed to kill the beast, and these people were helping me do this. I should thank them instead. They owe me nothing. I just needed them to understand.*

"It is what it's meant to be. Please trust me. Everything's under control."

"How do we know that you're not just saying that to cover your stupid mistake?" The fisherman's son insisted, "and besides, why should we trust you? We don't even know you."

"How about this?" Aary said calmly, "if you do exactly what I say, and if we fail to kill the sea monster, I will hand myself over to you. You can do whatever you like to me, feed me to the monster, or kill me, torture me, whatever you want. I won't fight back. But you'll have to listen to me for now."

"Deal! We'll do whatever you say, and if you really kill the monster, you can ask for anything. But if you can't, don't blame us for being cruel. You said it yourself."

"It's a deal."

The old fisherman spoke: "Please forgive my bad-mannered son. Of course, we will do what you ask. But are you really confident that we can do this?"

Aary nodded firmly, his hand pressing on the hilt of his dagger.

Having the promise he needed, Aary started acting according to the next part of his plan. He looked up to the sky. A narrow curve of a moon was still hanging by the end of the sky, but was so low that it looked as if it would fall down at any point. The sun hadn't come out yet, but the sky was lighting up. The string of cloud at the edge of the sky was daubed with a streak of light at its bottom. The ocean tide receded inch by inch. Every wave front rushing to the shore went a bit less further than the last.

Aary asked: "Are the fish ready?"

Five young, strong fishermen carried out ten large net bags each filled with hundreds of fish. All the bags were tied onto one thick rope, one after another, like beads on a necklace but with a gap between each. They usually put the offerings all into one giant net bag, but Aary asked them to prepare it this way. He also asked them to put some light-weight woods in the bags, so that they could stay afloat. Aary thanked the men, gesturing for them to put the net bags down for now, and asked again: "And the web?"

A bright ray of light broke through the horizon as the golden sun emerged from the ocean, lighting up the wavy surface of the water, like a piece of shiningly exquisite golden silk. Everyone and everything were ready in their places. It was time.

Aary looked towards the horizon, his eyes dazzled by the rising sun. He rolled up his trouser-legs and stepped into the cold water. Leading the others, he walked towards the location where he remembered the pit was until the water was thigh deep. They could already see the big pit from where they stood. But because they could only see the closest edge, where the color of the sand stopped and gave way to the dark color of deep water, and could not see the whole shape, it looked like the edge of an underwater cliff. And beyond the cliff, the deep trap lurked dark like a bottomless abyss, dangerous and mysterious. He told the men beside him: "Put out the fish."

* * *

She moved into his little cabin. Every day after work, he would come home to her. They were like all the other couples head over heels in love, having endless things to tell each other, saying all the vows in the world to each other. They never quarreled. He was overly indulgent and obedient to her, listening to anything she said, doing anything she wanted. And she loved him back with all her heart. They were immersed in the world of two, and spent the sweetest and happiest time together.

26

A Close Victory

With several huge splashes, the nets full of fish were thrown into the water at the edge of the pit. Then, a few other men carried forward a heavy thick wooden stick, and Aary helped them drive it into the sand around where he stood. He tied one end of the rope onto the stick, and gave the net bag at the end of the rope a push towards the pit. The rope straightened up, and the net bags lined up in a row in the water above the pit, wobbling back and forth with the motion of the waves.

Aary looked back to the villagers and said: "It's ready."

"God of the ocean! Please come for your offerings, and keep us safe!"

Everyone in the fishing village shouted in unison, almost like following an instinct.

Aary felt the hair on the back of his neck standing up. *These people have suffered so long because of this creature,* he thought, *it's about time it ended.*

After only a few seconds, a giant figure emerged from the water's surface afar, breaking the peaceful horizon. A tremor of fear and excitement spread across the crowd as the creature leaped into the air, rolling and turning in a beautiful long arc, and dived back into the sea. Jumping and diving, it came swiftly towards the people on the shore.

They backed up a little, but still stood in the water because Aary didn't want to move too far away and lose control. And they watched.

This was the first time Aary had seen anything like this. In the book he borrowed, there was an illustration of it, but it did not capture even a tenth of the magnificence of the monster in real life. It had very smooth skin like a dolphin, which glittered radiantly of a million colors in the morning light. Every time it leapt out of the water, a crystal-like water arc followed it closely behind, gliding from its body and shattering in the air into tiny water drops, like a piece of silk shaking off a thousand tiny jewelry beads that had been wrapped inside it. Aary was fascinated by its beauty.

In the blink of an eye, it was already very near the shore. People started to flee the water, their shouts of excitement souring into terror. Aary stood where he was, but lowered his body and put his hands on the sword, carefully watching the creature's movements. The sea monster had a pair of clear blue eyes, reflecting the color of the dawning sky. They looked so pure and clean, and left Aary doubting how these eyes could possibly belong to the mad killer they described. But the moment it opened its mouth full of sharp teeth like a trap of spikes, he doubted it no longer.

The monster violently tore apart the first net bag holding the fish. Hundreds of fish rushed out leaping and flipping, swimming with their best effort towards their last hope of life. The sea monster just held open its gigantic mouth, and the foolish fish all senselessly headed into it. Then it shut its mouth. Blood dyed the water red. Aary felt disgusted, and turned away from the scene to look at the clear water beneath him. A frothy white wave rushed towards him, broke around his legs, and closed again behind them, then started to pull back, sweeping away some sand under his feet back to the ocean. Before long, it came up again. After several minutes, Aary's knees that were once soaked in the seawater were exposed in the damp breeze again. He looked behind him, and saw a large area of wet sand emerged from under the seawater into the golden glow of the morning sun. The waves were still washing the flat surface of the shore again and again, rhythmically, but falling quickly behind. The receding tide had accelerated.

The greedy creature in front of everyone was still wolfing fish down happily, moving on to the next bag after finishing the last one, giving the crowd a scornful glance from time to time. It didn't notice the unfriendly new objects in people's hands or that they were staying closer to it than they usually did. It did not have the slightest idea that its life was already under threat. The water surface was dropping fast, but it paid absolutely no attention to that because the depth of the pit was holding its large body in the same place. Aary waited patiently as the monster devoured its feast. The edge of the waves gradually backed to where the pit was, and exposed Aary's feet in the air. When the monster finished eight bags of fish, Aary carefully took a small step forward, and another one, and another one... other people followed quietly and slowly enough so that the sea monster didn't notice anything. Not long after, the water completely backed away from the pit and the pool of water with the sea monster inside was like a pond in the desert. The trapped beast was still eating unconcernedly, and people were finally starting to see Aary's intention. When the sea monster was almost finished with the last bag, enjoying its last bit of the savory meal, Aary called out: "Cast the web!"

Several heavy big rocks were thrown out across the pit. But the pit was too big and the rocks too heavy, so a few didn't make it to the other side, but smashed directly on the monster's body. It gave out a very low and angry roar, and tried to leap towards the people throwing the rocks, but was held down by the net. That's when it finally realized the situation it was in. The sea monster tried to leap and flip and wiggle its way out, but its struggle only made the rocks sink deeper in the sand and the net tangle tighter. Several young fishermen couldn't hold their excitement and ran towards it with their spears and harpoons in hands, but were stopped by Aary. He patiently explained: "Don't rush it. Wait until it's tired. Although it's trapped, it can still take your lives. We probably don't even need to do anything. The sun is already burning bright and the water is evaporating. In no time the sea water left in the pit will turn into highly concentrated saltwater. Let it die of dehydration. It's the safest way."

But the villagers were too excited to sit back and wait for this to happen. They had already waited a hundred years. For so long, this little village had suffered too much from this terrible creature, had shed too many tears and blood, and now was the time they finally could do something about it, the time they'd been waiting for. The sea monster in front of them was at its most vulnerable, trapped in a pit under a heavy and strong web.

A young man called out: "Don't be so spineless! It's trapped! What can it do now?" Another shouted: "Aary is not from here. He doesn't know what it did to us. He caught it for us. We can thank him later. But for all the lives this thing took, how can it deserve an easy death?" Aary tried to calm them down: "No! Wait! Guys, please listen to me..." But his voice was totally drowned out by the villagers excited calls: "Aye!" "Aye!" "Smash the beast!" "Aye!" The first young man ran forward before Aary could stop him, and others followed. It was too late. Aary had no other choice than to follow.

With revenge in mind, the few villagers that first arrived used up all their strength to stick the pointy ends of their weapons in the sea monster. To their surprise, its skin was extremely thick and hard. Most of them didn't even pierce through its skin, even the strongest fisherman only managed a small, insignificant cut. But the pain once more provoked the sea monster. The giant creature screamed and tried to leap again, this time harder than before. In the meantime, it tried to open its mouth and bite the people beside him. The web restrained it from getting to the people, but its sharp teeth caught some strands of the web and when it pulled back, one of them snapped at its teeth. Aary panicked. He never thought that even a web as strong as this could be broken by the sea monster. On the other hand, when the monster saw that it could break the strands with its teeth, it started tearing the web savagely, and the single broken strand soon became an open hole. In no time, the web would be of no threat to the beast, and then the beast would become a threat to the people.

Aary took a quick look around. The few men that struck the first attack were all thrown back onto the sand by the strong thrust of the sea monster's leap. Others that were running towards it were all terrified by what happened in front of them and scattered running off screaming. No one dared to go near the sea monster again, but if no one was going to stop it, it would break free very soon. Even though it was trapped in the pit, it may very well leap out from it back to the ocean. They had already seen how high it could jump from the water. With no other option, Aary sighed with resignation. He grabbed a fishing spear from a man running past him away from the monster. And he dashed forward.

He ran to the sea monster, and didn't stop by its side, but leapt directly onto its body. The web covering the monster made it very easy to clutch and climb. Aary mounted the top of the sea monster, clung tightly onto the web with one hand, and used the other one to thrust the spear into the monster's gill on one side. The gill was much softer than the other parts of its body, and the spearhead sunk into the flesh. The pain made the monster give a strong and sudden shake. The jerk was too strong for Aary to hold on to the web or the spear, so he was flung into the air and landed in the water. The water slowed down his speed of falling, but he still crashed hard against the sand. Sea water poured into his eyes, nose and mouth, and almost drowned him. Coughing badly, he struggled to climb up and spit out the water in his mouth. When the villagers saw that the sea monster was not completely impenetrable after all, they also regained some confidence and over-came their fears. Many people came forward and surrounded the sea monster. Aary wanted to go back, but dizziness made him unable to walk, every time he tried to stand up, he would end up falling back into the water again. So, he gave up and shouted to the others: "Its eyes and gills are the most vulnerable places. Focus your attack!"

One man shoved another spear right next to the spear Aary left in the monster, another tried the other side, the third one went for its eye... the sea monster dodged several of the attacks by turning labori-ously, but with people attacking from all sides, and the web still holding it down to the pit, its strength was running out bit by bit. Finally, the sea monster did not have the upper hand anymore, its counterattacks slowed down and became less efficient. At last, the trapped beast managed a final round of helpless struggle, and stopped moving. The open wounds on the gills were bleeding deep blue blood.

The people around it looked at it quietly for a few seconds. Everyone was holding their breath, no one made a sound. The blood-soaked gills opened and closed weakly a few times, then closed forever. When they were finally convinced that this murderous monster was totally dead now, the crowd broke into the happiest cheer they had had in a hundred years. Everyone shouted and jumped, crying and laughing at the same time, hugging each other. Someone started to strike the dead body with the weapon in hand, and others followed. They released their anger and hatred that had been suppressed for a hundred years onto this mountain of a body that had lost all ability to fight back.

The old fisherman was the only one that remembered Aary was still struggling in the water. He walked towards him and hugged the boy that helped the little village out of this life-long disaster. Aary was still a little dizzy, so the old fisherman carried him back to the shore. Aary was surprised to see how strong the old man was. Now everyone surrounded him, they took turns to thank him and hug him. But he just felt really relieved and that he needed some rest to get over this dizziness.

He smiled faintly and politely, and tried to wobble his way through the crowd to the monster's body. The monster's body was bleeding everywhere. He opened the tiny flask and collected a few drops of the blue blood. Having done what he came for, he sat down wearily and looked at the sea monster's mutilated body. He didn't know why, but he felt sorry for the monster. *It's bad. It's evil. It killed many people. You did a good thing. You should be happy, and celebrate.* He told himself. But somehow, he just couldn't convince himself and chase away the guilt in his mind. *Did the sea monster really deserve this? Maybe it wasn't really bad. Maybe it had its own reasons. Maybe it had feelings too, like Blackwind.* But there was no way to know that now. Aary shut his eyes to avoid looking at it, but he couldn't get the scene out of his mind. The happiness of victory was soured by this absurd guilt. He wondered why he didn't feel this way when he fought the soldiers that came to Rocky Vill. Maybe because back then, he didn't really understand pain or death. It seemed to him that these years of suffering made him more empathetic to other creatures. He could relate to another's pain more, and it was a very uncomfortable feeling.

"Look!" Someone shouted.

Unwillingly, Aary opened up his eyes again, and what he saw made him feel even worse. A few people were still poking their weapons at the sea monster's body even after it was long dead, and the persisting attacks opened a hole in its belly. Aary looked at where a man was pointing at, and saw that, in all the blue blood and flesh, there were some translucent balls falling out from the open wound. Each one was the size of a fist, with a solid blue core inside.

Eggs? Aary thought, *the sea monster was pregnant? That explained why it suddenly needed more food in recent months. It was getting nutrition for its eggs.*

The villagers started crashing the eggs with their weapons, destroying every single one of them in a mixture of frenzy and pleasure. Aary wanted to stop them, but he felt so tired and didn't have any strength to do anything. Anyway, he knew that even if he did say something, no one would listen, and they might even start targeting him again. The villagers suffered too much from this creature to have mercy for its unborn babies, and they had no reason to leave them to pose future risks as well. But he just couldn't get over the thought that he had murdered so many innocent lives. He felt dizzy and sick again. All he wanted to do was to sleep, and the world blackened out in front of him.

When he woke up, he found himself in the old fisherman's home. The fisherman's wife was looking after him and their daughter was sitting by his bed anxiously. When they saw that he'd awakened, they all rushed towards him to ask him how he was feeling. The girl was obviously crying before he woke up, as her eyes were still red and wet. But she was really happy to see him awake. Hearing the sound in this room, the fisherman and his son came in. The big boy blushed when he saw Aary. He lowered his head and said: "I'm really sorry. I've been a jackass and mean to you. I shouldn't have distrusted you. I apologize for my arrogance. But your plan did work, and the monster is dead now, thanks to you. I'm a man of my words. Whatever you want, I will do my best to fulfill my promise." Aary smiled weakly. He struggled to sit up in the bed, and made space for the fisherman's son to sit down. Even now he still felt a bit dizzy. He looked at this embarrassed big guy, and lifted up the little flask: "I already got what I need, thanks to you and all the villagers' help. I never would have done it on my own."

The old fisherman came forward and said to Aary solemnly: "Thank you, son. Our village owes you big time, aye. You're a good lad, and a clever boy." Then he turned to look at his daughter, who blushed at his sight: "Our youngest daughter is the prettiest, smartest and kindest of all the kids, and she likes you very much. If you like her also, we would like you both to marry. You said that you don't have a family, but we can become your family and take care of you."

The smile on Aary's face was frozen from the shock. He stared at the old fisherman for a long time before he could believe what he just heard. Everyone was looking at him expectantly. The old fisherman, his wife, their son. And the girl. He somehow felt the feelings between the girl and himself, but he thought it was just his own pathetic imagination. Indeed, he liked her very much. The girl was very beautiful, and kind, and good to him as well. She was everything he had wished for in a wife when he was young. It would be like a dream come true. But right now, there was only one name in his mind.

He always thought of Lyna as a little sister, so young but brave. He knew she was still a child. But when this girl, beautiful, mature, of the same age as him, was standing in front of him, he just could not get Lyna's brave little smile out of his mind.

"I am really sorry." He turned to the girl, feeling a strong sense of guilt in his heart, "I like you very much. You will be a great wife to some very lucky man. But there is already another in my heart."

* * *

Gradually, their lives settled into a peaceful routine. He still loved her deeply, and she him, the only difference was that the vows and pledges at the beginning were replaced by small, ordinary contentments in their lives together. But to him, this kind of happiness felt from the company of each other seemed more intoxicating. He loved cooking meals with her, cleaning the house with her, and reading books with her while slouching on the couch together shoulder to shoulder. He wanted his whole life to be like this, with her, forever. Nothing needed to change. Until sudden, unexpected news disrupted their lives.

27

The Lava Demon

Aary wrote a letter to the fisherman's daughter and visited her in her room before he left on his next quest. He wanted to tell her in person how lovely she was and how much he liked her, hoping these words would somehow make his choice less hurtful, or himself feel less guilty. But it probably didn't work, since the poor girl was crying the whole time. Thus, his actions actually made him feel more guilty.

He needed to get his head off this matter. So, after saying goodbye to the old fisherman and his family, Aary went directly after the last of his three targets – the lava demon. As soon as he thought that he walked far enough from the village so that no one would see him, he pulled out the whistle and called Blackwind to take him to the lava demon's lair.

Lava demon, even the name of the creature sounded really scary. It appeared to be the most dangerous and mysterious of the three beasts too. In *The Evil Spirits* there was very little information about them. It only described where and how to find them, how deadly they were, but mentioned nothing about their weaknesses, like the bellies of bat-wing dragons, or the gills of sea monsters. There were drawings and illustrations for the other two, but for lava demons, there was not even a single word telling what they look like. So perhaps no one had ever seen one, let alone defeat one. Aary knew that he had been lucky with the last two, and this one would probably be a real challenge.

Blackwind brought him to the mouth of a cave by the foot of the mountain. It looked pitch dark inside, not at all like the place for an animal with "lava" in the name. Aary made a crude torch from a branch, some dried leaves and a shirt sleeve, and lit it up with sparks made from his sword striking a flint, before entering the endless darkness.

This time when Blackwind insisted on staying with him, Aary didn't force him to go. After all, compared to walking into this unknown dark cave alone, having a strong, giant dragon as a companion was something to be thankful for. The cave wasn't very wide or very high. Fortunately, when Blackwind crawled down on the cave floor and walked on all fours, or more precisely, on the strong thumbs of his wings which he used as front paws and those sturdy short legs, he was not much taller than two men's height, and could just fit in the cave without having to bump the crest of his head on the cave ceiling.

He didn't know how long they had been walking for, because it was impossible to tell what time of day it was in the cave. But he was pretty sure it had been a long time, at least a couple of hours. There was no sunlight, no blue sky, only infinite darkness, coldness, and dampness. If not for a huge friend walking beside him giving him courage, Aary felt that he might even want to give up and head back.

The pathway they walked on remained approximately the same width, but constantly winding and twisting, turning left and right, up and down. He even started to wonder if they had entered a maze, if they had been circling around the same tunnels all the time, and if there really was the mysterious monster somewhere in there.

They met several forks at which they needed to choose between paths, and Aary remembered what the book said: "Always go down instead of up. All the way down, to the burning hell deep beneath the earth, where even rocks melt from the heat. That's where you'll find lava demons, the rulers of the underground world."

He wondered if it was just a metaphor or if rocks could really melt. If that was true, how would a human like him survive? But he didn't really need to worry about that at that moment. For all he knew, they might not even find it at all. The cave became colder and damper as they went deeper, and there was no sign of the promised heat whatsoever. He started to worry, what if they were trapped in there? What if he would never see the sun again? As the cave tunnel extended endlessly in front of him, he thought of what would happen to Lyna if he would die in this cave. Poor girl, she would stay in his treehouse until realizing that he would never come back. She would be on her own again, with no way to get the blood she needed...

He was thinking about Lyna when he tripped on something beneath his feet. He lowered the torch and saw a bump on the stone ground, stretching from the wall on one side to the other. It seemed really abrupt and bizarre, as up till now the ground had always been pretty smooth, moistened by the dripping cave water. But it was when he raised the torch back up that he realized that something really was different.

The cave tunnel that had been about the same size all the way since they entered, widened up from where the bump was. The ceiling was higher and the walls further away, and as they kept on walking, he started to realize that the air had become warmer, and not as damp. A few steps further, he even felt a gush of hot air coming at him. Aary became really excited, but also a bit nervous. Luckily, with Blackwind by his side, he felt much more comforted. He hugged the dragon's neck, and received a gentle rub on the shoulder from the big guy. He took off his winter overcoat because it had become too hot to wear, and threw it on the ground. But as they kept on walking, Aary started to wonder, it was already so hot, his forehead was even sweating, but the tunnel still looked as dark as it had been the whole way. Why couldn't they see any light? Just where was this burning underground world?

Suddenly, he heard a large cracking sound beneath them. At the same time, some parts of the ground under Blackwind's wings, cracked and caved in. Blackwind managed to withdraw his wings and stand up on his hind legs before the piece of ground that his thumbs were pressing on sank and fell. Aary was startled. He pulled on Blackwind's wing to make him back up further, and stared in horror at where the stone collapsed. A hole had appeared, but it was not dark down the hole. Some sort of bright orange light was shining from inside.

Blackwind reached its head out curiously, wanting to check out what was shining beneath the hole, but Aary stopped him in fear that the hole might enlarge with more stone sinking around it. But after a while, when he saw that further changes in the hole didn't happen, he used an arm to hold back Blackwind, and carefully took a few steps forward, one at a time.

When he finally reached the edge of the hole, he stretched out his neck to look down through the opening. He couldn't hide his excitement at what he saw. Two hundred feet beneath the ground they were standing on, was a glowing and bubbling hot molten lava stream.

The cave was so wide at this point, that Blackwind could even spread his wings and flap them up and down. Therefore, to further open the hole, Blackwind kept balance with his wings and used his feet to stomp the ground around it, while Aary stayed a safe distance away. Following a few small falling rocks, some large pieces of ground sank and fell into the lava.

The radiance illuminated from the burning red lava lit up the whole space that had been too dark to see before. Aary put the torch down against a wall because he didn't need it anymore, and looked around.

It was a very grand, spacious cave, very different from the narrow tunnels that they had been walking through. He noticed that the stone walls around him had a kind of weird pattern. It looked as if there was a layer of sticky thick liquid on the walls, with smooth lumps that looked like liquid drops dripping down along the wall. But when he reached out his hand to touch it, it was nothing more than hard ordinary rocks.

In fact, everywhere he saw, everywhere were solid rocks, apart from the lava below. Even though the book only had a very vague introduction without giving any details about lava demons themselves, he didn't need a book to tell him that they must be hiding inside the bubbling lava, that was probably why it was called "lava demon" in the first place. He started to worry, how could they get the lava demon out from that molting lava? Because if it didn't come out by itself, it would be impossible for them to reach it without being melted.

He stared at the glowing lava beneath them and pondered, trails of sweat rolling down his back. The lava looked like boiling water, bubbles rolling up from the bottom and bursting at the surface. *The lava was like water, but hotter. Getting something out of it would be just like fishing from the sea. It couldn't be that hard. But we will need a very large fishing pole or fishing net, one that could endure the heat. Maybe we should get out of here for now, make the tools that we can use and come back tomorrow with those tools...*

Suddenly, he noticed a bulge rising up from the flat liquid surface. A sudden excitement rose from his heart. *It's coming out by itself! We don't need to waste another day!*

However, when the bulge became larger and larger, sucking and absorbing the pool of lava, until all the liquid was condensed into a huge moving shape, he knew he was wrong. The monster was not hiding in the lava, the whole mass of molten lava itself that he just saw was the lava demon he was looking for!

This elastic, shifting form of lava started climbing up the stone wall, dripping and burning with flames. Where it touched, the stone was melted into glowing red lava and slowly dripped down along the wall, but soon froze into stone again when the heat moved away. Now Aary knew where all the bizarre patterns on the stone walls came from. The creature slowly moved towards where Aary and Blackwind stood, like a giant piece of melting cake. Aary felt hotter and hotter, and sweat was running down his body like a waterfall.

But when the monster came even closer, all the sweat was gone. The air became so hot that Aary felt as if all the water inside him had evaporated and that his whole body was burning, on fire. He also felt extremely thirsty, his throat aching like hell. He thought he might not last long in this environment, so he needed to fight, and fast.

He reached for the dagger on his belt. But the grip of the dagger was also hot like a burning charcoal in his palm. He drew his hand back quickly the moment it reached the dagger, and put his burning finger into his mouth to cool down.

With no other option, he posed to fight with his bare hands. Blackwind also landed on all fours again, crouching down close to the floor and lowering its watchful head with hostility, like a leopard getting ready to jump onto its prey.

Suddenly, totally different from what Aary expected, the giant fireball talked. A hole opened up in the center of the flames, and closed and opened again like a human mouth. Its voice shook the whole cave with the longest echo Aary had ever heard, making it almost hard to understand:

"Who is this that's so audacious? How dare you come and intrude in my territory and disturb my rest! Do you know who I am? I am the demon of lava, the king of the underworld, the mightiest of the whole world! And who are you? You pathetic, weak creatures!!"

Creatures...-eatures...-tures...s... The echo answered.

Blackwind was deeply offended by this speech, and bared its teeth, ready to attack, but Aary calmed it down with a hand on its head. Aary himself was surprised, but happy, to hear the monster talk, and more than happy to have confirmation that they had indeed found what they were looking for.

Being able to talk meant being able to reason with, and this lava demon obviously had a large ego to be fed. So, Aary relaxed his fists, and replied respectfully while enduring great pain in his cracked, dry throat:

"We are terribly sorry to have disturbed you. We have heard of your mightiness for a long time, but have never had the honor to meet you in person. We thought that we couldn't continue living if we didn't see you in real life. So, we came all this way to admire how magnificent you are, and now, upon seeing you, I know it was definitely worth it. You are more fierce and powerful than any other thing we could imagine!" *-gine...* The echo was much weaker, almost unnoticeable.

"Of course I am! How could you inferior creatures imagine the mightiness of me? Now that you have seen me, you have already done more than your pathetic lives are worth. So even if I take your lives, you should still feel grateful!"

Grateful...-ateful...-ful...-ul...

It moved forward one step further, and Blackwind became more agitated, arching its back into a bow, like an angry cat pissed off by a barking dog. Aary tried harder to comfort it, while making more effort to talk to the demon in the unbearable heat: "I would be happy for you to take my life. But I want to go back and tell everyone in the world how mighty you are. Because they don't know, and they should know."

"Hmm..." The lava demon hesitated. Aary felt that his scheme was working. Then it said: "That would be a good use of your pathetic life. Ok, I will spare your life, so that you can tell the world about me and let them worship me. You may go now."

Go now... -o now...now...-ow...

Since they still hadn't gotten what they came for, Aary continued: "But they might not believe that I saw you. How could I prove it to them that I did see you in person?" He pretended to be thinking for a moment, then asked: "Could I get a few drops of your blood so that I can show it to them? If you could just be so generous to spare me only a few drops of blood?"

The lava demon answered: "That is no problem. My blood is the lava that's running down the walls of the cave right now. If you want it, come and get it."

Get it...-et it...it...t... It moved closer to Aary and Blackwind.

Aary felt like he was going to faint, but he had to keep going. He was so close to success. So close. But at that very moment, he lost control of Blackwind. The dragon roared and stepped forward, trying to protect Aary from the burning flames. The lava demon stopped and backed up a little. It seemed to have noticed Blackwind for the first time:

"It seems that your friend here does not want the same thing as you do. It seems that it is more honest than you are. If you have come here to admire me, why is your friend so hostile? Why do you have a sword? Don't think I haven't noticed. Nothing escapes my acute observation.

Are you lying to me, you low, vicious creature? How dare you lie to me? Who do you think you are that you can fool me?!"

Fool me...-ool me...me...e... Even the echo sounded angry.

Aary tried his best to stay clear-minded and mend this: "No I'm not lying. Please believe me. He is just afraid of you, that's all. He's here to accompany me, but I'm the one that admires you. The sword was just to protect myself on the way..."

But it was too late. The lava demon didn't trust him anymore: "This is too much! Admirer or enemy, the safest way is to kill both of you. I have too many admirers, all the creatures in the world are my admirers, killing one or two means nothing to me."

Nothing to me...-thing to me...-to me...me...

When speaking, the monster grew bigger and the flames burnt brighter. Aary knew that his plan had failed. Now all he wanted was to stay alive and get out of there. He backed up a few steps, getting ready to run away, but a sudden, scorching pain hit him in the back. He turned around to see that the back of his shirt was on fire. He hastened to take off the shirt and throw it to the ground, but already felt that parts of his back and arms were burnt. In this extremely hot environment, the burning wounds were way more painful than his normal whip wounds.

What set his shirt on fire was the bump they had just crossed. He should have realized that the bump looked like some kind of a threshold and have been vigilant when crossing it, but it was too late now. The stone threshold had turned into red-hot liquid, and "grew" taller by itself. The melting, hot liquid not only lit the fabric of his shirt, but it was also sealing up the whole tunnel right now like a closing door, blocking their only way out.

And in no time, just in front of his eyes, the tunnel was sealed, then the molten lava concreted into solid stone again. Whether red hot lava or solid stone, it was a dead end for sure. Looking at the sealed tunnel behind them, and the still growing monster in front of them, Aary thought desperately and miserably: *this is the end.*

* * *

Summer came and went. Autumn silently took over the world. It was the harvest season again, and the people in the village had already started their annual busy work for this time of the year. One morning, she came to him, with a mixture of emotions on her beautiful face. She opened her mouth to say something, but shut it again without saying a word. She lowered her head. The way she bit her lips like this made him worried and anxious. He cupped her cheeks gently with his hands, gazed tenderly into her black eyes, and calmed her with his soft words. She took a deep breath, placed a hand on her lower stomach, and said quietly: "I'm with baby."

28

Brave Blackwind

"Prepare to die!" *To die... die...-ie...* The lava demon shouted at them.

The monster seemed to be bloated with fire, and got bigger and bigger. Now the flames were only a dozen steps away from Aary. He thought that it probably didn't even need to use any physical attacks, because he would definitely die and melt from the heat long before the flames actually reached him. He didn't know how long he was going to stay alive in this hostile environment. The inside of his mouth felt chapped like the barren earth of a rainless summer under the mid-noon sun, and all the water inside his body was drying out. Suddenly, the big black dragon beside him gave a powerful thrust against the ground with his strong back feet, and lifted into the air.

Aary was horrified. He wanted to shout to Blackwind, but no sound came out from his chapped throat. He watched as Blackwind flew directly towards the lump of heat and light without any hint of slowing down.

"No!!" His mouth formed the shape, but only made a very faint coarse sound. It was impossible to be heard anyway. The sound of Blackwind snarling and the lava demon bellowing drowned out any sound he could possibly make.

When he saw his beloved dragon throwing itself into a burning fire, his heart broke into a thousand pieces. Like his name, Blackwind dashed into the flames of the lava demon like a gust of black colored wind, and a bolt of blinding bright light exploded from where they clashed, so powerful that it forced Aary to close his eyes. Almost simultaneously, a strong force thrust him backwards as if he were a piece of paper. He hit hard onto the stone wall behind him, then fell onto the ground on his knees.

Then he just kneeled there, held his hands over his head, and started to cry. Aary's tears were almost dried up by the heat, so even though he was already crying his heart out, the tears only stayed in his eyes and refused to drop. That made him sadder. He wasn't crying because of the unbearably violent pain all over his body, but because of the pain and guilt in his heart, of losing his friend. Blackwind was so good to him, but he let it die protecting him. The happy memories with Blackwind over these past few days, the despair and helplessness when he saw hit for the first time, and its tender and kind eyes when looking at him, all flashed through his mind. He couldn't believe that he almost left it to die when that hunter shot an arrow in it. He could not forgive himself. He should have treated it like family, should have been really good to it, as Blackwind was to him.

But now he knew that everything was too late. He saw with his own eyes that Blackwind rushed into the sea of flames. He kept on blaming himself, how could he be stupid enough to believe that he could conquer the lava demon? No man had ever beaten one, who was he to think that he could do it? He never felt so alone, or so helpless. Actually, he even felt grateful for the pain in his body now. He hoped that the actual physical pain may more or less atone for his crime, he hoped that the pain would get fiercer, that he might even die of agony, because it seemed that only this way could his mistake be fairly punished. He didn't dare stand up or look up. He just kneeled like this, his whole body curled into a ball, like a criminal kneeling in the corner of a dark, cold prison cell. He had been in prison before, though he hadn't committed any crime. This time, however, he had committed the crime.

Suddenly, a cheerful cry pierced Aary's eardrum. *Blackwind?* He flung his head up and opened his eyes still wet with tears. He couldn't believe what he saw: the monster was gone. Some molten rock on the stone cave walls was still glowing red, and Blackwind was flying towards him, its large black wings flapping up and down in the hollow cave, with something in its mouth. He was so thrilled that he wanted to jump up onto the big black dragon, but he realized that even getting up from the ground was very difficult and demanded all his strength.

Blackwind landed in front of him, and spit out the thing in its mouth to rub its head against Aary. Aary threw his arms around the dragon's thick neck, and hugged the big fellow for a very long time. He pressed his burning hot skin onto Blackwind's cold dragon skin, and whispered from his cracked lips: "I love you, Blackwind."

He didn't move until Blackwind withdrew its head, and gestured to him to look at the thing on the ground. That was when Aary paid close attention to it for the first time. It was something that looked like a giant dead toad, only without any legs. It looked seriously disgusting, slick and sticky, with large bumps covering the skin just like normal toads. Some of the bumps were even broken. Some sort of sticky yellow liquid ran from the wounds. Aary now understood, that the huge lava demon they had seen was not all lava and flames, but this sorry looking thing in the center. But how did Blackwind pass through all the flames to reach this thing in the center? Why wasn't it burnt by the heat? And where did all the lava and fire go?

Right at that moment, Blackwind gave out a sneeze, and answered all his questions.

Fire came out of its nose and mouth!

Aary looked at Blackwind in astonishment, his eyes and chin almost popping out. Blackwind seemed to be surprised as well. There was still smoke escaping from its nostrils, and when it tried to stare at its own smoking nose with disbelief, its eyes crossed in the middle like a fool. It looked so silly that Aary had to laugh.

Blackwind tried again to blow out some air, and another tongue of fire licked the ceiling of the cave tunnel. Then it tried again, and again, and again. When the dragon finally understood its new superpower, it emitted a call in ecstasy that almost deafened Aary. Blackwind was so happy about its new skill that he couldn't wait to show off again and again. Although extremely tired and in pain, Aary still felt the same happiness as his dragon friend, the first ever fire breathing dragon!

Their celebration was interrupted by a sudden round of coughing from Aary. It was so fierce that he fell to the ground again coughing, and had to support himself with his hands. Blackwind looked very shocked and worried when Aary coughed out some blood on the floor. The lack of water and burning wounds were really getting to him, and he desperately need some water right now. He leaned forward and collected the last drops of yellow blood from the last target of his quest.

He looked at the shirt on the ground that was already burnt into a pile of blackened dust, and was really glad that he had taken off the coat earlier. The wounds on his skin were still burning with pain, so he didn't dare to put it on. Blackwind nudged his head against the solid stone wall that sealed the tunnel they came from, and the wall broke down easily. Aary gently stroked Blackwind, and whispered: "Let's go get some water." Blackwind obligingly lowered its neck to let Aary on. Aary struggled to climb on, and laid his bare chest on Blackwind's smooth black skin. The dragon steadily carried him out of the lava demon's deep cave.

* * *

He widened his eyes and looked at her in disbelief. She nodded, with an incomprehensible expression on her face. It's hard to say it if was happiness or sadness, or perhaps confusion was the word. She was waiting for his reaction with a little bit of worry, but when he understood what he heard, his eyes lit up with excitement, like a child getting a toy he had long been wishing for. He cupped her head and kissed her affectionately. A short while later, he was seen running around the village like a madman, calling to anyone he came across: "I'm going to be a father!"

29

Two is Company

Winter's footsteps had been heard by people for a long time, but now it had finally come officially. The dry, cold wind started to penetrate straight into people's bones like a sharp pointy knife, and the forest was much lonelier. All the animals, chattering birds, cheerful squirrels, bouncy hares, that once filled the woods with joy and songs were nowhere to be seen. Only bare, darkened tree trunks and branches remained standing bravely in the freezing wind. But even the trees couldn't oppose the power of nature, and couldn't help constantly shaking in the biting cold. The strong wind was like an invisible saw, making a huge grinding sound when it moved across the black, withered branches. At times, one or two would be torn from the tree and fall from midair then thump onto the earth, like a sword that was covered with rust and no longer shining, thus no longer treasured by its owner. In this snowless winter, tree barks were cracking, and the weeds were dry and yellow. Only a crow or two would sometimes appear and croak hysterically from their hoarse throats, while flying to a branch to get some rest. But they were not alone. Among the withered trees and the ghastly crows was Aary's little tree house.

The door opened with a squeak, and Aary leaned on the frame with tiredness and unconcealed excitement on his face. He hid the little flask with the blood behind his back, and smiled to Lyna. Lyna was reading the books Aary had in his treehouse for the third time. When she lifted her head and saw Aary, she was so happy that she ran to give him a big hug. But she noticed Aary trembling slightly and a gasp of pain escaped when she wrapped her arms around him. "Sorry," she drew her arms back gently, and asked in worry, "did Elior hit you again?"

Aary shook his head with a crooked grin, and pulled out the little flask from behind.

"Look what I've got! The blood of the batwing dragon, sea monster and lava demon!"

He opened the lid and gave it a little shake. The blood mingled together, but it could still be seen clearly as red, blue and yellow color, not blended into black. It looked like a rainbow but with only three colors, surprisingly pretty. Aary looked back to Lyna with the proudest smile anyone could see on a boy.

Lyna froze.

Aary thought she would be very happy and smile when she heard the news, but right at that moment her eyes were filled with tears of blame and sadness.

He freaked out. The smug, bragging smile on his face turned into puzzle and worry. He didn't know what he had done wrong. "What...what's wrong?" He asked anxiously.

Lyna hugged him again, tears running down her face: "Why didn't you tell me? You promised that you wouldn't go on your own. Do you know how dangerous this task was? You could have gotten yourself killed! And how do you think I would be able to live with myself if you died for me? Did it ever cross your mind?"

"I... knew it was dangerous, so I didn't want you to get hurt." Aary tried to explain, a bead of sweat ran down from his forehead.

"You don't understand. You thought if you went alone, you'd be the only one that might get hurt? But do you know that it hurts me more when I see you wounded? You always treat me like a little child, always wanting to look after me and protect me. But I'm not a child anymore. I can take care of myself, I can even look after and protect you! Maybe if I went with you to protect you, you wouldn't have even gotten hurt!"

Lyna couldn't continue berating Aary because the crying got in the way. Aary was truly shocked by her words. He felt something in his heart that had always been hard as a rock suddenly turning soft as silk. Growing up as an orphan, he had got used to doing everything alone and bearing all the pain on his own. And since he was captured by Elior, he got even more used to suffering, struggling, and surviving all by himself. Licking his own wounds like a poor stray dog was like a daily routine for the boy. No one really cared for him, no one would be happy for his happiness, or be sad for his sadness, so he learnt to keep it all to himself. He never felt the love of anyone else, and never learnt to love himself. All he ever knew was how to face and endure whatever came his way, with teeth clenched and tears swallowed. He learnt to never show his pain or weaknesses, because it would only cause him more harm. He gradually developed a personality of extraordinary fortitude and perseverance, but love was what was missing in his life, until now.

"I'm sorry, Lyna." He lowered his head like a little boy that was being scolded for some naughty mistake, and said, "I didn't think... I didn't know. I thought you really wanted the cure for your mother."

"I do. And in fact, that was all I had in mind when I first came here," Lyna's voice became very soft, "but now that I know you, I care for you too. I care for you like I care for my mom. You are also very important to me. I cannot lose either one of you. If you died for this, I would be as sad as if I never found the cure for my mom."

"But... why? You have only known me for a few weeks."

"Why did you risk your life, risk everything, to help me? **You** have only known **me** for a few weeks." Lyna answered his question with another question.

"I..." Aary didn't know how to answer. His face turned as red as a ripe tomato, and he didn't dare look up into Lyna's eyes. He didn't even know why. Why?

Suddenly, Lyna leaned forward on the tips of her toes and gently delivered a kiss to Aary's cold, chapped lips.

Aary was startled by this sudden kiss. He didn't know what to think or how to react. His lips felt weird after touching Lyna's lips. He didn't know if they were his anymore. His mind totally blanked out. But his heart was hammering in his chest like a deafening drum. He feared that it might even pop out sometime soon.

He sneaked a peak to see if Lyna had heard his beating heart and felt his embarrassment, and saw her blue eyes looking at him. Somehow, at this moment, he didn't care if he looked embarrassed. Nothing else in the world mattered. He kissed her back and wrapped his arms around her skinny shoulders.

Later, Lyna carefully put the tiny flask with the blood that Aary risked his life to collect into a small wooden box. There were also the three red leaves she picked up before.

She offered to help Aary treat his wounds. At first, Aary felt a bit ashamed and wanted to do it on his own, but he remembered what Lyna said earlier and accepted. He had given all the medicine he made to Blackwind earlier, but Lyna made some more while he was away. She found the handwritten recipe that Aary developed on a paper note between the pages of *The Art and History of Alchemy in Healing*, and collected the herbs needed in the forest. She even added more ingredients using her past knowledge from Garden Valley.

Aary took off his coat a bit awkwardly. He only had a coat on directly, because the shirt he had worn had been burnt to ashes. When he came out of the cave with Blackwind, it was freezing outside, so he had no choice but to put on the coat. But now, parts of the coat were sticking to his wounds, and taking it off was even more difficult than putting it on. He couldn't imagine how painful the cleaning of the wounds and the application of the medicine would be.

He lay his belly on the wooden floor and closed his eyes in fear when Lyna kneeled beside him with the medicine. But he soon found out in amazement that it didn't hurt at all. Though young, Lyna's hands were gentle and careful like an experienced healer, and it felt so comforting when the cool medicine she made covered his burning wounds. It felt so much better than when he awkwardly treated his wounds by himself.

As he lay there, facing the rough wooden floor, tears of happiness swelled up in his eyes. He couldn't explain the feeling he was having right now, but he knew for sure that he had never felt this way before.

* * *

All the elders in the village, including Maire's father, thought they were too young and inexperienced to raise and parent a child, saying that they were still children themselves. People advised them to ask her parents to raise the child on their behalf, or even give the child away to some wealthy family that couldn't have kids, saying that it would be good for the child, and for them too. But when Jerre heard this, he got really angry. He swore to them that he would keep and bring up this child no matter the cost, and that he would raise this child into the finest and the most outstanding person they would ever see.

30

Surprise

When Elior came back from his royal trip, Aary knew there would definitely be some punishment waiting for him for escaping the journey. He was right. The moment Elior set his pair of light-colored eyes on Aary, he made the command. Aary had already prepared his mind for this, so he didn't really care. However, to his surprise, when Elior saw his wounds, the cruel cold-hearted king hesitated, for the first time that Aary had seen. Elior asked him what he did and how he got burnt. He lied that he accidently fell asleep when making a campfire to cook. Elior sneered at him contemptuously, then only ordered him to clean the stable for a few days, because his "stupidity had punished him enough, and thus no whipping was needed this time". Aary felt like he had received an unexpected award. "Well, I guess even Elior can be sympathetic." Later, he told Lyna happily.

Lyna was still staying in Aary's little treehouse, waiting for the first snowfall. She was a sensitive and observant girl. Every time that Aary experienced some upsetting things or received punishment in the castle, and came back and tried to conceal his emotions, acting like nothing happened, Lyna always saw through him at first glance. Young as she was, she knew much more about love. She grew up with a mother that loved her deeply, that taught her to understand and care about people's emotions. She knew how to love someone, and what it was like to be loved by someone. But Aary knew none of that. All he knew was that he liked this girl very much, that he wanted to do anything for her, but he had no idea what he should do or even how to be with her. But with Lyna's gentle encouragement, Aary's heart gradually opened. Little by little, he learned to initiate a chat by sharing his fun or not-so-fun experiences from the day, and he told her many of his happy memories from childhood. The more they learned about each other, the more they enjoyed each other's company. Aary knew Lyna's favorite books, and Lyna learnt Aary's favorite tunes.

Lyna didn't want to kill animals for food, but she was very good at picking berries and herbs. So, she would often spend the day collecting baskets of them, and make some good tasting soup for Aary when he got back from the castle. Sometimes she would go to the nearby village to trade some herbs for other food, potatoes, tomatoes, or freshly baked bread. Every day when Aary came back in the afternoon, he would be welcomed by Lyna's proud smile and a delicious meal.

But of course, he didn't need the food to give him motivation to come home. Every day, when he scrubbed the floor of Elior's room or shined Elior's glamorous white armor, or even when he was being beaten bloody, the mere thought of going back to his treehouse to be with Lyna, chatting with her and laughing with her, made everything he did worthy and rewarding. Because he knew that by the end of the day, when he rushed back to his treehouse in the middle of the woods, he would see Lyna's cheerful little smile, he knew that she would laugh when he told her that he secretly spat in Elior's soup, or curse when she learnt that Elior made him clean the privy again. Even when he was being beaten, it was not so bad because he would be expecting Lyna's gentle treatment and words of comfort. Every day no matter how tired or depressed he was at the castle, when he was with Lyna in his little safe space, his day was saved.

Sometimes Rudi would drop by and say hi, and the three of them would play games in the forest. Aary's favorite one was hide and seek, because no one ever found him when he hid on top of a tree. As winter deepened, days were getting shorter and the sun was setting earlier. So usually by the time Elior let him go in the afternoon, it was already quite dark, and that made the games more exciting. When Aary was the one to seek, he often sneaked up on Rudi from behind, and suddenly jumped out to scare him. Then they would all laugh so hard until everyone's belly hurt. It felt like childhood again, no kings or whips, no stress or worry, just laughter and fun. These were the moments when he could temporarily forget that he was captured and enslaved by the cruelest monarch, and he could be beaten to death by him any time soon. These were the times when he was just a boy again, not some prisoner of war, or some king's servant, just a boy with no duty or responsibility. However, no matter how much fun they had, the happy times always passed quickly and then it would be time for Aary to get back to the castle again and sleep in the cold, dark dungeon alone.

One day, after his day of work in the castle, Aary returned to his little treehouse as usual, excited to tell Lyna about a squirrel that ran into the castle kitchen earlier that day that caused chaos. But before he entered, he noticed that there wasn't candlelight leaking out from under the door. His heart tightened, and the smile vanished from his face, as an uneasy sense of foreboding arose. He rushed to push open the door.

"Surprise!"

Aary was taken aback as Lyna and Rudi jumped in front of him. The cup that was covering the candle was lifted up, and Aary found that his little cabin was not the same as before. His bookshelf, wooden floor and walls were all decorated with colorful leaves: red, yellow, green, and orange. There was also some tempting looking food on the table: bread, cookies, cheese, even apple pie and coconut cake. A very beautiful fruit cake was placed in the center. There was also something on the floor that was covered by a piece of cloth. Aary's eyes were so wide that they looked like they were almost popping out. He stared at his little treehouse that he could hardly recognize anymore, while his two friends were laughing at his surprised expression.

Lyna took his hand in hers and said: "We know you never knew when your birthday was or had a birthday celebration. But 16 is a very important age. So, we have decided to pretend that today is your birthday, so that we can celebrate with you."

"I... wh..." Aary was stuttering.

Lyna dragged him to the mysterious object under the cloth. "This is your birthday present. Take a look. I made it myself!"

Aary lifted the cloth doubtfully.

In front of him was the most beautiful piece of artwork he had ever seen. It was a sculpture of a dragon and a little person riding on the back of the dragon. It was Blackwind and himself! The sculpture was not big, but it was very delicate and well made. The body of the dragon and the little person were carved from wood. The details were amazingly exquisite. Even the tiny spikes on the dragon's tail were so vivid. The large wings used wooden frames for the bones, but the thin film was made with dried leaves sticking together. Tiny Aary even had a leaf cape flying behind its back. In the sculpture, Blackwind was standing on the ground with both hind legs and spreading its wings, as if getting ready to take off. It was so dashing and cool.

Lyna and Rudi were waiting anxiously for Aary's comments. But Aary seemed to be struck dumb by this sudden surprise. His expression was very confused. He didn't seem to understand what they were doing. After a long, awkward pause, he only managed to ask: "When... did you prepare for all this?"

"When you were in the castle, of course. We've been preparing for a month. Do you like it?"

"Why... are you doing this?"

"Because we love you! You're our friend." Lyna answered.

"Friend...?" Aary repeated the word.

Suddenly, the pale faced boy took a step back. His face seemed anxious and uncomfortable. He raised his hands to cover his face and head, and said trembling: "You shouldn't have..."

Lyna and Rudi were confused by his reaction, and asked him worriedly: "What's the matter? You don't like it? Or is there something wrong?"

Aary kneeled down to the floor, hands still covering his head: "No, no, I love it so much. You're too good to me. I don't deserve it."

Lyna said confusedly: "Don't be silly. Of course, you deserve this. You saved my life from the bear. You risked your own life to help **me** get the blood of the beasts. You did so much for me, more than anyone has ever done, when you had no reason to do anything. This is the least I could do. I can't help you with Elior, but I can make sure that you're happy when you're here."

Rudi agreed: "You are a very good friend, Aary. We wanted to do this for you. Seeing you happy makes us happy. That's what it means to be a friend."

Aary shook his head: "No, no, no. You don't understand. I'm not the kind of person you think I am. I'm a very, very bad person. I don't deserve to have good friends like you. I don't even deserve to live!"

"Why do you think that? Tell us, Aary, what on earth had happened?"

"I... I can't. If I tell you, you'll leave me forever."

Lyna and Rudi each put a hand on his shoulder and comforted him: "Don't worry. We promise, we will never leave you, and always be your friend, no matter what you did. But we want to know the truth. Please."

Aary's face was still facing the floor. He said weakly between his heavy shaking breath: "I... I killed my best friend."

* * *

He tried his best to prove with his own actions that he could be a good father. During her pregnancy, he looked after her in every single possible way. He was even more attentive than a mother taking care of her sick child. He paid close attention to her at all times, and treated any of her slightest discomforts seriously as if it was the only thing that mattered. He never let her do any housework. No matter how tiring his work was, he insisted on doing everything himself: cooking, washing, cleaning, and taking care of her. Yet he never felt tired, since he was immersed in happiness.

31

Opening the Old Wound

Lyna and Rudi were truly astonished by Aary's answer, and neither of them knew what to say for a moment. They exchanged bewildered looks, and then looked at the youth trembling on the floor. They really couldn't believe that a kind boy like him would do such a thing. Lyna lowered herself beside him, and took one of Aary's hands in hers. She said in a very tender voice: "Aary, it's alright. Can you tell us what happened?"

Aary shook his head in distress: "No... I don't know... I can't remember. And I don't want to remember."

"Then how do you know that you killed your friend?"

"Because he died!" Aary was almost breaking down, "please... don't do this! I don't know..."

Lyna calmed him down with a long hug, and said: "It's alright. Just try your best to remember. Tell us the story from the point where you do remember, before it happened. We may not be able to help bring your friend back, but as least we could help you take some burden off your mind. Bringing back the past won't hurt anyone, but keeping it inside might hurt you. Trust me, you will feel much better if you let it out. Come, have a seat. We are here, always, no matter what."

Aary sat down in agony. Like a child that did something wrong and was trying to hide it from his parents, Aary kept his head really low, with one hand in Lyna's hands and the other one twisting uncomfortably. Lyna felt the hand she was holding was twitching too. After a while, he timidly looked up to Lyna and saw her firm, encouraging eyes. Yes, this thing, this terrible, terrible thing, had always been hidden in the deepest corner of his mind. He never even tried to open it himself, let alone share it with anyone else. Every time he tried to approach it, he would be surrounded by misery, so he had to retreat to his safe zone. However, recent experiences with his two new friends had indeed made him feel the benefits of sharing happiness and distress with others. So, he decided to give it a try this time, to see if he would be able to reveal the secret buried in his heart for so long.

"A few years ago, I had a friend, named... Johan."

Even mentioning his name was hard enough. Aary closed his eyes to ease the pain and continued bravely.

"Like me, he was also an orphan in Rocky Vill. We were about the same age, and were closer than brothers. We ate together, played together, read together, and when we got into trouble, received the punishments together. Do you remember I told you that I was sort of a little leader among the kids in the village? Well, actually, it was the two of us. We always did things together and made decisions together. We seldom had disagreements, and even when we did, we would work it out quickly, so the other kids could follow us in the fun things we decided on.

"We told each other interesting or funny stories and took care of each other when either of us was sick. When I was young, unlike now, I was always very thin and weak. But he was very strong, even a little chubby, and taller than me too. He was also more mature than me, and was like a big brother to me and looked after me a lot, even though he was not much older himself. I remember sometimes when I was sick or felt sad that other kids all have their families, he would smile and tell me that he was my family and tell me that everything would be just fine.

"When we got older, he became an apprentice to the village baker, and he could bake the best bread and cookies in the whole world, even better than his master. At that time, I was learning to make musical instruments with my master. When doing woodwork, I always got too focused and forgot to have lunch. He was afraid that I might not have proper meals to eat when I got hungry, so he made a jar of cookies for me to eat whenever I wanted to.

"He also made the jar himself. He said that when he made the jar, he accidentally cut his finger and a few drops of blood fell into the wet clay. You've all heard of the widespread saying that if you add your blood to something while it's being made, the object will take on your own spirit because part of your life goes into the object with your blood? Well, it is real. Because when the jar was finished and fired in a kiln, it was like it became a part of him, taking on his skills and kind heart. Every time I ate one cookie, the jar would create another, and it always tastes as good as if he had freshly baked it himself. He always said that when we got older and were both married and had kids, our kids would be best friends too. He said he'd bake the best cakes for my kids, as long as I taught his kids how to play music."

Lyna thought she saw a hint of an exhausted smile on Aary's face when he recalled his happy memories. But even if there was, it was there for no more than a blink, before agony took over him again, when he said:

"He was so good to me. I never had anyone so good to me as he was. Until..."

He covered his face in pain, shaking. Rudi put an arm around his shoulders, and Lyna gave his hand a squeeze.

After a while, he continued with a shaky voice:

"One day, the two of us went into the mountains. I was cutting some wood for making instruments, and he was collecting some berries, mushrooms, and herbs to take back and make into pastries. It was a beautiful day, and both of us were finding a lot of what we were looking for. We walked and talked, and came to a cliff. And then... and then... no I can't do this! I can't remember! I don't want to!"

Aary suddenly buried his face between his knees, and drew back his hand to cover his head with two fists, as if someone was attacking him. Lyna felt sorry for Aary, and a bit worried. Part of her felt that maybe they shouldn't push him this way, to peel off the scab that had long formed and expose the wound in the open air. But the other part of her was convinced that this could help Aary finally get over it, to actually heal the wound instead of concealing it.

In her experience, telling her bad memories to someone she trusted always helped her recover from them faster. Since when she was very young, every time when something bothered her or saddened her, she would talk to her mother about it. When she was wronged and felt like crying, but didn't want to cry in front of her friends because it would make her look childish, she would often come home and let it out in front of her mother. And every time, her mother would give her the emotional support she needed. But even before her mother's feedback, simply telling her the experience and letting her tears run down freely made her feel that she was not alone, and the negative emotion would subside. She knew that Aary didn't have anyone to talk to growing up, and could only keep everything inside. So, she hoped that she could be the one for Aary to turn to when he had problems, although it might take a long time for him to really open up. That was alright for her. She could wait. But right now, she had to harden her heart and push him further.

"It's okay, Aary. You are already doing very well." Lyna said in her gentlest voice, "I believe that you can do this. You can remember everything. You just need to try a little bit harder. From when you saw the cliff, what happened? What did he do? Did either of you go near the cliff? Tell us everything you remember."

Aary's breath gradually calmed down, and he raised his head to give a soft nod. Lyna and Rudi could see the tears shining on his cheeks. Aary closed his eyes and pressed hard on his scalp, his brows knitting into a knot as he tried to pull out his long-repressed memories:

"Because we couldn't go any further forward, we turned left and walked along the cliff... And then... then, he saw something at the edge. Yes, he saw something, and said it was a kind of very rare and precious herb that could be used to treat many diseases, that he wanted to collect. I told him it's dangerous to go near the cliff edge, but he said the herb was so rare and it only grew at the edges of cliffs, and the cliff looked pretty solid too. He said that if I held his hand, he would be totally safe.

"So, I held his hand while he tried to reach for the damn herb, and then... then somehow he just died! I don't know what happened! I can't! I really can't!"

The most important moment was still not revealed, but Lyna and Rudi had to calm Aary's emotions again and encourage him to go on patiently. Lyna stood up and held Aary's hand. She said, very calmly and gently:

"I know this is hard for you, but you're getting very close. Here, let me help you. Try to imagine that I am Johan. You are holding my hand like this, and I am trying to reach the herb." She stood sideways and leaned over, stretching her arms out as far as she could. Her right hand was in Aary's hand, and her left hand was reaching for the imaginary herb growing on the floor.

Aary was startled at first. But when Lyna calmed him down again, he also formed his position. Squinting at Lyna, Aary slowly recalled:

"He was reaching for the herb. He lowered himself to keep his balance. Yes, just like that. Wait, no, he was facing the other side. I was holding onto his left hand, and he reached out his right hand for the herb. Yes, like this. We carefully and slowly moved towards it, and finally, it was within his reach. He grabbed the herb, and pulled. He pulled, but the roots were deep in the rocks and very strong. So, he added more strength and gave it a sudden yank."

Aary paused a moment to push his memory.

"And then... and then... I remember now! With that strong pull, the herb was finally coming out from the gap in the ground, but the loosened roots pulled up part of the rocks too, then the ground under his feet also started to totter. I pulled him backwards towards me, but it was already too late. The rocks started to break and fall one piece after another, and when he tried to move back, it just made it worse. Then he fell too, following the rocks that he was standing on. I grabbed his left hand with both my hands, and tried to pull him up. But he was heavier than me, and there was nothing that I could hold onto on the cliff. Also, my arms were cut by the edge of the cliff and were bleeding. No matter how hard I tried, we were still slipping slowly down the cliff.

"Then when I was almost falling off too, he suddenly loosened his hand, and told me to let go. I shouted "no"! I demanded that he hold on tight to me. I told him I could get him up here. I asked him to trust me. But he just looked at me and smiled, the kind of smile he always wore every time he told me 'everything's going to be alright'. But everything was not going to be alright. He was my best friend, and my only family. I could not lose him. I wouldn't let him go, but no matter how hard I tried, I couldn't pull him up either, and when he stopped trying and let go, it got harder for me to keep my grip. The blood from my arms ran down my hands and made them very slippery, and I just watched as he slipped from my hands and fell into the abyss. Oh Johan!"

Aary started crying like a baby. It was the first time Lyna and Rudi had seen him cry and both of them felt heartbroken. The boy had always been brave and fierce, shouldering all the responsibility and pain that was put on him. He had never shed a tear no matter how badly he was hurt. When Elior beat him, all he did was accept it all and heal himself. For all the things he'd been through and all the things that he did, it was still hard for others to remember that he was only a youth of 16. But that was all that he was, only a boy, at the age of 16. He should be able to get sad and cry too, for the childhood friend that he had long lost.

"After I lost grip of him, the force that I had been using to pull Johan pushed me back from the cliff edge." Aary continued quietly, tiredly, "my head must have knocked onto a rock or something, because I just felt a sudden strike and blacked out. When I woke up again, I found myself back in the old instrument master's house. My head was aching ferociously, and my forearms were wrapped in gauze, but I couldn't remember anything other than going into the mountains with Johan. I asked people where he was, but they just told me that he went away. I didn't believe it at all. He was my best friend. He wouldn't just go away without telling me. I knew something must have happened during that trip, but I just couldn't remember. The adults in the village were good to me as always, as if nothing happened. They acted as if Johan was never here. No one ever mentioned him or even spoke of his name. And every time I tried to ask anyone about him, they would hem and haw, and try to divert the topic. But the other children in the village started isolating me. They stopped calling me for the fun stuff and avoided talking to me. It was like after one friend was gone, I lost all my friends. I was really sad, and I had no idea why.

"Until one day, I accidentally overheard two kids talking about me. They didn't know I was listening, but I finally heard about the whole thing from them. On that day, when we didn't come back in the afternoon, some people went into the mountains to look for us, and found me unconscious by the cliff, alone. They said that Johan and I were having a big fight near the cliff, that Johan cut my arms and struck my head, and that in the end, I pushed him down the cliff and killed him. But I was hurt quite seriously too so I passed out. When I heard this, I ran out from my hideout towards the two kids. They were terrified to see me and tried to run away. But I caught them and knocked them down to the floor, striking them hard and demanding that they admit that they were lying. They cried in fear and called out for help. They were shouting: 'Don't kill me too!' or 'Leave me alone, murderer!' And that just made me strike harder.

"Later, their parents came and led them home. Both of them were bleeding from their noses and lips. I thought their parents were going to punish me or even drive me out from the village. But they just scolded their own kids and asked them to apologize to me. They did it in the end, saying that they were making it all up. But I already believed everything they said, because I couldn't find any other reasonable explanations. I felt that my whole world had collapsed, and I was the worst, evilest person in the world. He was so good to me, better than anyone else, but I on the other hand, killed him.

"I felt so guilty and ashamed, so I hid away anything that might remind me of him. I buried all the things he had given me, including the jar of cookies, in the mountains, because I couldn't bear to see them, but I didn't have the heart to destroy them either. I shut out everything about Johan from my life, including my memories, because anything could remind me that I killed my best friend... But now I remember everything! I didn't kill him. But I failed him. I tried my best, but still couldn't save him, and he had to choose death so that I could live. If it was me falling off the cliff, I'm sure that he would have pulled me up, like he always did. I'm so useless and worthless. Why did he have to die while I lived? Oh Johan, Johan, Johan..."

Aary curled up on the ground and cried heartbreakingly. Lyna and Rudi also felt sad for him and found tears in their eyes.

Lyna said softly: "What are you talking about? You are the exact opposite of useless or worthless. You saved my life and will save my mom's life too. You also saved the little fishing village when you killed the sea monster. You are probably the only person on earth that could have managed to collect all the blood. You are the bravest and the kindest person I've ever met. You couldn't save his life at that time, and it was not your fault, it was just fate. But you saved so many more lives after that. I'm sure he is very proud of you in the world he is in right now. And what you should do is to keep his memory forever and try to live your life to the fullest and do the best you can. If he were such a good friend, he would definitely want to see you happy and be happy for you, and feel sad if you are sad."

After a while, Aary's crying finally calmed down and subsided. He looked at Lyna with a pair of watery eyes and nodded. Although it was indeed a very sad story, his two friends felt happy for him in a way, that he could finally untie this knot in his heart. Johan was a good friend that deserved to be remembered forever, not imprisoned in a forbidden area deep in his mind. Memories were meant to be treasured and recalled, not forgotten. Now Aary wouldn't need to panic every time he heard the word "friend", and also understood more the true meaning of friendship.

In the end, he said in extreme weariness: "After that, I have never had a friend again, until..." He turned to Rudi. The little elf that had been listening to his story with compassion and sadness the whole time, now gave him a heartwarming smile. Aary smiled back, and repeated the sentence Johan said to him all the time:

"Everything is going to be alright."

* * *

Her belly was getting bigger and bigger, and he was getting more excited day by day. Every day he would softly stroke her belly and talk to the baby inside. He would tell their baby in the gentlest voice: "You have a father that loves you the most in the world, and the most beautiful mother in the world". Every time she would slap him lovingly while laughing and correcting him, that it should be "the mother that loves you more". They couldn't wait to meet this little life. And finally, the day came.

Aary's Theme

Chen Yuxiao

PART TWO

32

Commander Greig

Aary sat lazily against the wooden wall of his treehouse, yawning and staring blankly at the huge snowflakes flying outside his window. It was the heaviest snow of the whole winter, but he no longer cared. He remembered how excited everyone had been when the first snow of that winter started falling.

In the early part of the winter, after he helped Lyna collect the blood of the three beasts, life was quite peaceful for a while. No snow had fallen yet, so they needed to wait to get the final ingredients for Lyna's mother's cure. Every day when he came back from the castle, the two of them would sit together to chat or read. Sometimes Aary would play some music for her and she would listen in total enchantment. When Rudi came and visited, the three friends often played and chased each other in the woods. The happiness and freedom that everyone experienced made the chilling winter cold feel like spring.

Annoyed by his own reminiscence, Aary shook his head abruptly to interrupt his thoughts. He lowered his head and forced himself to get back to the book he was reading. But soon, the lines of words in front of his eyes were taken over by the memories in his head again.

He remembered, that on that one specific afternoon, he had gotten a rare treat – an early finish from his work at the castle. Elior was probably in a very good mood that day, so he let him go. On his way back to his treehouse, he suddenly felt something touching the tip of his nose, something icy. He looked up to the sky and saw thousands of tiny shining snowflakes fluttering through the dry tree branches towards him, one after another, elegantly dancing in circles. He excitedly ran back to his cabin and stopped Lyna from her reading to drag her out the door. It was the first time Lyna had seen snow. She opened her eyes wide and claimed that it was magic. Everything was white. The once bare, black trees that looked ghastly, now looked like fairies with white hair and white coats; the thorny bushes snuggled under fluffy white blankets like soft kittens; and Aary's little treehouse looked like a delicious chocolate cake with creamy icing. And when she closed her eyes and lifted her head, the cold refreshing snowflakes just landed on her face and melted into many tiny droplets. They climbed down the tree and lay on the ground, feeling the snow flattened under their bodies, smelling the moisture of snow and earth. The grasses were giving out a refreshing fragrance as they were finally moisturized by the long-expected snow after two months of a dry winter. In that snow, the two of them found the last thing Lyna needed for her mother's cure – three flowers that only grow in snow and ice. Actually, the flowers were not so hard to find. There really were flowers that were still blossoming in the winter. Only they were too small, and too white, so they were hard to notice if you didn't look carefully for them. When they finally collected everything needed for the cure, Aary was even more happy than Lyna. However, he didn't realize what it would mean.

Aary now sighed. In his extreme boredom he began counting the snowflakes flying by his window. He felt something was missing in his heart. Lyna had been gone for one month up to that point. Her mother may be cured by now, but Aary seemed to be sick. He felt like he had lost his soul, that he was incomplete. Every time he encountered some great or terrible things, he wanted to share them with Lyna as usual. But when he pushed open the door, he always found the little tree house cold and empty, and lonely. So lonely. There was no one to read with him shoulder to shoulder, no one to share his bitterness or happiness, and no one to take care of him when he was hurt.

The only consolation was that Rudi was still nearby in the forest. He felt that he could only be happy for a short period of time when the little elf came to visit. But even that would remind him of the happier times when the three of them were all there. Rudi was feeling bad for him too. He knew the boy was in love, most probably for the first time in his life, but lost it after they had spent such a short, happy time together. He remembered the day when Lyna left, Aary and Lyna hugged each other for a very long time. Lyna was crying. Aary didn't say anything, but looked totally wretched and in despair. Of everyone Rudi had ever met in his 112 years of life, Aary was the best at hiding pain, but the sadness was obviously too great to be hidden. He looked as if he had lost the will to live. Maybe he had. Rudi felt sorry for his best friend, but there was nothing that he could do to help him apart from just being there with him to keep him distracted.

The result was that Aary had become absent-minded during work at the castle, thus, he made so many mistakes and received so much punishment. The burn from the lava demon had healed quickly with Lyna's medicine, and there wasn't any reason for Elior to pardon him anymore. But he didn't seem to mind. He just numbly accepted it all, and didn't even have the motivation to treat his own wounds. He tried to persuade himself that he could be like before, as if Lyna had never shown up. But he couldn't do it. Lyna's cheerful ringing voice and light hopping figure controlled his every nerve like a spell. Time, the only salvation he was hoping for, not only failed to gradually reduce his pain, but also increased his longing day by day.

Elior's most loyal commander Greig never liked Aary. Now, he hated him even more. Greig was a sturdy man, but small in stature. A disheveled, thick red beard covered most of his face, only leaving bare his pair of naturally ferocious and suspicious beady eyes. Only when he took off his helmet and released the hair that was similarly disheveled and red, but much thinner, would you be able to see an amusing area of bare scalp on the top of his head. He had an extremely bad temper. As soon as anyone showed disrespect or dared to make fun of the defect on his head, he would break into a fury and even draw his sword to challenge the provoker. That was the reason why he was the only person that Elior demanded remove his sword every time he came to the palace.

However, of all of Elior's commanders, this peevish dwarf-like commander was the best at leading the army and fighting battles. He had been only a junior officer in the old king's troop, even though his abilities in battles and military strategies were obvious to anyone. But because of his overly irritable and uncontrollable temper, he couldn't get along with anyone and often caused troubles. So, he never had too much power. But as soon as Elior claimed the throne, he named Greig as his First Commander, the only person that could give orders to the whole army apart from the king himself. The original First Commander Bobor, on the other hand, who was known for his integrity and prestige, and had always been loyal to the old king as well as performing meritorious service, was demoted to an ordinary commander. Elior only asked him to help him with training the soldiers outside wartime, and did not even let him onto the battlefield.

Commander Greig had never been put into such an important position before and was very grateful to Elior. Although he would still lose his temper from time to time and cause some minor troubles, he absolutely didn't fail Elior's trust in war. For every battle, he would lead the vanguard or the main force, or wherever Elior stationed him, and charge into the enemies' army like an angry bull, leading the soldiers behind him and fighting their way through blood and flesh. In the great war of Hilldown Plain, he was either fighting side by side with Elior himself, or leading the second largest division of Elior's army to do the less exciting but still very important conquering that Elior trusted him with. It was only because of him that Elior could take the whole plain within such a short time. Therefore, he was Elior's biggest war hero, and the young king had always shown the maximum degree of tolerance and forgiveness towards his odd temper.

Greig was always very nasty to Aary, jeering at him whenever Elior wasn't around and then slandering Aary to Elior. Aary didn't know what he did to make Greig hate him so much. Maybe it was because Aary never flattered or admired him like everyone else in the castle did. That was apart from Elior, of course, and Commander Bobor. Elior didn't need to flatter or compliment anyone, and Greig and Bobor definitely hated each other. Aary didn't have any strong opinions about Commander Greig, actually. He thought he was respectful enough to him, but he just didn't know how to flatter anyone, and also didn't want to. Maybe that was what made Greig furious. He kept telling Elior how terrible Aary was and suggested that he get rid of the youth. But Elior never cared about anyone else's opinions and comments, let alone the malicious lies of this irascible little man.

However, Aary did wish that Elior would listen to Greig and kick him out. It might seem to other people that Elior was giving him a great honor, not only freeing a prisoner of war whose life was worth nothing more than a blade of grass, but also appointing him as the king's own servant inside the palace, the most privileged place in the whole kingdom. Only Aary himself knew that, Elior merely saw him as a plaything, an object for venting and torturing without any consequences. Elior had total control over Aary's life. If one day he found himself bored with Aary and didn't want him anymore, he could just kill him for any arbitrary reason. Aary knew that Elior didn't even like Greig, but just used him for his benefits. In fact, Elior probably didn't really like anyone, or respect anyone, apart from himself, judging from the contemptuous smile that could always be faintly seen on his otherwise expressionless face, even when he was acting respectful. Aary thought, compared to Elior, Greig might even be better, because at least he showed all of his opinions and emotions on the outside, while Elior hid everything inside his elusive mind, which was much more dangerous.

The rest of the winter passed blandly like soup without salt. Day after day, every day was just the same. But no one could deny that it was getting warmer. Chilly rain took the place of snow and the forest vaguely turned a little bit green. Aary was indeed feeling slightly better just as the vigor of life was coming back to the deathly winter woods, but he didn't stop missing Lyna. If anything, it only made him miss her more, because the sign of spring reminded him of Garden Valley, where Lyna came from. He had never been there, but it sounded like such a lovely place. He wanted to go with Lyna to visit that dreamy place and to meet her mother and friends. But he couldn't. He was stuck here in Elberkhan, with Elior, for the rest of his life, which most probably would not be a long life. He grew more resentful of this tyrant, and things felt more hopeless than ever.

Until, at the noticeable advent of spring, Elior decided to go on a royal hunting trip in the forest.

* * *

That beautiful, precious little life, the crystallization of their love, the continuance of their lives, came to this world in an ear-splitting cry. It was a boy, with his beautiful eyes and her thick dark hair. The moment he saw his own son for the first time, he fell deeply in love with the child. And when the baby saw his father, before the tears on his face dried up, he started giggling and reached out his tiny chubby hands.

<h1 style="text-align:center">33</h1>

❧

An Unexpected Reunion

Aary didn't expect that going out on a hunting trip would make him feel any better, but it actually did.

He was riding a grey colored mare named Cloud, and he felt like he was indeed riding on a cloud. He had loved horses ever since he was very young. There were only a few carthorses for carrying cargo and long distance traveling in Rocky Vill and every one of them was Aary's friend. These horses were not very fast, but huge and strong. Even when he was so small and couldn't reach the stirrups, he could ride and control a giant horse as if they were one. He could even stand on a horse and do all sorts of dangerous tricks. Since he came to Elberkhan, he had ridden some marvelous horses, but he always had to follow Elior and never had the chance to really ride at top speed.

But this time, Elior took a very large entourage with him. Everyone was focusing on the dashing young king and his extraordinary archery skills, complimenting him on how he shot an arrow through a boar's eye from a hundred feet away, and no one was paying attention to Aary. So, he slowly walked his horse towards the side of the group, until he was at the edge. Then, he gave a subtle squeeze with his legs, and Cloud vanished with him in the woods.

After urging his horse into a gallop, Aary loosened the reins and just let the mare run freely through the forest that was just starting to turn vividly green in the early spring. Bright but not dazzling sunlight surrounding them shrouded everything in a hazy golden brilliance. The air was filled with the faint fragrance of grass and wildflowers. It was so fresh that it almost felt like juice could be squeezed out of it. Aary felt like he was greedily sucking in more of the fresh forest air, and didn't even want to breathe out the waste air inside of him. The wind that was no longer freezing blew his black hair up and Cloud's mane shook at a certain rhythm along with the steps. It reminded him of flying on Blackwind's back, the feeling of conquering the blue sky and riding the wind. He hadn't seen the big dragon since the lava demon quest. He should probably use the whistle to call him back again, just to feel his cool black skin under his palm and enjoy soaring through the sky.

As Aary was totally losing himself in this wonderful feeling, he suddenly heard something. The sound was torn into pieces by the wind passing by as they raced at such a high speed, and only some fragments of it arrived at his ear. But how familiar this shattered sound was! It touched the softest spot in his heart, and this feeling of either pain or itch, made his whole body as soft as a newly baked cake. It seemed that a thousand different dreams from all the nights, and a hundred happy times he had from his past, came right back to him at this exact moment, as if they all just happened yesterday. It sounded like his name.

He pulled a sharp halt on the reins that almost made the poor mare falter, then he jumped down from the horse and walked her backward. He was looking for the source of the sound, but it seemed to have hidden itself playfully. All he saw were layers of budding trees, one after another, extending in every direction until the end of sight. Nothing seemed unusual.

Aary shook his head and smiled bitterly. He knew it was just a delusion created by his own mind. But he didn't have the heart to give up this slight hope, and called out the name that he repeated a million times in his dreams but never dared to speak out loud:

"Lyna?"

His voice disappeared in the air, followed by a dreadful silence that was almost rare in the forest.

Aary sighed and weakly leaned on a tree beside him. He closed his eyes and the side of his forehead felt the rough bark of the tree. It seemed that even opening his eyes was such a big effort right now.

"A... Aary?"

His whole body gave out a shake as if he had been struck by lightning. He opened his eyes and froze.

In front of him, through the gaps between the trees, stood Lyna in the coat she wore on the first day they met, her back against the sun. Her golden hair was lifted up by the spring breeze, and her beautiful contour outlined by the sunshine behind her reminded Aary of the first time that he discovered she was a girl. When Lyna saw Aary, she also froze in astonishment. But then, a joyful smile emerged on her face.

* * *

He had spent many years on the road before he met her. He was long used to roaming and wandering around, making a home wherever he went, and sleeping in a different place every night. It had seemed that this was and would be his life forever. Her entrance shook his world and turned it into a world of two. Nothing would ever be the same again. He would stay here in this little village with her forever. Or if she wanted to see the world that he talked about, they would go on this journey together. It didn't matter where they were or what they did, as long as they were together. Nothing and no one else in the world mattered to him anymore, and he thought that he would never love anyone else as much as he loved Maire. But right now, this newborn little life came into his life, and completely subjugated him.

34

Rebirth

Aary was still worried that it was just his imagination or a dream. He closed his eyes and rubbed them violently. But when he reopened them, Lyna was still there, and running towards him. He suddenly felt that all his strength had returned to his body. He ran forward himself and held Lyna tightly in his arms.

Holding the girl, Aary felt that he was like a fragment of broken emerald whose pieces had finally been collected and put together again. He felt like he had gotten back a part of his body, or more accurately, like a limb finding the body it belonged to, and he was finally a complete human being again. They hugged each other tightly for a long time without a word.

Lyna's hands were on Aary's shoulder. She could feel the new scars on his back even through his shirt, and his protruding shoulder blades. His face seemed paler and thinner. It broke her heart. But Aary was immersed in the joy of reunion, and asked concernedly: "How is your mother? Is her disease cured?"

The light in Lyna's eyes dimmed into sadness. Lyna looked at the pair of hopeful green eyes in front of her, lowered her head, and broke into tears.

"She's gone." She said in a whispering voice.

"What?!" Aary panicked. His head felt like a beehive and his breath seemed difficult. His voice sounded almost angry: "How?! What happened?!"

Lyna covered her face with her hands, and whimpered: "I'm sorry."

"Sorry?" Aary realized that he was yelling at Lyna, this poor girl who had just lost her mother. He suddenly felt very ashamed. He put his hands on Lyna's shoulders, and knelt down to look up to her face.

He said in his gentlest voice: "I'm so sorry Lyna. What happened? Didn't the antidote work? Was there something wrong with the ingredients we found? Tell me, Lyna. Didn't we collect everything in time? What did we do wrong?"

Lyna wanted to answer but couldn't speak. The flood of tears she had managed to control only a few days ago came back to her again. Aary didn't ask any more questions, and silently wrapped Lyna in his arms.

When Lyna gradually stopped crying in the arms of the black-haired youth, she started telling the story of what had happened.

She returned home in the early winter. At that time, her mother was already nearing her last breath. She cried when she saw her baby girl come home.

When Lyna left the village, her mother was devastated. Lyna told her mother that she was going to look for a cure. Her mother begged her not to go, saying that she didn't want a cure, she only wanted Lyna to stay with her for her final days. But Lyna was a very determined girl. She had made up her mind that she was going to find the cure and save her mother's life, and that's what she did, even though she didn't know how to.

Lyna's mother was terribly worried, but there was nothing she could do. She was too weak to go after Lyna. So, she just stayed at home and prayed day and night for her precious daughter to return. When Lyna finally pushed open the door that her mother had left unlocked since the day she left, the poor woman couldn't believe that she was real. She thought it was a delusion before death finally came to her. But Lyna ran to her mother's bed and hugged her tightly while tears ran down both their faces.

However, what Lyna couldn't have imagined was that not only her mother, but also more people in their village had gotten the Watchman's Curse. No one had even heard of it before her mother fell sick. But now, so many people in this one little village were affected by it, even though it wasn't contagious. If the book where we learnt about the disease was accurate, there hadn't been so many cases in one place ever since the Dark Era.

People started saying that the village was cursed by dark magic and began keeping a distance from the families with anyone that got the disease. When neighbors met on the street, they didn't stop and chat with each other anymore, but only gave a quick greeting before hurrying back to their own houses. Some families even abandoned the houses that they had lived in for their entire lives and that their ancestors had lived in for thousands of years, and ran away from the village. Fear and despair controlled the whole village that was once full of happiness and laughter... until Lyna came back with the medicine she and Aary collected.

Before Lyna returned, no one thought that this disease could be cured, because for everyone in this little village, the ingredients of the medicine seemed impossible to get. But when Lyna came back with the cure, hope came back to every house.

As soon as Lyna returned home, she carefully followed the instructions in the book and cooked the remedy from the ingredients she got with Aary's help on a little pot on the stove. Before it was even done, every family came knocking on their door to beg for help. They were all fellow villagers, neighbors, even good friends of Lyna's family, the people that had watched her grow up, the people that helped this family of mother and daughter without any question or delay when they needed it. Now when they came to ask for something that was a matter of life and death, how could they say no?

Lyna wanted to cure her mother first, and then save the rest for the others. But Lyna's mother was a very kind woman who always put others before herself. She insisted on saving the others first, especially the younger ones. But how could that little amount of medicine be enough for everyone? Even though everyone was very careful and only drank one spoonful, the little pot was getting empty quickly.

When it finally came to her turn, there was almost none left. So Lyna poured some water into the pot, and her mother drank the last bit of the thinned medicine.

Then they all waited anxiously for the miracle to happen. And it did. On the day that Lyna came back, when the night fell, the whole village fell into a restful slumber, including her own mother. Everyone that hadn't been able to sleep, no matter when they got the disease, enjoyed a good night's sleep on that day.

After drinking the medicine, Lyna's mother lay on her bed. She asked Lyna to lie down beside her and tell her everything that she did after leaving home. So Lyna told her everything- about the beautiful, colorful autumn and the magical white winter, about the bear, about how dragons were actually real, about the youth she met and how he helped her get the cure. She told her everything she saw and did and felt after she left home, and gradually, her mother fell asleep.

Lyna was very surprised and happy to see her mother falling asleep. She didn't know if that tiny little bit of remedy was enough to cure her mother, but her mother was lying peacefully on the bed. Her eyes were closed and her chest moved up and down with the rhythm of her breathing. Lyna lay by her mother's side, eyes filled with tears of joy, and watched her mother sleeping, until sleep finally conquered her as well.

But the next morning, when Lyna woke up to the bright morning sun, her mother never did.

Lyna's mother had been suffering from this disease for far too long that her body was already extremely weak, so when sleep finally took her, her body didn't have enough strength to wake up again. Thus, she was gone, quietly, peacefully, in a sleep that she had been waiting for so long, beside her daughter that she loved more than her own life, with the sweetest smile on her face.

* * *

At that moment, the world was not just the two of them anymore, and he suddenly had a plan for the future, had a purpose for his life. He would watch his son grow day by day, teach him to walk, to speak, and to read. He would teach him everything he needed to know to be a good man. He would see him fall in love with a girl and form his own family. Then he would hold his grandchildren in his arms like now. He would be there for all the important moments in this boy's life. He was thinking about all the things that were going to happen in the future years, and the baby in his arms chuckled.

35

Unwanted Guests

After Lyna's mother passed away, all the villagers came to her house to offer their condolences, especially those that survived because of Lyna's cure. People cried as if their own mother or daughter had died, and offered to take care of Lyna and raise her like their own child. But none of this could make her feel any better. She lost the person that she loved most in the world and who loved her most, the kind, loving mother that taught her everything, the wonderful woman that gave her life.

Lyna lifted her head and looked at Aary with her teary blue eyes:

"I didn't want to stay there anymore. Seeing their caring and concerned eyes only made me think of my mom, of her tender smile and wise words, her goodnight kisses and gentle touch. The better they were to me, the sadder it made me. My mom is in heaven now. She doesn't need my care anymore. But you're still here. You never take good care of yourself. Compared to staying there and being taken care of by others, receiving their pity and sympathy, I would rather be here and offer you some help, or even just some company, as long as I can. Besides my mom, you're the one that understands me the most.

"So, I put on the big overcoat once again and said goodbye to the people in the village. I left the little house that I had lived in since I was born, left the Garden Valley with spring all year round, and came back to you.

Aary gently stroked Lyna's golden hair and said softly: "You had an amazing mother. Even though she's gone, those that lived because she let others be treated first are continuing her life in a way, right? She'll be watching you from heaven, loving you, and protecting you."

Lyna nodded: "I really hoped that she would get the chance to meet you. She already really liked you when I told her about you. She said you were a very strong boy, that you remained so kind and positive even after all the hard times and pain you've been through. She said that if she ever got the chance to see you, she would give you the biggest hug you'd ever had. She was grateful for how you took care of me when I was away from her, and how you helped me collect the cure for her. She also said your own mother would be somewhere watching over you, feeling very proud." Lyna looked at Aary affectionately with her big teary eyes, and said: "And now my mom will be watching over you too."

Aary felt that his eyes were also getting a bit wet. Lyna reached up to put her arms around him, her voice trembled due to her sobbing: "Now, I'm giving you this hug, on behalf of my mom."

Aary put his own arms around her shoulders and allowed a drop of tear to secretly run down his cheek. He silently made a promise to Lyna's mother's soul in heaven, that he would take care of this little girl and never let any harm come to her...

Clip-clap-clip-clap...

A charge of galloping hoof beats abruptly broke the peace of the afternoon. Alert to possible danger, Aary turned his head toward the direction where the sound was coming from. The happiness of seeing Lyna again and the sadness of hearing her story completely made him forget about Elior and his troop not far away. But now it sounded like they were catching up.

He quickly ran his eyes over the surroundings and whispered to Lyna in an assertive voice: "Climb up the tree. Hide. Now!"

Lyna asked in apparent fear and worry: "Who are those people? What about you?"

"It's the king's men. They won't do anything to me. Do it, now!" Aary said as he lifted Lyna with his arms.

The sound of the hoofs was so strong and forceful that the whole ground was shaking when they drew near. But thick bushes all around them blocked any sight of what was coming at them. Just when Lyna had climbed onto a thick branch and hid herself behind the leaves, a tall, robust black horse suddenly leapt over the bushes and appeared in front of Aary. If the man on the horse hadn't pulled up on the rein the moment they emerged from the bushes, they might have crashed into Aary and killed him.

The man on the horse was a strong, magnificent looking soldier. The mighty look of him would make anyone fear and respect him before he even needed to say anything. The warhorse he rode was the same, the strong muscles looked almost like it was cast from bronze. The armor he wore reflected the afternoon sunlight and stunned Aary's eyes. Aary had to lift a hand to cover his eyes to avoid the blinding light.

Aary greeted respectfully: "Commander Bobor."

The Commander did not answer. He jumped down from his horse and glared at Aary harshly, and led the horse aside to make way for the new arrivals. When Aary saw Commander Bobor's movements, he knew who was coming next.

Another horse jumped over the bush in a manner that was as light as a feather. The horse was covered in a coat of short fur as white as the purest snow from head to heals, and its elegant movements represented the nobility of the rider.

Commander Bobor slightly bent towards the newcomer: "Your Grace."

Watching this from her hiding spot up in the tree, Lyna was totally taken aback. She always imagined Elior to be an evil, ugly tyrant with vicious eyes and a black beard, but never thought that he could be such a handsome, elegant, and noble young aristocrat. He was wearing a thin milk-white cotton garment. His silver hair was braided into several thin plaits in front of and behind his ears, and the rest of his hair was tied loosely behind his head. It looked simple, but elegant. His fair, calm face looked like it had been carved and polished for decades by the most skillful sculptor from the finest stone in the world. And it was as if the sculptor thought that his creation was still not perfect enough, so he placed two of the clearest, prettiest light green crystals as the eyes. However, beautiful as they were, those eyes looked so cold and emotionless that they made Lyna shiver.

When Elior saw Aary, he gave a contemptuous sneer from the top of his horse, and said in an icy, sarcastic voice: "Oh there you are. We thought that you were eaten by a tiger, not that I care, of course."

Aary lowered his head and answered: "Sorry, Your Grace. I got separated from the troop."

But at that time, Elior's crafty eyes already landed on a few scrapes on the bark, and slid up along the trunk. Lyna hurried to hide her head behind the thick branch, but a strand of golden hair betrayed her. When Aary saw the look on Elior's face, he felt his heart sink into an abyss and his blood froze in his veins.

Elior proded the silver horse to move a step forward, and looked at the girl in the tree with a kind of cruel amusement: "Hmm, now I can see why you prefer to be here than with me. Obviously, you've got better company that you enjoy more than your old king. But is that how you treat a lady, keeping her on an uncomfortable tree branch? Where are all the manners I taught you? You're not inviting your friend down to meet your king?" Before he finished his sentence, the young king drew the sword on his belt and swung it towards the branch that Lyna was on.

The thick branch was completely cut off from the tree by the sharp sword, and fell through the air.

Screaming, Lyna fell with it, and at that exact moment, Aary rushed over to catch her. The heavy branch hit his shoulder first and knocked him onto his knees, but he fought to hold his arms in place and caught Lyna before she reached the ground. In the meantime, Elior's men surrounded this tree from all directions, the iron hoofs of their warhorses stomping a storm of dust off the ground.

Aary struggled to his feet. By then, Elior had already slid his sword back to its sheath. He gave Aary one last scornful look, turned his horse and lifted his hand lazily, as he said casually to the others:

"Bring them to me, alive."

* * *

Since the day that child came to this world, he became the most important thing in both their lives. His life and her life that had evolved around each other's were now centered around the baby boy, the fruit of their love. He thought he must be the luckiest man in the world, because their life right now was the one that he wanted the most. There wasn't a single thing that he would like to change. He wanted nothing more than to be just like this, being with the woman he loved and their own child, living in this little beautiful mountain village for the rest of his life, like all the other ordinary people.

36

An Uneven Battle

A few soldiers hopped off their horses and pressed on towards the two youth.

Aary knew Elior too well. This cold-blooded despot had never stopped looking for new, crueler ways to torture Aary, and clever as he was, he would have already realized that the girl meant a lot to Aary. If he ever got his hands on Lyna, he would gladly try torturing and destroying someone Aary really cared about as an alternative way of torturing Aary, a worse way. Aary made up his mind that he would do absolutely anything to prevent this from happening. Of all people, he knew what Elior was capable of doing. This man had no kindness in his heart. Aary would rather die than watch him do anything to the only girl he ever cared about. He promised to protect Lyna, to take care of her, not lead her into danger, and that's what he would do, no matter what it took.

Since being captured and taken to Elberkhan, Aary had suffered from too much pain, endured too much humiliation, and he had never seen, not even once, the villagers from Rocky Vill. The faith that supported him through this had gradually turned into doubt, and now, he couldn't worry about this anymore. For the first time, he decided to fight back.

When the men coming for them were only a few steps away, Aary pulled Lyna behind himself, and drew the dagger. The soldiers exchanged a few looks and laughed. No one even drew their swords. Apparently, they didn't take him seriously, and that was his chance. The closest man reached out his hand to grab Aary's free arm. Aary didn't move until the soldier had almost reached him. Then he quickly dodged away and yanked the man's reaching arm, while at the same time knocking the hilt of the sword onto the back of his head and kicking the back of his knee. The big man yelled in pain and fell heavily on the grass covered ground face first. Blood came out of his mouth as he bit his tongue when his chin hit the ground.

All the other soldiers were shocked, and their laughs froze on their faces. A few of them reached for their swords. But Aary didn't give them the chance to get ready. He held Lyna's hand in one hand and his dagger in the other, and moved swiftly between the men surrounding them. A few tried to stop them or grab them, but Aary managed to block all the attacks with his short sword.

More soldiers were waiting beside Elior, including his most trusted commanders. When they saw that the king's young servant was rebelling, fighting the soldiers that were commissioned by the king himself, and trying to run away, many of them gasped and offered to go and take them. Meanwhile, Elior had been watching in amusement on his horse this whole time, like watching some fools acting on stage. He didn't seem to worry at all about Aary and the girl escaping or his men getting hurt.

However, just when Aary had almost fought their way out of the encirclement and was feeling hopeful that they might actually be able to escape, Elior glanced at the restless, wound up men waiting beside him, and pointed his chin towards the fight lazily. The new group of soldiers rode forward and surrounded the two youths in several rings. The warhorses under their legs formed a solid circular wall around Aary and Lyna.

No! Aary moaned silently in his mind. He tried to keep a brave face, because he didn't want Lyna to panic or Elior to sense his fear, but he did feel quite desperate. However, he didn't have the freedom to give up. He had already picked up the sword of rebellion against Elior, and now it was either fight or lose everything. Surrender was not an option.

He turned around to look in every direction. It would certainly be a very difficult fight for them to get out no matter which way. He decided that maybe the better strategy would be to wait until the others made the first move, and then try to break through their formation when they were moving around. But he couldn't think of a good way to protect Lyna while fighting. At that moment, Lyna leaned her back against his back so they were back-to-back, and whispered: "I've got this side covered."

Aary looked at her and was surprised to see Lyna holding a sword. She must have grabbed it from one of the soldiers Aary tripped, and she was gripping it with both of her hands. Aary suddenly felt a lot more confident and full of strength. He took a deep breath and held his battle position.

The soldiers surrounding them started to approach. Aary blocked several attacks, but he couldn't reach the men sitting on top of their horses with his short sword, and the men were pressing closer and closer to them. Lyna wasn't doing any better. She hadn't had much experience using a sword, and certainly not fighting with people. So, she was just holding it nervously, swaying it from side to side, pointing at anyone that tried to get closer.

Then the chance came. When a soldier was turning his horse sideways and wasn't looking at them, Aary reached out his sword and poked the horse on its side hip. He didn't do it hard, but the point of the sword was sharp enough to cause the horse to jump. The poor horse was startled, it kicked its hind hoofs in the air and started to run uncontrollably, bumping and kicking into several other horses on the way. The soldier that was sitting on its back lost his grip and fell from his saddle. Soon enough the scene became a total mess. Horses were running everywhere, soldiers falling off, horses stepping on people that fell on the ground; horses' neighing, people shouting, and the sound of hoofs' thumping filled everyone's ears. No one seemed to be paying attention to Aary and Lyna anymore. And that's exactly what Aary wanted.

He thought that they could just sneak off in the middle of the chaos, while everyone was trying to control or catch their horses, or simply protecting themselves from getting their brains kicked out. Even better, he thought they might be able to get a ride. With that in mind, Aary grabbed Lyna's hand in one hand, and tried to catch a free horse's rein with the other one. A horse was running in their direction at that moment, and he could see that freedom was just inches away...

Suddenly, a fierce stab of pain pieced his body from behind his right shoulder blade and a strong thrust pushed him to the ground.

* * *

People in the village said they had never seen a father that loved his child as much as he did. All the voices of doubt about whether they were capable of raising the child faded. No one said anything anymore, or dared to question him, the man that would endure all the hardship in the world to protect his wife and child from any trouble. Indeed, he might not be very rich in terms of wealth, or very powerful in terms of social status, but no one could deny that being his woman or his child would be the happiest thing in the world.

37

❧

A Twisted World

"Aary!" Lyna screamed.

Aary felt a sudden attack of dizziness. The world started spinning in front of his eyes, the sky falling down and the ground moving up. It made him a bit nauseous. Some kind of salty liquid was filling up his throat. He tried to stop it and swallow it back down, but failed. The liquid rushed out from his mouth like a fountain. In utter disorientation, he was confused to see that the liquid on the ground was red.

Everything felt so unreal, so distant. He felt like he was underwater. Everything he heard sounded so muddy and far away from him, and everything he saw was trembling under the sun. Time seemed to become slower. He didn't even know if he was dreaming or awake. Or maybe he was dead already?

Suddenly, the pain he was feeling attacked him again, and spread through his bones to his whole body. From head to toe Aary felt his body twitch and screamed in agony. Unpleasant as the pain was, it did prove that he was still alive.

Who shot this poisoned arrow at him? Was it Commander Greig? He hated and despised Aary, and he was the one that always lost control of his temper and let his weapons speak for him. It must have been him! He was the only one that might try to kill Aary without the king's command. Or was it the king himself? Elior must be really angry that Aary, the boy he thought he had total control over, would dare to rebel against him for some girl he didn't even know. If he could no longer do whatever he wanted to Aary, then Aary would be of no more use to him. There was no reason for Elior to keep Aary alive anymore.

After another wave of unbearable pain, Aary clutched his teeth and struggled to get back to his feet. He felt that he had been pulled out of the water, and everything around him became clear again. He heard people shouting, horses screaming, hoofs stomping and weapons clacking. He looked down, and saw a large pool of fresh blood. He felt that his whole body had no strength, and his legs were two floppy noodles that couldn't bear the weight of his body. Then his head fell back into the water again, his vision and hearing distorted and far away. He tried his best to keep his balance, but the ground was turning and rocking. He felt one knee crashing heavily onto the ground, and his face went towards it too.

"No! Aary!" A voice seized his heart and caught his whole attention.

Aary turned his head towards the direction of the voice before he hit the ground. Although the world was still spinning, he could see clearly what was happening in front of him. Two tall, strong soldiers had grabbed Lyna by the arms and were dragging her away from him, while Lyna was looking back at him, tears all over her face. Aary turned into a madman. He snatched up the dagger he had dropped from the ground where it lay, and threw it towards one of the soldiers grabbing Lyna, with all the strength he had left. The soldier fell as the dagger landed on his back.

Lyna struggled to free her other arm and ran towards Aary. Aary wanted to shout: "No! Wrong way! Turn around and run away!" But no word came out of his mouth. Then another soldier caught Lyna by the arm and rudely pulled her towards himself. Lyna tripped over a root and fell on the ground.

"No!" Aary tried to run towards Lyna, but his legs seemed to belong to him no longer. Trying to get up and run only made him fall harder on the ground. Then someone grabbed him too. He tried to fight but was too weak and dizzy. He knew that he wouldn't live for much longer, and probably Lyna too. He was like a dying lion surrounded by a group of wild dogs, desperate but never giving up its fight, fearing nothing anymore.

Finally, a second rush of blood gushed out from inside of him, and the world blackened out. The poison overtook his mind and he fell on the ground like a withered leaf. The last thing he saw before he lost consciousness, was the fear and despair in Lyna's eyes. That pair of beautiful eyes, on the sweetest girl, the girl that he failed.

I'm so sorry, Lyna. I'm so sorry.

* * *

The moment the child was born, this young couple turned from intense lovers into responsible parents. No one taught them what to do, but everything that they did and everything that they had somehow evolved around their son in the center of their worlds. They were so immersed in infinite excitement and joy, that neither of them felt the tiredness of looking after a newborn baby. They were fulfilling the baby's every need, and showered him with all the love in the world.

38

The Changes in Hilldown Plain

Lately, there appeared to be some crisis on Hilldown Plain.

It might have seemed that the sun still shone as bright as usual, the sky as blue, and people's lives were as peaceful as they had always been, busy and substantial. It was as if everything was just the same as usual, and nothing was happening. However, there were some changes indeed, during people's chats and laughs, work and study, when people weren't paying attention, changes so subtle that they were almost impossible to notice. No, everything wasn't as peaceful as it seemed. The sun and the sky may have been the same, so were the rivers and trees, it was what was going on inside people's minds and hearts that was the problem. Silently, little by little, evil had started to grow.

Bruke from Butcher's Vill sold beef for a living. Lately, he noticed that his balance scale wasn't working correctly. Every time when he measured the weight of the beef, after the balance was reached, the scale would always move again and tilt slightly towards the meat, so he would need to add more weight on the other side to find the balance again. However, before he tried to fix it, he found that the money he made from selling one cow was now more than he had made before. He discovered that this little trick could silently make some improvements to his life without anyone noticing. So, he secretly added some mud under the weighing plate to make the meat look even heavier. Later, he came up with an even better way: to kill the cows by drowning them in the pond. After doing that, the beef was a lot heavier than before. This way he would become rich and wealthy in no time.

Old Mrs. Keate from Hay Vill had always been very helpful and warmhearted. She lived alone and always offered to cook for children whose parents went out to labor, because she enjoyed the children's company. But lately, she felt that spending time with these children was a bit annoying. She realized that she was not getting anything out of this. So, she started asking the children's parents for gold as payment if they wanted to send their children to her place.

But these are still trivial matters. The troubles caused by this little crisis didn't stop there.

Maiki and his wife had always been a very loving couple. But lately, his wife seemed to be more and more impatient with him, always showing disgust and dissatisfaction. He realized that his wife had gotten bored with the ever unchanging, calm and happy life they lived. He found out that she didn't love him anymore, but had fallen in love with someone else. The man she fell in love with was their neighbor, young, handsome, and strong. Maiki's wife left him for this other man. Maiki was devastated and outraged. He came to confront the man that took his wife, with a large knife in his hand. That man was not scared. He knew that Maiki was very kind, and very weak. That's why he had the guts to steal his wife. However, when Maiki swung the knife, that man would never again see the woman he had just stolen. When the father of that man heard what happened, he was extremely grieved, and all he had in mind was to avenge his son. So, he grabbed the kitchen knife from the chopping board and stormed out of his house...

All sorts of new acts were put on the stage of Hilldown Plain. Thefts, robberies, fraud, rapes, and even murders, were happening more and more frequently. Hilldown Plain was no longer that harmonious, beautiful, and loving world that it used to be. Instead, it was filled with distrust and hatred.

Yes, it might have seemed that the sun still shone as bright as usual, the sky as blue, but nothing was the same as before.

Meanwhile, in a cave at the foot of the mountains not too far away, a group of dirty, disformed creatures were appreciating all the evil events happening on the plain, feeling satisfied with their achievements. They showed their blackened teeth and smiled evilly in the darkness.

* * *

They decorated their home for the newborn baby. She wove a basket from soft but sturdy willow twigs, and he used a few pieces of wood to build a frame. When the basket was hung on the wooden frame, it became a cradle for the child. They padded the cradle with the softest and cleanest cotton cushion, and when the baby was sleeping inside the cradle, he looked just like a little doll.

The Dark Kingdom

Chen Yuxiao

39

The Arrival of Spring

Spring gradually sprouted and flourished in the city of Elberkhan. Soft, slender grass looked like fluffy furs grown from the ground. It looked like a cloud of green smoke from a distance, but disappeared when coming near. In front of the castle, the ice on the river had melted, and was being carried away piece by piece by the flow of water. The ice and snow on top of the mountains also melted into a web of streams that ran down the slopes, washing away all the coldness, loneliness, and sadness of the winter. It was spring now.

The warm sunshine was caressing the reviving ground, and shining into every window of the castle. Even the ancient stone walls were radiating the glamor of freshness and vitality. It shone onto a bed sheet as white as snow, and into Aary's dream.

Aary slowly opened his eyes, and looked at everything around him uncomprehendingly. He found himself lying on a soft bed in a strange room. The room was filled with the bright, gentle sunlight of the morning. Outside the window, he could see that the sky was very blue.

An old, wrinkled woman in white linen was sitting beside his bed, smiling at him. When she saw him, she delivered a cup of water to Aary's lips.

"You're awake. Have some water. How do you feel now? Does your head hurt? Or your shoulder?" The old woman asked very gently and kindly.

Aary obeyed, he raised a hand to take over the cup, and felt the coolness of the water running down his dried throat, nourishing his cracked lips. After he finished drinking, the old woman took the cup and smiled at him attentively. He didn't answer, but blinked blankly at the old woman. She seemed familiar, but he couldn't figure out why. Who was she? He tried to dig into his memory, but realized that it was blank. He didn't know where he was or how he got there. He couldn't remember anything, apart from his own name.

He looked down and noticed that he wasn't wearing a shirt. His right shoulder was wrapped up tightly in cotton strips down to his upper arm, and there were a few strips going around his chest as well. When he lifted his arm to hold the cup, he felt a blunt pain in the back of the shoulder blade. Apart from that, his left forearm was also wrapped up, and he could see some minor cuts on the exposed parts of the skin. It seemed that he had been injured. But how? He couldn't remember anything about that. He tried to think harder, that made his head hurt. But he didn't stop, because he needed to know, why was he there.

He stared at the cup in the old woman's hand. It was a bronze goblet with some engraved patterns. He felt like he had seen it before, not long ago. Then some vague pictures gradually came to him. He had seen the cup. It was that cup, but not filled with water, with something else, thick and dark. It was in this same bed, same room, and he thought it was the same old woman too, handing him the same cup. But he had been too weak to sit up or hold the cup himself, so the old woman used one hand to gently lift up Aary's head from behind his neck, and the other to pour the liquid in the cup into Aary's mouth, carefully, slowly. He used the only bit of strength he had to swallow the liquid, but couldn't taste anything. He remembered that the old woman gently let down his head, and pulled up the cover to his neck. Even these memories were very fuzzy and didn't seem real. After that, he didn't remember anything. He must have fallen into a deep slumber, until now.

But that memory was already in this room. How did he get here? Where was this?

He looked around the room. There was hardly any furniture, only the bed he was in, the chair the old woman beside him was sitting on, and a bedside table. On top of the bedside table, there was a pile of clothes, and a sword belt with a sheathed dagger attached to it. He recognized the clothes and the sword. They were his own. They must have taken it off from him when they wrapped up his shoulder. The stone wall looked a bit familiar too, he felt that he had seen it somewhere. Or more precisely, he was very familiar with the texture of the wall, because... it was... the stone wall of Elberkhan castle!

Now he remembered it all! An absolutely terrifying picture came back to his head: the soldiers, the forest, the poisoned arrow, and Lyna! Oh, poor Lyna!

Aary pushed himself up from the bed and sprung to the ground. Blood drained from his brain and made his sight blacken. His shoulder ached unbearably like a knife stuck inside. But he didn't care about any of that. He grabbed the sword belt on the bedside table and dashed to the door of the room. The old woman called anxiously: "No, you're still very weak! You can't get out of bed yet!" But he didn't even hear it. The door swung open at his push, and he soon vanished in the dark corridor.

* * *

Every time when the baby couldn't sleep at night and cried, they would take turns to hold him in their arms, talk to him, sing to him, and tell stories to him, tirelessly. In that little village's tradition, handling babies was usually the mothers' job, because men needed to work during the day. But no matter how tired he was from work, he still liked to hold the baby and softly murmur to him until the baby fell asleep.

<h1 style="text-align:center">40</h1>

The Dark Corridor

Aary's world was like the corridor he was in, fallen into infinite darkness.

I'm so sorry! How could I let them take you! I'm so sorry! I should have protected you! I swore to protect you! But now I led you to danger! I'm so sorry!

Aary felt a wave of vertigo and fell against the corner of the wall. As he struggled to erect himself, scary thoughts spread across his mind, like poisonous weeds growing wildly in a cornfield, draining the existence of all the crops.

You're only 13, still a child! You should have had a wonderful life ahead of you, in the beautiful little village you grew up in, away from all danger and harm, hunger and cold, surrounded by people that loved you and cared about you; not alone in this strange kingdom, where the only person you knew here couldn't protect you and even led you into capture by the cruelest king in the world. Oh, poor Lyna, you should never have come back to this treacherous place for me! I'm a piece of trash. My life is already ruined. How could I let this happen to you too?!

He didn't know how long he had been in that bed for. The wound he suffered caused a continuous high fever, and he must have been delirious for days, unconscious for most of the time. He didn't know what had happened during this time. Did Elior imprison Lyna in the dungeon, that rotten, dark and cold place that Aary was more than familiar with? If so, she would be locked in the same place with all the murderers, robbers, and thieves, the most vicious and evil people in the whole kingdom. What would they do to this beautiful little girl? He couldn't even bear to think.

However, that was even the least terrible possibility, the best he could hope for. He might even be able to see her every day if she was really kept there. But as someone that took pleasure from other people's pain, Elior wouldn't let that happen. He might have been torturing her the same way he did to Aary. Aary would rather get 10 times the beatings he had already gone through than know that Elior had done anything to Lyna. She was so delicate and gentle. Her skin was soft and exquisite like silk, and fair and smooth like milk. What would happen if the tips of Elior's whip touched her skin? She hadn't suffered from much pain growing up, how could she take it? She was so small and soft, Elior's punishments would definitely be hard on her, might even break her bones!

And it could be even worse. The question that Aary tried to push out of his mind, but haunted him the most, was whether Lyna was still living in this world. If Elior had wished to destroy Aary completely by killing the young innocent girl, he wouldn't have hesitated a second to do that. And if Lyna was gone, what was the point of him still living? The arrow wound that was still throbbing between his shoulder blades was a bit towards the right. If the arrow had been aimed just a little bit to the left, it would have pierced right through Aary's heart. How he hoped that it had, and he had died back then. And it was a poisoned arrow as well. How could he still hear his own heartbeats? How could he be alive if Lyna was dead, because of him!

He fumbled his way through the dark corridor, and stumbled on aimlessly. He didn't know where he was in the castle because he had never been in that place, but he guessed that it should be somewhere in the gallery around the southeast corner, where all the chambers are vacant. This part of the castle had long been deserted and forgotten, left alone in the dark and damp. When he was younger, curiosity encouraged him to explore this area a few times. But the darkness always frightened him and made him fear the unknown. Every time, he made up his mind to go further and try to find the end of these dark corridors, but every time, once he reached the point where he couldn't see any light anymore, he would lose confidence. The furthest he went in this darkness was two minutes away from the light, until he could no longer hold the fear in his heart and ran back to the bright world. He never understood what these chambers were for, or how many of them were lurking in the dark. The only thing he knew was that, since he came to Elberkhan, they had never seen any light.

However, this time, he wasn't frightened, not even for a little bit. His mind was too deep in sorrow to know any fear. He just walked in the darkness and let himself drown in his thoughts, bumping into walls, and tripping on steps. He didn't know how long he was circling around in the dark when suddenly, a glimpse of light appeared at the end of the corridor. When he blinked to make sure that it wasn't a trick played by his eyes, he let go of the hand that was going along the wall the whole time and ran towards the light.

But when the light became brighter, he soon realized that it wasn't the exit of this maze, but one of the rooms along the corridor. The door was ajar, and light was streaming from the gap, like a lighthouse standing in the endless darkness. His heart was pounding from the run, which sounded extremely clear in the silent darkness. He took a deep breath, and pushed open the door.

* * *

She always saw him falling asleep exhaustedly on the cold floor beside the cradle after getting the baby to fall asleep. She was afraid that he'd catch a cold, but didn't have the heart to wake him up, so she would only put a cover a top on him. She couldn't bear seeing him so tired like this, so she told him to just go to sleep after he came back from work and leave the baby work to her. But he would not obey. He shook his head with a weary, but happy, smile on his face.

41

A Strange Room

The intense light stabbed his pupils that had enlarged in the darkness, almost blinding him. When the world around him gradually separated out from the paleness, his eyes were still feeling sore. He walked into the room and closed the door behind him.

It was a huge chamber. The many torches burning along the wall made the room bright and hot. The flames were reflected on the glossy floor tiles and ceiling too. It made Aary feel that he had fallen into a burning fireplace. But apart from that, there was nothing much in the room, only a crudely made wooden chair made from some rough, spiky branches, and a giant, dark, walnut wood desk with piles of books and parchments on it.

Aary went up to the desk to take a closer look at the parchments with writings. He picked up a pile of opened parchments and flipped through. They were letters written by different people, names that he didn't know, and most of these letters were addressed to the king.

He felt the hair standing up on the back of his neck. Did he accidentally find Elior's workplace, his secret hideout? But that thought didn't last for long when he ruled it out himself. That wooden chair looked very unrefined and uncomfortable, absolutely nothing like the extravagant throne of the king. It didn't even have a back or armrests, let alone cushions or decorations. The untrimmed smaller branches and thorns were sticking out from everywhere.

Aary felt that even the chairs in his treehouse that he made himself were a lot better than this. How could Elior, the lavish, ostentatious king, use a chair like this? It was probably just one of his minister's offices, someone in charge of the mail, perhaps.

After examining the room, Aary was convinced that it was nothing special and wouldn't get him anywhere closer to finding Lyna. The burning torches also made the air unbearably hot and dry. He turned around to leave.

Just when his hand was reaching for the doorknob, the ancient bronze knob started turning by itself.

Aary was startled and took a few steps back. He stared at the door tensely and felt the muscles in his body stiffening to prepare for danger. There was no window in that room, so he could only either fight, or try to escape through the door through which he entered, going around whoever or whatever was coming inside. He felt that escaping might be a better option.

He had put the sword belt back on, so fortunately he had his dagger with him. But he knew that he had not regained his full strength yet. The cotton wraps were so tight, making any movement of his right arm difficult, not to mention the pain.

He didn't really have much time to think about this until the door was opened.

A man was standing at the door. Aary's eyes widened in shock upon seeing him. White silk shirt, long silver hair, a bow and quiver across the shoulders, the man that was looking at Aary with a surprised, but still insolent look on his face, was no other than the king himself.

* * *

Every time when he saw some toys for sale, he couldn't resist buying them for his baby. Their son was still too young to play with any toy, and wouldn't be needing them until at least a year later. But he always enjoyed bringing them home, saying that they had to be prepared for the future, because the child would grow up in the blink of an eye, and he needed to make sure that he would have a happy childhood. Their little room was filled with building blocks that could build towers and castles, little people and horses carved delicately from wood, and even sling shots and wooden swords that the boy wouldn't be needing for years.

42

The End of the World

Before Aary even had time to think, he blurted out almost instinctively the question that worried him the most:

"What happened to Lyna?" After saying this, he realized that his tone was probably too terse and rude to Elior, and he might not even know who Lyna was, so he quickly added, "... the girl that was with me, if you would kindly tell me, Your Grace."

Although the room was still as hot as an oven, the cold look that Elior gave him made him feel a chill down his back. Aary flinched a bit. He was afraid that he would hear an answer that he couldn't bear, and couldn't accept. For a moment, he even considered storming out the door, as if as long as he didn't know the truth, it could prevent all the bad things from happening, because he knew that whatever he was going to hear, it would be too cruel to accept.

But Elior didn't give him a chance to escape. "You knew what would happen," he said quietly and coldly, "she's dead." After saying this, Elior closed the door behind him elegantly, and walked towards the desk as if this was just an ordinary conversation.

Aary knew that he heard something, but it also seemed that he didn't hear anything, or didn't understand anything. He stared at Elior blankly, without any thought.

"Wh... what?"

"Did that little arrow leave you stupid? That little friend of yours, I had her killed. What use can I make of her otherwise? Make you a baby?" Elior snorted a mocking laugh, "she did give out a fight though, that I can give you. Quite fierce for a little girl. Nearly bit one of my men's ears off. Didn't know you like that type. I wish you could have heard that sweet little cry of hers when the blade cut her open. But you were in a coma then, what a shame. Anyway, no need to talk about her anymore. She is dead."

Now Aary finally understood those three words. He felt like he was being struck by lightning. It was a feeling that was a thousand times more painful than being shot by a poisoned arrow. He couldn't say anything, couldn't hear anything, couldn't see anything. Any doorway that he used to communicate with the world was blocked: his eyes, ears, nose, and mouth, all slammed shut. His world caved into its core in a deafening crash, and trapped him inside, crushing and pressing him until his lungs were as thin as a piece of paper and could no longer breathe. *She is dead.* The three words echoed in his head like a bell, and became louder and louder, until it was the only thing left that he could feel, shattering his eardrums. *SHE IS DEAD!!!*

For a moment, he thought he was dead himself, because he couldn't feel anything outside his body. He almost felt relieved, even happy, that he would go and meet Lyna again.

But no. He could not go. Not now. The poor girl was murdered at the age of thirteen. And the murderer, the man who took her life, and the same man that destroyed his own life, was right in front of him, alive and well. How could he die calmly when this devil was still here! He failed Lyna once when he let this happen, but he could not fail her twice! He needed to avenge her death, avenge the destruction of his own life, avenge everyone in the world that suffered from Elior's existence.

He used all his strength to pull himself back to the mortal world, and saw him, Elior, who had already sat down behind the desk and put down the bow and quiver, who was at this moment shaking his head and looking at Aary with a smug, amused, and contemptuous smile on his face. Breathing heavily, Aary felt a fire of rage burning up inside him and controlling his whole body. He knew what he had to do at that moment.

His hand pressed the hilt of the dagger.

* * *

Surrounded by the deep love of his mother and father, the baby grew up fast day by day under their painstaking care. He inherited his parents' delicate appearance: a pair of watery big eyes always blinked curiously on the pink, peachy face, and a strand of soft hair always tamely sat on his forehead. He loved to smile too. Every time someone tried to play with him, he would open his mouth and giggle, showing his two tiny sprouting baby teeth. Everyone in the village loved him. No one could resist falling in love with him when they saw him smile.

43

The Last Duel

"Are you sure you really want to do this?" Still smiling and shaking his head, Elior was looking at Aary as if he was some pathetic, dying old dog.

"Are you scared of me? *Your Grace*?" Aary ground out the last two words from his teeth, sarcastically, "Can't fight with me when I have a weapon with a proper blade? All you could do was torture me when you had all the protection, isn't it? Well, don't say that I slew you without giving you a chance."

Elior laughed: "Sure. If you want to play, I'll play with you. But now that you are using a real weapon, I can't promise that I could manage enough control to prevent myself from killing you. It would be a shame if you were to die, where could I find another like you to play with?"

"Or maybe I'll kill you. You vile, inhuman, monstrous creature! You don't deserve to be a person, let alone a king."

"Try it then."

The young king calmly stood up from the desk, and leisurely picked up his beloved bow and an arrow from the quiver, and notched. However, this time, for the first time, Aary saw that he was having a bit of difficulty drawing the bow. His hands trembled a little, and there was a very subtle frown on his usually expressionless face. However small and fleeting those actions were, Aary caught them anyway. Only then did Aary notice that Elior's left wrist was bound with cotton strips like the ones on his own shoulder, and the outer layer was already stained with fresh blood oozing out from within.

Seeing Elior's injury, Aary felt some relentless pleasure of revenge, and then felt ashamed of himself. He knew that he could never take pride in defeating an injured foe, even if it was Elior. He was even thinking maybe he should wait for another chance to fight with him fairly. However, that thought went away soon enough, when he started thinking about Lyna again. It struck him that the wound on Elior's wrist was probably caused by Lyna herself when she was struggling for her life. He could almost see the indomitable girl trying her best to fight against all the armed and well-trained soldiers, like a trapped little tiger struggling defiantly until its last breath. Elior might have tried to grab her, and Lyna, the brave little girl that Aary knew, would have bitten his wrist to rip free of his grasp and run away. That must have made Elior furious and caused him to order his men to kill the girl. What could a thirteen-year-old girl do when an army of soldiers was trying to hunt her down with bows and swords? Poor Lyna!

This extreme sorrow was turned into motivation and strength for revenge. Aary looked at Elior again. He was injured and couldn't even draw his own bow, and also alone in this room with no guards around protecting him. How could he find a more perfect chance to kill him than this very moment! It was not just for Lyna, but also for the villagers in Rocky Vill, and for himself too. Before Elior could draw the bow, Aary pulled out his dagger, and reached across the desk towards Elior.

When Elior realized that he couldn't count on the bow anymore, he threw it on the floor and quickly drew his own sword. The action was really fast, but not enough to block Aary's attack with his sword, so in the meantime, he swiftly took a step sideways and dodged the edge of Aary's blade. As Aary landed back on his feet on the other side of the desk, Elior swirled around and struck Aary backhanded with the long sword in his hand. Aary didn't expect that Elior would be fast enough to dodge and strike back and was thus caught by surprise. Suddenly, he felt that his right shoulder ached fiercely. He looked back over his shoulder, and saw that Elior struck him right in the old arrow wound. The sharp end of the sword tore open the thick layers of cloth and ripped a gash in the flesh. Aary darted an ironic look at Elior. He couldn't believe that he was actually feeling sorry at first for fighting Elior when he was injured. Apparently Elior didn't have that problem. Now that Elior opened up Aary's own wound with the first strike, Aary had absolutely no need to feel guilty anymore. So he struck again, and again, and again...

As they fought across the room, the torches on the wall were shaking in the draft caused by their movements, which made the fires burn brighter. All the past torments, abuses, and humiliations that Elior had done to Aary came back before his eyes. The blazing fire on the wall reflected into his eyes while the fire of resentment and rage burnt from the inside. It seemed as if the fire was about to burst out of his eyes and burn Elior alive.

Aary could feel that Elior was not in his best state that day. He had fought Elior countless times, but only with a wooden stick or something not much better than that. This time he had his own dagger, the weapon that he was as familiar with as his own hands. That already gave him a much better chance. And as if he had some extra help from Lyna's spirit, he felt that Elior was also much weaker than usual. No matter how that wound on his wrist occurred, it was probably quite serious, since it was affecting his skill with the sword, which had never happened before as far as Aary knew.

But Aary himself was also recovering from the arrow wound and its poison, so he knew he couldn't defeat Elior easily. Even though the cut Elior made was not deep, it had opened the wound which was hurting badly. However, the urge for revenge and love for Lyna fueled his whole body with strength and made him forget about the pain.

Aary attacked Elior faster and faster from all directions. He could feel that Elior's strength was draining and the scale of victory was leaning towards himself. He was feeling that the battle was getting easier and easier for him and that he was able to block Elior's weak attacks without any difficulty. However, Elior's defense was always flawless. He just could not find an opening to reach him. And he felt that he was also getting weary and losing strength himself.

Up to that point, the cloth wrapped around his shoulder was soaked with blood and had turned completely red. The blood that couldn't be held anymore dribbled down his back together with his sweat. He was feeling a bit dizzy too, not knowing if it was from losing blood or the remaining poison, or maybe it was just the heat, or the effect of everything combined. He knew that he needed to finish this fast or he might not have the upper hand for much longer. Fighting someone as skillful and experienced with swords as Elior, one careless step may cost Aary his life.

Elior didn't seem to be affected by the heat at all. He wasn't even sweating. In sharp contrast to Aary, who was barebacked with a thick mixture of blood and sweat all over and some bloody torn cloth, Elior looked perfect as usual. His soft, silver hair and fine, white shirt were still clean and neat apart from a few stains where Aary's blood had splattered. Elior kept his injured left hand at his back the whole time while using the sword with his right hand. Even though Aary could feel that Elior was showing obvious exhaustion in his weakened strikes, he was still moving swiftly and elegantly, and had the same superior smile on his face. That made Aary angry as if Elior was just playing with him for fun.

Aary pressed on harder. He swung and hacked and stabbed his dagger at Elior at the fastest speed he could manage, and could see that Elior was slowly taking steps backward, until his back reached a wall and could go no further. Elior was surprised when he hit the wall, almost causing him to lose his balance. For a quick moment, he turned his head to look for possible ways to retreat. But just for that single moment, his attention was diverted from the fight with Aary, and Aary spotted a fatal crack in his defense: Elior had left his chest unguarded and vulnerable. Aary did not let go of this tiny and hard-earned opportunity. In a flash, he used what was left of his strength and shoved his short sword right into Elior's heart.

The young king gave out a faint moan, almost too quiet to hear. His sword that had been swinging towards Aary slippedfrom his hand, glided through the air past Aary's shoulder, and fell on the floor with a loud clank.

* * *

In everyone's eyes, they were such a happy, blessed, enviable family: man and wife that were so deeply in love, a baby that was so cute and lovely. Only he knew himself, how hard and precious this happiness was for him. He tried to forget everything he was before, and just be an ordinary man in this little village, spending his whole life in peace and quiet, with the wife and son that he loved more than his own life.

44

A Brand New World

It happened.

It was real.

He wasn't dreaming. Elior was dead. That man who destroyed his life and killed everyone he ever loved, the man that took away everything good he ever had, was dead, killed by his own hands.

Aary's dagger was still buried in Elior's chest. Blood dyed his clean white shirt bright red, like a beautiful, but deadly red flower blooming in the pure winter snow. He sat lifeless against the wall, head tilting to one side. His light-colored eyes were still half open, as they usually were, but the craftly lights in them were gone.

Aary's legs felt weak and boneless. He crumbled down onto the floor beside Elior. He knew he was supposed to be happy, or at least feel a sense of satisfaction, but he just couldn't. He had been wishing for this moment all his life. He had dreamt of killing Elior, and the joy of freedom, relief, and pride that he would feel after that. But right now, he did not feel any of those emotions. Lyna was dead too. When he learnt that Lyna died, the only things in his mind were desperation and revenge. But now he had killed Elior. He avenged Lyna. The hatred that supported his life and fueled his strength was gone. What else did he have to live for?

He probably wouldn't live for long anyway. He killed the king inside the castle. Someone would come in and find out very soon and seize him. Then he would be put into the death dungeon, and would be executed before next week, probably in the most painful way possible. But he didn't care anymore. He didn't even think of escaping. Yes, there may still be a chance to escape. No one else in the castle had seen Elior's body yet, since they were in a forgotten area of the castle where there was seldom anyone at all. Even the hallways were unlit. Yet, if he did escape, where would he go? What would he do? Both Lyna and Elior were dead. His life had lost its purpose completely, and a life without a purpose wasn't a life worth living.

The person in front of him was so familiar to him, and yet so strange. He never really understood Elior. *Was he really that evil?* Aary asked himself, *he could have killed me too... but how did I survive the poisoned arrow? Did he really deserve to die?* Aary shook his head violently to get rid of the thought. *What are you thinking? He left you alive to torture you more! It's even worse than death!* He shouted to himself in silence, *he killed Lyna! Just for that one thing, he deserved to pay with his life!*

But he was the king of Elberkhan, the ruler of Hilldown Plain. He was the first person to unite the whole plain. The Kingdom of Elberkhan had never been so powerful as it was under his reign. What will the whole kingdom think when the news that he was killed gets out? And what will happen to the kingdom now? Elior never married and has no heir. No one is there to rule this huge kingdom now that he's dead. Will it go into total chaos? Will there be wars and will the people suffer? Did I really do the right thing? Or did I just ruin everyone's lives and become a great sinner in history, because I acted on my personal resentment? What have I done?

He watched Elior's body leaning against the corner of the wall. All the torches on the wall couldn't warm up the cold marble floor or his gradually cooling body, nor could they warm up Aary's shaking heart. Elior seemed really peaceful, as if nothing happened and he was still the young, powerful, ruling king of the large kingdom. And Aary wasn't sure if he was mistaken, but he felt that he could even see a glimmer of a smile at the corner of Elior's thin, cold lips, like the unnoticeable smile that was always on his expressionless face when he was alive, the smile he had when he told Aary about Lyna's death, or when he saw Aary struggling to get up every time after a beating. It was as if he was saying: "Now look what you've done, you fool. See if life will get better for you after I'm dead."

That was more than he could take. He reached out to Elior's sword on the floor, and was ready to put an end to this.

At that moment, he heard the squeaking sound of the handle of the door turning behind him.

Startled, Aary turned to look. Someone was coming. Someone was going to see Elior dead and know that Aary killed him. Should he fight? Or let them take him? Or maybe he should just kill himself right then and there while he still had the chance, because there might be something worse than death waiting for him. Before he could find an answer, the door opened, and he never would have guessed who was standing at the door.

* * *

However, he wasn't just an ordinary village man, and never could be just an ordinary village man. He wasn't even an ordinary wanderer. Buried in his heart, were the deep, unknown secrets from his past. Those secrets were hidden inside a corner of his memory, forever shrouded by darkness, and never seen by anyone. Even the beautiful bright light Maire brought to his life couldn't shine into that corner. Because darkness was always a part of him, inescapable, unerasable.

45

Chaos

He didn't know if he should be happy or sad. He didn't know what he should think. His brain was a total blank.

The person standing at the door was Lyna.

When Lyna saw him, tears rushed down her face like a waterfall. She ran towards Aary, knelt down beside him and put her arms tightly around him.

For a moment, Aary was too happy and thrilled upon seeing Lyna to think about anything else. He hugged Lyna so tightly that she couldn't even breathe, since he thought he was never going to see her again. But moments later, he realized how strange and unreasonable it was to be seeing Lyna. He let go of her and put his hands gently on her shoulders.

"I... I thought Elior killed you. I made him pay for your life with his. But... how did you manage to survive?" He asked in complete confusion, "what happened?"

Lyna stopped crying for a moment and looked over Aary's shoulder. Only then did Lyna notice Elior sitting behind him. The young king sat silently against the wall with a dagger in the heart. His face looked calm and clean, like always, as if he was just taking a rest. Blood had stopped seeping from the wound, but his whole chest was already soaked in red. His longsword lay flat on the marble floor.

"No!" To Aary's surprise, Lyna cried even harder, "no... I'm... he..." She covered her face with her hands, and couldn't even speak.

"What is it?" Aary demanded, even sounding a bit angry, "are you telling me that I made a mistake? But he harmed you! Or... did he?"

Still crying with her face buried, Lyna shook her head. Aary was more confused. If Elior didn't kill Lyna, or even hurt her, he lied to Aary. But why?

He wanted to ask more questions, but seeing how sad Lyna was, he didn't have the heart to push more. *It doesn't matter,* he told himself, *Lyna is safe and sound. That's what matters. You thought you lost her forever, but now you can still hold her in your arms. What else could you ever wish for.* He wrapped her in his arms again until she stopped crying.

Sobbing, Lyna pointed towards the door: "Nana Hadden told me everything, Aary. It's not what you think it is."

Aary looked up along Lyna's hand and saw an old woman standing by the door. She was leaning on the doorframe with one hand and covering her mouth and nose with the other. Her eyes were closed as if she was in great pain. Aary realized that it was the same woman that he saw beside his bed when he was in the sick chamber. Nana Hadden, Aary felt that he had heard this name somewhere.

"She's Elior's wet nurse." Lyna explained, "she's one of the few people left in the palace that knew Elior before he left. She will tell you the whole story."

Lyna stood up and walked to Nana Hadden. She took her by the hand and led her up to Aary.

* * *

It was only after some strangers took him away that she knew he had secrets that he could never tell her. She never would have thought that their wonderful, happy life would be changed so completely and abruptly. Their lovely son hadn't even reached his first birthday, ignorance and curiosity was still written all over his clean little face, but he would never again see the father that loved him more than his own life.

46

A Kingdom's Downfall

The Kingdom of Elberkhan used to be a very prosperous and powerful kingdom, almost like it was during Elior's rule. The old king Estor, Elior's father, did not get a child until he was over fifty. However, his wife, who was a kind and gentle queen, died while giving birth to Elior, their first and last child, their only son. Estor had loved his queen very much. He was devastated when she passed away, but he didn't let himself drown in sorrow. Instead, he turned to give all the love he had for her to their son, as if he was the extension of her life. Old Estor loved and treasured little Elior in every possible way. He looked over him day and night, and had his strongest guards stand outside the little prince's room, lest anything should happen to him. Because Elior didn't have a mother, Estor asked the kindest and most attentive woman in the kingdom to feed him and take care of him. However, misfortune still befell this poor old king and his precious son.

When Elior was about to turn ten, King Estor planned to hold a huge feast for his birthday. He invited his most prestigious officers and commanders, and the kings and highborn lords of all the nearby kingdoms to join the feast, and celebrate the young prince's tenth birthday. The planning for the feast started several months in advance, and a week before the big day, all the best chefs in the kingdom came to the palace to prepare the courses. All the commoners in Elberkhan were also extremely excited. Everyone took out their best vintages from the cellar, cooked their favorite dishes, and put up decorations that they had been saving for the most important events. And this was exactly one of those events.

They hadn't seen the little prince yet, not since he was born. The reason was that the little prince was quite thin and delicate, and the old king protected and treasured him as if he was a fragile piece of artwork, fearing that he might catch some sickness if he came into contact with too many people. Only the people closest to the king and those who lived inside the palace could see and play with the child, and word had it that he was the most beautiful boy one's eyes could ever see, and anyone that did see him fell in love with him right away. For most people in the kingdom and nearby kingdoms, this was the first time they were going to see him, as King Estor believed that he was finally old and strong enough to meet his people and see the kingdom that he was going to rule when the old king himself was taken by time.

On the day of the celebration, everyone was at the climax of bliss and ecstasy. People were dancing and singing in circles, musicians played cheerful tunes everywhere on their spotlessly clean instruments. The old king Estor was so happy that he couldn't stop laughing and smiling. His baby, his precious boy, was finally turning ten and the whole world could see how strong and beautiful he had turned out to be.

But, bad things always happen when people are least prepared. On the morning of the feast, half an hour before the official ceremony began, all the important lords were gathering in the throne room with their gifts for the young prince. Drinks were served and people were chatting happily. Musicians stood in the gallery and played upbeat airs to accompany the mood. King Estor sent a guard to the prince's chamber to escort him to the throne room. Meanwhile, he was sipping a glass of wine, happily appreciating the music and the delighted guests, listening to the lords and officers sitting at the high table beside him commenting on the crowd outside.

Suddenly, someone stormed into the throne room with a loud bang of the door. It was just a guard. The musicians stopped for a beat but quickly resumed in a quieter manner. Some people's conversations were interrupted by the intrusion, and turned to discussions about the bad manner of this guard. Everyone's eyes were on the person entering the hall. Before the king could get angry about the abrupt entry, the soldier knelt onto the floor in a loud crash and said in a trembling voice: "Your... Your Grace, the prince, his Grace is gone... disappeared!"

The hall suddenly turned quiet. There were some gasps and whispers in the crowd, but no one continued chatting. The music stopped completely, and the king's face turned as pale as milk.

"What are you talking about? Are you certain?" An officer at the high table spoke to the soldier on the floor, "it's punishable by death to lie to your king."

"Please forgive me Your Grace, I would never lie." The guard answered, tears running down the big man's face, "the guards outside his grace's bed chamber said the door was never opened. But when we knocked, no one answered. So, forgive me, Your Grace, I pushed open the door. The chamber was empty and the window was open. And... and... I found this on his Grace's pillow..."

He presented a piece of paper to the king and held it over his head. Estor didn't need to go anywhere nearer to see the words written on the paper, as the two words were big and eminent in bright red ink: Dark Kingdom.

The king collapsed onto his throne. It looked as if his heart had been dug out from his chest and thrown onto the floor, and he lost any strength to move. He always feared something like this would happen since his son was born. He lost his dearest queen when he was the happiest, and he knew he just couldn't lose his prince too. That sweet little boy was all he had left. He gave only the best of everything to his son, hoping that he would grow up healthy and strong. But still, tragedy happened.

The festive and joyful atmosphere in the whole kingdom turned into extreme darkness and depression, and the old king Estor completely gave himself up to despair. He didn't even send people to look for the little prince and simply took it for a fact that he had lost his son forever.

No one knew what had happened to Elior or what he had gone through. What they did know was that not long after Elior's disappearance, a challenge raised by the whole plain against the Dark Kingdom failed.

The original plan was initiated by Estor three years before the kidnapping.

Thirty years ago, even before Estor became the king, his father was the king of Elberkhan. He noticed that the number of reported crimes in his kingdom and people coming to him to beg for protection had increased gradually, especially in the northmost villages and small cities. Meanwhile, his patrolling troops had also found an increasing number of abnormal signs and unnatural elements around the same area, which might indicate the usage of dark magic: strange carvings on tree barks with thick black liquid seeping out, animals' carcasses arranged in bizarre patterns, and even some twisted human skeletons.

Estor's father sensed that these two things could be connected. To make sure that this wasn't some kind of a prank, he sent a special army to investigate. He picked seventy of the most seasoned, skillful, and fearless soldiers in his army, and armed them with the best weapons in the royal armory; and he chose seven of the wisest, most experienced scholars, with whatever books that they could carry about dark magic. The expedition lasted for a whole year. They recorded the densities and patterns of the crimes and the signs, and followed them beyond the northern edge of their kingdom, until they discovered a cave entrance looming in the shadow of the mountain, stretching into endless darkness. One soldier returned to the kingdom to report to the king, while the others went inside the cave to carry out a deeper inspection. But no one ever saw any of them again.

Folklores of the Dark Kingdom had always been popular tales on Hilldown Plain, but no one really believed in them, and they were mainly used by parents to scare their misbehaving children. According to legend, they were located right there, the place that today's people called the Hilldown Plain, and they were the most powerful kingdom in the Dark Era. Their magic was so strong that they covered the whole sky with black clouds, so there was no sun or daylight at any time of the day, only darkness, endless darkness. Their castles were made from the white bones of dead people and animals, which made them almost seem as if they were glimmering gruesomely against the dark sky, and they had more towers and fortresses than all the kingdoms on today's Hilldown Plain combined. They controlled the whole world with dark magic and fear. Plants, animals, and people died in droves, and their power was getting ever stronger.

But the Dark Kingdom was defeated, marking the end of the Dark Era. The black clouds dispersed, and the sun shone once more on the death-covered earth. Life gradually recovered and flourished again. Dark magic, or in fact any type of magic, had been gone for thousands of years, and the Dark Kingdom was reduced to no more than a scary tale for the children. That was, however, all changed with Elberkhan's new discovery.

Alarmed, the king wrote to the other kings on Hilldown Plain, and shared with them the things that he discovered. He suggested that they should unite their forces to destroy this reemerging dark force, root and branch, before they became too powerful for them to control, and bring the world back to another Dark Era. The last one was ended by the power of magic, at the cost of numerous kind magical creatures. But now that magic was basically gone from the world, if it really came to another Dark Era, who would be there to stop them?

Estor's father was the king to one of the largest kingdoms on the plain, and also a very highly respected person himself. A few small kingdoms supported his proposal. But still, most other kings on the plain would not follow. Some said that they were over-suspicious, saying that it was probably just some local bandits trying to scare people, and there was nothing to worry about; some said that if it was really so serious, then their own forces needed to remain on their own lands, protecting their own people, when the danger came. It was difficult to ask kings to send out armies that were supposed to protect themselves, to fight an enemy that they weren't even sure existed, and knew absolutely nothing about. So the plan was aborted before it was even started.

That was thirty years ago. Since then, Estor's father had passed away and Estor became the king of Elberkhan, and the power of the Dark Kingdom had grown like wildfire. The abnormality that Estor's father observed thirty years ago had spread to all the kingdoms on the plain, and was getting more and more conspicuous. Along with the increasing number of thefts, robberies, rapes, and murders, there were also an increasing number of animals and people just disappearing completely. The threat became real, and the fear of the Dark Kingdom became a shared feeling between people all across the plain. But whatever they did, they always did it in secret, and could never be caught. No matter how many guards were patrolling the streets day and night, they could always find their way in and leave without a trace.

Finally, three years ago, Estor called all the kings on Hilldown Plain to a meeting, and brought up his father's proposal again. This time, most kingdoms agreed that they should do something, but they couldn't agree on how many men they should send, or how the plan should be made. It took a whole year of sending letters, talking in person, and meeting together, for Estor to persuade all the large and small kingdoms on the plain to work together and agree on contributing all the forces they could muster. It took another two years of countless meetings for the heads of every kingdom to scheme and come up with a plan that was so thorough and detailed that everyone thought it would be successful and no unforeseen problems could arise.

But no one saw it coming, that the little prince of Elberkhan would get kidnapped by their enemy before the war even started. His disappearance ruined the whole plan. Estor, the king of Elberkhan, who was the most important link of the alliance and held the strongest core of the force, lost all his will and ability to fight when his precious son was in the hands of the foe. Actually, he had already probably lost his sanity the moment he learnt that his son was gone. He couldn't even function on a daily basis, let alone be the king of such a vast area with numerous subjects, or the leader of such a powerful league.

Three of the highest commanders in Elberkhan couldn't stand by and watch such a perfect plan fall through, so they ignored Estor and took over the army of Elberkhan by themselves. The other kingdoms were doubtful, but they still carried out the plan as it was. Everyone agreed that the plan was already complete, and the armies were all full and strong, what could go wrong with just one commander missing? But the truth was, they probably should have just aborted the project when it happened. The problematic start foreshadowed a tragic ending. The Dark Kingdom was no ordinary enemy and any flaw in the plan could cost everything.

When the battle started, it seemed that nothing was working out as the Hilldown Plain alliance had planned. The plan they made was to join forces outside the castle of Elberkhan because it was the closest to the Dark Kingdom. The armies from a few of the larger kingdoms would march in two groups towards the cave entrance which they knew was a gateway to the Dark Kingdom, while the main part of the forces would spread out and set up ambushes in the forests, and the rest remained in the Kingdom of Elberkhan as backup. They hoped that when the Shadow Knights saw a relatively moderate army marching towards their base, they would ride out to meet them, expecting to destroy them before they reached their entrance. But then more men would come and destroy whatever forces they sent out, and press forward. If they had other routes to escape, the ambush in the forests would ensure that they wouldn't go very far.

But even before the armies reached Elberkhan, every one of them was ambushed and attacked on its way, resulting in a loss of a large proportion of its forces. The armies that were marching directly towards the cave didn't encounter any enemies, but the remaining forces in Elberkhan received envoys from their allies that were ambushed in the forests with a call for backup. Before they could reach the forests, some men from the forest forces came to meet them, saying that they were the only survivors who managed to escape from the massacre.

It seemed as if their enemies knew exactly what their plans were, so they could always stay one step ahead of them. The kings and commanders from each kingdom started arguing amongst themselves, and with the absence of Estor, there was no one else who could settle the arguments. The alliance broke down and the plan completely fell apart. The troops started fighting against each other. In the end, of all this grand allied army crusading against the Dark Kingdom, including all the elite forces and chief commanders of all the kingdoms on Hilldown Plain, none came back.

All the while, Estor, the old king of Elberkhan, just stayed in his castle doing absolutely nothing. When it was reported to him that his entire army was lost during the battle against the Dark Kingdom, he just nodded indifferently and took a sip of his wine, as if none of this had anything to do with him. It seemed that he had always known that this would happen and didn't care at all.

In fact, he stopped caring about anything, not the news of his kingdom, not the suffering of the people. Instead, he just wasted away the days in an almost trance-like state, walking around like a dead body. He didn't pay any attention to the increasing riots occurring that degraded his kingdom. Nor did he pay attention to his officers' sincere pleadings. The prosperous, peaceful kingdom that he and his ancestors ruled and managed well for hundreds of years was turning into a waste land of wailing and despair and he just let it happen. He abandoned his kingdom and his people, and gradually, his kingdom and his people also abandoned him. They no longer thought that this person was their king. Laws were ignored, rules were forsaken, the whole kingdom had fallen into darkness.

* * *

That night, when everyone had fallen into sleep, a group of strangers broke into the village. They rudely banged on every door asking for a specific person. They were wearing filthy dark hoods that totally covered their faces and bodies so that no one could see what they looked like. The villagers thought they must be mistaken, for the name they were asking for sounded very strange. In their little village everyone knew everyone and they all knew that there wasn't a person with that name there.

47

The Return of the King

Over the years, the Dark Kingdom's power grew daily and spread across the plain. After the defeat of the Hilldown allied armies, people lost all hope to ever again try to stand up against their great power. They gave up the fight for good and gave in to their control. Darkness ruled over almost everyone's heart. The great alliance broke up for good, and the kingdoms turned from allies to deadly enemies, fighting and killing each other over land and resources every day. With the king doing absolutely nothing, the kingdom of Elberkhan lost its power, people, and land to nearby kingdoms, and gradually degenerated from the greatest kingdom on the plain to a minor, unimportant piece of land that no one cared about. In the whole kingdom, up to the highest officers and commanders, down to the poorest peasants and tenants, no one ever mentioned Elior again, as it seemed that he brought them nothing but disaster and despair.

However, fifteen years later, when everyone believed that he was long dead, Elior came back, riding alone through the gate with a bow over his shoulders.

He had grown from the little boy he was when he was last seen into a handsome young man. His exquisite face and perfect build showed a royal temperament. Most people who had served in the palace when he was younger were gone, either because they were too disappointed in the old king and went to seek other wiser lieges or because the kingdom couldn't afford them, and the old king sent them away. But a few remained, and Nana Hadden was one. Elior recognized his wet nurse at once when he saw her and hugged her tightly. When she recognized that this elegant, handsome young man was the lovely little Elior she nurtured and fed, she cried with tears of joy. Everyone was thrilled.

Nana Hadden stroked Elior's long silver hair while looking at him lovingly. "I'll have the chef prepare a large feast to celebrate," she said, "How have you been? Where were you all these years?"

"Don't worry about the feast." Elior smiled, "Where is my father? Take me to him, Nana."

Nana Hadden sighed, a sad look appearing on her face.

That worried Elior. "Is my father alright? Did anything happen to him?"

They explained to him that after his disappearance, his father had never quite been himself. He had spent every day of the last fifteen years doing nothing but eating, sleeping, and sitting in his bed chamber staring blankly at the window. And now that he was getting too old and feeble to even get out of his bed and always slept for most of the day, he still spent the little time that he was awake staring at the window from his bed. He wasn't responsive to anyone, and talked to no one but himself.

They still took him to the old king. Elior insisted, and the others were hoping that the good news might cheer the poor old man up and return him to sanity. When Elior entered his father's bed chamber, fortunately the old man was lying in bed with his eyes open. Elior came up to him, sat on his bed, and said gently: "Father, I'm home."

The old king slowly moved his eyes away from the window, and looked at Elior. The strangeness and hollowness in his eyes made him feel cold.

"Father, it's me, Eli, your son." Tears filled his eyes.

If the old king heard it, he did not show. Elior stood up and turned away, disappointed and remorseful, and started walking towards the door.

"Eli...?" The king's throat made a scratchy sound, so quiet that he almost missed it. He turned back.

"Yes! Father! It's me, Eli, Elior. It's me! Do you remember me?"

"Eli..." The king whispered again, more faintly, and then, slowly closed his eyes. A teardrop slid silently from his old, wrinkled eye corner onto the pillow. That was the first time in years anyone had seen him showing a hint of lucidity and the last time he was seen awake. Three days later, he died peacefully in his sleep. It seemed that he had always believed that his son would come back one day, and had been waiting all his life for this day. And now, he could finally rest in peace.

Elior held a funeral for the old king as grand as the kingdom could afford, followed by his own crowning ceremony. That was when the common people of Elberkhan first knew that he was back. No one had seen this young man before, and the fact that he suddenly became their new king came hard for everyone. Many still remembered how his disappearance changed the whole kingdom and their lives, and blamed Elior for everything that had happened since then. Others distrusted him, saying that he was a fraud, just claiming to be the heir to the throne because no one had seen him. Elior had been taken by the Dark Kingdom, and no one ever escaped from the Dark Kingdom, let alone a small, weak ten-year-old child. How could the real Elior possibly have lived after that? Some even say that he had become one of them, turned and assimilated by the Dark Kingdom and now coming back to control the kingdom for them. Some said that he murdered the old king. How else could the old king just happened to have died conveniently right when he came back.

But Elior paid no heed to any of these doubts or accusations. He had a contemptuous, insolent attitude, and ignored any counsel of others. As soon as he was crowned, he started calling for all fighting men in the kingdom to become new recruits for the army he was forming. He opened the iron vault that had been locked for years, and took out all the weapons that had been collecting dust to sharpen and polish them, and even had new ones forged. He picked and deployed his soldiers one by one, led the training himself. In no time, he created an elite cavalry army unlike anything the kingdoms on the plain had ever seen. He just had one goal: take back all the land and people his kingdom had lost.

The war started, and the young king shocked the world. People found that during the time of his absence, he not only acquired unerring marksmanship and unbeatable swordsmanship, but also became an excellent commander. He led one troop himself to tackle the most difficult battles, and maintained control and order of the other troops through messenger riders. They swept across the plain and took the major cities of the other kingdoms in no time. Within two months' time, with his newly formed army, Elior had conquered the whole plain, taking back all that had belonged to him, and more.

* * *

When they banged on their door and shouted that strange name, she woke up from her dream and turned sleepily to him lying beside her, hoping that he could answer the door and send them away, telling them that they were mistaken. But the look on his face at that moment gave her a chill and chased all sleep away. His face was frozen with fear, and she could see his lips trembling, but making no sound. His eyes were fixed on the door as if a monster was going to break through it, wide open and filled with despair. It seemed that all the strength he had had been sucked out of his body, leaving only an empty shell with no soul, and no hope.

48

The Start of Everything

When the war was almost at its end, something happened. One day, the troop Elior was leading had just taken the capital castle of one of their most powerful opponents with only very minor casualties. Elior was leaning against a pillar in the palace, waiting for his men to inspect the city's granary and armory, when someone came to report on another battle that was happening. The herald told him that there was a little village in the kingdom's countryside that was especially tough. It was a small troop that went to that village, because no one thought that there would be any difficulty. But the villagers were fighting back, and even did quite a lot of damage. Elior was very intrigued and decided to go and have a look.

When they arrived, the battle was halfway through. Elior rode onto a small hill next to the village to get a better view of the battlefield. Dead men lay on the bloodstained streets, mostly villagers with plain clothes, but also a surprising number of his men with metal armor and helmets. He knew how strong and well-trained his army was, but the villagers of this little community were not giving them an easy time. They used the plainest and crudest weapons, tools from their daily labor, to fight against proper steel swords and spears, and had managed to maintain their survival until now. He was fascinated by their determination and fearlessness. They probably knew for sure that they didn't stand a chance, but they would rather fight and die than bend their knees to the invader. The bloody scene had some kind of tragic and heroic beauty to it, and it made him heartbroken. He loved that loyalty, even if it was not to him.

That was when he saw the boy. He was probably not even ten, small and skinny, and therefore was very conspicuous in the chaotic clashes of big men. But he was no less a fighter than any others. He held a little dagger in his hand, and ran and jumped nimbly between the much taller and stronger men, stabbing the dagger into armed soldiers' throats and bellies, knees and elbows, before they even had time to realize what was happening. The villagers outnumbered the soldiers, so most soldiers were dealing with several villagers at once, and could hardly spare any attention for the little, short figure that was flashing here and there quick as a shadow. The boy was bleeding all over too. Blood and dirt and sweat mingled together, and gave him the perfect cover. Elior was shocked. He had never seen a young boy that could fight like this, or bear the pain of all the wounds he had. He couldn't let this boy die. He just could not.

Elior told three of the men with him to go down to the village and find their way to that boy, and capture him alive and unharmed, as least not harmed more than he already was. And told the rest of his troop to go and finish the battle. He was extremely grieved and distressed giving the order to kill everyone, but also really firm. If they wouldn't surrender to him, he could at least let them have their last dignity and die defending their honor.

When his men found Aary, he was already lying unconscious on the ground. But they felt that he was still breathing, and didn't find any fatal wounds on him, so they carried him back to the king. Elior ordered him to be taken back to the castle, carefully treated, and put into the dungeon with other war prisoners. At that time, he had already conquered the whole plain of Hilldown.

He had a plan of how to train the kid and observe him. Elior didn't want him to know that he was specially picked, so he pretended to be coming to the dungeon to pick an attendant, and set the conditions especially for him. The boy was very resistant, as Elior had expected. That made Elior like him even more. The more he fought back, the more it made Elior believe that he was the boy that he was looking for, the boy to take his throne when the time came.

All his officers and advisors thought that he was completely out of his mind, to choose a boy with low birth from another kingdom as his successor, and someone who hated him intensely. Nothing was known of the boy's family, who his parents were. The royal line of Elberkhan had always had the purest blood, following very strict succession laws. Elior's family ruled it for hundreds of years. The old king Estor was past the age of fertility when Elior went missing. And next in line for the throne, the old king's younger brother, was an extravagant prodigal, who spent all his money on drinks and women, and produced countless baseborn children. No one thought he could be a good king, not even he himself. And he had absolutely no interest in ruling. When Elior disappeared and Estor was eaten away by despair, the senior advisors of the kingdom wrote to the king's brother, begging him to come back to court to assist the king, but didn't even receive a reply. As the old king got older and sicker each day, people became very worried that when he died, no one could rule this kingdom, and the leaderless kingdom would finally fall apart and be destroyed completely. So, when Elior, the rightful successor, came back, the officers in the kingdom were more than relieved, especially after he proved his own ability with the Hilldown Plain conquest. Elior was young and handsome, smart and brave, no one doubted that he would marry some beautiful princess and have plenty of children. But Elior surprised all his advisors by refusing to see any woman anyone introduced, and naming a random boy out of nowhere who absolutely despised him as his successor. The old advisors that used to give advice to his father lined up to persuade him, listing all the things that could go wrong if he did this. But Elior listened to no one. He made that very clear as soon as he claimed the throne. The boy was chosen by him to be the next king of Elberkhan, and so he would be. But he didn't let Aary know anything about this, and forbade anyone else to tell him too. He wanted Aary to keep hating him, that would make the training easier.

He had a short sword forged especially for Aary, with the best steel that could be found on the plain. In the old days, great swordsmen usually put their own blood into the forge when their swords were being made. That would make the swords more resilient and stronger as well as taking on their owners' characteristics. Elior wanted his own spirit to be with Aary and protect him, so before the sword was finished, he added a few drops of his own blood into the mold that contained the melted hot steel. When the sword was done, he dumped it casually at Aary's feet like a piece of garbage. But when Aary picked it up, the sword was already connecting Elior's spirit with his.

Elior knew that hardship and pain would toughen a man, and he wanted Aary to grow up to be a much stronger man than he ever was. Every time Elior ordered his men to beat Aary, he felt as if his own heart was being strangled with a wire until it was bleeding. Every time, he would secretly look away, because he couldn't bear the sight of Aary suffering, he would rather bear the pain himself. But he knew how important it was to let him get used to pain as part of his training. He also asked Aary to fight with him with blunt weapons. At first Aary was no match to him at all. Elior was skillful enough with the swords to make sure that Aary was taking some hits every time, but not wounded so seriously that he wouldn't be able to heal by himself. He felt that Aary was learning fast, and improving each time. After a few years, Aary could almost keep up with him in a fight, even though he couldn't do him any harm with the lame weapons he was given, and would still get hurt by Elior's sword. Elior knew in his heart, that if given the same weapon, Aary would by that stage be able to beat him. That was his intention. He wanted Aary to be better than himself and was more than glad to see that it had already happened.

Even though Aary suffered less and less from the fights, the beatings were anything but lighter. He knew Aary hated him more and more. *Let him hate me*, he thought to himself bitterly, *I took away everything from him, his friends, his family, his happy and careless life, and put him through this endless suffering, at least he could have the freedom of hating me.*

Elior hadn't touched a woman since he came back to Elberkhan, let alone take a wife. And therefore, he had no children of his own. Instead he loved Aary in his heart as if he were his own son. He knew how much he wished that he could just let him have everything, comfort, safety, and love. But no, he had to put him through all that suffering to make him stronger. He could only watch with extreme pain in his heart, when his own men beat the boy bloody under his own orders, watch as the boy fell into a pool of blood again and again, but each time stood up stronger and stronger.

He knew it would be hard to let Aary go along with his plan and take the throne as he wished, since he had made Aary hate him so much. The torture of his own soul was also getting unbearable. He came up with a solution for it all – he wanted to let Aary kill him with his own hands. Elior had brought too much pain to the boy, it seemed only fair that he gave Aary at least for once what he had wished for, the final vengeance. Also, it might be the only way that he could redeem his soul.

Elior had this in mind for a long time, but only told a small group of people that he really trusted. He didn't want too many people to know about it, because he knew what a commotion that might cause. He knew that this was an idea that no one would understand, or support, and people might do all sorts of unexpected things to mess it up. But he needed to let someone know, at least the highest commanders and advisors. Or else if Aary actually killed him, he would be hanged for regicide.

About half a year before his death, he called a secret small meeting of no more than ten. He had the royal parchment ready, the king's will. He told them that they needed to keep the letter secret and safe, and not let anyone else outside that room know, until he died. After his death, they needed to show the letter to Aary and everyone else that had any objections to Aary's claim. He told them if anyone leaked the message or tried to act against it, it would be penalty by death. He was hesitant about calling in Commander Bobor and Commander Greig, because he knew that neither of them liked Aary. But they were two of his highest commanders, and he also knew that they despised each other too, so they would never plot together to sabotage Aary's claim, so he included both of them in this secret meeting.

Elior closed the door of the small meeting room, and passed his will to the people around the table. After reading it, every single one of them was totally shocked and speechless. But if the king had made his decision, no one could talk him out of it.

In the name of Elior, son of Estor, King of Elberkhan and Ruler of the Hilldown Plain, I hereby name Aary, the orphan of Rocky Vill, to be my rightful heir. If it occurs that he is the one that ended my life, it is my own will. Therefore, he will not be held responsible in any way for my death. I command that this letter and its contents should be kept safe and confidential, and shown to Aary as soon as I die. He should at the same time be informed of the responsibility that falls upon him, and crowned as soon as possible.

Elior
(The King's Seal)

* * *

He was the person they were looking for. She didn't understand. It must have been a mistake. Her gentle, caring, Jerre, that good man, good husband, good father, the man that she loved with all her heart, the man she thought she knew everything about, how could he have anything to do with these filthy strangers? But now, even the name she knew him by was fake. And there wasn't even any surprise on his face, just infinite agony, as if he had always known that this would happen. He stood up weakly and opened the door. He whispered something to them, and returned to the room as pale as a dead man.

49

The Choice

In the past few weeks, Elior began to worry a little when he noticed that Aary was absent-minded most of the time. So, he decided to take him on a hunt to get some fresh air. When they were in the woods, he saw Aary cheer up a little, so he decided to just let him enjoy himself for a while, and didn't watch him closely. When it was time to return to the castle, he realized that Aary still hadn't rejoined the group. So, he sent the larger troop back to the castle, and went looking for Aary with a smaller band, including his closest advisors and commanders, and dozens of riders.

Later, they found him in the woods. He was just going to play the cruel king as usual and have him punished. That was when he saw the girl. Elior was really happy. He had guessed that there might have been a girl involved in the explanation for Aary's unusual behavior. He hid the joy inside, and tried to act with his usual cruelty. He hacked off the branch of the tree that the girl was hiding on and asked his men to take them captive when he saw that Aary was ready to fight back, as he expected. All this time he had been waiting for the right opportunity, and he knew that this could be it. If he visited Aary alone in his prison cell one evening, and told him that he killed the girl, the boy would not take it easily.

However, what he didn't expect was that an arrow would be released from someone just beside him, and strike Aary in the back. Then, when he saw Aary throwing up blood, he knew that it was not just a regular arrow. Elior was terrified. He jumped off the horse and ran towards Aary, but the boy was already unconscious when he reached him. He held Aary in his arms, and ordered his men to take Aary to the royal physician on the fastest horse, and to command the physician to save him at any cost. After they'd gone, he turned to the person that shot the arrow – Commander Bobor.

Commander Bobor had always been one of the highest commanders and most prestigious people in the kingdom when the old king was alive. He had been in charge of the army for many years, and served the kingdom well and loyally. A few years after Elior's disappearance, some people in the castle started saying that if the old king died, and his brother refused the throne, Bobor should be the person to rule until the next rightful heir, maybe one of the king's nephews, came of age. At first, Bobor thought it was complete folly, but more and more people echoed this voice, until even the old king heard it and thought it was a sensible idea. Then, Elior suddenly came back and claimed the throne. Secretly, Bobor was a little bit disappointed, but he knew better than to show it and be considered a traitor. He wished that he could at least maintain his status in the army. But even that wish was not completely fulfilled.

He only became the high commander after Elior's disappearance and after all the old commanders died in the Dark Kingdom campaign, so Elior never met him or knew about him. After Elior came back, he let the old commanders and officers stay in their old positions, but quickly built up his own team by promoting the people that he appreciated to higher positions, and gradually distributed real power towards those people that he advanced. He preferred younger people, with ambition, rigor, and possibilities, to the spiritless, conservative old men that the old king valued. While most old officers thought that Elior was too young and hasty, the young people in his new team absolutely worshipped him. Elior still named Bobor as one of the highest commanders in the army, but in the battles, he always sent his troop on a relatively simple and unimportant task, while putting others on the main vanguard, such as Commander Greig. Bobor resented this, but he still tried his best to aid Elior and serve the kingdom.

Then, things got even worse when Elior chose Aary as his heir, and even planned to let Aary kill him. Bobor did not trust Aary at all. To him, Aary was just a random village boy from a conquered kingdom. If he took the throne after Elior, the whole kingdom could become a complete mess. He appreciated Elior's battle skills, but he thought he was completely out of his mind for making this decision. He knew what the kingdom had been like before Elior returned, and he would not allow it to go back to that way, or maybe even worse. He also knew that if Aary really became the king, his own life would not be easy. He had always been very harsh on Aary, and he expected that he would do the same if he was in control. He decided that Aary must go. Once the seed of that idea was planted in Bobor's mind, it rapidly grew stronger and deeper, until he decided that he would find a chance to kill Aary and stop this nonsense entirely. He knew it wouldn't be an honorable thing to kill a teenage boy, but he told himself, that it was for the good of the realm.

When they went to the hunt, he secretly inserted a poisonous arrow in the quiver. He thought that he could kill Aary without anyone noticing, because there would be a large group of people and hunting trips were usually quite chaotic. He would make it seem like only an accident, and Elior would forget about this boy soon enough, and hopefully, name a more reasonable successor, maybe even Bobor himself. But he lost sight of Aary before he had the chance to do it. Later that day, Elior commanded that he join the search for the boy. But things got completely out of control. Bobor didn't expect Aary to fight back, and that it would turn into chaotic combat. *Now his grace can finally see the treacherous nature of this little urchin.* Bobor thought, as he nocked the poisonous arrow on his bow. *Time to end this folly. There never was an opportunity as good as this, and probably never would be. His grace will thank me for helping him get rid of this ungrateful rat.* He aimed it at Aary's heart and loosed the arrow.

But Elior wasn't thankful. He was horrified and furious. Bobor had never seen the king like this. Elior always looked calm and confident in front of anyone, even in battles. But at that moment, fear and helplessness could be seen in his light-colored eyes. Aary's blood and dirt from the ground was on his clean white tunic. Even his hair was messy from his hasty actions. Elior breathed heavily. It seemed that he was almost going to cry. He looked at Bobor in extreme disappointment and reproach, until he could weakly make out the words: "Put Commander Bobor in the dungeon, death section."

When Elior got back to the castle and looked for the physician, Aary was still lying unconscious on the bed, but the arrow had been taken out and lay bloody on a bench, and his wounds were wrapped up.

"How is he, doctor?" Elior asked, politely.

The physician looked hesitant: "Your grace, I pulled out the arrow and sealed the wound. But the arrow was poisonous. I studied the essence residue on the arrowhead, and it seems most likely to be a poison called the 'sleeping beauty'. It does not kill as fast as most other poisons, but it makes people unconscious with excessive loss of blood, and dead within a few weeks. Currently... there is no cure that can reverse the effect."

"No! That can't happen!" Elior moaned, almost angrily, "Is there any other way? Anything you know that might save him? I want you to try every method possible, at whatever cost. Do you understand?"

"Y... yes, Your Grace," the physician was startled by the king's reaction, "there is one way that might work, but..."

"But what? Tell me!" The king demanded.

"Y... yes, Your Grace. The books did record one successful treatment case in the history. The treatment involved having the patient drink as much blood as they lost with some dissolved essences. I have all the needed essences on my shelf, but we need the blood, sire. It has to be human blood, and it has to be from one person. But losing that huge amount of blood might put any healthy man's life at risk. In other words, we might be trading the life of this person for his life. Maybe... Your Grace can pick someone from death row and collect the blood when the person is executed? Only... the side effect is, that he might gain the personality of the blood provider..."

"He can't use some prisoner's blood." The king said, disgusted, "what will he become? A thief? A rapist? No that can't happen." Elior paused for a second, and continued with a firmness in his tone, "He'll use my blood. He needs a king's blood."

"How is that possible, Your Grace? This is too dangerous! Your grace still has a whole kingdom to rule! Your Grace..."

"How much blood? Give me the container."

The commanding tone in his voice made the physician shut up. He took a large bronze goblet from his shelf and handed it to the king with shaking hands. "It will be seven of these cups, Your Grace, given one each day, across seven days. He will start regaining consciousness towards the end of the treatment."

Without a word, Elior drew his sword and sliced open his left wrist. As blood came pouring down, he sheathed the sword and held the goblet under, filling it to the top.

He gave the goblet to the physician and said weakly, "Now do your thing, doctor."

Every day, Elior came to the physician, re-cut open his wrist and fill up the goblet with his blood. And every day, the physician wrapped up his wrist, added medicine to the blood, and gave it to Aary. As Aary's skin started turning less pale little by little, Elior turned paler and weaker. In the end, he couldn't even climb the stairs to the physician's chamber. Therefore, he moved Aary from the physician's chamber to an empty chamber near his own bed chamber to be able to see him often, and asked Nana Hadden, the person that he trusted the most, to look after him. On the fifth day of the treatment, Nana Hadden said she saw his eyes moving when she fed him the blood that the physician brought over, but he still didn't wake up. Then, three days later, he was surprised and happy to find Aary standing in his own office.

As he had expected, Aary snapped when he heard that Lyna was dead. Elior knew Aary very well. Aary reminded Elior of himself when he was younger. But apparently, Aary didn't know Elior at all.

And therefore, this young and capable king, who wrote the most glorious page in the history of Elberkhan, closed his eyes forever with a sword in his heart, the sword that was forged with his own blood, and held by the youth that he raised and trained to be his successor.

* * *

He walked to his son's little cradle, and kissed his little, pink cheeks one last time. Teardrops rolled down like strings of pearls and broke on the baby's little hands. How much he loved him! He stared at his son's face, not willing to move his eyes away for even one second. And the innocent child was smiling sweetly as usual, blinking cutely at his loving father. To him, it was just one of the usual times he spent with his father. He had no idea why his father was dropping water on him, less did he know that the man in front of him, the man that loved him the most in the world, was saying farewell.

Elior's Theme

Chen Yuxiao

50

Aary stood there, like a stone sculpture. He didn't know what to say or what to make of this. Elior, the person that he thought he knew all about, turned out to be the person he knew least. The person that he hated the most, was actually the person that loved him the most. Everything he knew was not true, not real. All this time, he was living a lie that Elior made up, unaware of the plans Elior had for him.

Yes, now it all made sense to him. Past memories flashed back into his mind and the things that he didn't understand before were all explained, expect... why? He felt like such a fool. Elior played him at the cost of his own life, but why did he have to play this game?

Aary was so mad at himself. How could he have not figure it out? He must have been too blinded by the pain and hatred. It's so much easier to hate someone, think of him as a monster, and blame him for everything, than try to make sense of the things he didn't understand. But now he understood. Only, it was too late.

He fell to his knees and knelt in front of Elior's body. This "cruel" person now looked so kind and dear.

He devoted so much thought and effort for you, but you took his life when he was at his weakest and most vulnerable, because of saving you! Aary said to himself. *You ungrateful, worthless fool!*

He didn't understand why. Why must Elior have chosen this way to tell him? Why did he have to give his life for it? Elior's thoughts were so hard to understand, as always. But at that moment, he was just sitting on the cold floor, face as calm as usual, as if he was just taking a rest.

Aary looked at Elior. Infinite sorrow, guilt, and regret filled all his veins, and took away his breath that was already very weak from the wound and the fighting. When Lyna realized that he hadn't moved for a long time and shook him lightly, she found that he had already passed out from excessive grief and pain.

What's done was done, Elior was dead, and nothing could change this fact. Elior's body was transferred to a white wooden coffin in the throne room. Only a few high officers and commanders that Elior trusted with his will were allowed to come and say goodbye to the young king, as Elior had commanded when he was still alive.

Aary was sitting on a chair in a corner of the room with his face buried in his hand, Nana Hadden beside him.

Elior's body was lying inside the coffin placed at the center of the room with pure white flowers clustered around. His face was calm and peaceful as a quiet lake with no wind to disturb the surface. His pale skin and silver hair all matched the color of the wood and the flowers.

White was his color, everyone knew that. His horse was white, so were his usual clothes and cloaks. The only dark color on him was the black on the leathered boots that wrapped around his legs up to the knees, and the sword belt that was tied around his waist, dividing his white shirt and white breeches.

And there was some green too. His closed eyelids hid away his snake-like, yellowish-green eyes, but his emerald ring was still on one of the fingers of the hands that were crossed on top of his stomach. The few people that were in attendance lined up at the foot of the coffin and stepped forward to pay their tribute one by one.

When it was Aary's turn, he stood up weakly and walked up to the coffin, not daring to look anyone in the eye. He looked over the coffin walls at Elior. Aary's sword had been removed from Elior's chest and the wound had been sewed up and cleaned. He was changed out of the blood-soaked shirt into a new one and all traces of their fight were nowhere to be seen. For a moment he thought Elior was about to wake up and order Aary to be beaten bloody. He never thought that one day he would actually wish for this, more than anything.

But when he leaned forward to kiss Elior on the cheeks, the cold skin that touched his lips made his heart shiver. He knew that he had really made a mistake this time, a mistake that he could not undo.

"Your Grace," one of the officers said, "it would be wise to have a public succession ceremony to let the common people know that King Elior has passed away and Your Grace is their new king now."

Your Grace? There is no king now that Elior is dead. Confusedly, Aary looked up, and realized that he was talking to him. He was startled. *He's speaking to me as if I'm the king now. But I'm not a king, I'm a murderer. Why did he pardon me in his will? Why am I not punished by death? And why am I suddenly the king?*

Aary just stood there and looked at him, speechless, full of pain, as if he didn't understand the words.

"Your Grace?" The officer repeated.

"I... I'm no king." Aary spoke the words with difficultly, "Sorry to disappoint you, but I... I can't take the throne. I don't know why Elior chose me. Any of you can do this better than me. I should be punished. It was my fault that he died. And I should pay for it with my life. That's what is supposed to happen."

"It wasn't your fault." Nana Hadden put a hand on his shoulder, and spoke gently, "It was Elior's own decision, and he tricked you into doing this. He trusted you and put in a lot of effort training you. He worked so hard to lead the kingdom to where it is now, and he believed that you would make it even better than he himself. I hope you won't disappoint him and let the kingdom fall back into desolation?"

"No, of course not. But... why me? I'm not even a warrior like him. How could I protect the kingdom and its people?"

One commander who had always been quite friendly to Aary said: "He picked you from the battlefield at Rocky Vill. I was there myself. Even as a child, you were fiercer than anyone else. Then he trained you by fighting with him. You could even match him when he was using an edged sword while you were using a training stick. He was the most skillful fighter I've seen and you're now better than he ever was. If you're not a warrior, who is?"

"He also kept you close to him in all of the important meetings with his advisors and officers," an officer added, "so that you could listen and learn about all the necessary things involved in ruling a kingdom. You might not have noticed, but after seven years of attending the meetings, you already knew everything that you needed to know."

All the encouragement and trust in him made Aary even more uneasy: "But, but... I didn't even want to be a king. I don't like to tell others what to do and I hate wars. I only ever wanted to be a... a wood maker or a musician."

Nana Hadden answered kindly: "You love peace and hate fighting, and that was the exact reason why he thought that you would be a good king, and trusted that you could make the people of the kingdom live a safe and happy life. You are kind and righteous, even under the most difficult circumstances. You are also brave and smart. Lyna told me all about how you helped her conquer the three beasts to save her mother. You have a good heart. But now, you have more responsibility. I know it must be really difficult and almost suffocating for you, but remember, you're not in this alone. You have us, all of us."

Aary looked up, and saw everyone around him looking at him kindly and nodding. He felt tears swelling up in his eyes.

"Still, I don't think I'm ready yet. If he was still alive, I could have learned more from him before I took over."

"He thought you were ready, and you need to be now. He also wanted to be there for you for longer, but time was running out for him."

"What do you mean 'time was running out'?"

Nana Hadden took out a leather covered notebook from the pocket sewed onto her dress and passed it to Aary. It wasn't very large, but was quite thick with many papers sticking out between the pages. Aary felt the weight of it when he took it in his hand.

"This is Elior's diary." Nana Hadden said, "He told me to give it to you. You'll understand after you read it."

* * *

He turned around to Maire. Fear and confusion were all over her beautiful face. He didn't explain to her who these people were, what his real identity was, or why this was happening. He only gave her the most affectionate kiss and held her tightly in his arms for one last time. As he let her go, he whispered in her ear with a trembling voice: "Goodbye Maire. I'm really, really sorry. Please love him and take care of him for me."

51

The Shadow over Childhood

Aary spent days reading Elior's diary carefully from the first page to the last. It recorded his entire life, and the strongest and most secretive feelings that no one else knew. Elior kept this diary with him all the time, and never showed it to anyone, not even Nana Hadden. He asked Nana Hadden to give it to Aary when he died, so that Aary could know everything about him, including the things that he had never told anybody else. For Aary, the first reader of the diary, the process of reading was a heart-to-heart communication with Elior. Elior's writings were sensitive and sincere, making Aary feel like he had experienced Elior's life himself, feeling all his happiness and sadness, and the other emotions brought to life by his words.

Aary learned that, the strongest and deepest emotion in Elior's life ever since he was a boy, was his hatred for the Dark Kingdom.

When Elior was taken away by some "thing" from the Dark Kingdom, he was terrified. How he regretted opening the window of his room out of curiosity, when he heard a tapping sound with a strange rhythm on his window. He should have been at his own birthday celebration at that moment, surrounded by all the highborn lords and his royal father's officers, enjoying the great feast with countless dishes. His father told him that he would be able to see everyone, including the people that he was going to rule when he became king one day. He had never seen so many people in his whole life...

But now, he didn't know where he was, who he was with, or what would happen to him. He didn't even know what time of day it was because the place where he was held captive was extremely dark. Only a few glowing worms hanging from the ceiling made it possible for him to see anything at all, but they looked utterly disgusting. The people, or creatures, around him all hid their faces under black hoods, and it scared him. No one wished him happy birthday. Instead, they tied his hands tightly behind his back with coarse ropes that broke the skin around his wrist and locked him in this dark, cold, and damp cave.

Disgusting worms and bugs were crawling all around him and some even ventured onto his skin. His knees, which had been scraped on the hard ground when they dragged him around, were now in contact with the dirty, damp floor and hurting like hell. He was the sole son of a king and the heir to a great kingdom, the king-to-be! Until now, he hadn't even had a taste of what real pain was like, because he was always watched over and protected by several servants when he played. They would even catch him if he tripped over something and see to his needs immediately if he had any. But now, he was crying till his tears were dry, and his wrists and knees had gone numb from the pain. Still, no one cared.

In the meantime, he had been thinking about the things they said when they first put him there. After they removed the dirty black hood that they put over his head when they captured him, Elior found himself in this dark, scary place, surrounded by a few strangers in black cloaks. One of the creatures whispered to him: "Tell us everything that you know about the plan, and we'll set you free."

He was only ten, but very clever. He knew at once what plan they were talking about. His father and his allies had been scheming for so long. His father thought he had become old enough to be a part of all the important discussions of the kingdom, so that he would know what to do the day he became king. Ever since he reached his seventh birthday, the little prince of Elberkhan sat through all of the meetings their king attended, including the ones in which they discussed the plans to destroy the Dark Kingdom. For Elior, it was like listening to an interesting story, how they were planning to deploy the army, who was going to lead which company, and when they were going to attack as well as from where. He loved the map that spread across the whole floor of the room, with little wooden horses and soldiers that they played with. He was not allowed to move anything, but he could touch them as long as he put them back where they were. They were like his own toys, but more delicate and advanced. He knew everything about every step of the plan, and now, he was in the prison of the Dark Kingdom.

But Elior was a thoughtful child. He knew that he shouldn't tell them about it, or the plan would fail. He knew that his father had put so much effort into this, and the allies were quite confident that this time it would work, so long as it remained secret. He pretended to be ignorant: "What plan? I don't know anything."

He hoped that they would just let him go if they realized that he knew nothing. After all he was just a child. But they didn't seem to believe that at all.

"We could give you anything that you want if you make us happy," the same one said, "and make your life a living hell if you don't."

Elior was scared, tears fell down his cheeks. "I really don't know anything. Please let me go. My father will give you what you want if you just let me go."

"You already have what we want, and you're going to give us that. Then we'll let you go. Be a smart kid."

"I told you I don't know!"

"Okay, let's see what you remember tomorrow."

They left him in the dark cave and locked the door. For a whole day, he didn't have any food or drink, and couldn't even get up with his hands bound. It was just endless darkness that accompanied him, and the bugs. He cried himself to sleep and woke up still in the darkness.

They came again. The one that talked to him before was holding a roasted chicken in one of his filthy hands. Elior was starving after a whole day without eating, and his eyes were shining at the sight of the chicken.

"Do you know anything now? You little lying rat?"

Hearing this, Elior quickly shut his eyes and swallowed a mouthful of saliva. "No, I really don't know anything."

"Alright." Elior heard him say to the others, "this little fool wants to go the hard way."

He tore a leg from the chicken and bit through flesh and bones, while another one went outside. When he came back, he was holding something in his hand. When he came closer, Elior saw that it was a whip.

* * *

Even though she was extremely distressed and confused, she didn't ask anything. She trusted him, and knew that he loved her and their baby more than his own life. If he didn't tell her what was going on, he must have his reasons. They just hugged each other as tightly as possible, letting the hot tears mingle together. He would rather die than to leave them, but it was not his life that he was worried about. When he finally let go of her and turned around, he felt that he heard the sound of his own heart breaking into pieces, and the pieces were all stabbing him until blood came out.

52

Betrayal

Two of the things came towards little Elior. He was extremely frightened and didn't know what they would do. He wiggled his body, but that brought him nothing but more pain to his tied-up arms. They lifted him up by the collar, and tore his shirt around his neck. He shrieked when the clothes bit into the flesh of his neck when they were trying to tear it apart. They stripped it down his body until it couldn't go any further when it reached his bound hands. The clothes restricted his hands even more, but his shoulders were bare now.

"No!" Elior screamed, when the one with the whip lifted his hand and slashed it down at him. He was held by the two that stripped his clothes or else he would have been pushed straight to the ground by the powerful thrust. It pushed all the air out of him, and he felt like a burning snake was crawling on the skin of his back. Before he had the chance to get some air into his smashed lungs, the second lash came.

"No! Please stop!" Elior cried out. The whipping paused for a second.

"Do you have anything to tell us?"

"I... don't know. Please just stop." He sobbed.

"Hmm... I don't think that's the answer, young man."

The third one came, followed by another one, and another. Each one was accompanied by a heart tearing scream.

"

"Please stop! I'll tell you what you want to know! Please just stop! I can't... I... just don't hit me anymore! Please!"

"Now that's a smart boy." The one with the whip stood aside, while the talker came near him, with obvious satisfaction in his voice.

Crying, Elior told them everything that he knew, in a coarse voice as a result of all the crying and screaming.

When he was finished, the talking one said to the others: "See? I know this is a boneless chicken. They all are. Little spoiled brats from highborn families. Just need a little bit of pushing for them to betray everyone."

Compared to the whipping, this was even more painful, like the stab of a knife in his heart. That creature was right. He was a boneless chicken, a coward. He hated himself.

Then, the talker said to him: "You've been a good boy. We'll let you go now, with a little parting gift." Before Elior could answer, one of the creatures holding him grabbed tightly at his right leg with his claw-like fingers. Elior moaned in pain and fear, as the fingers started growing and stretching around his ankle, until it closed tightly around it. Then the creature took out a knife with the other hand, and swung it down. Elior almost screamed, thinking that he was going to cut off his foot. But to his surprise, the creature cut off his own hand, the one that was grabbing him, and shrieked in pain, but the hand that was grabbing him held on even more tightly, cutting into Elior's flesh like a living thing.

The talker explained: "My friend here was kind enough to give part of himself to you. When you walk out of here today, you can go back to your father and kingdom and carry on with your pathetic little life. But whenever we need you, we will send letters with your orders or find you directly. And if you don't obey us or try to play any tricks, his fingers will dig into your veins, climb all the way to your heart, and tear you apart."

As his words finished, one of the fingers on the hand clawed into Elior's skin. He screamed in pain and then the finger was out. Blood ran down his ankle from the hole where the finger bit though and mixed with the mud.

"Do you understand now?"

Sobbing, Elior nodded.

Then they let him out, like throwing away a piece of chewed up chicken bone. The same one that took him from the castle put him over the back of his horse, a huge black horse with a skeleton helmet, put the hood back over his head, and carried him out. When Elior was finally out of the cave, he was thrown on the grass just outside the mouth of the cave. The sky was dim but still not entirely dark, and stars were coming out, so it must have been dusk. The creature removed the hood and untied the rope around Elior's wrist, but he was too weak and hopeless to get up. He just curled up with his face on the prickly grass, crying and trembling. His clothes were all in rags and hardly doing anything to cover the whip wounds on his back, which were still hurting like hell. But he didn't want to go home. He had betrayed his father, his kingdom, his people. He betrayed everyone on the plain. He was less than a dying old dog, because a dog would at least bark at strangers instead of selling its master out. He didn't deserve to be the prince of Elberkhan, even less the future king. He wanted to kill himself, but he didn't even have the courage to die.

He thought maybe he could just lie there and starve to death, but later that night, it got so cold and windy, and he became so hungry, that he gave up on that plan too. It was too hard and painful to die, and he was too useless and boneless. So, he had no choice but to stay alive. He struggled to get up from the grass and look around, and saw the dark cave opening of the Dark Kingdom beside him, like the mouth of a monster waiting to devour anything that came near. Freaked out, he started running down the hill. The darkened woods were so spooky and scary, and the howls and shrieks of animals could be heard from time to time. It was all he could do not to scream out of fear. He ran as fast as he could, tripping over rocks and roots several times, and his knees and elbows were all bloody and hurting like hell when he saw a farmhouse at the foot of the hill.

Shaking and crying, he knocked on the door. He begged for food and cover, and the kind farmer and his wife that lived there took him in. They gave him some soup that looked just like yellowed water with nothing but a strand of withered leaf in it. He would have lost all desire to eat if he had seen soup like this before, but now it tasted better than all the lavish cuisines he had in the castle. They put some herbs on his wounds and gave him some old rough-spun clothes that their son used to wear when he was younger, which were still way too big for Elior. But he didn't mind any of this. He was so tired of everything, tired of regretting, tired of self-blaming, tired of self-pity, tired of thinking what was supposed to happen. He decided that he would forget about everything in the past, including the luxury and the wealth, the shame and the mistakes, forget about who he was before. From now on, he would be just a poor homeless orphan boy, wandering about and begging for food. He knew that he would never go back to his life before, and he was fine with it. He was no longer Elior, the prince of Elberkhan whom everyone loved and spoiled, but a nameless, hungry orphan boy who no one would spare a second look at when he was walking on the street.

He said goodbye and thanks to the farmer couple, and went on the road. When they asked him what his name was, he thought of a wandering hunter from Nana Hadden's bedtime stories, one that would poach on the rich people's lands, but who no one could catch. He had never hunted anything before or broken any laws, but somehow, the thought of that brave hunter gave him some courage.

"Jerre," he said, "my name is Jerre."

* * *

He left, leaving her and their child. She didn't know why, but she didn't blame him. She knew that he would not have left them unless he had to. She also knew that this goodbye might be forever. But she didn't let herself drown in sorrow or distress. She had a child to raise. THEIR child. She had the pliable resistance of a woman and the unbending strength of a mother. She needed to be strong for him, to play both the role of mother and father.

53

The Prelude of Vengeance

After years of wandering around, Jerre had seen everything, and forgotten everything about being Elior. He had seen the most beautiful and the ugliest of the world, the best and the worst of men. He had met people who didn't even have enough food and clothes for themselves but were still willing to share with him whatever they could, and he had met people who were wearing jewels and furs but kicked and chased him away as if he was a dirty, stinky stray dog contaminated with plague. He had been to the very edge of starvation, being frozen to death, and being torn to pieces by wild beasts. He had been so close to the gate of death countless times, but he never felt the slightest fear. He knew that his life was not his anymore, not since he was ten, and the severed hand around his ankle that grabbed him ever so tightly reminded him of nothing else. It bit into his skin and bones like a toxic vine that ate away the tree that it clung onto. He knew that he was dead to the world when he was taken away from the castle, and these vile creatures that had control of his life could take it away from him any day. And that was exactly why he wanted to see as much as possible while he still could. Every new day that he was still alive was one more day extra for him. He never allowed himself to stay in one place for more than three nights or get too close to anyone. He never knew where he would go next or what he would encounter the next day. Let it be excitement, danger, beauty, horror, he welcomed everything, even death.

But that was all until he met Maire, the woman that changed everything. For the first time since he became Jerre, he wanted to stay somewhere and never leave. For the first time, he was afraid of death, because that would mean that he would not be able to see her ever again. He loved her more than he ever could love himself, and for the first time in his whole life, he had a purpose. He married the beautiful woman and gave her the best that he could, including a son.

However, he kept the secrets from his past to himself. He never told Maire anything about who he used to be, or what he had been through. He pretended that if he didn't mention it, it would just fade away and leave him alone. To her, he was just a poor wanderer. When Maire saw the hand on his ankle for the first time and asked him about the bizarre looking bracelet, he lied to her and said that it was just a decorative wooden bracelet that he'd had since he was a child, and had some particular significance to him. Maire did not suspect at all that he was lying to her, because why would her kind, loving Jerre lie to her about a funny bracelet? Even he started to believe that he was the person that Maire knew, just an ordinary guy who had wandered a little bit further than the others, who was finally settling down because of love and ready to start a family.

But fate played a trick on him once again. It kicked him hard in the stomach just when he was starting to taste the sweetness of life. All he ever wanted was to live a life like any ordinary person, spend a nameless life in a nameless little town. But when he was taken away once again, he finally knew, that was impossible for him.

Those monsters found him again and forced him to accompany them, because they wanted more use out of this weak, pathetic coward. He was so scared that they would hurt Maire and their son, that he begged them to leave them alone. He told them that he would do any-thing that they asked, as long as his wife and son would remain safe, even if it meant leaving them forever. He said farewell to them with the greatest guilt. She had the kindest and most beautiful soul in the world, and she could have had everything she deserved – happiness, safety, and peace – if not for him. She could have had a loving husband that stayed with her and cared for her until the end of time, and many, many loveable children and a happy family. It was him that came and stole her heart, only to let it go heartlessly. It was him that took it all away from her, that made her suffer from his own mistakes. But there was nothing that he could do now.

He went back to the Dark Kingdom and listened to their evil scheme. The one that could speak human language told him that he needed to go back to his own Kingdom of Elberkhan and take the throne. They said that the old king, his father, was getting very old, and that if he died, Elior would become the new king. Then he would need to start a war, and somehow find a way to conquer the other kingdoms on the plain. He would need to establish his authority in the new giant kingdom, amongst the common people and highborn alike in a few years' time. Then when the time was right, the Dark Kingdom would march towards the Elberkhan castle, and he, Elior, the King of Elberkhan, would open the gate for them, and hand the kingdom over. Only that way, could they conquer the whole plain with the least amount of effort. Elior didn't like that plan at all, but he knew that he had no choice but to obey, if he wanted Maire and their son to be safe. He listened to the whole plan attentively and nodded solemnly.

They kept him there for a few weeks, going into the details of the plan and making him recite everything. Elior did everything that they asked for until they told him that he could go.

The first thing he wanted to do was to go back to Maire and their son. He thought that he would never see them again, and didn't think that those monsters of the Dark Kingdom would let him out so easily. He missed them so much and wanted to give them countless kisses and hugs. Then he would tell Maire everything. He would apologize for not telling her the truth before, thinking that it would protect them, but there would be no more secrets from now on. Then he would ask her if she wanted to come back to the Kingdom of Elberkhan with him and be his queen.

The creatures said that they would come after a few years when the time was right, so there was still time, and Elior thought that he might have been able to work out a plan before then. If Maire and the baby were in his own kingdom, surrounded by his own army, at least they would be safe. Even if they could kill Elior with that hand on his ankle, or make him hurt so much that he wished he was dead, they couldn't touch Maire and their son. They would be protected well, and Elior was ready to welcome death, or anything worse than death. He would find a way to fight with the Dark Kingdom, or even if his son was old enough at that time, he could become the new king after Elior and lead the battle.

He was so excited to be able to see them again, and include them in his plan, that he urged the horse he was riding into a speedy gallop. When he entered the little village that he was so familiar with now, he almost cried with excitement. He pulled to a sudden stop in front of their little house, swung off from the horse, and pushed open the door with the biggest smile on his face. Only, it was an empty house that welcomed him. Everything was placed exactly where it was before, but covered with dust and spiderwebs. The smell of mould and rot took the place of the sweet flowery fragrance, and ants and flies were crawling all over the blackened food on the dining table.

He rushed out of the house like a madman, and grabbed the first person that he saw, demanding to know what happened. The startled villager told him that a few days after he left, those strange people that were knocking on the doors came back again, and killed both his wife and his son. The village elder, Maire's father, also killed himself in the excessive grief of losing both his daughter and grandson. Elior couldn't believe it. He shook that person so hard that he almost broke the man's neck, as if that would wake him up and make him tell the truth. But the villager just shrugged sympathetically. He said that they found their bodies by the river. Maire had her throat cut open, while the poor baby didn't even have a head. Her father buried them himself before he stuck a knife in his own throat.

Without saying a word, Elior let go of the villager, and went back into the house. His world was crushed. The sky was tumbling down and the earth cracked. His whole world was built around Maire and the baby, and now they were gone. And worst of all, it was his fault. How could he believe those faithless creatures when they promised not to harm his wife and son! They knew that Elior was a coward, but they needed to make sure that his son would not become a future problem. They knew that if his son was alive, he might be less afraid of death, and harder for them to control. They wanted to destroy all his hopes of ever escaping their hands, so that he would be their puppet completely. But what they didn't know, was that he wasn't afraid of death anymore, not after the important things in his life were gone. Death was probably the sweetest thing for him right now.

He saw the meat knife on the kitchen bench and thought that he should probably follow the path of Maire's father. There was nothing left in this world for him, and his life was absolutely worthless. No, it was worse than worthless. He was the one that had brought this fate upon them, he was to blame. He was the source of all disasters and tragedies, he deserved to die, to pay for their lives.

He moved into the kitchen, ready to end it all. Accidently, he stepped on something and almost twisted his ankle. He looked down and saw that it was one of his son's little toy blocks on the floor. He knelt down and picked up the toy. Holding this cute, little, yellow wooden block in his palm caused his sight to blur with tears. It was as if his son was trying to stop him from killing himself. He wanted to tell his father something, to tell his father that he wasn't ready to die yet, he needed to do something before that. He needed to avenge them.

An unstoppable rage rose from inside him and a powerful strength filled his body in the place of sorrow. He could put all the blame on himself and kill himself, ending it the easy way, or he could face the creatures that were really responsible for this, for everything, and make them pay. He had been a coward. Last time, he let fear and despair take control of him, but this time, he needed to gather himself up, not for himself, but for them. His weakness killed his wife and his son, and now, he needed to get rid of it, in order to avenge them.

He knelt down onto the cold floor of the house that they once lived happily in, and swore to Maire and his son that he wouldn't let them die for nothing. He clenched the toy block in his fist, so tight that it broke the skin and made his palm bleed. He concentrated all the sorrow, pain, anger and hatred, into a deafening roar that echoed in the whole village, and a punch on the floor with his fist. The wooden floor shattered on impact and the sharp broken edges of the wood cut into his fist and arm. But he was no longer the weak whining child that cried at a little bit of pain. The hatred and thirst for vengeance made him as strong as steel. He welcomed the pain, because it was the only thing that could still make him feel alive. When love and happiness were gone, all he had left was pain, and it reminded him of what he needed to do. It was time to correct all the wrongs that had been done.

Before leaving, he tied a piece of cloth around his chest, and wrapped his son's yellow toy block inside so that it was touching his ribs at the most vulnerable and tender spot. He tied it so tightly that the corner of the block dug into his bones. He used this physical pain as a constant reminder of his son and Maire.

He didn't want to go back to the kingdom as useless as he had been when he left, so he spent years training himself. He visited everyone that he thought he could learn something from. During his earlier years of wandering, he met many people with great skills, good swordsmen, archers, fighters and even hired killers. He went back and found every one of them that he could recall and asked them if he could do some work for them in exchange for food. While being close to them, he secretly observed every movement and memorized it. Then, at night or on days when he was not working, he trained by himself and tried to copy those movements. He didn't have a sword, so he used a thick tree branch much heavier than a sword. He didn't have a bow, so he made one himself with wood and the tendons of animals.

He would train by himself for hours even after the hardest day of work, in the hottest sun or the coldest snow, even the simplest thing that he noticed from the expert, until he could master it and even do it better than the person that he had learnt it from. He would train until he could no longer lift his arm, then he would train his legs. He would train using every last bit of strength, until he could fall asleep the second he closed his eyes.

Once, he worked for an old man who used to be a great archer in his younger days and learned from him. One morning, the old man ran into him secretly practicing with his self-made crude bow. He was really impressed by his skill, and gave him a real bow. He said that it was the best bow he had, but he could no longer draw it now that he was old and weak. It would be better off being used again by a good archer. Elior thanked him dearly and treasured the bow from then onwards.

He spent seven years training himself until he thought that he could beat anyone he met. At that time, he was a completely different person from when he left Elberkhan and even Maire's village. He was skillful with any weapon, fearless of any enemy. He was thirsty for revenge, thirsty for war. His heart and his muscles were as hard as stones. He had no emotion, no love, no fear. Then, he returned to Elberkhan.

* * *

The son was his last and greatest gift to her, and she treasured the baby more than ever. He was all that she had left now, that cute, sweet child, and he needed her. She had only one wish, to raise their son to be a man, a good man, a responsible man, a kind man, a man like him. But fate was always so cruel, that even this little wish of hers would be shattered.

54

Preparation

Aary closed Elior's diary and pressed it on his chest.

He finally understood. Everything. Everything about Elior that was so mysterious and unexplainable, it was all clear now. He learnt about his whole life. The happiest memory and the deepest pain, even the moments that Elior himself wanted to forget, all were now revealed to Aary. Now he finally understood why Elior was the way he was, why he felt that Elior always had a protective shell around his soul that no one could see through. He also understood everything that Elior had done for him. His own son was dead and he was never able to love again. Yet, he loved Aary as if he was his own son.

His son had Maire's black hair and Elior's green eyes, and Aary's appearance must have reminded him of his little baby from the first time he laid eyes on him. He put all his hopes, his wishes, and his expectations on Aary, because he knew that he couldn't face the Dark Kingdom himself. But he didn't want the same tragedy that happened to him happen to Aary, so he made only a few people aware that he had chosen Aary as his heir. To most people, even Aary himself, he was just a service boy or a toy of his. He also had to make Aary strong and tough, much stronger and tougher than he was himself. He did every-thing he could to train Aary to be better than him, to get used to pain and be a better fighter, and also to learn everything that he should from the books and the meetings. But still, he needed to pretend and act in front of him, hide away all his emotions, and bear the unbearable pain in his heart every time he had Aary punished.

Pain, that was the theme of Elior's life. How much pain he had gone through in such a short life! Pain had pierced through most of his life, from his childhood to his death. His one final wish was for his life to be ended by Aary, before the darkness came and tore him apart. At least this time, he got what he wished for.

Between the last page of the diary and the back cover was a letter. On the outside of the letter were some words written in blood. The dried old blood was a kind of dark scarlet color, but there was no mistaking what it was from the disgusting smell it still bore. The handwriting was very difficult to read due to the running of the blood, but Aary managed to make out the words: "To Elior" and "Dark Kingdom". The seal was already broken, so he just unfolded the parchment.

Dear Elior, our old friend,

Thank you for uniting the plain for us, you have done well. You know that we have one more task for you. As we agreed, you would open the gate and hand over your kingdom to us when the time was right. That time has come now. Next autumn, when the first full moon ascends, we will march towards the castle in full strength. All you need to do is to announce your submission and loyalty to us in public, and order that for anyone who disobeys, the penalty will be death. Then no harm will come to you or your people. You have served us well and we remember that. We also hope that you still remember the wonderful time we spent together.

Prince of the Dark Kingdom,

Nameless

Aary could almost feel the outrage and pain Elior must have felt when he read this letter. He must have wanted more than anything to face and eliminate the Dark Kingdom himself, but he knew that he had no choice. That was why he had decided to leave this task to Aary, whom he personally trained to be a warrior and a thinker, hoping that Aary could accomplish what he couldn't.

But... could he? Aary felt the weight on his shoulders was almost unbearable. "Next autumn, when the first full moon arises", that's less than half a year from now. How could he, a half-child with no experience in leading a battle whatsoever, get ready in half a year and lead this most important war in which no defeat was allowed, facing the most powerful and dreadful enemy? He knew that it would determine the fate of everyone on the plain. If they failed, the world would be ruled by darkness. How could he do it? He just couldn't!

Then he remembered Nana Hadden's words. "Remember, you're not in this alone. You have us, all of us." Those words calmed him down and put sense back into his mind. It was true. He wouldn't be facing the Dark Kingdom alone. He had the wisest advisors and commanders in the whole kingdom, whom Elior trusted. He had the invincible army made of the fiercest fighters that Elior trained himself over the years, which was so much larger now than when he conquered the plain.

There was still half a year's time to prepare. He needed to have confidence, have faith in himself and the others. If even he didn't believe in himself, didn't believe that they would win, how could the others trust him and follow him? The Dark Kingdom was best at playing with people's minds, and they could locate even the slightest doubt in their enemies and magnify it, until the enemies collapsed from within. Time was short. Instead of wasting it worrying and doubting himself, what he should be, and must be doing, was to grasp every second they have to prepare for it, so that they could be ready by autumn. After all, before the darkness falls, there's still time for everything.

Within a week's time, Aary held a public succession ceremony. But he knew that, to really have people accept him as their king, he needed to do more than that. Before calling a Grand Council meeting for the preparation of the war, he visited all the advisors and commanders one by one, to let them know about the war to come and make sure that he had their support. He did this to show his respect, and let them know that this war couldn't be won without them. Some visits were easy, and he got full support of the person right away. Others were more difficult, especially the older, more experienced, and highborn people, who didn't trust this young, inexperienced boy without royal blood. But Aary wasn't angry at all. He just said to everyone, in a calm but firm voice:

"I know you might think that I'm not qualified to be your king and lead this war. I'm not Elior's son, and I might be even younger than your children. I totally understand. But the war is near and we don't have the time to fight among us. If we don't work together, the war will most certainly be lost, and the whole plain will be shrouded in darkness. Therefore, I will be the king during this time because Elior named me, but once the war is over, I would like to hand the reign over to whoever made the greatest contribution in the war. Anyone will be eligible, and this decision will be made by everyone in the Grand Council in the form of a vote. But before that, may I please have your full support in both strength and counsel? Will you give everything you can to this war?"

Every person who heard this was totally shocked when these words were spoken. They were surprised by the wisdom and modesty of this young man. There wasn't a single king in known history that would voluntarily give up his reign, let alone letting other people decide who will succeed. Anyone was eligible. It also meant that even they could become the king themselves if they give out their best for the war. What reason did they have to refuse?

One by one, but quickly, Aary got the support of all advisors and commanders. However, he didn't forget about one last person. This might be the most difficult visit of all, and he could almost still feel the pain in his shoulder when he thought of the name. But he knew he needed to do it. He needed him if he wanted to win this war. He had to put all personal feelings aside now, because had a greater responsibility. He needed to do what was right no matter how hard it was for him. He needed to do it.

* * *

A few days later, those beings came back. Their purpose was clear: to kill his son. They went directly towards Jerre and Maire's house with swords in their hands. When she saw them through the window, she knew their intention right away with a mother's instinct. She was almost paralyzed by the fear, but she knew she had to protect him. She was all that poor baby had, and she needed to be there for him. Whether the person she loved was Jerre, the name that she knew, or Elior, the name the strangers were calling out for, it did not matter, because she loved him. And this was his child, her only hope.

55

Commander Bobor

Aary knew that Bobor used to be the most respected commander in the kingdom before Elior's return. Elior didn't give him many important tasks, because he thought that Bobor was too old and conservative, especially when he offered too much advice that he didn't need or want. But Aary knew that Bobor still had an unfaltering position in the hearts of the soldiers because of his ability and experience. Compared to Greig, Bobor was more thoughtful and strategic. Unlike Elior who dominated all the decisions, Aary needed others, and he needed Bobor's commanding abilities and counsel. And, hard for him to admit it, but personally, Aary admired him. He was frustrated that Bobor didn't like him and was even more frightened of him after he was shot. He really wanted, and really needed, to gain the trust and support of Bobor, however hard it would be.

When the jail keeper opened the iron bars to Bobor's cell and announced Aary's arrival, the man was eating. Weeks of prison life hadn't changed him much. He was still dressed very neatly, with the usual stern, upright manner. When Aary entered, he continued his meal as if nothing had happened, not even looking up from his plate. Commander Bobor thought that Aary must have come to humiliate him before executing him. He made up his mind that he would rather die with honor, than kneel and beg in front of this boy king.

Aary, on the other hand, was acting like a child being blamed for a mistake. He lowered his head, and said respectfully: "Commander Bobor, I'm here to pardon you and reinstate your position as the High Commander. That is, of course, if you would accept it."

Bobor was obviously surprised, as the cutting action of a piece of broccoli on his plate stopped. After a few seconds passed, he continued the cutting movement and delivered the broccoli into his mouth with the fork, still without looking up.

"Is this some kind of a trick?" Bobor said, with a bit of sarcasm in his voice, "If you think offering me pardon and reinstatement can make me do whatever you want and make a fool of myself, save your breath and send me to the guillotine. Do you think that I can't see what you are doing? If you want to kill me, do as you wish. But if you want to see me beg for mercy and kiss your feet like a dog, sorry to disappoint you, but that won't happen. And who knows if you will still kill me in the end. Don't take me for a fool."

"I take you for a man of honor, Commander Bobor, a man that is loyal to the kingdom and the people." Aary said sincerely, "There is no trick. I won't ask you to do anything unreasonable. I don't even ask that you kneel and call me your king. I don't care if I'm king or not. All I care about right now is the fact that the Dark Kingdom will be coming for us in less than six moons time, and if we lose, we lose everything. Believe me, I don't want the responsibility, but Elior gave it to me, and I have no choice. I can't abandon all the people on the whole plain and just run away to save my own life. You are the most experienced and respected commander in the kingdom. The soldiers look up to you, and trust you. If you don't resume your position, half of the army's strength will be gone, and we can't afford that. There's no one that can replace you in the army. At this critical moment, we need all the power and intelligence we can get, and you are far too important to stay out of it."

Aary stepped outside the cell, and returned a second later with a bow and a quiver, Bobor's bow and quiver. It was the bow that he had used to shoot Aary and the arrow that was pulled out from his shoulder was cleaned and put back in the quiver. Aary knelt down on one knee and held out the bow and quiver.

"Please, Commander Bobor. I beg that you set aside whatever feelings you have about me and go back to your military position. You're not doing this for me, but for thousands of innocent people: farmers, fishermen, their wives and children. They can't protect themselves against an enemy as powerful as the Dark Kingdom, they need the army to protect them. And the army needs you, the kingdom needs you. I would willingly take another hundred arrows if you would go back to your position and lead the army."

Bobor suddenly felt a shiver in his heart and something that was hard as a rock softened like melting ice. He realized that Aary really meant it.

When he was put in the dungeon, he knew that he wouldn't live for much longer, especially when he heard that Aary survived the poison, and became the new king after Elior died. He was getting ready to embrace death any time soon, and all he hoped for was that it would be clean and quick without too much torture, though he knew that even that was too much to ask. No one in history ever had the luck of an easy death when being caught after a nearly successful assassination. Also, considering how much torture Aary had suffered at Elior's hands, Bobor was expecting that this boy who was used to living in pain would probably think of the worst and cruelest punishment for him. But now, Aary, this young, lowborn boy, who only just learnt that he was the heir and then became the king, was kneeling down in front of the person in the dungeon, the person that shot him with a poisoned arrow that almost killed him, begging him to resume his position. His wound had not even healed yet and still wrapped up tightly in cotton.

Bobor felt unbearable shame rising in his heart. Aary was begging him to fight for the plain and the people. He was willing to forget and forgive all the wrong that Bobor had done to him because he was thinking of the whole picture. Young as he was, he had the biggest heart and broadest mind of all the men that Bobor had met. He had the qualities that Bobor himself never had. It seemed that Elior had made the right choice after all, and this young man that was kneeling in front of him, might be the wisest and greatest king the kingdom had ever seen. And what did that make him? A foolish, blind, arrogant old man who always thought his own cause the most righteous one, a criminal that had done something terribly wrong.

Bobor's knees touched the ground in a loud *thump* and he reached out his shaking hands to receive the bow and quiver that Aary was holding out for him. Tears of shame, regret, apology, and gratitude shone in his eyes. He looked at Aary's sincere pleading face and said in a trembling voice:

"I am so sorry. You are the true king, the real king. You are my king. Your Grace, please forgive me for the unforgivable sins that I've done. I will do whatever Your Grace commands. You have my sword, my bow, my life. I will protect, fight for, and die for Your Grace, the kingdom, and the people, to the best of this useless old man's ability."

* * *

At the last minute, she grabbed the basket which the baby was sleeping in, and jumped out the back window. She ran as fast as possible, away from the village, away from those hooded bandits. When they saw her, they all jumped on their horses and chased after her. But the strength and speed that a mother can reach when protecting her child was unbelievable. Even the horses couldn't reach her. She ran and ran, while the hoofs of the black horses followed closely behind, until she could run no further.

56

Peace before the Thunderstorm

As the tiresome summer heat gradually turned into cooler breezes, the endless calling of the bustling bugs also quietened down to let people breathe. Undoubtably, everyone could read the signs that summer was ending. If these days had been in the past, it would mean that the harvesting season was coming, and everyone would be excited and getting ready for the last round of busy work before they could rest for the winter with abundant food in their barns and warming fires in their houses. But this year, no one could spare any mind to think about that anymore. Summer was ending. It also meant that the war that would determine everyone's fate was drawing near.

Aary gained the trust and respect of people quickly during this time. When he first claimed the throne, more people doubted and questioned him than obeyed and followed him. It definitely wasn't easy. And Aary's solution was to try to do his best and prove himself worthy, instead of punishing anyone that didn't obey him. He knew that in order to have the best chances of victory in the war to come, he needed the support of as many people as possible. And by support, it meant real support from the bottom of their hearts, it meant knowing that he could count on them to try their best in the face of danger, it meant that they needed to believe in him and what they were doing. He would not force anyone to obey him, because pretend support that was given under pressure or threat would mean nothing when the real enemy came.

At the start of summer, after talking to everyone in the Grand Council one by one, Aary knew that he was getting there, albeit slowly. The officers and commanders in the Grand Council were the most prestigious men and women in the whole kingdom, the best in their fields. Gaining their individual support meant gaining the support of their supporters, and in turn gaining the support of the kingdom. Aary was doing well.

Aary also invited Rudi into the castle and named him one of the King's High Advisors. He did this because he knew very well that he needed all the brains he could get, and Rudi often had some bizarre but good ideas. It raised some eyebrows at first, because many people had never seen a tree elf before and thought Rudi was a monster. Some people even thought he was a Shadow Knight. But Rudi was neither evil nor did he know how to ride a horse.

He did act quite silly, though, and that was the main reason, or excuse, many people mentioned when they advised Aary against including Rudi in the Council. Aary could see why they thought that. Rudi never concealed his amazement and surprise when he saw something new that he had never seen before, and the city was full of those kinds of wonders. He would suddenly shout out and run to a marble statue and gaze at the magnificent stone man with eyes and mouth wide open or marvel at some delicious food with utter exaggeration and tears in his eyes. He always acted like a little kid, despite being 112 years of age. But Aary just explained patiently to those people, that Rudi was actually very old, and thus very experienced and wise, and that he was his personal friend as well, until they shrugged and accepted the fact that this weird little creature was indeed staying.

As soon as Aary felt that he was ready, he called a Grand Council meeting, in which he invited both Lyna and Rudi to attend.

"My lords, advisors, and commanders, thank you all very much for coming." Aary began, "You must already know the reason why I called you here today. The Dark Kingdom is going to come for us in a few moon's time. You all know their reputation. This is not going to be easy, and we be well prepared, if we want to have the slightest chance of defeating them. And I cannot do it without every one of you. I know that you are the best minds and swords of this kingdom, so I trust that together, we can come up with a perfect plan. So now, may I ask that everyone please speak out any ideas and thoughts that you have, even the ones that sound irrelevant? I'll take notes."

At first, all the high officers and commanders seemed at a bit of loss. The last king Elior had never asked for anyone's opinion. He only trusted the words of a few, and for the others, he had only commands. But now Aary was asking for opinions from every single member of the Grand Council, and acting as if he, the king, was just a secretary that records the meeting. They didn't know if he actually meant it or had some other plans in mind. A few of the most prestigious advisors were digging hard into their brains, hoping to come up with some really clever and brilliant plan that would impress the king and every-one else. However, none of them could think of anything elaborate and sophisticated enough, and they didn't want to get laughed at if they said something that might sound silly and simple. But there was someone that wasn't afraid of saying silly things.

Rudi was the first to break the silence.

"Well, I don't know much about them," Rudi spoke as if he was talking to Aary alone, "but since it's called the Dark Kingdom, I guess they are afraid of the light, right? Or else they wouldn't be called the Dark Kingdom, would they? So maybe if we shine bright light at them, we can blind them to death! If only we could save the sunlight during daytime and bring it out when they come at night... not that I know how to do it... just saying..."

Some suppressed laughter could be heard in the silent hall.

"Thank you, Rudi, that's a very good point." Aary responded, con-templating the words that Rudi had just said, "Maybe we can use fire. Fire arrows, oil barrows. We can dip all the weapons in oil and light them up, that will definitely make us more powerful when dealing with the Shadow Knights." He jotted something down on the parchment in front of him.

The laughter from just a moment ago was gone. People realized that, in this meeting, there were no stupid ideas. The king wouldn't laugh at anything people offered, but he would be disappointed if there were no ideas.

"Your Grace," said an old adviser that Elior used to trust more than anyone, "the Dark Kingdom's greatest weapon is fear and mind-control. They like to show off all the power they have and let their enemy break from inside, and submit to them, before the real violence even starts. But we can actually turn that to our advantage, because we can hide our power, pretend to be scared, and surprise them. Because of how powerful they are and their successes in the past, they are arrogant, and believe that everyone is afraid of them. True, they practice certain types of dark magic that allow them to live for thousands of years and easily kill a man in a one-on-one combat, and they might play a trick or two that can scare an ordinary person to death, but they are not invincible, as a lot of people tend to believe. We must take them seriously and do the best we can, but we must also have faith in ourselves and believe that we have the power to defeat them. They are very good at locating the negative feelings in people: fear, doubt, jealousy, selfishness... and magnifying them by a thousand times. So, we must control our own minds, leaving them no gap to break in."

Other people started to speak up, saying things that might sound obvious or not thought through. Even those warriors, who only knew how to fight, and had never even said a single word apart from "yes, Your Grace" in all of the past Grand Council meetings, were saying things that they thought of. Aary listened carefully to the ideas and thoughts coming to him from all across the hall, and took down each one of them.

The meeting adjourned at dinner time, when Aary asked the royal kitchen to cook a feast to show his gratitude, and resumed the next morning. It lasted for a total of three days, and Aary continued to work into the evenings to reorganize the scattered ideas, deleting some that were repeated, and rephrasing some that he jotted down in a rush.

From all the ideas, Aary gradually made up a rough plan, which was refined over time with more ideas. Then he listed the things that they needed to prepare before the war, and assigned suitable tasks to everyone. He already knew the strengths and weaknesses of most people in the Grand Council from all the meetings that he attended with Elior over the years, and he also knew about people's relationships, who hated whom and who could work well with whom. He never really thought about these things that he knew, and less did he expect that they would become useful one day. But there they were, all coming to him naturally, which surprised even he himself.

He also appointed a smaller council that would meet regularly, to further perfect the details of the plan and update him on the progress of the preparations. Commanders Bobor and Greig were both leading training sessions but safely away from each other. The advisors that Elior trusted the most were also the ones that gave Aary the most useful ideas.

The longer Aary was King, the more he realized that Elior was such a wise and smart ruler, and had put everything exactly in place, so he didn't really need to do much apart from maintaining the work that Elior had already done. Sometimes, he even felt as if Elior was still there, helping him, guiding him, and smiling at him through his half-closed, contemptuous, light-green eyes.

But compared to Elior, who listened to no one and looked down on everyone, Aary's attitude and personality was very different. His modesty and sincerity won him hearts more quickly and easily. He would go and personally check every link of the chain in the preparations. Regardless of the fact that he was the King, he would help anyone with anything, whenever he could, even if it was helping a laborer carry a dirty heavy rock. Actually, he often forgot the fact that he was the King himself, and acted like a humble no one, like what he used to be. He never asked to punish anyone that was failing to do their work, but would go and ask the reason and try to help them if he could. From the highest officers and commanders, to the lowest and poorest workers, not a single person disliked their new King after meeting him.

The blacksmith in the city offered to make Aary a suit of armor. He had never worn armor before. But on the other hand, he also had never been in a battle, apart from the one in Rocky Vill, where he was just a kid without even proper weapons. He was really excited when the blacksmith presented him with a dashing light-golden armor with gilded red patterns on the shoulder plates and chest, and a black cape behind it. The armor was really lightweight but strong. When he put it on, he could move as freely as he did wearing his usual clothes.

The first leaf turned from green to red, announcing the arrival of autumn in a silent, beautiful way. Autumn was the most beautiful and the most comfortable season on Hilldown Plain. The sun had shed the intoxicating heat and cruelness of summer, yet still bringing warmth to the earth even when it was swept by the cooling breeze. The sky was infinite and transparent. The blue seemed unrealistically pure and clean, with not a single cloud at most times.

When there were clouds in the sky, they were always white and unstained. Some huddled up in soft fluffy bundles of cotton, some were wiped by the wind and spread in a thin layer across the sky like butter on a piece of bread. But no cloud could block the bright light of the sun, and the earth fell into a sweet little nap under the gentle caress of the sunlight. The weather was extraordinarily pleasant that autumn. It would have been a perfect season, if not for the coming war that threatened to dye the beautiful earth the color of blood.

But the war was inevitable. If they won, they might be able to free Hilldown Plain from the threat of the Dark Kingdom for good, and Elior would get his revenge. If they lost, however, the Kingdom of El-berkhan would be gone, and darkness would rule over the whole plain, maybe even the whole world.

All the preparations were done. The traps were in place all around and inside the city, the granaries were all full with enough food to support the city for months in case of a siege, the army was well-trained, organized, and rested with the best commanders in charge, weapons had been sharpened and armor shined. Everyone and every-thing were ready for them, waiting for their arrival. No one knew if the Shadow Knights would come at the promised time in the letter, though. They seemed to have eyes and ears everywhere, and surely, after several months, they would have heard that Elior was dead. Aary tried to keep all the war preparation as quiet as possible, but he needed to warn people about their coming. If the Dark Kingdom knew that he was preparing for war instead of surrender...

The night when the first full moon arose, the whole city held its breath. No one could fall asleep, but everyone was pretending to be sleeping. Sentries stood on top of every wall and tower, watching closely into the darkness of the night. All the women and children, the sick and the old, were hidden in the city library, the grandest and, oddly enough, strongest tower in the whole city, to give them one more layer of protection in case the enemies breached the gate and sacked the city. Aary himself was waiting in the throne room dressed in his new suit of armor. It was ordered that if anyone saw any movement, instead of blowing the war horn like they usually did, they should report to the closest of the messengers posted at each corner of the city, who would then inform the King and the commanders.

Lyna and Rudi waited with Aary in the throne room. He told them to hide in the library as well since they wouldn't be fighting in the war and couldn't defend themselves, but they insisted on staying with him before the battle started, which he really appreciated. Even though he had been acting like a confident King who knew what he was doing, so as to give his people strength and faith which they desperately needed in the face of such powerful enemies, Aary knew that, deep down, he was still a frightened boy who needed his friends' comfort and support, and they knew that too.

So, they waited, and waited, and waited... Several hours passed. Rudi and Lyna said a few encouraging words from time to time, but no one was in the mood for a lengthy conversation of substance, so most of the time they just waited in silence. The moon outside the window rose and fell, and Aary started to doze off. He dreamt that Elior walked into the throne room, wearing his light silver armor and carrying his bow and sword. He gave Aary a contemptuous sneer, and said: "Can't believe someone was stupid enough to actually think that he could be the King and defeat the Dark Kingdom." Then he called out to his men, who followed him into the room in orderly lines, "give this unabashed boy the punishment he deserves. But do it after the battle. I need him to lead my right wing. Greig, you take the left. Bobor, ready my horse. I'm leading the vanguard."

Aary had never felt so happy to see Elior in all his life. He was even excited about being beaten. What was a beating compared to all the pressure and responsibly that he faced when Elior wasn't here! He didn't need to play the King anymore. He promised to himself that this time he would really pay attention to what Elior did, and learn from the great King...

Suddenly, a round of hastened knocks pulled Aary violently out of his dream. He was alone in the throne room again, only with Lyna and Rudi accompanying him, both of whom had startled looks on their faces at the sudden knocks. Elior was gone. A soldier pushed through the door.

"Your Grace," the messenger said, breathing heavily from the running, "they're here!"

* * *

A wide river blocked her way, and she could hear the sound of the hoofs coming towards her. The water flowed endlessly in front of her, relentlessly. It had been flowing for thousands of years, and would keep on flowing for thousands of years more. There was no point in hoping that it would stop at this moment, even if it was obstructing the way to survival of two beautiful souls. It was just a river, with no feelings. The clear water reflected her grieving, beautiful face. In despair, she put the little basket into the water.

The War

Chen Yuxiao

57

⚜

Crossing Swords

Aary hugged Rudi and Lyna farewell, and jumped onto his horse to ride to the city gate, where the first sentry had noticed movements. He climbed atop the gatehouse, his mind lingering on the dream he had just had. He was wondering if he was still dreaming, when he saw a large patch of shadow creeping towards the castle. He tried to see it more clearly and make some sense of it, but realized that it wasn't possible. The moon was hanging low in the sky, round and big. And the silver moonlight was shining bright on everything, but that was, everything apart from the shadow.

The area that the shadow covered was nothing but total darkness, pure, pitch-black, like looking down into a bottomless abyss. Aary wondered if there was something wrong with his eyes, because he had never seen anything like this. It reminded him of the cave he went in to look for the lava demon, where the light of the sun never reached. But this wasn't in a cave, it was on the plain, under a bright full moon, but still, no light reached the area of the shadow. It was growing quickly, too. It was leaking out from the darkened forest and spreading across the open ground, covering the earth like a thick black blanket, or black ink spilt over a table, devouring all the lights it reached. Aary felt an indescribable fear rising in himself. Growing like this, the darkness would cover the whole plain and swallow them all. It seemed like the end of the world. In addition, he could hear a low, rumbling sound, and felt that the ground beneath him was trembling, shaking the bricks of the gatehouse he was on. His heart was shaking with it too.

"Your Grace? What is the order?"

The question from Commander Bobor brought Aary back to reality and his senses. When he started thinking clearly again, Aary realized that the enemy that they were facing wasn't the mysterious, impenetrable, untouchable darkness, but the creatures of the Dark Kingdom, real, living creatures that they could touch, that they could kill.

But that would be easier said than done. There must be hundreds of thousands of them. The dark blanket covered the whole area all the way from the forest to more than halfway to the castle, and was still growing without any hint of an end. And they must be on horses too, judging from the rumble and tremble. And worst of all, he couldn't see them. He couldn't see anything but the thick, seamless darkness. How could they fight an enemy they couldn't see?

"Ready the fire arrows," Aary commanded, "but don't make any movement visible from outside the castle. They might be still thinking that they can take the castle without any effort, that I or whoever the King is would hand it over to them. If it's like that, we need to take full advantage of it. Tell our troops to pay attention to the signal."

"Yes, Your Grace."

Instead of yelling out the command in the way it used to be done, a line of messengers waiting next to the King got the order and spread out. Each of them ran to the location they were assigned to, and reported to another line of messengers, who then ran to each commander on the wall. Each commander was in charge of twenty archers, twenty free soldiers carrying spears or swords and torches, and three oil barrels. Behind the battlements, thousands of arrows had their heads dipped in oil, lit by torches, and nocked on bows. But all of these actions were done in silence. From outside the castle, the castle looked as peaceful as the moon in the sky. It seemed that everything and everyone were in a deep slumber, far away in their dreamlands.

Aary held his breath as he watched the darkness spread in front of his eyes. He could see the dust kicked off by the hoofs of the horses, like a yellow smoke rising from the plain. His pupils enlarged in the dark of the night, and the torches on the wall were shining and dancing in his eyes. *Just a little closer,* he told himself, *a little more...*

When the front line of the dark riders finally reached within the range of the arrows, Aary put two fingers in his mouth, and blew out a clear, melodious string of four notes, like a bird's call in the morning forest. In no time, the bird-like whistle vanished in the dark sky, drowned out by the increasing sound of the horses.

Throop... Thousands of burning arrows left the top of the castle wall, drawing lines of dazzling light in the air and rushed down towards the enemy like seabirds diving into a school of fish. Everyone's eyes were fixed on the arrows and the moving shadow beneath them.

Their enemies didn't seem to notice the arrows, and didn't show the slightest hint of slowing down, until the arrows reached them. Then came the horrible sounds. Aary could identify the sound of horses screaming in pain, the sound of riders crashing into each other and tumbling down, but there were other sounds too, sounds that didn't sound like any animal and were definitely not human, sounds that he had never heard in his life. Aary felt a chill and the hair on his back standing up. The other men on the wall must have been scared by that sound too, because there was a moment of complete silence, before a cheer suddenly broke out. Their scheme of taking them by surprise worked.

Some arrows lit up small patches of fire on the dry autumn grass, and the whole area of shadow was finally not completely black. It was very chaotic, but Aary could still make out figures of horses and riders in black capes and hoods in the dim light. He opened his eyes wide, but it was still impossible to see what weapons they were carrying and if they had other facilities for sieging and storming the castle. Before they could be happy for too long, the fires were all put out by the hoofs and the dust, leaving nothing but darkness again.

Suddenly, Aary heard a coarse whispering voice in his ears: "You foolish people. We gave you the chance to hand over your kingdom in peace. We gave you the chance to live, and you threw it away."

Startled, he turned to look, but saw no one beside him. He realized that everyone else that he saw was also looking around themselves with unconcealable horror on their faces. *They all heard it*, he told himself in disbelief, and the voice started again.

"However, the generous Shadow Prince will give you one more chance, your last chance. Throw down your weapons and hand over the kingdom now, and we will take only the same number of lives to make up for our deaths. We will even grant the rest of you eternal life. But, if you choose to fight against us, death will befall every one of you. The era of darkness has come. Our era has come. There is no point in fighting against what must come to be." Then it repeated, "The era of darkness has come. Our era has come."

Aary felt light-headed and confused. The whispering voice seemed to be putting him to sleep. He felt really tired. For a moment, he forgot what he was doing there, forgot why he was there. He just wanted to lie down and let sleep take him away.

No! A voice inside himself called out to him, *fight it! Resist it! Don't let it take you away!* It sounded like Elior.

He shook his head violently and cleared the sleepiness away. He also noticed that everyone else was in a trance like he was.

"No!" He shouted, like the voice inside him, "fight it! Resist it! Don't let it take you away!" He shouted and shouted again, and shook the people standing close to him by the shoulders. One by one, they came back to their senses, looked around in confusion, and finally joined Aary in waking up the others after this realization.

"Don't let them control your mind!" Aary called out, when most people were awake now, "That's what they're best at! Resist the voice! Make noise yourselves. Then you won't hear it."

"Yes, Your Grace!"

"Yes, Your Grace!"

There was no need to hide and be quiet anymore. War horns were blown, commanders were shouting commands, and more fire arrows were shot from the castle wall. But during that short period of their immobility, their enemies had already managed to cover the rest of the ground and reach the moat of the city.

The army of darkness arrived in front of the wide, torrential river, and stopped. The drawbridge was long pulled up, and the river was deep and treacherous enough to drown any horse with its rider. Fire arrows showered like rain from atop the wall, but they didn't seem to cause damage anymore. What they did do was light up the air so that people on the wall could see their enemy more clearly. They saw that all the beings below were wearing large black capes with hoods pulled over their heads. And when the arrows reached their black capes, suddenly they acted as if they had forgotten what they were doing there in the first place, losing all their direction and their fire, then falling onto the ground like autumn leaves. Even their horses were wearing skull helmets. Only the very few arrows that happened to reach a horses' shoulders or legs would cause the horses to rear in fear and shake off their riders. But for the number of Shadow Knights outside the castle walls, those casualties were nothing.

One rider stepped forward from the army. His whole face was covered by the black hood he was wearing, so no one on the castle wall could see his face. The rider drew his long sword and pointed it downward until the sharp tip of the sword reached the bank of the river. He whispered something, and under everyone's astonished gaze, the river began to freeze under his sword. More riders came forward and drew out their swords, touching the bank of the river and whispering spells. Ice started to form from the outer bank where they were, slowly growing across the river. Everyone in the castle knew that the Green Water never froze, not even during the coldest of winters. The constantly rushing torrents just made it impossible for any ice to form without getting crushed and drifting away. And yet there it was, right in front of their eyes, forming a solid, thick layer of ice across the river. A few horses already stepped their hoofs on the ice and got closer to the castle walls.

Everyone in the castle felt it too. The cold. A gush of wind blew, and

Aary felt as if it was suddenly the middle of the winter. The chill penetrated his thin armor that was designed to be light and flexible instead of warm, went past his clothes, and cut right through his bones. The ominous wind blew out several torches on the wall, and pulled some clouds over the full bright moon. The world darkened.

The Elberkan archers continued to shoot fire arrows, but with little effect. Many of them were blown off by the wind before they even reached the enemy, others were extinguished by their capes. The arrows that did reach the ice did no more than melt a little dent on the surface, before they too were put out by the cold ice.

Aary knew that they needed something else, something more powerful.

"Cast the fireballs!" he commanded.

The "fireballs" were actually stones wrapped up in cotton tied with straw and soaked in oil. On each ball, one thread of straw was left especially long. One soldier lit up the extended thread with a torch in his hand and put it on a sheet of wet hide that was held by another two soldiers between them before the fire reached the main part of the ball. Then, just as the ball itself started burning, the two soldiers tossed their arms forward in unison and the fireballs were flung into the air like dazzling suns. The range was definitely shorter than catapults, but they didn't have time to build enough catapults and the advantage of this was that they could reload and shoot again in much shorter time.

It worked. When they designed this strategy, the fireballs were intended to be shot a little bit further than the other side of the riverbank. But now they didn't even need to throw that far because the enemy was going onto the ice. The heavy stones on the inside dragged the balls down to the ground, and gained enough speed on the long fall from the top of the castle walls. Then, when they finally reached the surface, the heavy, burning fireballs crushed people, horses, and ice alike.

Aary heard another round of cheers on top of the walls. But he knew it was too early for that. He watched closely everything happening below. More and more Shadow Knights were coming forward and joining the forming of the ice. The holes that the fireballs made were closed up shortly after the glaring fire vanished in the dark water. The Shadow Knights seemed to be coming endlessly. The moving dark shadows covered every inch of ground from the castle to the edge of the forest. For every Shadow Knight killed another took his place. The ice kept forming, and the riders kept pressing on closer and closer to the castle gate.

Suddenly, within ten feet from Aary, one of the soldiers throwing the fireballs shouted in pain and fell down on his back. He let go of his corner of the hide, and the fireball that had already been loaded bounced off and hit another solider, setting his sleeve on fire. The soldier that caught on fire screamed and rolled around on the ground. That caught Aary's attention. He ran over to help, and threw the wet hide over that soldier, which finally stopped the fire. Just when everyone around them was praising the King for saving a common soldier's life and checking the burnt wound of that soldier, Aary turned to look at the first soldier that fell down and realized that he was gone.

Surprised and confused, he turned around to look for him. His brain almost blanked out in shock, when he saw that, the exact soldier that he was looking for, was standing right behind his back, raising his sword, and hacking it down at him.

* * *

She took the ring he had given her off her finger, and hid it under the little blanket that her son was lying on. The ring was so pretty, with delicately carved patterns and her name on it. But more importantly, he made it for her. He was the love of her life, the father of her son. She knew that she would never see him again, but if someone could find their child and save him, maybe this ring made from pure gold might be worth a few coins, that could be exchanged for some clothes and food for their baby.

58

Light and Heat

At the last moment, Aary drew his sword in horror, and was just in time to block the attack. But that first blow was so hard that it brought Aary to his knees. That soldier didn't stop. He slashed and hacked at Aary with full strength and speed. Aary struggled to defend himself but he was at a disadvantage and was pressed down almost to the floor. Just when he felt that he was about to break, a sharp, shiny sword's end appeared from the soldier's chest and the sword that he was using to hack at Aary fell from his hand.

Commander Bobor pushed the soldier's body aside and withdrew his own sword from the soldier's back to give Aary a hand and help him up. Aary thanked him, but his tongue froze when he saw that the blood left on Bobor sword was not red, but black. Bobor saw it too.

Aary flipped the dead man over. There wasn't any obvious wound apart from the hole in his heart that Bobor made. He wasn't shot by an arrow, as Aary expected. Both he and Commander Bobor knelt down beside the body to take a closer look and noticed that there was something on his right cheek. Aary tore a piece of cloth from the dead soldier's sleeve, and pulled the thing out with the protection of the cloth. Commander Bobor grabbed a torch, and the two of them closely examined the thing under the light of the torch.

It was a very small, pointy object, like a wood splinter, but purely black. The pointy end that was buried in the man's cheek had some kind of sticky black residue on it.

"It must be this." Aary said, frowning, "somehow they shot it from down below, maybe with something like blowpipes."

Commander Bobor agreed, "It must be poisonous, or had some kind of a spell on it, that turned our man into theirs."

"We have to warn everyone." Standing up from the corpse of the dead soldier, Aary shouted: "Watch out for anyone that suddenly falls down or anyone that behaves abnormally! They might be controlled or turned!"

"Yes, Your Grace! But... you might want to have a look at this..."

Aary leaned over the edge of the wall and looked down between the battlements. While he had been dealing with the chaos up there, down below, the enemy had managed to form solid ice all the way across the river and had ridden their horses to the castle gate.

"Okay..." Aary murmured to himself, then called out the commands: "Archers! Keep showering them with fire arrows. Don't give them any break! Fireball crew! You don't need to throw them anymore, just tip them over the edge and the weight of the stones will do the work. Whatever you do, don't let them climb onto the walls!"

But soon he realized, the Shadow Knights weren't thinking about climbing up the walls at all. The ones that reached the walls jumped off from their horses and started digging on the ground. And the speed was unbelievable. Not even moles could dig that fast. In less than a minute, the holes were deep enough to conceal the Shadow Knights that were digging them. Aary had never seen anything like it.

Of course, Aary thought, blaming himself for not being prepared for this, *the whole of Dark Kingdom was said to be hidden in tunnels and caves, they must have some special skills for this.* Aary pressed hard on his temples. What should they do now? All the things they prepared were for keeping the enemy from going over the walls, because no one had ever imagined that it'd be possible to get through under the walls.

The foundations of the walls were buried deep under the earth. Even the iron gate had metal bars buried beneath it with dangerous spikes poking out to prevent any tunnel diggers. It would take a normal army of men with spades days, or even weeks, to dig a tunnel under the walls from outside of the city. But judging from the digging speed of these creatures, it might be less than a few more minutes before they appeared on the other side of the wall.

The fire arrows and fireballs continued to shower down on them, but they were doing little harm to the Shadow Knights that had already hidden themselves in the tunnels. Even those that remained outside were protected by their thick filthy capes, which normal fire arrows could hardly penetrate. The fireballs were more deadly for sure, but they were impossible to aim and took too long to load. So, they were doing little good to stop the endless waves of Shadow Knights rushing towards the wall and starting to dig. Unlike the dry grass on the plain that could be easily lit by fire, the ground up here was frequently moistened by the splashes of water from the river and covered with wet moss. So, when the arrows or balls landed on the ground, the fire went out like lifeless fallen leaves.

"Your Grace, look!" Someone shouted. Aary turned around following the voice, and saw that the enemy had managed to get a first tunnel opened inside the castle gates. A big hole appeared on a street inside the city and the Shadow Knights in the tunnel emerged from it with their horses. Commander Greig's troop went over to meet them. They had been waiting inside the city under Aary's command and this was the exact moment that they were prepared for.

Their men surrounded the hole and the Shadow Knights and the first close encounter started. The sound of steel clashing, men yelling, and horses screaming came up and reached the wall. Aary saw that their own men out numbered the enemy, but the Shadow Knights fought like no human. He saw a Shadow Knight cutting a soldier in half with its sword, through armor and bones like slicing a piece of pudding. Other people on the wall saw it too, and Aary could see extreme fear in their eyes.

Another hole opened up in the ground not far away. Aary knew that

Greig's people wouldn't be able to hold them for much longer, and there were always more of them coming. Soon enough these merciless creatures would be all over the city, killing everyone they came across, and not long after they would find the library and start a massacre. Something had to be done to stop them, and had to be done right away.

Aary looked around aimlessly, his mind searching hard for any strategy to use. They needed something that could reach into the tunnels and kill the Shadow Knights in there, something that wouldn't stop even when it hit the ground, but would go all the way down, something that could fill all the tunnels with death... His eyes landed on the oil barrels.

"Commander Bobor, would you give me a hand?" Aary asked, as he grabbed two handles on the oil barrel next to him.

They had prepared those barrels only to soak the arrowheads and the cotton on fireballs. But to make it easier for the soldiers to carry the wooden barrels up to the top of the walls, iron handles had been fixed on the sides. No one had given an extra thought to those handles, but now they became of great use, as Aary was going to turn the barrels, which were originally prepared as storage facilities, into weapons.

Bobor grabbed two other handles on the barrel. Together they tried to lift it, but the barrel was so heavy that it hardly moved at all. Then Aary remembered. The barrels were empty when they were brought up and filled with oil later using smaller buckets. But now as they were full of oil, it was impossible for two men to lift it up. A few other soldiers saw them and came to their aid. Some reached their hands through the gaps between the bottom of the barrel and the floor, while others grabbed the iron hoops that were used to bind the wooden boards. Then, together, six of them lifted the barrel off the ground.

Under Aary's command, they slowly and carefully moved the barrel towards the outer edge of the wall and set it back down on the floor. Then, even more slowly, they tilted the barrel little by little on the bottom edge, until the oil inside started pouring out from the opening, along the wall, like a flood breaking the dam. Aary looked down. As the oil poured on the Shadow Knights beneath them, they grumbled angrily. One of them looked up, its face still hidden in the shadow. It was less than a second before Aary realized something, and yanked his head back. Something flew past his nose within an inch, and he knew immediately that it was the same thing that was shot at the soldier who tried to kill him.

Aary stepped back from the edge, and made a gesture to the three soldiers handling fireballs. One ball was already soaked in oil and loaded on the wet hide before the oil was poured out. The soldier with the torch lit up the thread, and the two soldiers holding the hide cast the ball out in three, two, one...

The ball burnt and flew. It seemed to take longer than usual for it to reach the ground, as Aary and other people's eyes were all fixed on it. But when it finally hit the ground, fire broke out like when a freshly fueled fireplace. The oil that had already soaked the ground and the Shadow Knights was lit up immediately by the blazing flame, and the world beneath became a sea of fire.

When Aary saw that it worked, he passed the words to other commanders on the wall. The oil barrels were poured out one after another, and fire arrows, fireballs, or even torches were thrown down to light up the fire. The burning flames soon connected, and became a new moat for the city, surrounding the walls and even down into the tunnels. The city was like an island standing in the middle of a fiery sea, and the men on the walls were looking down on the burning world. The flames burnt bright as the mid-day sun. The whole city, and the night sky, was gleaming in the flickering orange light. The Shadow Knights were like ants torched in the burning sea, screaming horribly and making crackling sounds as they burnt. This was even worse than the sounds they heard earlier. When those hooded enemies caught fire, the flames became a kind of dark purple color instead of bright orange, and suffocating black smoke arose, together with some kind of disgusting, pungent smell. Aary saw that a lot of them were crawling back out from the burning tunnels, stepping on their companions, dead or alive, to struggle for their own survival. But everywhere they went, it was all the same. Fire, smoke, and death.

Those Shadow Knights that were still a bit further back started pulling on their startled and uncontrollable horses to try to head back. Many of them were thrown off by the screaming horses, and got their skulls cracked open by the heavy hoofs, as their mounts decided to run for their own lives. Even the ones that managed to stay on the horses didn't have much more luck. The ice on the river started to melt from the heat of the fire. Large cracks split through the ice, opening up holes to the running water below. The horses struggled to even stand on the slippery ice and the broken ice tilted from their weights, opening up more holes that devoured the horses and riders on top.

The larger part of the Dark Kingdom army was still on the other side of the river. Seeing what happened to their confederates, they stopped going forward, watched from where they were for a while, and retreated, leaving the less fortunate of their kind burning and dying in the flames.

Cheers of victory burst from inside the castle. Soldiers hugged each other, ready to throw down their arms and start the celebration. But before long, the voice that whispered in their ears sounded again:

"Do you foolish people really think you can hide behind those walls forever? You people are even more ignorant than we think. Let's see how much cooking oil you have stored in that tiny city of yours. You better start working on your last words now."

Aary knew, however reluctant he was to admit it, that the enemy was right. They couldn't keep the flames going forever. Before the war, they collected almost all the oil that every family in the city had, and now they had already used it all. The fire at the foot of the walls was burning hot and bright, licking up the stone wall and pushing waves of heat towards the people on the top. The Shadow Knights that already crossed the river when the fire started to burn had all turned into ashes and smoke, the rest vanished at the edge of the forest. Even the few that already entered the city had been wiped out by commander Greig's troop and other soldiers waiting and patrolling inside the city, but not without cost. However, in less than a few hours, the fire would burn out. The Shadow Knights that they killed were only a negligibly small part of their army, and the main force of the army would come back, as they promised.

They needed fire that could be used without limit, fire that they could create any time they want. That was not a silly fantasy. Actually, Aary knew exactly how he could get that, but he was unwilling to do it, and with good reason.

After the Grand Council meeting in which they first drafted the plan for this war, Lyna talked to him in private: "Aary, you know that apart from the fire arrows and oil barrows that you mentioned, there's another way to create and use fire."

"What is it, Lyna?"

"Blackwind is your friend, and he can spit fire freely from his mouth. He said he was willing to do anything for you, so maybe he will be able to help us."

She was right. A fire breathing dragon would increase their chances of winning drastically. But Aary felt that he already owed Blackwind his life, and that he shouldn't ask the batwing dragon to risk his life again for Aary. He had absolutely nothing to do with this war and it wouldn't seem fair to drag him into this most dangerous situation. Also, what would the people think? A dragon in their army? Would they even trust him? Batwing dragons were usually considered vicious creatures that bring death to people. They probably would even consider him as part of the enemy's army. Aary had contemplated this for a very long time, and decided that he wouldn't call Blackwind unless he really needed to. Nevertheless, he put the wooden whistle, their agreed signal, in the pocket inside his armor.

At that moment, he was wondering if he should use it. It seemed pretty clear that the Shadow Knights didn't have any archers, nor any weapon that might reach high up into the air. So, it shouldn't be too risky. Also, they were indeed running out of oil, and there was nothing that they could use to stop the Shadow Knights from coming back and digging hundreds of tunnels under the walls, apart from normal arrows and stones, which hardly did any harm to them. So, in order to protect the city, they would have no choice but to charge out and meet the enemy in the open field.

They had seen the Shadow Knights fight. The average human soldier might stand a chance if three of them were fighting against one Shadow Knight. Even the greatest warriors and fighters, like Commanders Greig or Bobor, would have a really hard time fighting even one of the most unremarkable Shadow Knights. Hundreds and thousands of people would die. And the worst thing was, even the numbers were not in favor of them. They couldn't see clearly how many Shadow Knights were there, but they did cover up the whole area of thousands of acres as far as the castle could see, and there were probably more of them than the soldiers of Elberkan. How could they even stand a chance?

With a very mixed feeling, Aary reached into his pocket and took out the little wooden whistle, put it in his mouth, and blew it harder than he ever had before.

Not long after, a cheerful shriek arrived into Aary's ears from a distance. The sound was so familiar, exciting, and comforting at the same time. During the time that Aary waited for Blackwind, he passed on the order that no one was allowed to shoot an arrow into the sky and asked someone to fetch Lyna from the city library to be the translator.

In the meantime, the dimmest morning light started to turn the dark sky into a kind of lighter grey. Aary knew that the darkness wouldn't last for much longer. The Shadow Knights were known to seldom come out in daytime because they didn't like the sunlight. So most probably, they would be safe for now, until the next night arrived.

A black dot appeared at the edge of the sky, flapping up and down, and gradually grew bigger. Aary was thrilled. In no time, the little black dot turned into the familiar giant dragon that Aary owed his life to. The soldiers on the walls were terrified, but no one dared to disobey the king's order. Then, everyone opened their eyes wide when they saw that the dragon glided down from the sky and landed next to Aary. Aary threw himself on the big fellow, and hugged his neck tightly.

Shortly after Blackwind's landing, Lyna arrived too and was also really happy to see Blackwind. Aary had already told Blackwind everything when he hugged him, and Blackwind told Lyna what he wanted to say.

"Blackwind said he was happy to help." Lyna translated, "He asked if you could wait for a few hours. He could bring back three more dragons like him."

"What do you mean dragons like you?" Aary asked in confusion.

Blackwind lifted his head and spit a fire snake out of his mouth.

"You mean fire breathing dragons?" Aary asked, "aren't you the only one?"

Lyna answered for Blackwind: "He was, until his children were born."

"What?!" Aary gaped in surprise, "you are a father now?!!"

Blackwind called out proudly in response.

Aary hugged Blackwind again happily, but he hesitated about the offer. He already felt very bad for putting Blackwind at risk, how could he bring his children into danger too? But on the other hand, four fire breathing dragons could really turn the odds in their favor, and the dragons would be able to protect each other as well.

Blackwind read Aary's mind before he could figure out the words to say. The dragon rubbed his head against Aary, and lifted into the sky.

"Wait!" Aary called out. But it was too late. Blackwind only turned his head around and made one last call, before he vanished in the sky.

"He's going to bring them." Lyna said, "he said they were not fully grown yet, but they were almost as large as himself and very strong. They will help you defeat the darkness."

* * *

Accompanied by the baby's joyful giggles, the little basket swirled and turned and floated away with the river's movement. Maire felt a strike of happiness and relief. She hoped that the water would flow faster, and faster, taking her son away from these murderers. It would be just like a game for him, a rocking cradle in the arms of nature. Then someone with a kind heart would find him, adopt him, and raise him as if he was their own child. He would live a better and happier life than both of his parents, and he wouldn't remember anything of them, because that would only bring him sorrow.

59

The Aid of Blackwind

The sun came and went and the fire burning at the foot of the walls gradually subsided. Aary knew that the Shadow Knights would probably come again at night, so he told all soldiers to go and rest, all but a few sentries, who were instructed to blow the war horn if the Shadow Knights came back, and to call Aary if the dragons appeared. Even Aary himself managed to get a little bit of sleep. When the red sun set behind the silhouette of the Soulkeeper Mountain, everyone was back on the walls, well rested, fully armed, and prepared to greet their enemy again.

As if on cue, as soon as the sun vanished, before it was even fully dark, the shadows reappeared from the edge of the forest, like vultures appearing at the death of a lion. The city was no longer protected by the blazing fire. Only black, scorched ground, and one or two cinders were left. There was still no sign of Blackwind. Aary sighed. They had to start on their own.

Aary descended the wall. The army already rallied in formation inside the city gate. Commanders Bobor and Greig each led a wing. Riders and foot soldiers were packed in the big square in front of the gate and more were waiting in the streets. Aary jumped onto the horse that his men had readied for him, walked to the front of the army, and turned around. The faces of the soldiers looked determined and unafraid. That gave him courage.

"Darkness is not ruling the world now, and it never will. They will not take Elberkhan, as long as we are here. This is our city, our home. Here live our family, our friends. Here live the most righteous, kind, and loving men and women. We won't allow those evil creatures to breach the city walls and lay their filthy hands on our people. Aren't you always wondering what's hidden under the shadow of their black capes? Let's go find out!"

Aary raised his sword: "For Elberkhan!"

"For Elberkhan!" Hundreds and thousands echoed.

Along with the clanking sound of the iron chains, the drawbridge was lowered, and the iron portcullis lifted up, slowly and steadily. As soon as the end of the drawbridge hit the other bank, Aary gave his horse a squeeze with his legs, and the horse set off like an arrow from a bow, running into the cloud of dust stirred up when the bridge landed on the other side of the moat.

Commanders Bobor and Greig followed Aary closely on each side. Seeing that their king was charging at the very front, the soldiers in the army were highly encouraged. The ice that the Shadow Knights formed on the river had melted completely, and the wooden drawbridge shook above the splashing currents as hundreds of iron hoofs pounded on the bridge. The soldiers gripped their weapons and reins, urging their horses to charge at the highest speed towards the army of shadows. All their fears and worries were chased away, and all they had in mind was to kill their enemies to protect their homeland, protect their families.

The soldiers charging from the city gate were like a metallic flood, rushing towards a tide of black soup in deafening shouts. And their opponents, silent and indifferent as ever, drew their swords slowly from under their dirty black capes.

It seemed like a long time for Aary, almost a lifetime. He held his sword high up in the air, and felt the up and down of the galloping warhorse beneath him as if he were riding a wave. There was no one in front of him except the dark shadows that he was running towards, the shadows that swallowed countless lives and shrouded the whole plain with fear.

But strangely, he didn't feel scared at all. In fact, he didn't feel anything. His mind hadn't been so peaceful since the death of Elior. He had been waiting for this moment all along, and it finally came. He had the army of Shadow Knights in front of him, and his own army following closely behind. Soldiers holding fire torches, swords, and bows were charging at the same speed as himself, hundreds of thousands of strong, brave, young men who would do anything that he asked them to do, and wished for nothing but fighting for their kingdom and the people on Hilldown Plain, for their king. That was a peculiar feeling. He had never felt anything like this before. But he knew that, that was the reason why there was no fear in his heart.

The two floods of riders crashed into each other. Gigantic waves were stirred up where the two fronts met. The sound of weapons clashing, men yelling, and horses screaming were accompanied by inhuman screeching sounds made by the Shadow Knights. Soldiers from either side twisted and wrestled together like black and white sand on a beach, unable to tell them apart.

Aary discovered that the Shadow Knights could be killed by a sword just like any human being. They were not immortal after all. But they were indeed harder to kill than any man. Their strength was much greater than normal humans, and they were fast too. Few men could defeat one Shadow Knight in a one-on-one fight. Only when several soldiers worked together did they stand a chance. Aary did manage to take down one Shadow Knight by himself, but that almost cost him a leg. He was only lucky that when the Shadow Knight slashed his sword down, his horse was startled by some other bloodshed nearby and jerked, so only the point of the sword managed to reach his thigh, causing nothing more than a shallow cut. But the sword cut through his armor of steel as if he wasn't wearing any. Later he found himself teaming up with other soldiers too.

The night sky was shaken by the shouts and screams from the battle, and not long after, the whole expanse was red with blood and covered with bodies. Aary felt his heart grow heavier and heavier. He knew that most of the bodies lying around were his men. They left their homes just a few hours ago, said goodbye to their mothers and fathers, or perhaps hugged their wives and children, promising that they would come home before they knew it. But now, all that was left of them were cold, lifeless bodies, some of them were left only in parts. Aary knew that many families were now broken, and many people in the city library right now would never see their loved ones again. Was he really doing the right thing? Or did he just send all the men loyal to him to die for nothing.

How he wished that he were just a normal soldier, with nothing on his mind but killing enemies and fighting for his homeland, fearing nothing and worrying about nothing. But now, he was the King of Elberkhan. He was responsible for all his people, he needed to think about everything, if they could win this war, if so, at what losses, and if not, what would happen then. Was this really the best way? Was this really the only way? What would Elior do if it were him leading this war. Would so many people still die like this? Or was it purely Aary's fault? What had he done!

Suddenly, someone shouted: "Look!"

Aary looked up and saw a black cloud at the edge of the sky, and it was moving swiftly towards the battle. At first, Aary was startled. Was it another magic trick that the Shadow Knights played? But soon enough, he recognized the shapes of wings and tails flapping up and down. Blackwind! He told Aary that he was bringing three more drag-ons, but now he was bringing hundreds of them.

Aary shouted to his men: "Don't panic! They are ours! They are here to help!"

Before long, those huge black wings covered every inch of sky above them. The Shadow Knights didn't pay any mind to them at first, until one of them, the biggest one of them, plunged down, and before it hit the ground, spit out a long snake of fire and lifted back up into the air. The fire caught the Shadow Knights right in front of Aary, and the sword that was swaying towards Aary stopped midway, and, together with its owner, tumbled down to the ground in burning flames. The dragon that did this didn't stop to enjoy his victory, but went directly for the next target, and then the next.

Aary recognized that dragon as his own friend Blackwind. Where the fire burnt, the Shadow Knights screamed and struggled and fell from their horses. The aim was perfect. Aary's men and the Shadow Prince's men were tangled up all over the place, but every single time, the fire only reached the Shadow Knights and left the soldiers intact. Aary joyfully realized that night was not only the time when the Dark Kingdom was active, but also the batwing dragons' hunting time. While men were unable to even know where their enemies were without the help of torches, the dragons could see every bit of detail of everything happening on earth.

Other dragons couldn't breathe fire. Instead, they dived and caught Shadow Knights with their claws, carried them up in the air and dropped them at other Shadow Knights. But Aary could see that three other dragons, Blackwind's children, were copying their father, shooting fire towards the enemies. They were smaller than all the other dragons, a lot smaller than Blackwind, but no less swift and agile.

The backup forces from the sky greatly encouraged the soldiers on the ground. The fire of hope in their hearts that was already gradually going out once again blazed high and bright. Those that felt like they were running out of strength suddenly felt strong and powerful again, and those that were thinking about giving up immediately felt that they were going to win this war. The Shadow Knights' attention was forced to split between both enemies from the air and the ground, and when they were looking up to dodge the swords of fire, the swords of steel might send them to their death, which most of them had been avoiding for hundreds or thousands of years.

The dragons had a great advantage over their land-bound opponents, especially the fire-breathing ones, and they were able to deal with the Shadow Knights with great ease. But the infamous legends of the Shadow Knights' skills hadn't come out of thin air either. The dragons without the fire breathing skill needed to come near the ground to be able to attack, which put them into danger. Aary saw one of the smaller dragons dashing down towards a Shadow Knight, who reached out his sword a blink before the claws of the dragon reached him, and cut a long gash on the unprotected belly of the unfortunate little dragon. Aary's heart was bleeding when he saw the dragon crashing down into the chaotic mix of men and Shadow Knights. The soldiers tried their best to keep the Shadow Knights' attention on the ground, but still one or two would manage to kill a dragon with great speed and strength.

The aid of the dragons turned the situation from the absolute advantage of Shadow Knights to an almost equally balanced field. But still, it wasn't going to be easy. They had been fighting for almost the whole night, and all Aary's men were becoming tired and were running out of strength. But the Shadow Knights didn't seem to be affected at all by fatigue. They were just as strong, and as fast, as when it all started. If it went on like this, it was just a matter of time before the army of men would break down.

At that moment, Aary saw him. The short, crooked rider was on the top of a low hill at the edge of the forest, sitting on the back of his horse and watching it all. His face was hidden in the shadow of his cape, but the skull helmet of his horse glowed dimly and ghastly under the silver moonlight. The sword hanging from his waist didn't have a sheath, but it was covered here and there with some dark substance that could be nothing but dried blood. The mere look of him would make the hairs stand up on any man's back. Aary had never seen him before, but he knew that he could make no mistake. He knew it the second he saw him: the King of Cruelty, the Prince of Darkness, Nameless.

Aary tightened his hand around his sword, and urged his horse in that direction. He hacked down a few more Shadow Knights on the way, and the thick black blood of the enemy was dripping from the tip of his sword.

Just when he was a few more steps away from Nameless, suddenly, his target turned towards him. He still could not see the face in the shadow, but he could sense that there was a pair of eyes staring at him in the dark. He suddenly felt that he couldn't breathe, as if a hand clutched his throat, he wanted to shout but could make no sound. The world started to turn dark before his eyes, like the time when he was shot by the poisonous arrow. He was going to fall off the horse!

No!!! Resist it! It's not real! It's just an illusion! Aary shouted to himself, or was it Elior's voice again? *Fight it! He will not control you!!* He shut his eyes and focused his mind.

It worked. Aary felt that he had gradually gotten his balance and breath back. Then the feeling was completely gone. He reopened his eyes.

But his target was gone. That short, crooked figure was nowhere to be seen. Aary scanned the area around anxiously looking for him, and suddenly realized his real problem. When he went after the Prince of the Dark Kingdom, he unconsciously left the main battlefield, leaving all his men and dragons behind. And now, he was surrounded by several dozen Shadow Knights, all facing towards him and pushing closer. He could feel all their eyes were fixed on him, but he couldn't see any of them. A chill crept up his spine.

He knew that if he stayed here there was no way that he would get out alive. Even dealing with one Shadow Knight was almost impossible, if he was going to fight with dozens of them, he might have a better chance of survival jumping from a cliff. He had to run, that was the only way. The direction towards the forest had a few less Shadow Knights than in all other directions, and there was a bit of a gap between them. The forest was dark and bushy, which would give him an advantage for concealment. If he was lucky, he might actually make it.

He showed no hint that he was going to move until he suddenly squeezed the horse with his legs as hard as he could while giving a powerful slap with the flat side of his sword on the horse's haunch. The horse dashed, and he wielded his sword swiftly at the Shadow Knights that were coming towards him, aiming at their sword arms instead of heads, to be as fast as possible. Difficult as it was – and he definitely received more open wounds – he fought his way out of the death circle and darted into the forest.

Dozens of Shadow Knights on their black horses with skull helmets followed closely behind.

* * *

Even though she knew that the truth was always cruel, that the end of the baby would break her heart. The river wasn't fast enough, since the creatures were coming for him on their horses. Even if he could somehow miraculously escape from their grasp, it was almost impossible for him to be found by anyone before getting drowned, starved or frozen to death, or found by a hungry beast first. The chances of him living until the next sunrise were as tiny as none. But just that tiny bit of hope, was enough to support her to heaven. She smiled weakly and painfully at the little basket as it floated away.

60

The Deadly Crevice

The sky was already turning bright as the morning drew near. Aary pushed his horse to its limit, making his way through the forest with a group of Shadow Knights at his heels. He was used to riding in forests, and swam between the trees like a fish. He thought that he could lose them like this, but the Shadow Knights were no less skillful than himself, and he lost none of them.

After riding a while, he reached the end of the forest, and realized in horror that the ground in front of him had changed. Where it had been flat with high trees growing all around, the ground now rose abruptly and vertically, forming a solid rock wall that was blocking his way, and which extended endlessly on both sides. The rock wall flattened out on top, creating a deep, long plateau that seemed to continue as far deep as the rock wall continued long. There were also trees growing on top of the plateau a little distance away from the edge. The height difference between him and the plateau on top of the rock wall was not big, probably no more than the height of two people. But still there was no possible way that he could jump or climb onto it to reach safety.

Aary knew that stopping was also not an option. The moment he slowed down even the slightest, the Shadow Knights behind him would definitely get to him and kill him. Turning sideways was not much better, because several of his pursuers were already dangerously close to him, and turning towards any direction might make him crash into one of them. The only way was forward. But if he continued to run straight, he would die inevitably by smashing himself into the hard rock wall.

Just as Aary was ready to take the risk and make a sharp turn, he saw a crevice in the rock barrier. It was quite narrow, not much wider than a man's arm length. Aary couldn't help but smile. He was not going to die today. Even the rock wall didn't want him to die and opened up a door for him. He rode towards that gap without a second thought.

But soon after he went through the opening, he regretted the decision. In front of him, the rock walls on either side did not open up, but pressed closer to each other. It was not a gap between two rocks as he expected, but just a crack in one rock. Instead of running into a doorway to life, he put himself into a trap of death.

As Aary was feeling desperate about his situation, a loud crash came from behind him, followed by a cluster of chaotic sounds: horses screaming, rocks falling, steel clanking... He quickly glanced back and saw that many of his pursuers had crashed into each other and the rocks at the entrance. The ones at the back must have failed to stop their horses in time and crashed into the ones that had managed to pull to a stop. Aary would have felt really lucky, if he hadn't seen the ones that made it through the fissure. Only a few of them were still chasing him now, but they were close behind. Since the gap was so narrow it was impossible for even two riders to ride side by side, they rode in single file. The closest one was just two swords away from Aary.

Aary urged his horse to run faster, but he could see that the rock walls were closing in on him. The crevice was getting narrower and narrower, and he knew that soon enough it would be too narrow to ride. If he kept on galloping like this, there would be but one kind of ending for him: crashing into the rock walls and dying. But if he pulled the reins up right now, the Shadow Knight that was right behind him, who was riding as fast as himself, would crash into him and his horse, killing everyone all at once. He realized that for the Shadow Knights, this was a suicidal pursuit. Since Aary was already trapped in the crevice, they could have just slowed down and taken their time to deal with him. But they did not slow down even the slightest. So no matter what Aary did, he would end up as a pile of crushed meat and bones, and the Shadow Knights with him. But that didn't matter to them, their goal was to kill him, and they would achieve it.

He quickly accessed the situation. It was rock to his left and rock to his right. In front of him, the fissure was getting narrower and closing in to smash him, and behind him were Shadow Knights galloping at the greatest speed. He looked up.

Fortunately, the rock walls hadn't gotten any higher than at the entrance, but they hadn't gotten any lower either. So it was still too high for the horse to jump up. If he stood up on the horse's back, he might be able to reach his hand close to the top opening. But the upper edge of the rock was round and smooth. It would be impossible for him to grab and he would no doubt fall back down and end up under the horses' hoofs.

Suddenly a name came into his mind. Wild with joy, Aary pulled out the little wooden whistle from inside his armor, and gave a deafening blow.

Seconds later, a pair of huge black wings covered the sky above Aary.

The first thing Blackwind did, was to turn his head around and try to burn Aary's pursuers. But the situation with the rock gash and the high speed made it really difficult to aim and reach them. He tried a few times without success. There wasn't much time left. Aary decided to take the risk.

He tucked the rein under the saddle, and put both hands on the neck of the horse. Then, he took his feet out of the stirrups, and carefully put his knees on the saddle. Blackwind at once understood his intention, and reached his clawed feet down. Standing on horseback wasn't a new trick to Aary. When he was young, he loved performing like that for the villagers. But those horses were of course much slower than the one he was riding right now, and there weren't rough rock walls pressing against him from both sides, let alone deadly enemies chasing closely behind. Now, it became a game of life and death. He had no audience apart from the Shadow Knights that were chasing him and Blackwind, his only chance to survive. If he succeeded, no one would applaud him. But any minor mistake, one tiny slip under his feet, would shatter him in a thousand pieces.

Slowly and steadily, he put one foot on the saddle, then another, and stood up on the back of the galloping horse. The moment his body straightened up, he reached out his arms, and his legs pushed him up from the saddle.

His hands caught Blackwind's claws in the air, and the dragon held tightly onto him at once. The next second, his horse crashed into the hard rock wall, followed by the Shadow Knights. Blackwind flapped his wings, caught the wind, and lifted up into the sky, away from the deadly crevice.

* * *

Her pursuers reached the river. When they saw her empty hands and desperate smile, they knew what had happened. They laughed contemptuously, and chased downstream along the river for the little basket. Only one was left behind, and urged his horse towards Maire. Almost leisurely, he drew his sword and swung it towards her. She didn't dodge or even step back. She had already used up all her strength when running with the baby and now she knew that it was her time.

Blackwind's Theme

Chen Yuxiao

61

The End of the War

I'm alive!!

Aary almost broke into tears. After thinking that he would die in that fissure for sure, now he didn't have anything else in his mind apart from enjoying the pure, simple happiness of being alive. Blackwind swung his feet and threw Aary in the air, while ducking beneath him to catch him on his back. Aary sat on Blackwind's shoulders and put his arms tightly around his dragon friend's neck. They hadn't flown together like this for a while, and Aary missed the feeling of flying freely in the air, and the sound of the wind whistling pass his ears. But more than anything, he missed the feeling of knowing that he would live to welcome a new day.

The morning sky was transparent. Aary took in a deep breath, feeling cool fresh autumn air filling up his lungs. The world seemed to become quiet, and he almost forgot about the war going on below.

Oh no! The war!

As soon as Aary realized that there was still a war to fight, Blackwind dived down towards the battlefield. As the King, Aary needed to be there for his people no matter what happened. If they thought that the King was dead, how could they still believe that they could win this war?

When Aary returned flying above the battlefield all he saw was a pool of blood. Dead soldiers, horses, Shadow Knights, and even dragons spilled across the grass, coloring it red and black. Aary could see that the fighting was still going on, and his men were barely holding up with the help of the air force of dragons. The surviving men were exhausted, wounded, just like Aary himself, and worst of all, desperate. They knew that they were not going to win this war, and everyone was going to die.

If this situation could get any worse, another large group of Shadow Knights were creeping out of the forest to join the battle. Aary realized that they must have been the ones that went off to chase him. They probably thought that he was dead already and had come back to help their comrades finish the work.

His soldiers thought so too. When they saw the troop that went to hunt their King had returned, everyone knew what it meant. Already, they were barely keeping up with their enemies, with the arrival of so many more, they were certain to break down. Some soldiers even crashed down to the ground out of desperation, throwing down their weapons and giving up the fight.

Not now! Aary thought, as he looked at the brightening horizon, *we are so close...*

"Don't give up!" Aary shouted, "The sun is rising! The darkness will soon be over!" Then he raised his sword, "For Elberkhan!"

Men and Shadow Knights alike looked up into the sky, and saw there, high up in the air, Aary sat on the shoulder of the largest black dragon, his black cape waving in the wind. In the meantime, Blackwind dashed down towards the field and let go of a long, fiery breath.

"The King is alive!"

"Long live the King!"

"For Elberkhan!"

The whole Hilldown Plain echoed the earth-shaking call of the soldiers, and hope once again came back to people's eyes like a fire spreading on a dry grassland.

At that time, the first golden light of the rising sun broke through the horizon.

The night ended, and the new day arrived. It was no longer the Shadow Knights' home field of darkness, but the men's world. The cruel, evil, disgusting creatures that always hid in the dark were brought into the bright sunlight. Aary knew that, it was their time to make the move.

Blackwind brought Aary to the castle gate so that he could shout out the commands. Hundreds of giant steel plates were brought out on top of the wall. The surfaces were polished to such an extent that a person could see the reflection of his own face in them. In the meantime, all the soldiers on the battlefield turned their shields around, showing the insides of the shields that were polished the same way.

When the Shadow Knights realized what was happening, it was already too late. The sunlight reflected off the shields and the plates were like daggers of light, cutting into the darkness under their hoods. Some fell directly from their horses miserably, as if the light beams were real swords that pierced through their hearts; others tried to cover their faces with sleeves and hands, and in turn got cut down by the soldiers. In the meantime, dragons attacked from above, snatching and burning Shadow Knights on the ground. When Blackwind landed on the castle wall, Aary borrowed a bow and a quiver from an archer, and carried it with him while Blackwind flew back to the battlefield. Now as Blackwind was flying across the sky shooting fire towards the Shadow Knights, Aary himself was shooting wooden arrows. The team they made was like the stars in the sky, bringing hope and strength to Elberkhan's soldiers and fear and death to the Shadow Knights.

The situation of the battle was completely turned around. The Shadow Knights started to run, trying to get away from the battlefield that had turned from their killing ground into their graves. Soldiers chased after them, hunting them down one by one before they made it to the forest. The Shadow Knights would never have exposed themselves in the daylight, if they didn't think that they were already winning, and were so drunk on their glory and the taste of blood that they stayed even when the night was ending in order to finish off their massacre. There was a massacre after all, but not what they had hoped for.

Their own arrogance and greed became their end.

Many soldiers hadn't even realized what happened when there were no more Shadow Knights sitting on their black horses with skull helmets, or even standing. They were all lying on the ground, in pools of black blood. Their black hoods were torn into pieces by the horses' hoofs, and the faces that no one ever saw were finally exposed in the sunlight. Those faces were even more hideous and twisted than what people imagined, making them hard to even look at. Evil and cruelty were soaked in every deep wrinkle and cut on their faces, and stained by the thick, black blood they bled. But now, all those faces were lifeless, with angry or painful eyes staring blankly ahead, staring into the blue sky and the sun that they had never dared to look at. Right now, the sunlight was so bright and warm, softly caressing all the lost souls lying across the field, evil or kind alike.

* * *

With a light call and the blinding flash of sharp steel, her beautiful life ended in a gush of bright red blood. Her soft body fell lifelessly down on the ground like a petal falling from a withering flower. Her fresh blood flowed into the clear water of the river and blossomed, before it was brought away by the river, following and escorting her baby in the basket, into the distance.

62

The Dark Kingdom

However, among all the dead Shadow Knights, Aary did not see Nameless. The Prince of the Dark Kingdom must have escaped when he saw that they were losing, and, most likely, he went back to their den, the corner of the plain where the sun never shone.

Aary knew that, as long as Nameless was alive, it was just a matter of time before he recruited more Shadow Knights and came back for revenge. After all, the world was never short of greedy, selfish people that would gladly trade their souls for eternal life. All his soldiers would have died for nothing, if everything would just go back to how it was in a short time.

Right now, the Dark Kingdom was at its weakest, and the Prince did not have his usual protection. There would be no better time than now to try and get to Nameless himself, and if they succeeded, they would be able to free the world from the power of the Dark Kingdom once and for all. It was now or never.

The next day after the bloody battle, Aary led a troop towards the home base of the Dark Kingdom. Needless to say, it was still going to be a very perilous task. The Prince of the Dark Kingdom was the most powerful of them all, and it was said that he had already lived for tens of thousands of years, and as of yet had met no enemy that could compete with him.

Moreover, compared with fighting the Shadow Knights on an open field, it was a completely different matter to be fighting in their own home. No one knew what it was like in there, because no one had ever gone inside the Dark Kingdom, and lived to tell the story, no one but Elior. However, he had been there as a captured prisoner, with a black hood over his head both times. And now, even he was lying in the crypt under the castle, forever.

However, it was no secret where the Dark Kingdom was located, because everyone had to know where it was, to be able to stay as far away from it as possible, in order to stay alive. It was at the foot of the Soulkeeper Mountain, a place where the sunlight never shone. But that was only the entrance, the mouth of a cave that stretched deep and far underground.

Unlike the battle on the previous day, this time, Rudi was a member of the expedition. Even though he was completely useless with a sword, being an elf, he did have a much better sense of smell and hearing than humans, and his vision was especially acute in the dark. He was also much smaller and quieter, thus less likely to be seen. So, he acted as a scout to check out the situation at the very front.

Commander Bobor was appointed as Aary's bodyguard. Strangely enough, even though he shot Aary once and almost killed him, now Aary found him to be one of his most trusted commanders. Also, Aary knew that this task needed to be handled with extreme caution and care, and Commander Greig's unpredictable temper might kill everyone. On the other hand, Bobor was cautious and thoughtful, and Aary knew that he could count on him.

Lyna also begged Aary to take her along. Aary thought it was a terrible idea to bring a young girl to such a dangerous place, but Lyna insisted that she had read all the books related to the Dark Kingdom in the city library during the time she was there, and the knowledge she learned could be helpful. Aary still said no, and told her to stay in the castle until they came back. But when they were almost there, Lyna rode up from behind on a young grey mare, and Aary had no choice but to let her stay with the troops, and told her to stay closely near him so that he could personally take care of her safety.

The mouth of the cave was not big, nothing compared to Elberkhan's city gate. But it was no doubt an important entrance, as the area outside was covered with the prints of horse hoofs, and no grass could grow because of the frequent traffic, just like the gate of Elberkhan.

Rudi was the first to enter, wearing his dirty robe, which also acted as some kind of a disguise due to its similarity to the Shadow Knights' cloaks. Aary and Lyna, and the other men followed, keeping a moderate distance away from him. Several dragons brought up the rear, including Blackwind and his children. The whole troop entered the dark cave that ordinary people didn't even dare to look at, and walked quietly into the silent darkness.

Because fire torches would be too bright and might expose them, they carried glass jars filled with many fireflies as lamps. The dim light of fireflies was not even visible in daylight, but as they went deeper and deeper, and when the last bit of sunlight from the outside was gone, the faint lime colored lights seemed more precious than anything. When people's eyes adjusted to the darkness, even the slightest light helped them see their way.

In the beginning, whenever they saw an intersection, they divided the group into several smaller divisions to go into every tunnel. But some ended up back together, some just walked into dead ends and had to return. Soon enough, they discovered that the inside of the cave was similar to a giant ant nest, with hundreds of tunnels and chambers crisscrossing into an extremely complex structure.

But there was one tunnel that was wider than all the rest, and all the chambers that probably used to be where the Shadow Knights spend their days were all empty. So, they stopped wasting time exploring the other tunnels, and followed the main one as one group, deeper and deeper. The tunnel stunk with a disgusting foul smell, and white bones could be seen hanging from or stuck into the walls, maybe as some kind of decoration.

Everyone felt a chill when they saw that at one place the bones of a person were put together into the shape of whole skeleton, but with every body part at a wrong location. That morbid "artwork" was so disturbing that they all hurried past without giving it a second look.

They also found the stable where the Shadow Knights kept their horses, a very big round chamber with countless bones stuck in the ground, probably some large animal's shank bones. But only a few horses were in there alone, tied to the bones in front of them, indicating that most Shadow Knights were not here. Aary was a bit relieved, and told the others to get the horses out when they finished their business.

They followed the tunnel, and walked deeper and deeper, until the tunnel disappeared into a black hole at the end. Rudi hesitated before he stepped into the hole, so Aary walked up to him, and together they entered the dark hole.

"Wow..." Like Aary and Rudi, everyone following them couldn't help but giving a low cry of amazement when they walked through that hole, because what they were looking at in front of their eyes was unlike anything anyone had ever seen.

They found themselves in an enormous cave chamber that was even bigger than the Elberkhan library. The chamber was connected to countless tunnels, each one with a platform at the entrance, one of which they were standing on. And the tunnel they just came from, which they thought was the main tunnel of the underworld kingdom, was just an extremely ordinary one of many. This must be the place where the Shadow Knights gathered for meetings.

The platforms were connected by bridges or ladders, all made from human bones. Some bones were bound with strands of human hair to form suspended bridges, others were stuck directly into the cave walls to form stairs along the walls. It was hard to imagine that there was such a giant, complex kingdom hidden inside the Soulkeeper Mountain. Aary thought that maybe the whole mountain was probably already dug hollow inside and could collapse anytime soon.

The bottom of the chamber was too deep and dark to see, but there were some cone-shaped, tower-like structures standing from the bottom all the way up to where they were, of which the one at the center of the chamber, the tallest and the grandest one, was obviously different from the others. All of these structures were connected to each other, and to the platforms along the walls, with more bone bridges.

Aary took a closer look at the tower in the center. It looked like a giant ant nest or a volcano from the outside. The top of the structure seemed flat, but they couldn't see it from the lower platform where they stood. There were stairs spiraling down from the top along the outer wall, with more platforms in between that were connected to the other ones. Aary thought that the tallest tower must be where the Prince stood to give orders to all the Shadow Knights of the Dark Kingdom.

Aary decided to go over to have a look. There was a bridge connecting the platform they were standing on to one of the platforms on top of the towers, which was then connected to the spiral stairs on the central tower. But the bridges were just a bunch of bones tied together, without any arm rails and were extremely narrow. Below it was unknown darkness. But whatever it was at the bottom, any person that fell from the bridge probably would be shattered into pieces.

Aary thought about having the dragons carry people to fly over. But it might create too much noise and could be dangerous. So, he told the dragons to wait in the tunnel, and told Rudi to stay with them, because he trusted Rudi to make the right decisions if an emergency happened. While unhappy that he couldn't explore with the rest of the team, Rudi knew the importance of that position, so he grumpily agreed.

Aary didn't even dare to stand up on that swaying bridge. He first put two legs down, and stepped carefully on the bones, while his hands grabbed tightly behind his body to stabilize. After he passed the lowest point of the bridge, he carefully swapped his hands to his front, and climbed up as if he was climbing a ladder. Seeing his example, everyone else became braver too, and followed behind him. Only two soldiers that were extremely afraid of heights couldn't even make it to the edge of the platform, so Aary told them to stay with Rudi and the dragons.

Safely and smoothly, they made it to the spiral stairs one after another. Although these stairs also didn't have arm rails, and had big gaps between the bones, at least the bones were stuck in solid walls instead of hanging loosely in the air. They could even put one hand on the wall to keep balance. It was already a great improvement over the last situation. Going faster than before, they reached the top of the tower.

The roof of the central tower wasn't completely flat like the other ones. There was a giant stone platform in the center, raising several feet above the ground, like some kind of stage. The whole structure showed extreme centralization, so even though none of the explorers had been in there before, they didn't need anyone to tell them where the Prince would stand. Aary could imagine Nameless standing on top of this stone platform, maybe even riding his horse, whispering evil ideas to his followers, and as a result having absolute control over the whole Dark Kingdom.

But how would Nameless arrive at this platform? Where was he hiding? He couldn't be sharing the filthy, stinky chambers with other Shadow Knights, he was like a god to them. He must have had his own private entrance, a place like the royal chamber in a castle, that only he himself and maybe a few trusted servants were allowed to enter. But where could it be? This tower was standing tall and alone in the center, away from all other platforms, with bridges of similar sizes connecting to all directions. Apart from this tower, there was nothing that looked special and different from everything else. Only this tower, and this stone platform.

"Come, help me move this thing." Aary said quietly, squatting down and putting his hands on the edge of the stone platform. The others followed him. And together, the platform moved. When it was several footsteps away from its original location, a soldier suddenly stepped back in fear. A hole appeared in the ground right next to where he was standing.

When they moved the stone platform further away, more of the hole appeared from beneath. When half the hole was exposed, they saw a spiral staircase, similar to the one on the outside of the tower, winding all the way down along the inner wall. They looked down from the opening, but still couldn't see the bottom. It was like a well in the ground, deep and dark inside, but here stairs stretched down as far as the eye could see. Aary walked down the staircase and the rest followed.

They descended the stairs silently. Only the rustling of their clothes could be heard. But the well still magnified the sounds, making everyone nervous. However, they did not hear any other sound. This well seemed as dead as the rest of the Dark Kingdom.

When they finally reached the bottom, all they could see was another horizontal tunnel. They kept walking deeper, and deeper, and deeper, into the den of the creature.

Finally, Aary could see a dim blue light at the end of the corridor. The light grew bigger and brighter as they approached, and then it was finally clear enough to see a silhouette, a figure in a hooded robe, sitting with its back against them, next to a candle in a blue glass lamp.

Aary paused for a moment, his heart pounding heavily, but the figure seemed to be still as a stone statue. Then, even more slowly and quietly, Aary moved forward.

* * *

As the light of life faded away from her, her whole life flashed in front of her eyes. She saw the peaceful and ordinary life she had lived before meeting him, and the earthshaking change he brought to her life. She saw the moments when they first met, got to know each other, and fell in love. She saw her excitement when he proposed to her, her happiness when they had their wedding, and her joy when their son was born.

63

Nameless

Just when Aary was about a dozen steps away, the figure suddenly started moving. Everyone stopped, held their breaths, and pressed their hands on their swords. Under everyone's stare, the figure slowly turned around, and when he showed his face, Aary felt a chill creeping up his spine.

Elior was sitting by the blue lamp, with a hood over his head. His long, soft, silver hair was tied loosely at his shoulders, and his half-closed eyes reflected the blue light. But his hands were tied by a rope behind his back.

"What took you so long?" Elior asked, in his usual lazy voice, "I've been bored to death."

Aary didn't know what to make of this. He stared at the figure in front of him, the person that he killed with his own sword, and his head was a blank. His men were as speechless and astonished as himself. No one said a thing.

"Are you dumb?" Elior said impatiently, "Your King is asking you a question. I've been waiting for you for a long time."

"But..." After a long, awkward silence, Aary finally got himself to talk, voice trembling, "I killed you. You're dead..." When he said those words, he could feel his eyes getting misty with tears, and a lump stuck in this throat.

"Do I look dead to you, you fool? You really think you'd be able to kill me?" Elior sneered contemptuously, then his voice softened, "If I didn't play dead, would you do the things you did? Would you defeat the Dark Kingdom? This was my last challenge for you, and you didn't fail me. Now get me out of here. I've had enough of this." He turned his body a little to show the ropes that tied his hands together.

Aary could see blood oozing out from where the rope cut into the flesh, and thought of Elior's diary. Somewhere soft in his heart ached terribly. He walked towards him. But Lyna chased after him, and stopped him with a hand on his arm.

"Wait," Lyna said, "you didn't tell us how you ended up in here."

Elior was getting annoyed, "Why do I have to explain everything to you? Get me out of this rope first, it's an order."

Aary pushed away Lyna's hand and said to her: "You heard him. Let's get the rope off first. You can ask all the questions later. This man had suffered enough for me, this is the least I can do."

He hurried forward.

Just when his hands were reaching Elior's hands, Lyna suddenly pushed past him and stabbed a dagger towards Elior. Aary was terrified by Lyna's abrupt behavior and tried to stop her, but it was too late. Then, what happened after was even more shocking: a black snake whipped out from Elior's sleeve, and crashed itself right into the point of Lyna's dagger. Lyna let go of the dagger and it fell onto the ground together with the snake. The snake jerked and hissed in extreme agony with the dagger buried in its throat for a few more seconds until it finally stopped moving.

Meanwhile, Elior dodged the dagger, and his face was twisted with anger. Before Aary realized what was happening, Elior's hands broke free from the ropes, caught Lyna by the wrist, and gave it a violent twist. Lyna's thin arm made a cracking sound, and Lyna screamed as she fell to the ground. The soldiers ran forward to help them, but they had their own problems to deal with: several more Shadow Knights appeared behind them.

When Aary finally understood the situation, he struck his sword towards who he thought was Elior. He missed, and "Elior" opened his mouth to stick out his black tongue. Then Aary realized that the tip of the tongue looked like the head of a snake as well. The tongue seemed to be endlessly long, as it stretched out from the mouth as fast as lightening while the other end was still attached to the monster's mouth. In no time, the end of the long tongue reached Aary's thigh. The snake head opened its own mouth, and buried its sharp fangs deeply into Aary's flesh. Aary felt the most acute pain that he had ever experienced in his life, worse than being hit by a whip, worse than getting shot by an arrow. His brain was blinded by the pain and the world darkened in front of his eyes. That's when he heard the voice in his head.

It was a voice softer than whisper, quieter than breathing. Or more accurately, it wasn't like something that he heard, but more like his own thoughts. *Lyna, she's the source of all the trouble. If she never showed up, all of this pain would never have happened. I never would have got shot by a poisonous arrow and never would have killed Elior. It was supposed to be Elior's war, but because of her, now I am caught up in it. I didn't kill the King, it was her.*

That soft, gentle voice was so peaceful and calming, it made Aary let his guard down. The pain in his leg also disappeared, and he seemed to have gone back to being an infant in his mother's arms, listening to the mother's gentle murmur and falling asleep. He felt a sense of safety and comfort that he remembered from the past, yet had almost forgotten what it felt like. An extreme fatigue crawled over his whole body, and he just wanted to sleep, forever, in the darkness.

Kill her, end it all. Kill her, and everything will go back to how it was.

He looked at Lyna, and lifted the sword in his hand. A sudden terror broke the comforting peace in his heart.

Lords of heavens! What am I doing!!

He suddenly came back to himself, realizing that he could no longer control his own body. He felt that he was falling, sinking into an endless abyss of darkness. There were walls all around him that were covered with a kind of black, slimy substance, making it too slippery to grasp and impossible to stop the fall. He seemed to be in a dirty dry well, and everything outside the well had nothing to do with him. Everything he saw seemed strange and far away, covered in a black mist.

The feeling of not being able to control himself and losing his senses to the outside world was similar to when he was shot by the poisonous arrow, but much worse, and much more terrifying. His arm felt like someone else's, and it was swinging the sword towards Lyna. He was drowned by fear and despair, until he saw Lyna, sitting on the ground, looking at him in shock and tears.

No, he had to fight it! He had to seize back control of his own body before it was too late. He had to chase the fear and doubts away. He started trying to crawl back up from the bottom of the black pit, while his "other" body took a step towards Lyna and raised the sword. He used all the strength he had to punch the walls of the well with his fists and kick it with his feet. The hard, solid walls suddenly became unbelievably soft and made a painful scream. All the walls around him were now surging up and down like ocean waves or some soft sea creatures, bouncing back whenever he punched a dent.

He used the force he made when pushing back the wall, and struggled towards the only bit of light he saw. The light became larger and larger, and then the walls started to break apart, with lights shining in from the holes he made. Finally, when he was already exhausted, he came back to his own body. The second before his sword was about to stab into Lyna's skinny little body, he fought back the powerful strength that was still controlling him, and ripped the sword away. The sword flew from his hand and hit the wall in a piercing clash.

At that time, he once again felt the heart-tearing pain in his leg. The monster gave the snake tongue a pull, which almost ripped off a piece of flesh from his thigh. Aary cried out in pain and fell to the ground next to Lyna. The monster in front of him did not look like Elior anymore. He, or it, was the scariest thing Aary had ever seen.

Black veins were crawling underneath its skin like some kind of vine and squirmed like worms, and its mouth was wide open with blackened teeth. The long, black tongue sticking out from the mouth still had its snake head locked tightly on Aary's leg. And the monster's hands turned into skeletons with skin, crawling towards Aary.

But true fear only came when Aary saw his own leg. The clothes of his pants were torn, and he could see similar black vines as the ones on the monster's skin under his own skin, growing and expanding from the wound.

He knew he had to get it off him, but he no longer had his sword on him. He looked back to the other soldiers, but they were all busy fighting the other Shadow Knights. Seeing the bodies on the ground, he knew that there was no one there to help him. So Aary made up his mind and clenched his teeth, grabbed the snake tongue by the head and gave it a hard pull.

"Ah!!!!!!" His painful cry echoed in the whole tunnel. The extreme pain forced him to let go, and he almost fainted.

At the same time, Lyna pushed herself up and supported herself on her elbow. She pulled the dagger out of the dead snake with her left hand. The monster reached its claw towards Lyna, but before it could reach her, she used all her strength and hacked off the snake's head on Aary's leg from the long tongue that it was attached to.

The snake's head still had its fangs buried in Aary's leg, but the rest of the tongue whipped back to the monster's mouth. Thick black blood gashed from both ends. The monster screamed and twisted in agony. Aary put an arm in front of Lyna, gesturing her to move back, as he also struggled to move back. Lyna made it to her feet with the help of Aary and her left hand, but Aary couldn't possibly stand up with the current state of his leg. He took the dagger from Lyna's hand, and threw it towards the monster. The monster tried to dodge, but the dagger still managed to land in its chest. The blood colored the dagger black, but the monster was still not dead. Instead, it was furious. It crawled towards Aary, its mouth opening angrily, and Aary could see the black teeth and the black blood dripping.

"Get down!" A shout came from behind Aary. After finishing off the last Shadow Knight, Commander Bobor ran up to the monster. He jumped over Aary, swung his sword at the monster, and hacked its head off. The distorted head of the monster fell to the ground next to Aary.

At that moment, a gust of black smoke rushed out from the open neck that was bleeding thick, black blood, flew through the gaps between people, and vanished in the darkness.

* * *

She also knew that, if it wasn't for him, she probably was still living her peaceful, ordinary life like everyone else in her village. She probably would live until she was old and grey, and die with many children and grandchildren around her. But she didn't want that possibility at all, because that would also mean a life without him. She didn't blame him or regret letting him come into her life, because those three years that she spent with him were the best and happiest three years of her life. He gave her life meaning, and she gladly traded those three years with the rest of her life.

64

The Real Victory

After being carried back to Elberkhan, Aary and Lyna received full medical examinations and treatments.

Lyna's arm had a broken bone. The physicians reconnected the bone, and locked it in place by binding her arm tightly to a piece of wooden board. She would need to carry this board for months before the bone totally recovered.

Aary, on the other hand, had a much more complicated issue. The snake head was still stuck firmly in his leg. When the royal physicians examined him, they found that it was not only the fangs that were the problem. The black vines that stretched out from the snake's mouth, like how the snake head stretched out from the monster's mouth, were also buried deeply in his leg and clutching onto his flesh so tightly that it was almost like they grew there. That was why Aary couldn't just pull the snake head off.

The process of removing it was extremely painful for him since it was like cutting his own flesh. But he insisted on not taking any drugs that would dull his senses. His screams were audible throughout the whole castle, but it was finally completely removed from him. The physicians then used leeches to suck out the black blood, until the blood coming out from the wound was finally its normal red color. Even the leeches died after they drank the contaminated blood.

By the time Aary's treatment was finally done, he was soaked with sweat and had a face pale as milk. He passed out not long after with a high fever. The physicians told him that the wound didn't reach the bone, so he could still walk, but not without difficulty.

When Aary woke up at last, the first thing he had in mind was Lyna. Against the strong objection of the physicians, he insisted on visiting her at once. He needed to tell her how grateful he was that she saved his life, and how sorry he was that he didn't listen to her at first and let the monster hurt her. He was having strong, mixed feelings of love, guilt, and gratitude towards her, and he needed to let her know.

When he entered Lyna's chamber, she was sitting at the side of her bed reading. Aary felt his heart broken when he saw Lyna's arm fixed on the wooden board. But when she saw Aary, she smiled happily and came running to him, putting her left arm around Aary. Aary hugged her tightly, but none of the words he had prepared came out. At that moment, he knew that she already knew everything he was going to say, and they just hugged each other for a very long time.

The war was finally, completely won. The reign of the Dark Kingdom was over. The dark power influencing people on Hilldown Plain, turning all good things sour, was removed at its roots. Everyone felt an unprecedented delightfulness and easiness. This fresh feeling was indescribable, untouchable, but unignorable. It felt like even the dark corners in people's hearts had been cleaned out and all that was left was brightness.

Once again, people started greeting each other with friendly smiles and helping each other with warm hearts. When the sun set, families would still gather by the fire, telling each other stories of the day, but no one would be afraid to go out at night again, because there was no more darkness hidden in the nights, only the bright moonlight. Everything returned to the pureness and happiness that it once was, and there was a feeling of rebirth.

Aary held a grand ceremony to honor the soldiers who gave their lives for the victory as well as giving compensation to their families, and to reward the ones that made it to the end. The people that made great contributions in the war, including Commander Greig, Commander Bobor, and Lyna, were rewarded with the prizes and gratitude they deserved.

Batwing dragons became friends and honored guests in the whole Hilldown Plain. A new law was passed forbidding anyone from hunting them. Instead, the commoners all considered it to be a great honor and a charm of great luck if a batwing dragon landed on their property, and they would bring out their best food to serve them in warm welcome. The burnt city wall was painted again and oil production was increased so that the scarcity was eliminated.

Elior's last wish was fulfilled and now he could rest in peace. His funeral had been done privately on a very small scale, but Aary held another grand memorial, giving everyone in the kingdom the opportunity to say farewell to their beloved young King. In his life, Elior had been through too much hardship, suffered too much pain, so death actually allowed him to rest at last. Aary believed that, even though Elior had made some mistakes, he blamed himself for much more than he should, and paid off much more than his debt. He was not a perfect man, and he did some controversial things that might have been done better other ways, but all things considered, he was a good man, and a good King.

Now that Aary had finished what he was doing as King, as promised, he was going to step down from the throne and let the kingdom decide its new King. He once again called a Grand Council meeting, to gather all the commanders and advisors in one room. He thanked everyone for their support in the war, and announced that he would keep his promise and hand over the throne. The new King would be chosen by vote and anyone would be eligible.

But this time, the attitudes of the people were completely different from when he first claimed the throne. All the doubts, distrust, and criticism anyone had against Aary in the beginning, had melted away when they saw how smart, valiant, responsible, and mature this young

King appeared to be during the war. They accepted this commoner boy as their King from the bottom of their hearts.

Commander Bobor spoke first: "Your Grace, Elberkhan only won this war against all odds because of you. Your Grace is our true King. If we vote a hundred times, a hundred times I would vote for you as our King without hesitation."

Someone else followed: "I will vote for Your Grace too! Your Grace is the best King this kingdom has had in a hundred years."

"The kingdom cannot do without Your Grace! We need Your Grace!"

"We will have no better King than Your Grace! Please don't walk away from us!"

"King Aary is our one true King!"

"King Aary!"

"King Aary!"

"King Aary!"

Everyone in the room pulled out their swords and raised them into the sky as they called out Aary's name. Aary looked at their supportive faces and couldn't say a word. A few months ago, he never thought about becoming a King. It seemed further away from him than the distance between heaven and earth. Even when he read Elior's will naming him as successor, even when he acted as the temporary King during the war, he never thought of himself as a real King. But now, all these people in front of him, the people that devoted their whole lives to the kingdom, the people that he personally admired and respected from the bottom of his heart, all wanted him to be their King. He didn't know how to react. He received the love from all these people, but did he really deserve it?

At that moment, a white-bearded old man pushed open the door at the end of the room and walked in. The old man was wearing a coarse linen robe, his bare feet standing on the cold marble floor.

Everyone in the room stood up respectfully, including Aary. Aary had never seen him, but he had heard stories about an old mage on Hilldown Plain, who could see everything that was happening, had happened, and was going to happen, in every corner of the world; who couldn't be harmed by anything, not even sword or magic; and who, was the only person that could go into both castles of the kingdom of men, and the caves of the Dark Kingdom of Shadow Knights, and leave intact. He never took sides in any wars, never supported any kingdoms, even though with his wisdom and knowledge he could defeat any kingdom if he wanted to. He knew everything that was going to happen in the future, but he never took part in it and tried to change it. He would only show up when it was needed. No one ever knew where to find him, but if anyone needed him for something that no one else could do, he would come himself, for example, when the Prince of the Dark Kingdom wanted to deliver the letter to Elior.

But now, seeing him at a Grand Council meeting of the Kingdom of Elberkhan, everyone was surprised and confused. He nodded courteously towards the people in the room, and walked up to Aary.

"Child," he asked gently, "may I speak to you alone?"

Aary was more surprised and confused. He looked at the Grand Council apologetically, but no one showed any discontent, even a few nodded to him. So, he excused himself from the room, and entered a small chamber adjoined to the meeting room with the old man. The chamber was usually used as the King's resting place, and when the heavy velvet-covered door was shut, no sound from the grand meeting room could be heard from inside. Aary turned around after closing the door, and waited attentively for the old prophet to speak.

* * *

But she did hope that their son wouldn't need to go through this, and hoped that she would be able to hear his story, to be able to understand why this would happen. She loved him with her life, but she never got the chance to really know him, and never would. As she drew her last breath, she thought about the name that those people called him by, his real name. Elior, she repeated to herself again and again, it was such a beautiful name.

65

Revealing the Secret

The old prophet told Aary a story.

Once, there was a nobleman wandering alone far away from home. He met a beautiful woman in a little mountain village, and like in all the fairytale stories, they fell in love. Years later, the woman gave birth to a baby. But before the child had reached his first birthday, his father was taken away by a group of strangers, who later came back to kill the baby. Trying to protect her son, the child's mother ran away with him, and, before losing her life at the sword of the pursuers, she put the little baby in a basket on the river, together with a golden ring that her husband had given her. In the slight hope that her baby might be able to live, she closed her eyes forever under the blade. The strangers chased after the little basket along the river, but lost track of it before they could catch it. They reported to whoever sent them to kill the baby that they had finished the task, believing that a baby would be close to dead floating on the river alone in a forest. They didn't know that the little basket did not crash, nor did the baby get eaten by beasts. The basket floated along the river, circled around swirls, bumped against rocks, accompanied by curious little birds, and floated all the way to a little village downstream.

A woman went down to the river to fetch some water and saw a little basket stuck on a branch in the middle of the river. She waded across and picked up the basket, and to her surprise, she found a little baby lying inside. The baby was still alive when she found him, but was extremely weak because of hunger and cold. She took the baby back home and found a golden ring under the little blanket. She asked the women in the village with milk to feed the baby, and took care of him gently. Under her attentive care, the child gradually shed off the marks that the lonesome trip had left on him. Unfortunately, the woman that took him in passed away from disease within the year. But the villagers took care of him after she was gone and he grew up happily like any other child, into a healthy, strong boy.

That nobleman's name was Elior, but he went by Jerre in the little mountain village. The woman he married was named Maire, and the village their child grew up in was called Rocky Vill.

Aary blinked at the white-bearded man in disbelief. He had learnt so many unbelievable truths in recent months, and he needed time to digest.

He was Elior's son.

Elior was his father.

He reached inside a secret pocket sewn on the inner side of his shirt and took out a little golden ring. He had carried it with him for as long as he remembered, because he knew that it was the only thing his mother left for him. When he was young, he often played with the ring when he was alone, running his fingers along the beautiful patterns, and it felt as if his mother was with him. But he always thought that his mother was a villager in Rocky Vill, and thought that he had been born there. The ring wasn't even a perfect circle, but it had delicate hand carved patterns and a name in cursive writing: Maire.

"Did he know?" Aary asked.

Smiling, the old man shook his head.

Elior did not know, which meant that he died without knowing that his only son was still alive. Less did he know that the heir he picked himself, out of a little village that he conquered during the war, was his own blood, his own son.

While Aary was still trying to make sense of the things he just heard, the old man opened the door and walked out. After saying what he came here to say, there was no need for him to stay any longer.

"Wait!" Aary called out, just before the old man vanished from his sight, "But, why did you decide to tell me? Why now?"

The prophet paused, looked back, and smiled at Aary, then quietly closed the door.

Before Aary even realized it, the old man was gone, leaving him alone in the empty room. He did not even manage to thank him. But he knew that there would be no point chasing after him, because he knew how things worked with the old prophet: the things he wanted you to know, you would find out; and the things that he didn't mean to tell you, you wouldn't get any answer no matter how many times you asked.

After the old man left, Aary pondered the shocking news for a few more minutes. Was it just pure coincidence or was it something else? When Elior picked him from the battlefield, did Elior himself make the choice, or was it the spirit of the Kingdom of Elberkhan, as old as time itself. Aary was born as the son of a King, but grew up in a little village, and never yearned for power nor the throne. Nevertheless, everything that happened after he was born led him back to where he was right now. If it was fate that brought him here, he should know better than to disobey. He finally understood how it all worked. He always thought that it was luck that brought him there, that he didn't deserve to be King, that someone else would do a better job. But it did not matter what he thought. He did not pick the throne, no one did. The throne picked its King.

Aary closed his eyes and took a deep breath. He pushed open the door to the grand meeting room, behind which hundreds of officers and commanders, the most respected people in the whole kingdom, were still waiting for him to make the final decision. He promised himself, that he would never let them down, he would never let Elior down, he would never let the kingdom down.

If it has to be me, Aary thought, *at least I can try my best.*

Epilogue

It has been many, many years since the Great War with the Dark Kingdom. Aary did not fail the expectations of Elior, the Grand Council, or the people of Hilldown Plain, and became a great king. He succeeded Elior's brilliance and courage, but was gentler and more modest, making him loved by all. He always had his ears open to any opinions from anyone, and considered every one of them carefully, to make the best choices for his kingdom and his people.

He married Lyna three years after his coronation. The lovely, kind, and bright little girl from a foreign little village grew into a beautiful, compassionate, and wise queen. If Aary brought peace and safety to the kingdom, she brought happiness and prosperity. Her sensitive, understanding nature allowed her to always notice if something wasn't right – lords oppressing common people with violence, or merchants controlling markets with schemes. She could see inequalities, sufferings, or lies, and she would act, together with her king, to try and make them right. Everyone in the kingdom loved her as much as they loved Aary, if not more, from the noble lords and officers, to the common people from the capital to the most distant little villages.

Under their reign, Elberkhan was more prosperous and plentiful than ever, and all of his people lived happily and peacefully.

Yes, the power of darkness was always there, but it never again formed a threat to the kindness and righteousness in people's hearts.

Everyone in the story, everyone that witnessed it all, everyone, apart from me, has long been resting in eternal peace. Even I, Rudi, am almost at the end of my journey. Life is wonderful, but I have lived for seven hundred and seventy-seven years, and to be honest, enough is enough. I've seen everything, good things, bad things, good people, bad people. I've even met a few of my own kind, rare as we are nowadays. I've been living in the castle of Elberkhan since Aary brought me in, and since then I have advised and aided twenty-one kings on the throne. The last king built a new castle and moved the capital here, because the old castle was getting too small for the growing prosperous city. The old castle of Elberkhan, the one in which I spent most of my years, was given to the king's nephew to remain a smaller city. I went there a couple of times in the past few years, but nothing was the same as I remembered.

To tell you the truth, I don't really like this new castle. It's too big and busy for my taste. As the highest honored advisor, I have my own tower and servants. But what good is a tower for an old elf like me? I'm still half a man's size, skinny like a bunch of wooden sticks. The huge empty chambers make me feel lonely and all the stairs are killing my old legs. And above all, I could sense that the fire of my life is burning low.

As my time draws near, I have had a stronger and stronger yearning for the forest, where I spent my childhood in the scent of the old pine trees. I want to go back to where I belonged, find a tree as old and grumpy as myself, and spend the rest of my days in the tiny tree hole, like a child in his mother's arms.

But, before I leave, there's something I think I need to do, something that no one else can do apart from me. Therefore, I believe I have the responsibility to do this, to write down and share with you the story of two of the greatest kings in the history of Elberkhan. Today, when their names are mentioned, all that people can say is that together they saved Elberkhan and Hilldown Plain from the claws of darkness and provided happy and peaceful lives for their people. Yes, they were responsible for that, but they were also much more than that. They were human too, humans of flesh and blood, humans that experienced happiness, love, fear, grief, confusion, hatred, and forgiveness. The victory was built on their sacrifices and sufferings. But they, too, made mistakes, like everyone else. I have my own feelings and opinions about them, but I won't let that control what you think. I've written their story down for you, and I entrust it to you to give your own judgment and do them justice in your hearts.

Time will gradually wash away everything, and all living things will fade and die. No matter how long and lasting a life is, it cannot stand the trial of time. Even things that we thought were eternal might change. Mountains might flatten, rivers might go dry, and castles might crumble down into a ruin of gravel, until finally turning into dirt and scattering in the air. But words remain, and the stories they carry. When I tell you a story, the details, the plots, or even the story itself may fade out from your memory after a while, but it will not disappear from you completely. It will become a part of you, and will live with you, forever.

I open the window and a breeze of cool morning air makes its way into my chamber. The morning light has gradually seeped in from the dark sky, and the solid black canvas is turning transparent. Birds' chatter comes from outside my window, as the plain starts to wake up. Early risers have already gotten out of their beds and kissed their kids goodbye to start off a day's hard work. Others are enjoying the feeling of lingering at the edge of their dreams and walking back and forth between the state of sleep and wakefulness. In less than an hour, the world will be bustling as usual, people yelling and bargaining in the markets, kids running and chasing in the streets, hoes rising and landing in the fields, food steaming and sizzling in the kitchens. I stack the parchments with my writings in a neat pile on my desk, and put the metal lid over the oil lamp to put it out. Just the way I came to Elberkhan on that first day, I leave quietly without taking anything with me. The guards smile at me and greet me with a good morning. Suddenly, I was that little elf again, brought into the castle by my friend Aary, the new king. Everything seemed so novel and strange to me, even the sun seemed to be shining brighter than usual, and the air fresher.

About the Author

Dr. Yuxiao Chen (1995 -)

Born and raised in Beijing and currently living in Sydney, having completed a Doctor of Philosophy from the University of Sydney and a Bachelor of Architecture from Tsinghua University, Yuxiao is an engineer in architectural acoustics during the day designing world-class concert halls. At night, Yuxiao is an artist, musician, adventurer, and writer.

This story first came to her when she was in high school, as if transmitted through an electromagnetic wave from a parallel universe. Holding the belief that the story actually happened somewhere in the infinite space-time, and that every story needs to be told or it will gradually die and vanish, she felt obliged to write it down. Then, after years of translation work and detail refinement, the English version is finally ready to meet its readers. The English writing was proofread and edited by Dr. Bethe Schoenfeld, an English educator and friend of the author's.

All the music pieces and illustrations in the book are created by the author herself, apart from the portrait below.

A live performance of the theme music Kingdom of Elberkhan composed and conducted by the author, performed by the Sydney University Wind Orchestra, can be watched online: https://youtu.be/9I41lpn_9sw

Oil painting of the author by Wenhao Cheng, the author's mother